ALL THAT WILL BURN

Written & Illustrated by

Judd Mercer

All That Will Burn is a work of fiction. Names, places, characters, and incidents either are the product of the author's imagination or are used fictitiously. Any resemblance to actual persons, living or dead, events, or locales is entirely coincidental.

Copyright © 2017 by Judd Mercer

Artwork copyright © Judd Mercer. All rights reserved.

To my family, for telling me what I wanted to hear.

To my friends, for what I needed to hear.

To Katie, for listening.

Acknowledgments

Thanks to KM Editorial, for helping a first-time author like me turn a mess into something to be proud of.

Special thanks to Dan Marshall, for helping me learn patience, and how to appreciate the beauty of a single brush stroke.

And thanks to you, reader, for giving me a chance to share my ideas with you.

Prologue

"You're not gone."

"Not yet," said Luquitas. "Soon."

Despite Luquitas' best efforts to keep the outside world at bay, it filtered in with potency. But it didn't matter. Soon all of it would be behind him. Sunlight fought its way through the closed shutters, illuminating airborne dust as it penetrated the unnatural gloom. Outside, the streets of Ilucenta bustled with the sounds of life. Music and the familiar, sweet aromas of freshly baked goods seeped in through the closed shutters.

Tomas watched him from the corner of the room. His bulky, bronze frame leaned against the wall, finely attired, as always. Tiny beads inlaid in the stitching of Tomas' trousers caught what little light there was and threw it back.

Tomas always did care about the most useless of things. Luquitas tried to recall when last he had spoken to his old friend. Many years ago. Decades, perhaps. Time was a fickle thing in this place, easily lost and hard to keep track of.

Luquitas broke the silence. "How did you know I was leaving?" He arranged his meager belongings on the room's sole cot. On it lay a pile of papers, quills and inks arranged in a wooden case with an ebony inlay. A thick book sat nearby.

"I didn't know you were leaving," said Tomas. "Not really. I just had a feeling." He peered through the slits in the blacked-out windows. "I met someone recently, practically still dripping wet. As a newborn, remember? Hard to believe we were that...*young* once." Tomas savored the irony of the word. "Anyway, he reminded me of you, so I thought I'd check in. It's been over fifty years, after all."

"Has it?" Luquitas replied. He didn't look up.

Tomas sighed. "You always did have trouble adjusting, Luqa. I know."

"No, my friend," said Luquitas. He ran his fingers across an ancient-looking tome, tracing the square runes chiseled into the oiled, crimson leather. "You don't. No one does."

"You're not the first person to...well, *you* know." Tomas avoided saying it directly. "But that doesn't mean you have to leave. And I know what you think of the *Sang*, Luqa, and you're wrong. Dammit, they're here to help you. They're here to help all of us." He placed a hand on Luqa's shoulder. "You don't know what's out there."

Luquitas shrugged Tomas away. "You think they know everything? Think they care? No, Tomas. It's the blind leading the blind. I listened to their preachments and read their writings. I spent time inside the *Conventa* and endured centuries of those fools debating their moral authority. Now I know the truth, the true nature of the *Orvida*. This place. This *prison*."

Tomas shrugged, unconvinced. "And?"

Luquitas said nothing, his stone face an impenetrable wall. Tomas sighed and slumped down on the bed, hefting the large tome onto his lap. He paged through the heavy parchment, casually scanning the pages. "All these years you've been hiding out, slipping further and further away. What have you *really* been up to, Luqa?"

"Searching. For answers."

Luquitas eyed Tomas thumbing through the book, waiting. He debated whether to tell his friend, his *only* friend in this city of lies, the truth. Locked away in ancient libraries for years, Luquitas poured over taboo writings and obscure texts to understand the nature of his situation. *Everyone's* situation. Why were they in this cursed place? What was the point of it all? For centuries, the answers eluded and taunted him, but no longer. The only question now was whether to share them. He eyed Tomas like a predator and wondered if his friend was ready.

Tomas' curiosity drove him deeper into the text. As he watched Tomas in anticipation, an inkling of power leaked into Luquitas' veins, and a mad excitement stirred in him. He nurtured it like a tiny flame, patiently breathing life into the embers.

A mess of chaotic symbols and inscriptions replaced the fine scripture of earlier pages. Tomas turned the pages over more quickly now. Smeared ink obscured whole sections of text. Luquitas' scribbled phrases appeared over and over in the margins. Shadowy illustrations scrawled on parchment appeared in motion as Tomas frantically flipped through faster and faster. He stared in growing horror at the object in his hands.

Luquitas tasted Tomas' growing fear. In the dimness of the room, it was palpable. It filled him up, mixing with hatred into a kind of energy that made him alive. It was the only thing that did. The only thing that *could*. He knew that now. It was the dark secret Luquitas never spoke of, that *no one* spoke of. For years, he'd kept it deep inside, tended the fledgling fire and waited for this moment.

"Luqa?" said Tomas in disbelief, staring at the obscene pages before him.

Tomas was not ready. *Unfortunate, but not a total waste.* Luquitas would, at least, know for sure if one aspect of his theory was right.

"I am sorry, my friend," said Luquitas. His voice was a calm whisper. "I have found my path, and it is clear I must walk it alone."

Some remnant of Tomas' primal being sensed danger coming. He threw the book aside, scrambling to the door.

Despite Luquitas' large size, he was swift and nimble. He charged at Tomas. The caged animal was free.

The power coursing through Luquitas' body washed over him completely and drowned his senses. Rage and ecstasy blended into a potent concoction of pure bliss. Luquitas threw Tomas against the wall, the fragile plaster facade exploding in a puff of smoke. Tomas, on his knees, coughed and struggled to speak. Luquitas gave him no opportunity to protest. He silenced him with a blow that split bone and then dealt him another. He hammered Tomas' face into a bloody mess, the euphoria of violence as familiar and natural as breathing. Long had he awaited its embrace, having denied his nature for so many years.

But no longer.

Luquitas knelt over his friend's broken body, clamping his giant, bloody fists around Tomas' neck. Tomas fought for life-giving air, thrashing desperately as his eyes bulged with terror. Sprays of blood erupted as he choked in vain. The look excited Luquitas and stirred up a frustratingly vague memory, a swath of unspeakable pain and unbridled pleasure. Luquitas' massive forearms torqued harder.

With a jerk, Luquitas crushed the last of life from the thing resembling a man before him. Then, the room was silent. Blood pooled on the floor, and Tomas was still. Luquitas rose to his feet and drew a deep breath, satisfied with his work.

Tomas was more than dead. Although Luquitas had destroyed the body, he knew he had accomplished something so much more. *Desipar,* it was called. Luquitas whispered the ancient word aloud with satisfaction. Before now, he'd considered it merely a possibility. He'd tried before, of course, on some of those unfortunate wretches behind the walls, hidden in the mist, but had never been able to do anything more than mangle their already malformed bodies. This was different. Luquitas had discovered something wonderful.

Freedom.

He eyed the corpse, allowing the beast within a moment to bed down. Once his faculties returned, Luquitas sat on the bed and detailed the incident in his journal. Blood mixed with ink upon the parchment—an appropriate accent to the account. When he was finished, he placed the book and all his belongings in a satchel, slung it over his shoulder and walked to the window. He pried the shutters open. The blindness passed as he gazed at the sprawling Ilucenta skyline that terminated against the sea. Spires and towers and stepped pyramids scattered the golden metropolis, but to Luquitas, it was nothing more than a vast pasture where dumb, grazing animals lived in ignorance. He would bring the truth to them. He would bring them peace.

Luquitas smiled. "I will set them free."

PART I

BIRTH

*Lo! She did come by way of the sea,
And washed by the sea, though not cleansed.*

Liba di Halphyus 2:1

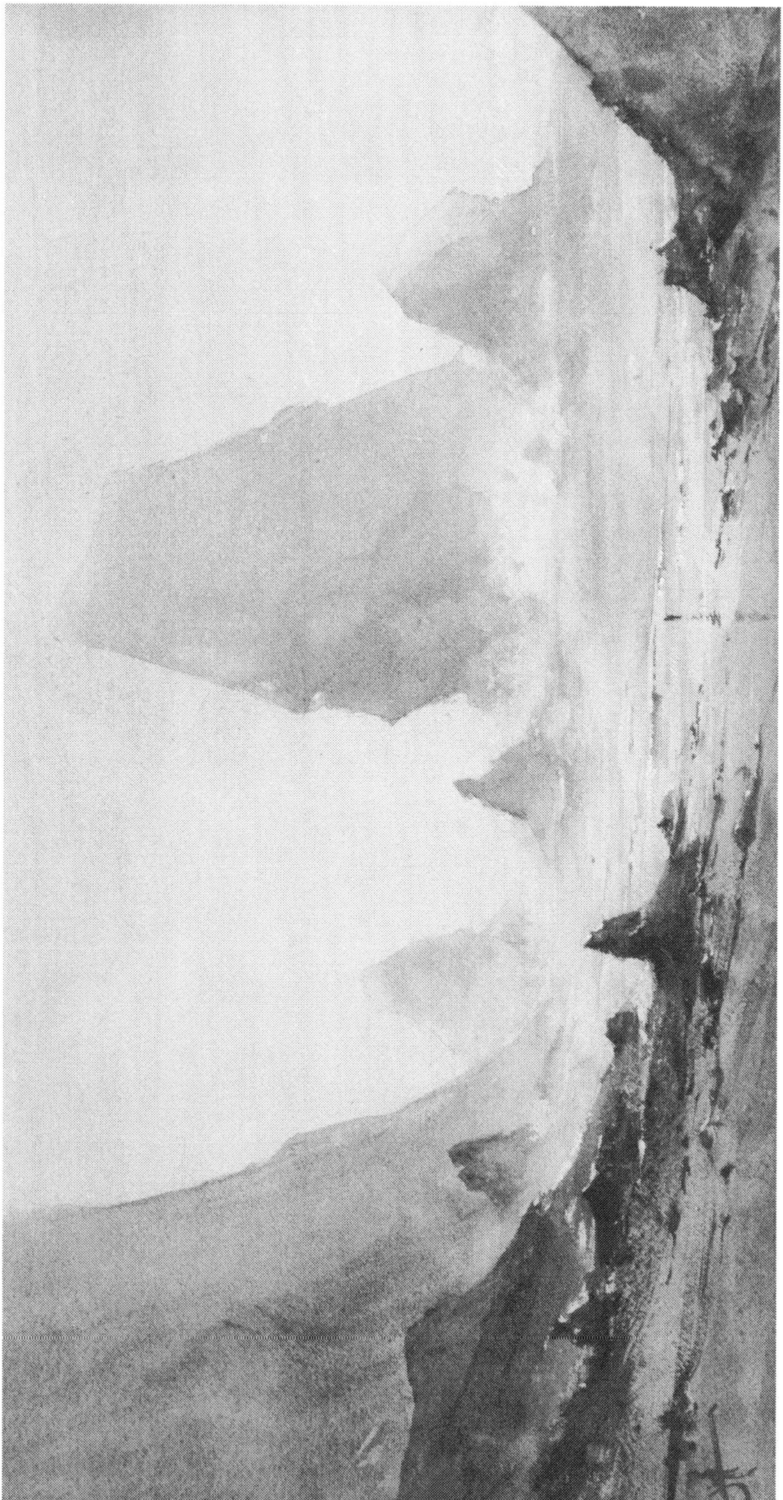

1

Sofia gasped for air, splashing about the surface. *Salty.* She was in the ocean; that much was obvious. She blinked intently and tried to get her eyes to work. They were near useless, blurry and throbbing from the sting of seawater. *How did I get here?* A thick fog obscured the horizon in all directions. Sofia cried out. There was no cry back.

Stay focused, don't panic, something inside of her said. The sloshing of seawater mixed with her own heavy breathing. *Get your bearings, head to shore.* Assuming shore was near, that is. Assuming she wasn't a thousand kilometers out to sea. With no sign of land, she easily could be.

Oh, God.

No. She told herself to stay calm as she bobbed, the waves lapping at her throat. *Think, think, think!*

Sofia fought the urge to panic. Looking in vain for some semblance of hope, she became aware of the cold current streaming between her thighs. *What is that?* She looked down at her milky limbs churning against the dark sea below. *Why am I naked? Oh, God, what happened?* Fear pierced her defenses, slunk into her mind. The abyss below ate away at her nerves. It conjured all kinds of primitive fears of the dark and unknown. She thrashed and cursed with frustration until her voice and muscles were spent. The gentle sounds of the waves persisted, undeterred. The otherwise peacefulness of the scene mocked her.

Is this how I die?

The instinct to survive lingered and kept Sofia's limbs pumping. *Come on, think. Breathe.* The bleak haze made it impossible to clearly see the sun. She strained to sense a wind on her face, but the air was heavy and still and dead. The cold current at her toes could be moving in any direction in relation to land—or not. But staying still wasn't an option. She had to do *something*; there was no other choice. Even if that meant picking a direction at random and swimming for it. So, she did.

Sofia followed the sensation of the current and took her first few strokes. It was difficult to keep her head above water, and she choked and spit. After a while, she found the rhythm and drifted along with the swells.

Time passed. Questions lingered. *How did I get here? Where am I?*

Her toes found something.

Sofia recoiled, screaming. She imagined a hundred terrible things lurking below. Scaly, nightmarish things with teeth and black eyes. She tucked her legs instinctively toward her body, thrashing at the water. She scanned the deep for signs of movement, but there was none. Only her pale limbs in broken silhouette against the murky deep.

It's nothing. It's nothing. Sofia felt silly. After a tense moment of waiting for something that didn't come, she defiantly thrust her feet downward. Her toes did not, as predicted, find the back of some leviathan, but silky sand. *Sand!* She plunged below the surface, probing for more ground and finding purchase in the silt. Bliss between her toes. She made headway shoreward, encouraged by the faint and gentle sound of breaking surf and firm ground beneath her feet. *I'm not going to die.*

Sofia wanted to cheer, but the moment was fleeting. Standing there on the gray, desolate beach, alone and naked, she felt no better off than she had hours before. Surf pushed past her ankles, and she was vulnerable again. Sofia wrapped her arms around herself, instinctively covering her exposed breasts, and knelt down in the shallow water. She considered her situation. *Try to remember. Was it an accident? Shipwreck?*

The air was cooler than the sea. She sensed it but seemed hardly affected by it. *Strange.* Why wasn't she shivering uncontrollably? *Must be the shock. Where am I?*

A quick scan of the area ahead revealed little: there were no footprints on the shore, no buildings or boats. Only dull sand in every direction, the oppressive, heavy fog and the splashing of waves rolling in around her. Sofia felt the urge to move, the same urge that had kept her swimming. It would not let her sit idle.

With a breath of determination, she marched out of the surf, trading one unknown for another. She stumbled. Walking felt strange, foreign. Dizziness struck and threw her off-balance, almost as if she hadn't used her legs in a while. *Was I drugged? Maybe something worse.* She shuddered and squeezed her arms tight.

How did I get here? Working backward, she found no recollection of a time before the sea. There was the water, and nothing before. *Nothing.* She couldn't remember where she was or how she'd gotten here. She couldn't remember *anything.* Anything, that is, but her own name. *Sofia.*

She kneaded her scalp and knocked her knuckles against her skull as if to jog her memory. *Family?* Nothing but faceless, amorphous figures. *Home?* Blurry lights and distance sounds. The more she grasped for any shred of familiarity, the less there was to hold on to. It didn't make sense. She knew how to speak. She knew how to add, recite the colors of the rainbow, and spell words like G-A-T-O and A-M-I-G-O, yet specifics about who she was remained a mystery. Her mind was as shrouded as the damned beach.

"I'm Sofia," she said aloud, reaffirming the one thing she *did* know. *But how can I remember my name and nothing else?* She was obviously herself; she knew that. But what about the rest? It was a hollow feeling, as if a part of her that was once there was missing. Almost *removed.*

Having no better option, Sofia started walking, once again choosing a direction at random. The beach was completely still save for the lapping waves. The kind of stillness that made her own breath sound like thunder. *Need to keep moving. Find help.* There was something unsettling about the shore. Paranoia clung to her like the damp mist. She glanced once or twice behind to confirm her footprints—and nothing else—were still following her. The sopping mass of thick, black hair tugged at the back of her head. With the fog obscuring her vision in all directions, it was hard to tell if she was making any progress. Not that it mattered. *Here* was hardly different from where she had started.

Sofia took note of her body as she walked, still searching for something recognizable. Her lean frame was toned, strong, but altogether unfamiliar. Visible knots of muscles hugged her ribs, plunged toward her hips and twisted as she walked. There was little excess or softness to her body. Flexing her arms, Sofia felt potential there. *Maybe I am an athlete?*

There were no stiff joints or discernible calluses on her hands that might confirm the theory. In fact, she had a hard time finding even the slightest hint of a blemish anywhere. *How old am I?* She didn't feel particularly young, but then again, she didn't feel old, either. *Thirty? Thirty-five, maybe?* A woman that age ought to have *some* imperfections. Yet there were no bodily signs of a life lived at all.

Sofia jogged a bit, further testing her muscles. She felt stupid at first, but her body responded quickly, honed for a purpose. She darted back and forth, sprinting for a few moments across the firm sand, then walked once more. A hard dash down the shoreline barely increased her breath. Her confidence grew, and despite the fact she was still exposed and alone on the beach, she felt a little more in control.

Hours passed, and discouragement soon set in. Sofia weighed the choice of moving inland, when an object emerged from the fog ahead, startling her from her thoughts.

The thing was a pale ghost against the gray sand. *Another person like herself, washed ashore?* She called out hesitantly—whether a plea for help or warning, she wasn't sure. But the thing didn't move. Sophia glanced over her shoulder before approaching. What at first seemed like a human form soon revealed itself to be a stone object half buried in the sand. *A sign!*

She bounded naked across the beach, exhilarated by a sign of hope. A kind of altar carved from a single piece of white stone materialized from the mist. It was a circular disc with a look resembling a felled tree stump, a single meter high and two across, covered in geometric designs. *Trees. I remember what those are.* From the stump emerged a pillar much taller than she, with square edges, a pyramid top, and strange, blocky symbols carved into its surface. Sofia stepped up onto the structure. She traced the designs with her finger and wondered how stone could be hewn so precisely. It was flawless, unmarked by chips or wear, but it *felt* ancient.

Sofia reasoned whoever had put the stone object on the beach had done so with a purpose in mind. *But what does it mean?* She gazed into the mist leading inland and considered for a moment what might await her away from shore. *A kind of marker?* Sofia sat down on what should have been cold stone to think, but it wasn't cold at all. She glanced back at her lonely footprints leading back into the mist, to nowhere. It seemed logical to wait for help, so Sofia sat for a while, listening to the gentle waves roll across the sand.

But impatience stirred her to action. The restlessness felt familiar, even if everything else didn't. When pacing failed to alleviate it, Sophia inspected the geometric carvings on the stone slab, which seemed to converge in a design pointing inland. With no better ideas, Sofia marched away from the sea and left the mysterious stone obelisk in the mist.

Fifty meters away from the shore, a towering cliff appeared. It loomed overhead like a black tidal wave, threatening to devour her. *Why would the maker lead me here?*

The rock face was devoid of any natural cracks or other formations, almost artificial as opposed to a more natural-looking crag. It spanned in both directions, parallel to the shore, a vast, obsidian barrier. From her vantage point, Sofia couldn't see the top of the rise. It disappeared above, swallowed up by the impenetrable fog. What she could see was series of holes, shoulder width apart, bored in regular intervals up the rock face. *A ladder?* They did seem appropriately placed, although only a few of her fingers fit inside each hole. It didn't seem like they were made for climbing. But whatever they were, they weren't natural. And they led up.

Gazing toward the fog above, hands on her hips, a frustrated Sofia weighed her options. On the one hand, she could continue following the beach and look for more signs of civilization. If the stone marker hadn't been placed by some long-dead people, she might find more signs of life.

Then again, she could climb to who knows where. Sofia glanced up the stone wall. The scattered holes leading up into the mist *felt* like a path, at least, more than anything else up to this point. *A little direction is better than no direction at all.* The mystery of it gnawed at her. Now she needed to know.

Sofia approached the stone face, imagining the climb ahead. Her stomach turned over, and dizziness disrupted her balance. She clawed at one of the holes, struggling for some purchase until the sensation passed.

Well, I guess I'm afraid of heights.
Shit.

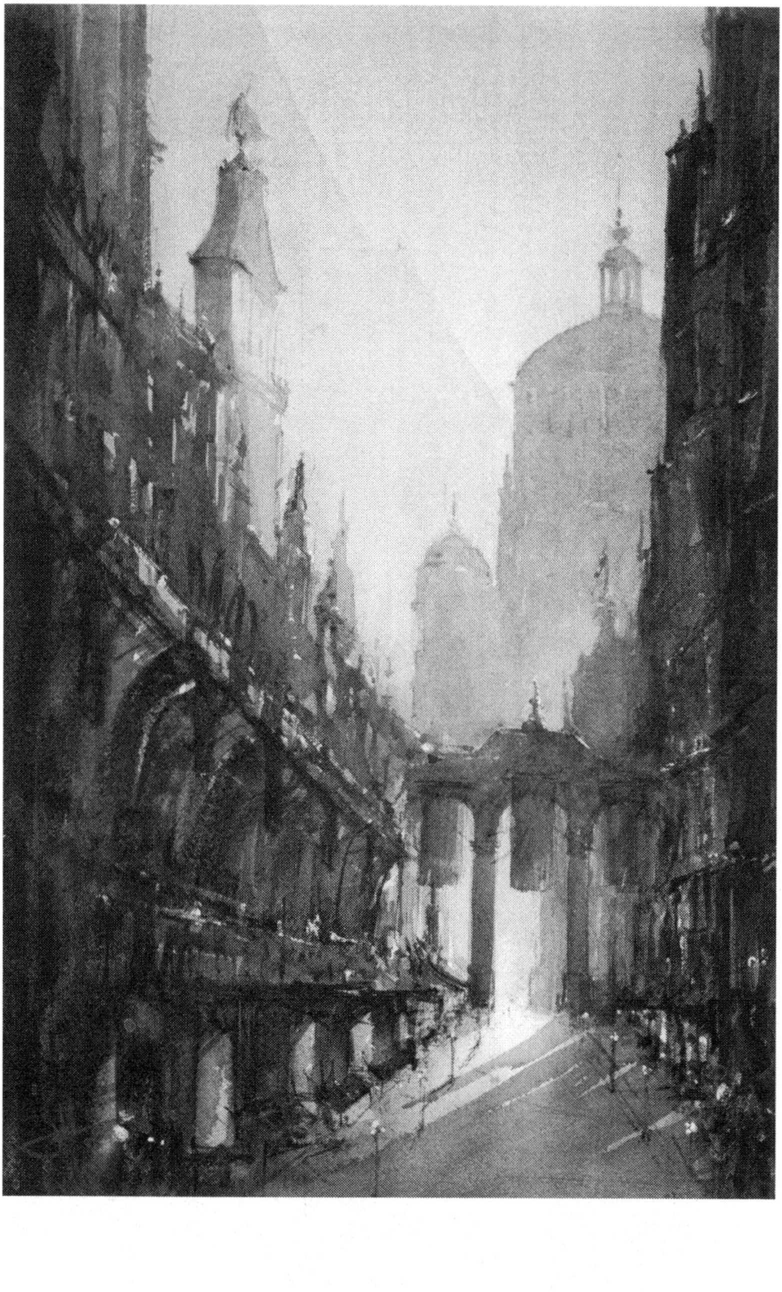

2

After fifty sets of hand-over-hands, Sofia lost count. She squeezed her eyes between each one and swallowed the panic down. Her face was never far from the stone, so close it rubbed the tip of her nose raw. The rock was equally unkind to the rest of her naked body as she climbed. It scraped and scratched every part of her.

She drew breath in quick bursts. Amnesia or not, a fear of heights was a part of her. But somehow, so was the drive to push through it. It was an odd contradiction. Each time she imagined the distance between her and the ground, dizziness attacked her senses and she reminded herself of the two simple options she had: keep going or climb down. *Or, I could fall.* A very real third possibility. She shook off the thought and stretched out to the next hold.

Something inside the bored-out rock tickled her hand. Sofia recoiled, crying out. Her feet slipped for a moment as she fought to hold on with one strained hand. She cursed under her breath and slowed her breathing with her forehead against the cool stone. *What the hell was that?* She glared at the hole and reached for it. Her fingers inched into the divot. It was empty save for a bit of moss. *Goddammit.*

Sofia continued to climb, more cautiously than before, until she reached blindly for the next anchor. A sheer ledge. It was the top of the cliff, and Sofia grasped it greedily. She scrambled up the face and, once she was a good distance from the ledge, sighed with relief to be on solid ground. Sweat glistened on her body uncooled by the damp, still air. *Strange.* Hours in the sea hadn't given her so much as a chill, either. *How could that be?*

Her hands throbbed. Sofia shook them vigorously and flexed her digits, taking note of the ache. Her hips and knees were red and scraped. She came to her feet and noticed for the first time, through the thinned mist, the stunning view before her.

A crumbling wall followed the perimeter of the cliff face, perched neatly on top of the rock as if an extension of the crag itself. It spanned the summit in both directions, and some of the original structure was intact, towering ten times Sofia's height at least. Most had been reduced to rubble. But what she saw beyond the wall ruins snatched the breath from her still-naked chest: a sprawling, silent city standing watch in the mist.

Sofia scaled a short section of the wall to gain a better vantage point, minding her more sensitive parts while navigating the coarse debris.

The city descended the sloping backside of the cliff, offering her a long view of its expanse. Massive spires and domes rose from cobbled streets. They were cylindrical and sat on stepped, angled bases—larger kin to the altar that had led her inland. Occasionally, a grand, faceted pyramid emerged, nestled between the spires. The pyramids commanded special attention. But Sofia noted unnatural gaps in the skyline as she scanned the horizon. More than a few towers were hacked off at the knees, and some appeared as little more than crumbling stumps. Still others bore scars of violence on a huge scale.

It was a lonely sight. Even so, Sofia was hopeful. *Where there are buildings, there are people.*

She maneuvered through the stone rubble, minding her bare feet, and found her way into the city proper via a narrow cobblestone street lined with patchwork structures on each side. An eerie stillness permeated the place. Even the air was old. Sofia hugged herself and made her way to one side of the street where at least her back would be safe against a wall. So many bridges crisscrossed the streets above that it seemed the roads themselves were slowly disappearing, strangled by progress.

There were signs of damage everywhere: caved in roofs, broken windows, and dark stains on the streets that Sofia didn't want to think about. But the structures weren't *worn*. There was no sign of the earth trying to reclaim the abandoned city. The buildings themselves were brightly painted—Sofia could *feel* the warm hues—but something had dulled them into sad shades of gray. The trees that lined the streets were tamed and well manicured, and yet they too lacked color and warmth. Time itself seemed to have abandoned the city along with all the vibrancy of life.

Sofia wandered through the city in silence. The soft padding of her feet gave a loud echo as she moved through the narrow streets. There was a heaviness about the place. The longer she walked, the more acutely she could feel it. It weighed heavy around her neck and slowed her senses. A kind of drowsiness, like the first moments after waking.

The patchwork buildings and towers loomed above. They dimmed the light and cast gloomy shadows across her path. Night came. The weak sun faded away, and the still-burning street lamps provided the only illumination. The tiny burning bulbs she saw through the mist, made Sofia think of glowing insects, though she could not say why.

She yearned to rest. Not from fatigue, but to find some comfort, some warmth. She peered through the windows of what looked like shops and cafes nestled at the base of the giant towers. She hoped for some place suitable to think for a moment and to maybe find something to cover her backside.

After an hour, Sofia chose what looked to be a promising storefront. The elaborate sign outside was unreadable but welcoming with a formal-looking name. The door was ornately designed, too, covered in carvings and symbols like the rest of the city. She pushed. The door resisted. Sofia thrust her elbow through the window without a moment's pause. The sound of shattering glass pierced the night. She might just as well have split the world in two. She froze and listened for sounds in response. Silence.

Sofia reached in and unlocked the latch. *Damn!* An errant shard of glass opened her hand. The blood appeared black in the gloom. Sofia shoved her way in, cursing her luck and clutching her hand. No lamps burned inside, and Sofia fumbled between heavy furniture. Her eyes slowly adjusted, and she laughed. It was a clothing shop. She could see the garments hanging in the window now, silhouetted against the light from outside. She grabbed the nearest one and wrapped her hand with it.

Frustrated and unable to see, Sofia left the shop and went back to the street, minding the scattered broken glass. Glancing around, she noticed an ornate sconce, its pale glow flickering in the dark haze. It was one of the few fixtures she could reach without climbing uncomfortably high. Sofia unscrewed the glass orb to find another, smaller sphere of glass inside. Within it, a tiny flame flickered like an imprisoned candle. Sofia held the light in her good hand and wondered how the flame could breathe inside of the sphere. It was small and weak, but something about it settled her nerves and relaxed her stiff muscles. She carried the sphere back into the store, holding it like an infant in her arms.

With more light, Sofia saw the store for what it was and all that it contained: richly embroidered robes and elaborate gowns lined the walls. She meandered through the displays and touched the beaded inlays and thick stitching. Sofia expected a thin layer of dust on everything in sight, but once again, she could find no sign of time passing.

Sofia passed by the more elaborate pieces to what looked to be more practical attire for men and grabbed the simplest pair of trousers she could find. She threw a loose tunic over her body, wrapped herself with a belt, and after placing the soles of knee-high boots against her dirty feet, found a suitable pair and slid them on. A scarf wrapped around her hand covered her wound. She couldn't remember ever wearing clothes before, but by the way her spirits strengthened, the garments may just as well have been armor.

Sofia tied her hair back and explored the tiny shop with the sphere of light. She riffled through the desk. Old papers were stacked neatly among heavy books, both of which contained writing Sofia could not understand.

Through a small doorway, Sofia found a small office with a handsome, high back chair. The thought of rest jumped into her mind, and immediately her body ached for something soft to sit on. She slumped down with the glowing orb on her lap, staring at the painted ceiling.

But sleep did not come. Every time Sofia closed her eyes, the oppressive feeling of the city—an acute loneliness mixed with dread—became stronger and condensed around her as if the very world were collapsing in. It would become too much, and she'd snap to attention again. Sofia gave up after a few hours. She didn't need rest; she needed some answers. *Where the hell is everyone? Where AM I?*

Sofia left the shop and moved deeper into the city. She walked through the night, still carrying the glowing orb until the sky began to change from a dark gray to a lighter one. The streets became wide enough for a hundred people or more to walk hand in hand, and the avenues and canals funneled to one central thoroughfare. Sofia reasoned the area of the city was important and might have some sign of inhabitants. Though the general opulence of the city was obvious, here it was even more so. The ornamentation of every facet was dizzying in its details, but still only evidence of a civilization long past. Sofia wondered how many centuries it had taken to create such a place.

A distinct sound drifted through the still air. *A voice.* It could have been a hurricane compared to the oppressive silence. Sofia followed the murmuring, peeking down alleys to find its source. She ducked down one narrow offshoot as the voice grew louder. The street was narrow and crooked, and Sofia used her free hand to feel the walls as she maneuvered the curves.

There, in the middle of the street, Sofia came upon a figure of man hunched over and sobbing.

Sofia wanted to run to him, to celebrate and laugh and sing. She took a step forward, craving the embrace of someone, *anyone,* but she stopped. Her smile faded. Something was wrong. It was a feeling of fear so profound her elation vanished in an instant. The hair on her arms pricked to attention. She crept toward the figure that was twitching and convulsing in bizarre ways. His sobbing continued, intermixed with harsh, guttural language. It was indeed a man; that much was clear. His clothes were tattered and soiled, the only sign of wear Sofia had witnessed. But there was something else.

Sofia glanced behind her, debating slinking away from the strange man and leaving him be. For the moment, curiosity overcame her fear.

"Hello?" Sofia said, after a short pause.

The man said nothing, still whimpering and muttering to himself. Sofia inched toward him so as to not startle the man and reached out. She gently tapped his shoulder. His head snapped around to find the source as if woken from a dream. Sofia reeled at the milky, lifeless eyes staring back at her. They were the color of the mist, impenetrable and frightening. Sofia nearly dropped the glass sphere she was holding, but caught it at the last moment and clutched it tightly.

The man was once handsome, with a square jaw and broad nose, but his features seemed permanently contorted. Like the city itself, it seemed all life and color had left him long ago. Animated, but without life.

His head jerked about as if he were a blind animal, listening in the darkness. Sofia stood frozen, and he seemed not to notice her. The point of his brow pointed upward, and the corners of his mouth plummeted into an expression of utter, pathetic sadness. Despite the man's grotesqueness, Sofia couldn't help but feel a flash of pity for him.

"Can you—Can you help me?" Sophia whispered. It was the first time she remembered speaking to anyone before. Her voice was rough, parched, but the words rolled off her tongue quickly and as one long phrase.

The man twitched again. Sofia wasn't sure if he was deaf as well as blind. He made no reply. The man muttered something to himself and scratched his head. Sofia caught sight of his arm as his baggy sleeve fell. Strips of skin were flayed off in thin ribbons about a finger's width wide, revealing oily, black flesh underneath. The wounds looked as if the skin had been peeled off intentionally. *Meticulously.*

Horrified, Sofia stumbled back and ran to the main street. Terror coursed through her. Instinct drove her to flee and put as much distance between her and—whatever it was she'd seen—as possible.

She darted across the uneven cobblestones, down a curving avenue and through a large intersection where the street opened to a large public square, a vast courtyard so wide Sofia could not see the other side. When she could run no longer, she held her knees to regain her breath, panting. *Dammit! I dropped it.* She had lost the glass sphere as she'd fled. The loss of it cut deeper than it ought.

She felt more lost than ever, once again adrift in the gray sea. *What was that?*

In the mist, she saw a few shambling forms meandering across the square. Then more. What should have been a morning scene of a bustling metropolis filled with the chaotic energy of life was but a hollow reflection cast from a hazy, ancient mirror. The forms of people aimlessly shuffled across the courtyard, in between defaced statues and pruned foliage, seemingly oblivious to their surroundings and one another. Wails and murmurs, cries and cursing mixed in the air. It was madness. A kind of horror without immediate danger or threat, but with a passive, almost sleepy, unease. The kind that doesn't care whether anyone else is there or not. *God, what the hell is this place?*

Sofia scanned for a route around the plaza, but its architecture seemed designed to guide her forward, through the square and into the fog beyond. Sofia debated turning around, but the more she watched the figures in the square, the more she began to think they meant her no direct harm. Maybe they would ignore her.

Sofia took no chances. She crept through the square, keeping as much distance between herself and the strange people as possible. They indeed seemed unaware of or uninterested in her presence. One woman was shouting at the sky, her skin covered in filth and strange markings, and her hair was a knotted mass accented with feathers. She wore the remains of what had once been an elegant gown.

Another man wearing a metal helmet was digging at the stone with what was left of his fingers as he rambled aloud. Still another performed crude dentistry on himself and laughed, speaking gleefully in a foreign tongue as he yanked another tooth out. Sour bile crept up Sofia's throat as she watched them, though she tried not to for long.

At the far end of the square, desperate for reprieve from the disturbing figures around her, Sofia approached a massive pyramid. It appeared from the fog like a giant resting with crossed legs, its tiered levels topped by a bulbous dome. Spires and obelisks marked its vertices, and at the base was a dark cavity leading to the interior. By its placement and ornamentation, it was important.

Whatever its purpose, it would do for now. She needed a safe place to think. *Anything to be away from...them.*

She passed through a pair of large doors and made her way through the gloomy interior. Large, ornate windows provided some light, just enough to reveal some history of the place. Sofia navigated piles of debris, broken furniture and the ruins of old columns. Huge chunks of the walls lay upon the floor, and the stained rugs were shredded in some areas. Frescoes adorned the roof above: detailed scenes of a war in the clouds.

Sofia turned her attention to the middle of the chamber where a kind of shrine sat, lit by an orifice in the dome above. The light drifted down and dissipated, but it was enough to see by. The shrine was reminiscent of the altar she'd found on the beach, only much larger and more ornate. This was a place of reverence; that much was clear. Perhaps for ceremony?

A long, creaking groan that called out from behind shattered the relative peace. Sofia scrambled for cover and ducked into a nearby antechamber, heart pounding. She peered out from behind a makeshift barricade and could see, just beyond the shrine, a figure moving about. It was a man, or *like* a man, though he loped around more like a beast on all fours. He growled from beneath a mane of black hair that masked his face. Compared to the milky-eyed stranger from before, this *thing* was far more unnatural. Seeing it in motion made Sofia think of joints moving in the wrong direction.

She fought to keep calm, silent, creeping backward with her eyes still on the creature until the floor fell from beneath her. She tumbled hard. Only by landing at the bottom of a stone stair was she brought back to the world. Various parts of her body throbbed with pain. *That thing is still up there.* She ignored the pain for a moment as her eyes adjusted, listening. *Is it following me?*

Sofia sensed she wasn't alone. She glanced behind to see a corpse lying next to her in cold silence. Sofia choked back a scream.

Even in the dim light, Sofia could see it was clearly the body of a woman. She was on her side. Her skin pallid, almost transparent. Sofia squirmed, instinct willing her away from death. Yet the gentle expression on the woman's remarkably beautiful face, elegant and noble, eased Sofia's fear. Tattooed lines ran in parallel across her cheeks and nose. Fine, pale hair, elaborately braided and adorned with jewels, sparkled, even in the gloom.

Sofia's fingers reached out to touch the armor covering the woman's chest. The plate was gold and cool to the touch, heavily gilded and highly contoured for a female form. Inscribed on it were words and symbols Sofia could not read, but in the center of the design was a stylized visage of a lion's head with a sun above it. *Lion? Yes, that's it.* At one side of the plate, a gaping, black wound. *What happened to you?*

Sofia stared at the armor and wondered what other things lurked in the city above. She glanced at the sword at the woman's side, sitting just outside of the warrior's reach. She'd never held a sword before, but Sofia imagined she'd be better off with it and the armor than without.

She listened for signs of movement at the top of the stair. Carefully and as quietly as possible, she unclasped the leather straps holding the woman's breastplate together. It was easier if she kept her eyes from the woman's dead face. The chestplate consisted of two pieces that creaked and pinged as she removed them from their previous owner. The back piece had two large openings on either side, for what purpose she couldn't say. But the armor was covered in blood. Sophia gently leaned the corpse away from the wall to find two symmetrical wounds in the woman's back, black and gory. Sofia held back her revulsion and laid the woman to rest once more.

Sofia slid the armor on, and while it wasn't the most comfortable, it did provide a certain confidence. She tightened the straps and reached for the sword, accidentally kicking something hard and metal as she did. A helmet tumbled down another set of steps, clanging and echoing as it fell. Sofia froze in terror until it stopped far below. Heavy shuffling. It was coming from above and growing closer.

It's coming.

Sofia fumbled for the sword and flew down the steps as fast as she could, tracing the walls with her hands. The air was damp down here. Small sources of light flickered ahead. Sofia darted through the corridors, watching the low ceilings and catching glimpses of side passages and other small rooms. Sacks and barrels filled some of the chambers off the main corridor, along with crates and ancient-looking tools and other supplies.

A guttural howl called out behind her. Lonely and terrifying. She pressed on, trying not to collapse from fear.

Sofia ducked into one of the rooms and dove behind a pile of laden burlap sacks. Even in the cellar of sorts there was no dust, no sign of age.

Beyond, Sofia could hear loping footsteps of whatever followed. Its labored breathing—raspy and erratic—let Sofia know it was close. *Very close.* She put her back to the barrier and squeezed the handle of the sword tightly, readying herself for what might happen next. Her muscles tightened. Her heart thundered. As her mind raced to imagine how best to swing a sword, she felt a warm breeze on her face. Sofia reached out a hand, noticing a hole dug into the wall leading *somewhere*. She only hesitated for a moment before crawling in.

The tunnel was a black void inside She scrambled on her hands and knees through the cold mud, sword still in hand. She imagined the thing at her heels, sniffing her out in the darkness. She crawled until her limbs ached and burned.

Light! There was a light ahead, soft at first but growing fast. The breeze strengthened. She kept moving, kept crawling. *Don't stop.* Meters turned into tens and hundreds after that. In the blackness, it was hard to tell. Sofia pushed on until the tunnel widened and she could pull herself to her feet. She tripped and stumbled through the muddy passage, finally emerging from the earth into the light.

Sofia slumped to one side of the tunnel entrance, catching her breath, waiting. The bleak morning gray overwhelmed her vision. Sofia blinked her eyes back in focus, wiping her sweat-drenched hair from her filthy face with one hand and holding the sword overhead with the other, ready to come down hard on the thing barreling out after her. But it never did.

Her heart slowed. *What was that thing?* The tunnel seemed to have led her outside of the city, beyond the wall and away from those things, back to the cliffs overlooking the sea. *Am I back where I started?* She glanced back into the tunnel. *An escape route?* She wondered why the woman wearing the armor hadn't made her escape the same way. The more she saw of this place, the less, it seemed, Sofia understood.

Sofia grasped the collar of the breastplate as a sign of thanks, happy to have not put it to the test. As she sat there on the rocks, she studied the sword.

It was less than her arm's length long with a generous width and sharp point. But the metal was deformed and blackened and even sagged in parts as if melted. *What could do that to a sword?* The handle was a rich, reddish wood carved and inlaid with gold. It, too, was charred and damaged.

Sofia swung the sword around, not having any idea how to do so. It felt good, in any case. As she sliced the air, she spied something in the distance. It was a light burning through the fog. And it was from no natural source. It flashed in sequence as if speaking to her.

A signal.

3

Light pulsated from the tower, intensifying as Sofia navigated the rocky shore toward it. Gray tide pools, devoid of color and life, mirrored the equally sterile sky above. As she walked, Sofia's thoughts lingered on the dead city. The farther away from it she got, the more implausible the ordeal seemed, yet the sensation of fear was still there, fresh and potent. A city frozen in time, inhabited by shadows—a beautiful gray nightmare.

But as unsettling as the thoughts and images were, the experiences were the only memories she had. She considered the strangeness of...wherever she was. She felt no cold, no hunger, no thirst, no fatigue. But the cuts and scrapes beneath her clothes reminded her that pain was real. Flesh and blood. Still more questions, and she held on to them tightly as she pushed onward along the shore.

Twilight descended as she walked. Warm grays deepened and cooled and transformed the shrouded shoreline into a bruise-colored veil. No moon or stars followed the coming of night, save for the one beckoning Sofia onward with its steady rhythm. She compared its pace to the surf meeting land, counting the seconds. They aligned perfectly. *Strange.*

Sofia chose her steps more carefully in the dark, negotiating the jagged hazards in time with the flashing light as she approached it, using the reflections to avoid dropping into a deep pool or twisting an ankle. Sometimes she missed, and her boots filled and sloshed with seawater. Sometimes she saw dark figures silhouetted against the light, and then they would vanish a moment later. But a person could only be on edge for so long until the feeling became normal.

She climbed the wet rocks toward the light, and the crowned spire materialized in full. The tower's architecture resembled that of the ruined city: a pale stone obelisk covered with carvings and rooted upon an angled base. The fixed torch at its top rotated rhythmically, like a sturdy heart pumping out warmth into the darkness. *What is this thing?* There was a word for it, but it remained just out of reach, lost in the mist.

As she summited the rocky outcropping, Sofia saw more light emanating from the base of the tower: a warm, flickering glow that danced chaotically in comparison to the regimented signal above. As she drew closer, winding her way up the beach and onto the small peninsula, she perceived more detail: secondary structures flanked the tower, all squarish, ancient-looking and stone. They crowded around their taller kin obediently and stood watch over the fire. A low wall encircled the area. On the far side, a stone stair led away from the structures, down a small incline to a jetty that extended toward the sea. There, a smaller tower kept its own vigil, a miniature version of the larger one.

Sofia used the darkness to hide her approach. *More of those...things could be waiting here.* She drew the sword from her belt and held it at the ready as she crept in the direction of the tower and the adjacent buildings. Firelight flickered through the gaps between them. Then, on the breeze, Sofia heard people talking. *Talking!* Not the mad ramblings of the inhabitants of the abandoned city, either. Sofia listened to the cadence of conversation, even laughter.

Her body willed her to move toward something familiar, but she hesitated. Yesterday, she might have run toward the voices without a thought. But that was before. For all she knew, these people were responsible for whatever had befallen the ruined city. For all she knew, they'd brought her here.

Sofia slipped down a narrow alley between two squat buildings and crept closer, staying low. Piles of thick logs and unused stone blocks offered perfect cover.

Peering from her hiding spot, she took in the scene: A collection of burning iron braziers scattered across the stone courtyard bathed the area in warm light. Even though she felt no chill, her skin itched for the comfort of the heat. The *idea* of it. Around the fires, people sat on benches, conversing quietly, eating and drinking. They wore plain linen garments, ill fitting and as drab as the gray shore.

Sofia inched closer to eavesdrop properly. The words were not unlike the ones she'd heard in the ruined city. But these seemed friendly. *Human*, like people ought to sound. The sounds rolled together in a pleasing rhythm with long sounds that fell off the tongue. Sofia closed her eyes and began to hear words she recognized. "Wait" and "watch" and "come."

She didn't notice the man until he stood above her. Sofia jumped to her feet, clumsily pointing the sword at his throat. He seemed as surprised as she.

"Who are you?" demanded Sofia. The man said something Sofia didn't understand. He held up his hands as he backed up toward the center of the courtyard. He was shorter than she, and his limbs seemed a little too long for his frame. Pale blue eyes set wide apart darted between hers and the sword.

As he retreated into the courtyard, the people there cried out and gathered around them. Some of them began to shout. Others seemed afraid. The man in front of Sofia gestured for stillness, to wait. He spoke again, calmly, but Sofia couldn't understand him.

She held the sword with both hands, kneading the grip, unsure of what to do next. If the crowd all rushed her, it was over. A woman pushed her way through the mob. She called out something to the rest of them. Sofia interpreted her meaning as "stop," but she couldn't be sure. The woman was undeniably beautiful and petite, with keen, sharp eyes. Warm, ash-colored hair hung far past her shoulders. Sofia's skin was tanned leather compared to hers.

She approached Sofia slowly with outstretched hands. She spoke delicately, the reassuring tone clear. Sofia lowered the blade, and the woman nodded, smiling. *She smiled.* After the hell of the last day, the power of that smile almost brought

Sofia to tears. The woman nodded again and waved. *Come.* Sofia scanned the dozens of eyes on her as she slowly slid the sword back into her belt. There didn't seem to be a choice now. The woman took Sofia's arm and led her away. No one said a word. The crowd watched.

Sofia put their number at around fifty; all were dressed the same in nondescript woven garments, nothing like the elaborate clothing she'd seen within the clothing shop she'd sheltered in. Sofia studied their faces as the young woman led her past them. They were all striking—beautiful, even. As diverse as any fifty, random people might be, but each more attractive than even the best of luck could produce.

The woman motioned for Sofia to sit at a long, wooden table built into the earth. She whispered something into the ear of a nearby man before sitting herself. The onlookers sat at a distance, watching Sofia with intense curiosity. The sound of fire cracked and popped. The stillness was agony. The woman across from Sofia folded her hands in front of her. She smiled as she finally spoke, slowly and deliberately.

"Chota," the woman said. She waved.

Sofia shifted in her seat. "Hello?" Sofia replied deliberately. To the people watching her, it sounded like "oh-la." The man from before reappeared, carrying a loaf of bread. It steamed in the coldness of the night. He handed it to the woman, who broke off a piece and, in turn, handed it to Sofia. "Cotacua," she said pointing to her mouth.

Sofia took the bread. It surprised her that, until this point, the thought of food had barely crossed her mind. The ache of hunger was simply not there. But the smell was warm and tempting, and soon her appetite appeared with a fury. Sofia took a bite. The sweet taste melted across her tongue. It was the only thing she had any recollection of ever tasting, but it was more than satisfying. The sensation of eating was *remarkable.* Like eating warm air, spiced with things she could not recognize. The woman across from her smiled once more. "Eyeh es *good,* nah amsi?"

"*Good,*" Sofia repeated, but what she said wasn't the familiar sound of her native tongue. It was *theirs.* "How is this possible?"

"We don't *sabemati. Eyeh lentiza* slowly. Listen."

As Sofia ate, the woman spoke to her and to others standing around. They still eyed Sofia with an uncomfortable intensity, but the fact that Sofia was *communicating* with people made her quickly forget about it.

Within an hour, Sofia began to hear words she recognized in the conversation. They shone through the unfamiliar, ancient sounds. The woman pointed at objects and said their names: table, fire, sky, ground, and the words came to Sofia faster. She repeated them back using the *feeling* of her own speech, but the words came out in the new tongue. Soon, the strangeness faded and the new language was as natural to Sofia as breathing.

"Can you fully understand me now?" the woman asked.

"I think so," Sofia said using her new words. "How?"

"We're not sure," the woman replied. "The words just come after a time."

Sofia nodded, though her thoughts raced. "Where are we?"

"We don't know that either, unfortunately. None of us remember anything. We all washed up alone on the beach and made our way here."

Sofia's heart sank. They were as lost as she was. "The only thing I remember is my name," she said. Murmurs rippled through the crowd. The woman pleaded silence from them with a wave.

"Your name?" the woman asked. "You...*remember* it?"

"Of course. I'm Sofia. You don't remember your names? None of you?" Sofia scanned the crowd of shaking heads. They looked at her with wide, astonished stares.

"No," said the woman with a raised eyebrow. "You're the first person we've met who can remember anything. Where did you come from?" She peered at Sofia's clothing and the sword hilt sticking out from her belt.

Sofia felt anxiousness creeping over her. The armor strapped to her chest was partially covered in ancient blood. She understood how it might appear. "From the water, like you," Sofia said, which was true.

"But where did you get those?" a man called out from the crowd. "The sword and that armor? Where did those come from?"

"Tell us how you remember! How did we get here? Will we remember, too?" called another.

"What about our families?"

"What's out there? Are we in danger?"

"No! I mean, I don't know. I—" Sofia struggled to find the words. She couldn't begin to describe what she'd seen in the ruined city. She wanted to run and hide from their stares.

"Enough, enough!" said the woman with more authority than her small size seemed capable of. "Leave her be. We don't know what this woman has been through, and we all have strange stories to tell if we choose to. Everyone lost is welcome here; let's remember that. Come with me, Sofia."

The others took their cue from the woman and dispersed, but their eyes lingered. They watched Sofia with interest as she made her way to a large dormitory lined with cots. Exposed rafters pitched the roof high. Through the few windows, the light from the tower flashed in sequence. Sofia found an empty cot at the end of the row and slumped down. She was glad to be away from the crowd for the moment. Weariness caught up to her.

"Don't worry. They're just scared," said the woman.

"How long have you been here?" Sofia asked, pulling her boots off.

"Fourteen days. I was one of the first. I suppose that's why they listen to me."

"Hmm. And you really can't remember anything?" Sofia asked. The woman shook her head.

"What do I call you?"

"Alana," the woman said. "I chose it. Goodnight, Sofia. We'll speak more tomorrow."

The others filtered in one by one to find their beds, yet sleep did not come to her. Sofia stared at the ceiling for hours, listening to their breathing as the others slept. She wondered when she might drift into dreams like they did. But there were too many questions, and no one here seemed to have the answers. *Who made this place, and why?*

She quietly changed into the fresh set of clothes she found under her cot. They weren't as finely made as the ones she'd found in the shop a day ago, but there was something to be said for trying to fit in. *But where did these clothes come from? And the food?* Once more she felt there was purpose to it all, but a purpose she could not see.

With little chance of sleep, Sofia slipped out of the barracks and walked the length of the peninsula as it reached to the sea. She sat on the rocks until the morning came and transformed the dark fog into a slightly brighter gray haze. It was still early, and the cluster of dwellings slept quietly by the still-burning firelight. Overhead, the signal flashed. Sofia explored the ancient stone buildings with their arched doorways and tiled roofs, poking her head inside the dark interiors. She half expected to find those things from the ruins lurking in the shadows. Sofia could still hear their wailing in the back of her mind. But this place was different than that one, she reminded herself. There was warmth and life here.

As daylight strengthened and people began to mingle around the encampment, Sofia engaged everyone she could to learn what they knew. Some seemed open and curious. One attractive, slender man with dark skin and finely cropped, black hair talked at length about his week inside a cave by the ocean. He had chosen the name Milo because he liked the sound of it. He and another man, Luiz, had spent time in the cave together after meeting on the beach. Milo said there were creatures living in the cave wanting to eat them, and the two men had rested in shifts to protect one another. By the fifth day, the creatures were getting too close, so he and Luiz had started walking. Sofia nodded politely. Given what she'd seen, there was no reason not to believe him.

A stocky woman with thick cheeks and ruddy hair, happy to have an ear to fill, inundated Sofia with her theories regarding the oddities of their surroundings. She followed Sofia as she paced the perimeter of the compound, talking the entire time. The stout woman, who had taken to calling herself, Isa, pointed out obvious facts like how the fog never seemed to lift, as well as more obscure observations such as the apparent lack of tides and wildlife. There was an *artificialness* to the place, Isa said, that was difficult to describe. Were they being watched, she wondered? Sofia didn't think so, but she could not deny the oddities nor offer better explanations.

At no point during her dealings with the others did Sofia reveal anything about her time in the ruined city to anyone. Each time the conversation redirected toward her, she vaguely described her time on the beach and little else. How could she tell them about the horror of the abandoned city? And if she did, would they believe her? Sofia was unsure if she believed it herself. Besides, no one here seemed to know any more than she about the things she'd seen. No sense making things worse by scaring them. Nothing good would come from that abandoned city; Sofia was sure of it. But despite her intentions, she began to sense an air of suspicion among the small community. Some eyed her from a distance, watching. Whispering. When Sofia did manage to strike up a conversation with them, the subject of the sword always came up. It was obvious they didn't believe her story about finding it in the sand.

"So, what is it?" Sofia asked as Alana led her through the door at the tower's base. Sofia liked talking to Alana; it was easy somehow.

"It's a lighthouse," said Alana.

Lighthouse. The word felt familiar. "What's a lighthouse for?" Sophia gazed upward at the hollow interior. There was no clear way to reach the top.

"To guide ships from danger, I think. But this one seems meant for us. It's what drew the others and me from the beach. Take a look at this."

Alana pointed to the floor. At the center of the hollow tower, etched into the stone tiles, was a great circular glyph made up of hundreds of interlocking symbols. They wove in between one another in intricate patterns, and all rotated around a central point—a long, teardrop shape. The end of it pointed farther inland. It looked remarkably similar to the marker Sophia had found on the beach. "Have you seen something like this before?" Alana asked, watching her reaction carefully.

Sofia said nothing as she pondered the connection. Alana knelt down and pointed at the symbols. "Some people here think it's some kind of calendar, that something is going to happen soon. What little sun there is comes in from that hole there," Alana said, indicating the hole in the lighthouse wall. A thick, round piece of glass was set there, somehow able to magnify the weak sunlight filtering through the mist into a pale beam. "And each day it has been getting closer to this point." Alana pointed to the shard of white light, which, by design, looked to be inching toward the inscription's zenith.

Sofia shrugged. "I know as much as you do about all of this."

Alana sighed. "All right. I'm sure you have your reasons; I can accept that. But the others…" She nodded toward the door. "They need answers. The armor, your clothes—where did they come from? And your name. No one can remember a thing except for you, Sofia. They think you know something about this place, more than you're saying." Alana looked Sofia square in the eyes. "I do, too."

Sofia felt a flash of anger. "They should worry about themselves."

"They're frightened," said Alana, gently. "We all are."

Something about Alana made Sofia wonder if she should trust her. Maybe it was Alana's directness or her authority. Perhaps it was something deeper, something innate that one needed no memories to judge. There was a genuineness in Alana's concern for the people here that Sofia admired. "I saw...things," Sofia finally said. "Strange things. And I've seen symbols like these."

"Where?"

"I don't know. Not far from here, there is a city, high up on the cliffs." Sofia shuddered. "You don't want to go there. Believe me." She said no more, and Alana did not ask.

Sofia left Alana and the others behind to take a long walk along the beach to settle her mind. She left her boots on the rocks and let the surf roll over her toes as she walked across the steel-colored sand. The mist thickened once again as darkness began to fall. The fog was a relentless force that never diminished. Each day the sun would fight back, and each night the mist would return in a never-ending cycle.

Sofia's mind was spent. The questions piled up, one after another, until she felt the weight of them would crush her completely. Why didn't anyone remember anything? Why could she? Who built this place, and more important, why? There seemed to be some intent to it all, but it remained a mystery.

She felt like running, like screaming. She felt on the verge of breaking down completely or doing something harm. She needed some time to think and to rest. Guided by the lighthouse's rhythmic glare, Sofia retraced her steps. She considered going to the barracks but decided against it. Enough stares for one day. Instead, she found a comfortable spot at the tower's base overlooking the dark, turbulent sea. There, Sofia sat alone, clutching her knees, and tried to let the sounds of crashing waves drown the endless questions running through her mind.

And finally, on the third night, she slept.

4

Colored paper masked the windows, a cheap alternative to stained glass. It did the trick. Reds and yellows bathed the room, drawing attention to the worn carpet, peeling paint and water-stained walls. The small apartment was more rathole than rectory. A double-stacked mattress sat on the floor flanked by a nightstand piled high with cheap holy relics—candles and icons on a particleboard altar. Nearby, a woman sobbed softly on the bed. Sofia almost didn't notice her at first. The woman's dress, pale blue-green and covered with worn stars, barely covered her swollen belly. The woman caressed her stomach instinctively with one hand and fiddled with beads in the other. Dark curls hung low, masking her face. A gold symbol hung from her neck.

Sofia took in the room, unable to say a word. Unable to move. She was there, living it, but at the same time, watching from a distance. She spoke. The words were not her own. But she felt the anger behind them sure enough. Pure, uncut rage. It coursed through her like hot venom. Sofia drove her fist clean through the cheap drywall for reasons unknown.

The woman on the bed started screaming. Sofia ripped the nightstand from the floor with single, powerful movement, sending the congregation of glass candles crashing everywhere. Another scream. Sofia inched closer as a predator would, savoring her fear. Powerful and fierce, yet still a passenger in a body that was not her own. Woman became beast, untamed and wild. Impulse devoured reason. *Is this happening?* Sofia couldn't be sure. But at that moment, she felt completely free do as she pleased. To take what she pleased. Kill whom she pleased.

And so, she did.

The woman screeched a final time as Sofia loomed over her. Her hands found their way to the woman's neck with little effort. She squeezed with a force her slender hands shouldn't be capable of. The blood pulsing within the woman's thin neck quickened for a moment, then slowed to a crawl. Sofia looked into her eyes. They burned like fierce emeralds, red with tears and terror. She clawed at Sofia's face in vain. Eyes bulging, skin crimson and ready to burst, she managed one word before Sofia crushed the life from her.

"Sofia."

***

Am I a murderer?

Sofia awoke in a cold sweat. Some words came slowly to her in this strange place, their meanings distant and vague, but "dream" had not been one of them. But in the groggy aftermath of sleep, she knew this thing called dream, called *nightmare. Or was it a memory?* She hoped not. The thought of killing another human being, especially a pregnant woman, disgusted her. But with no memories to ground herself, Sofia couldn't be completely sure *what* she had done—or was capable of.

No. Just a nightmare. Just a dream. Between the encounter with the thing that had chased her through the ruins and her utter exhaustion over the past few days, it was no surprise disturbing thoughts had crept into her sleep. It seemed logical enough. But the woman's face lingered in Sofia's mind. It was sharp, vivid. It didn't fade as Sofia imagined it should. *What if it wasn't a dream?*

It was still early, the fog not yet brightened by the rising sun, but she felt as rested as she could expect. Sofia pulled herself to her feet and spent the morning walking the perimeter of the lighthouse compound as caged animal would, tracing the confines of its pen. She contemplated the dream again and again. *Am I a murderer?* The thought twisted her gut.

She made her way to the far side of the settlement, behind the small cottages and other structures, where she found the beginnings of a road. It disappeared into the mist, following the same direction as the symbol on the lighthouse floor pointed to. Farther inland, she guessed. The allure of the unknown and the possibility of more answers pulled her toward it. She wanted to follow. Yes, she was safe here with her fellow amnesiacs, or so it seemed. But there had to be more to it.

An hour later, the sound of commotion drew her to the dormitories. A crowd had formed at its entrance, and their bland clothes blended together into one beige organism. Sofia wove through to find them surrounding the thin man with the blue eyes who had first startled her two nights before. He was examining her sword. A lanky girl stood at his side, holding Sofia's armor. Together they slid the blade through the hole punctured in the side of the plate, talking as they did so in a kind of reenactment of sorts. The crowd murmured.

"What's going on?" Sofia demanded. "What are you doing with my things?"

"Looking for the truth," said the man in a detached way, examining the sword. He picked at the bloodstain on the armor and rubbed the flakes between his fingers. "Where did you get these?" He paused, letting the words linger. "Did you kill someone and take them?" The crowd turned to her in silence.

"*No,*" Sofia said defiantly. She loomed over him, using her height advantage. "I found them." The smaller man seemed unconvinced and unimpressed. Others in the crowd shifted uncomfortably. Even Milo, whom Sofia had talked with at length the day before, avoided her eyes. Alana appeared from the crowd with a bewildered look on her face.

"Something will happen soon," the blue-eyed man continued. "Good or bad, we don't know. But if you know something about it, tell us." He did not point the blade at Sofia directly, but she took his meaning.

Anger tingled in Sofia's spine. "Is that a threat?"

"No, Erado. It isn't," Alana said, with arm outstretched toward the sword. The man named Erado stood for a moment before handing the blade over to her. The woman holding the armor let it fall in the dirt.

"This isn't how we survive here!" Alana said, addressing the entire group. "It's true we don't know what's going to happen next. And I am afraid, the same as all of you, but we can't let it divide us. It'll only make things worse."

Erado grunted. "Tell that to your friend." He turned and walked away.

***

A noise shook Sofia from her rest. She wasn't sleeping, really, just staring at the ceiling of the dormitory with every intention of not falling asleep. Thoughts of the ruined city mixed with the face of the murdered woman. And after the incident in the courtyard, it was clear she needed to watch her back.

Another sound. Murmurs drifted from the door leading to the courtyard. Sofia slid quietly from her bunk. Her fingertips found the hilt of the sword that had lain beneath her. Blade in hand, she tiptoed barefoot between the cots toward the door. She eyed the entrance from the safety of a corner and the shadows it contained. Beams of orange light fell across the floor, for the fires in the braziers outside never waned. Like clockwork, a flash from the lighthouse intensified the light all around and vanished just as quickly.

Sofia listened. She flattened against the wall and inched closer to the door. Only the sound of crackling fires and dozing people. Sofia relaxed. *Just nerves.* She started to make her way back to her bed when a hand cupped around her mouth and another around her body. Two more stripped the sword away and helped drag her from the dormitory. Her muffled screams failed to wake the others.

They sat her on the stone floor. It was cool against her feet. Her hands and feet were bound, dry, brittle rope around them. Sofia unwillingly hugged a thick wooden post that supported the ceiling. A roll of linen stuffed in her mouth kept her from speaking, and another over her face prevented her from seeing. Rustling of feet across the floor was all around her. *How did I let them surprise me?*

"I'm sorry," a voice whispered. "You didn't leave us any choice. Understand, we don't want to hurt you." The voice stopped talking for a moment, probably conferring with others Sofia couldn't see. *Was it Erado? If I wasn't tied up...*

"I would like to remove the gag so that we can talk. Please don't scream." Sofia didn't see a choice and nodded. A hand unbound her aching jaw. She thought about calling for help but decided against it. Maybe because her captors appeared reasonable, maybe because her pride wouldn't let her. She waited.

The voice whispered again. "Please, tell us what you know. Where did the sword come from? What is out there?"

"Erado? Is that you?" Silence. "Why should I tell you anything?"

"Prove to us you're not some kind of spy."

Sofia scoffed. "I'm not the one tying other people to a post." More whispers Sofia couldn't make out. *They won't do anything. It's a bluff.* The sound of metal scraping across stone filled the room. Sofia sensed heat nearby. Embers popped. Her heart jumped.

"Please," the voice pleaded again. "Don't make us do this." The whispers flew back and forth in disagreement then fell silent.

The logical thing to do would be to tell the whole story. Explain the ruins, the shadowy people living in the city and the dead warrior, but stubborn pride wouldn't let her. They didn't deserve to know. "Go to hell." The gag found its way back around her mouth, and the fire, her fingers.

The pain materialized slowly, then came to a blinding head. She strained against the ropes binding her, cutting into her flesh. Pairs of hands held her in place as she choked on the gag with muffled screams.

Sofia focused on the pain. She imagined herself as a piece of steel in a forge; white-hot from the heat but still sharp, still strong. A rage within flared to life. It overtook all notions of fear and reason and surged through her. And then, the pain was gone.

For a moment, Sofia thought she may have passed out. All feeling left her. She sensed hands holding her wrists, the prickly wood pillar between her legs and the cool floor underneath. She felt the waves of heat from the flame licking at her fingers. But the pain was gone. Without another thought as to why, Sofia leaned forward, plunging her hands deeper into the fire. Her captors cried out as the dry rope ignited, weakened and disintegrated, just as fast as she'd imagined it would.

Sofia pulled off the blindfold and saw three figures illuminated around her. She recognized them but knew only one of their names: *Erado*. The lanky woman from earlier was there, too, and another man, tanned and tall. They tried to restrain her. Sofia lunged once more at the brazier, pulling it toward her and toppling it over. Hot coals and ash sparked everywhere. The rope holding her ankles ignited. Everything dry in the room followed suit. Sofia, somehow immune to the flames, scrambled free from the burning restraints. She found her feet as her captors stared in disbelief. She looked down at her charred hands. They were black with ash and smoking but otherwise completely unscathed.

I...don't burn?

The sword in Erado's hand came quick.

He cried out and lunged at her, swinging wildly. Sofia caught sight of it and ducked at the last moment. The blade found its way deep into the post behind her with a thud. Some unfamiliar instinct took over. Time stalled. Sofia's vision narrowed. She did not think. She moved. Erupting from her crouched stance, her fist connecting with Erado's jaw, hitting with such force he crumpled to the ground a moment later, out cold. She stared at her blackened fist, surprised. This was not luck. This was reflex, something her body remembered.

Whatever it was, she liked the feel of it.

Only then did Sofia notice the growing flames around her. Erado's two companions were already fleeing the inferno. Sofia turned to the sword lodged into the now-burning wood. *Fire cannot hurt me.* Sofia grasped the hilt and heard a sizzling as she yanked it free. She looked at Erado's crumbled, unconscious body. She wondered for a moment if the world would be better off. She squeezed the hilt. Her muscles tensed...

The dream flashed before her. The woman in the little apartment screamed. The lonely, milky eyes of that wretch in the alley stared through her. Sofia felt a wave of nausea come over her, shaking her from her rage. She tossed the sword into the courtyard and dragged Erado's heavy body through the door and away from the flames.

Outside, the fire had caught the roof of the structure, and the flames churned and danced. Awoken by the commotion, sleepy people filtered out of the dormitory toward the blaze. They covered their mouths and stared at the burning building behind her. Some rushed toward it with an impulse to help, to do something. They threw dirt upon the flames and fetched water. As they did, Sofia saw fire reflected in their eyes. Everything around burned but her.

"What happened?" Alana asked, out of breath.

Sofia gazed at her shaking, inky hands. "They came after me...with fire."

"I'm sorry," Alana said. "I'm so sorry, Sofia. I had a feeling something like this would happen." She glanced down at Erado and knelt beside him. "Is he...?"

"No, he's fine," Sofia said. "Better than he deserves, anyway."

"People act stupidly when they're afraid," said Alana, shaking her head. Tears glistened in the light of the fire. "I should have been here to stop this."

"I have to leave," said Sofia after a moment. She picked up the sword, knowing full well what the crowd of onlookers must be thinking. There was little she could do about that now.

***

Alana and Sofia stood at the trailhead leading away from the lighthouse as dawn broke. In the distance, smoke still rose from where the fire once burned. Alana handed her a sling filled with bread and a pouch of water. Sofia was wearing her old clothes again, the ones she'd found in the city. She'd washed them in the sea, and although they were visibly clean, they smelled freshly of salt. So, too, did her hands. The soot had washed away to reveal no burns, not even a scratch.

I do not burn.

"What does the lion mean?" Alana asked, noting the design on the breastplate strapped across Sofia's chest. Sofia glanced down, shook her head and shrugged.

"Don't think too badly of them," Alana said, changing subjects. "Most of them are good people, I think. Just...lost. I will make sure they don't hurt anyone else." Sofia wasn't sure she completely agreed but didn't argue the point.

"I need answers, Alana, and I don't think they are here."

"And what if help is coming?"

"What if it isn't?" Sofia nodded toward the road. "If I find help, I'll bring it back."

Alana smiled. "And if it comes to us, we'll find you. Be careful, Sofia." Alana wrapped her arms around Sofia's neck. Surprised by the gesture, Sofia squeezed back.

With the dirt road at her feet, Sofia slid her sword into her belt, feeling the confident weight of it at her side, and took her first step into the gray unknown.

She didn't look back.

5

As the mist thinned, Sofia made her way inland. She trekked for days over dark, barren hills before stumbling upon a vast graveyard of charred, leafless trees. The forest had not risen gradually. Like the wall that encircled the ruined city, the perimeter of trees merely appeared fully formed and ominous.

She stood at the border of the woods, staring into the tangle of ancient corpses. Blackened fingers pierced the fog like withered hands grasping at smoke. Connecting the limbs were dark trunks that disappeared into a blanket of gray covering the ground.

Sofia sat down next to the road to rest for a moment. Something caught her attention above. *A bird!* It flew overhead, the first sign of an animal. At least, she didn't remember seeing one before. It soared over the trees and disappeared. *A good sign, I hope.* The longer she sat, the more the stillness of the forest reminded her of the ruins and the shambling figures wandering its streets. The same eerie quiet enveloped this place.

She'd considered turning back many times. It was safe there. But there was an itch that would never be satisfied if she did. And there was no going back to the lighthouse after what happened. Not now. The road Sofia followed had remained true and, even now, plunged headlong into the forest, unhindered. *All roads lead somewhere,* she reminded herself.

So, she swallowed a mouthful of water from her leather vessel and starting walking into the forest. After a few minutes, she noticed the gradual darkness descending around her. Huge, ancient branches overhead shrouded what little light there was before. It was unnerving.

A tree, damp and black, lay across the road ahead. It was wider than Sofia's arms could stretch, and she had to scramble over the slick bark to reach the road on the other side. As she did, she noticed the roots still anchored firmly to the earth and splintered where the trunk had once connected. More fallen trees lay in her path, and farther from the road, even more. The damage didn't seem to be a natural sort of chaos. There had been intent at work here. Something had raged. A fire. Climbing over the trunks covered Sofia's hands in greasy soot. Her thoughts returned to the burned building near the lighthouse. She had decided then the fire wouldn't burn her, and somehow it hadn't. The forest had not been so lucky.

A while later, Sofia sat down on a felled log and gnawed on a piece of bread from her sling. She wasn't particularly hungry, but it felt good to eat something. The sweet taste made her think of first meeting Alana and how she missed having someone to talk to. But the memory of standing over Erado lingered; sword in hand, the sense of power running through her. The urge to do something terrible tempting her. She didn't want to be that person. It made her wonder if losing her memory was a blessing, or a curse. *If I am a murderer, maybe it would be better forgotten.*

The time passed, and the dark turned darker. Had she been walking for days now? It was difficult to tell when one day ended and another began.

Sofia slipped off the road, keeping it well in sight, and found a small clearing where the ground was less damp. The snapping of tree branches cracked loudly, echoing through the dreary place. Sofia gathered twigs and kindling nearby, a seemingly simple task that, in practice, took entirely more effort than it should have. The trees were tough and unyielding, as was the soil when she tried to dig it with the blade of her sword. It was as if the land was permanently fixed and resisted any kind of change. The forest, charred and moist as it was, should have been half rotten yet appeared freshly burned. But there was no hint of smoke.

Sofia piled her kindling in the pathetic hole and, using her sword, attempted to coax a spark from the blade with a stone. Occasionally, she stopped and listened for anything the noise might have attracted, but always the silence endured. A fire probably wasn't worth all the effort, Sofia thought as she labored, but it seemed like a good idea. She missed the warmth of the lighthouse braziers. Sleeping at the base of a tree or in a dugout near a fallen log night after night should have been uncomfortable, but the chill hadn't bothered her. At least not physically. Each time she'd lain down to rest, the same disturbing dream had come to her: candles in the small apartment, the woman screaming and the feeling Sofia had been part of something terrible. And so, she chose not to sleep and avoided it if she could.

Sofia pulled the blade across the stone again and again. Sparks flew. Sofia cursed. Each attempt to build a fire ended with same results: a sad pile of sticks in a wet hole and filthy hands. She knew *how* to build a fire, in principle, anyway, but something prevented the wood from igniting no matter what she tried.

She slumped down, frustrated, staring at the indifferent forest. *If I can't get even a spark to catch, how did this whole place burn down? Or that building by the lighthouse, for that matter?*

A voice drifted through the trees. Whispers. Sofia froze for a moment, then peered over the felled logs, straining to hear. The sound was ancient, far away not in distance but in time, as if faint voices had been echoing for a thousand years. She could not understand the language, and her heartbeat quickened. *Did that thing in the tunnels finally catch up to me?*

She drew her sword from her belt with trembling hands. She crouched, waiting, and after a minute or two, the whispers began to fade.

Sofia pulled her hair back with a cord and went after the sound. Moving slowly and occasionally pausing to listen, she tracked the sound like a predator through the underbrush. It would drift one way, and Sofia would follow it. Other noises began to appear amidst the unintelligible whispers. Voices, yes, but also distant screams and desperate cries of anguish. The sound of metal and fire and drums beat inside her head. Beads of sweat ran down her neck, soaking the tunic under the armor strapped to her chest. Sofia ran, chasing the strengthening whispers deeper into the forest. Far behind, the road faded into the mist.

The source of the noise eluded her as Sofia followed her ears, darting to and fro at random and tripping over logs and holes obscured by the mist. Mad curiosity replaced fear, for the sound was now deep under her skin, in her bones and behind her eyes. Her own thoughts began to fade away, and all she could hear were the chaotic sounds of pain, of anger. She no longer cared what the voices were, only how to make them stop.

A misstep. A steep ledge sent her tumbling. Down a gully, over thick roots and rocks, Sofia crashed through the underbrush. Sharp brambles tore at her. *Or were they grabbing at her?* She came to rest at the edge of a large hole, gasping for the wind that had escaped her lungs. There were no trees here. The mist stretched out into the distance but was thin enough for her to see the forest floor.

Bodies. As far as Sofia could see, twisted, blackened bodies lay tangled in the massive pit.

A grave.

A surge of revulsion blindsided Sofia as she put charred faces to the screams in her head. It was as if the corpses were frozen while trying to escape a lake of tar. Where one person ended and the other began was indistinguishable. Burnt arms and hands and feet stretched out from the dark soil, reaching for some salvation that would never come.

Sofia hung her head between her knees. Hot nausea washed over her, and she retched, spitting into the dirt. *Make it stop, make it stop, make it stop,* she whispered to herself as the sound in her head grew louder. She covered her ears in vain. Sofia skirted the rim of the pit, stumbling across the uneven earth and the limbs reaching out toward her, threatening to drag her down into the darkness. She willed her legs to move, running at full speed through the mist. Branches tore at her face and roots at her ankles. Faster and faster, she fled from the mass grave until exhausted.

"MAKE IT STOP!" she screamed.

And then, it stopped. Silence returned to the forest as Sofia's voice echoed and trailed off. Once again, she was alone with her thoughts.

***

The next day, Sofia woke groggy and met a muted sky. Her mind was a haze. Clouded by the fantasy— or recollection—of murder in the dingy apartment, her dreams mixed with the terrible memory of the mass grave. She kneaded her forehead and squeezed her eyes tight to clear her mind. Coming to her feet, she realized she had no idea where the road was nor how to go back to find it. Her sense of direction was as dull and featureless as the landscape. But as she looked around, Sofia noticed the forest looked different here. It was thin and patchy, and the mist was weakening its hold across the land. Above, the white disk of the sun shone through the haze with almost a hint of warmth to it.

The sun! However weak, its light inspired her. She had no memory of how sunlight felt, but something inside of her knew what she'd been missing. She headed east, and the sun's power grew. It burned away the mist to reveal pale hues across the barren land. A steel-colored sky cooled to cerulean, and the earth warmed to ruddy shades of gold. Sofia's eyes drank the color greedily, having starved for so long on the monotonous gray of the coast.

By the second day of walking without rest, she left the forest far behind, and a vast, dry plain now stretched out before her. Stubborn scrub brush dotted the dusty hills and gullies. Dry creeks severed the earth's flesh with deep cracks where she labored to dig holes and find fresh water. She never did.

There were more birds now, too, and other living things. Signs of movement in her periphery put her on edge at first, but they soon became normal. Insects trekked across the earth doing whatever it is insects do, chased by mice and other creatures Sofia did not know the names of.

The sunlight fatigued her eyes as she surveyed the new landscape, taking in the view. The mist had always kept the horizon shrouded, but now, Sofia could see far. And at night, as she continued to walk to keep the dreams at bay, she saw her first glint of stars. She connected them to make shapes in the sky and wondered if anyone else had ever imagined the same images she did.

Four days passed. Sofia crested a small hill to get a better view of where to head next. To the west where the sun was setting, she spied what looked to be a patch of green in the distance, low in a valley. *Green!* It glinted like an emerald half-buried in sand. She began walking toward it, glancing away for a moment and then fixating on the patch of verdant green once more to make it sure it was real. After an hour, not only was Sofia confident the green was real, but she could also make out the shapes of lush trees and foliage surrounding what she hoped might be the shimmer of water. She quickened her pace. Bracing the sword hilt with one hand and gripping her sling in the other, she bound over the rocky land as it gently sloped down from the hills toward salvation.

A particularly thick section of underbrush slowed her descent. She cut her way through to find the edge of a ravine that opened wide and deep beneath her feet. Nausea and vertigo came hard and fast. Sofia took a breath and a step back and surveyed the view from a safe vantage. Only then could she see what lay below.

The oasis was at the bottom of the valley, nestled at the base of hills a kilometer or two away. Clusters of trees clung to the hills in thin patches that grew thicker near the valley floor. They were a hearty bunch and congregated around a pond.

"Beautiful," Sofia said, satisfied with herself.

She studied the slope of the ravine beneath her feet for the safest route down. Everything in her brain was telling her to find a long way around. It was steep and sharp in all directions. As she scanned the rock, something moving caught her eye in the valley below. She almost didn't register it. After seeing so few signs of life other than the occasional bird or rodent, it was surprising.

This creature, however, was altogether something new. It was alive, black and gleaming, but it moved with an unnatural and lopsided gait. It reminded her of the thing that had chased her in the ruined city, but larger. Though awkward, it moved surprisingly fast and with purpose. It bounded, unhindered by the terrain, working its way down into the gully where the trees were denser. *Was it chasing something or being chased?*

Just then, a huge shape buzzed by Sofia with a *whoosh* that kicked up the dust around her. She saw the approaching mass out of the corner of her eye and cried out, dropping instinctively to the ground. Looking up a second later, Sofia could see what looked to be large bird—an *enormous* bird—swoop toward the grove and bomb the black shape. A huge cloud of dust erupted around them.

What the hell? Sofia stared for a moment with her hand shielding her eyes from the glare. There was no sign of either shape, but there was a sound on the breeze. Unlike like the horrible whispers in the forest, it almost sounded like...*singing*. Something about the melody, faint as it was, struck a deep chord. A clear feeling of determination bubbled up inside of her. It washed away the days of dreariness and despair and pushed her into action. Not even the fear of falling slowed her down.

She found a patch of loose scree and rode it down the incline with speed. Toward danger, possibly, but the song drew her toward it, calling to her.

She struggled to maintain her balance as she barreled downward, dodging boulders. The incline steepened severely toward the bottom, and Sofia lost her footing, toppling backward. She gasped as the impact stole the wind from her lungs, but the rocky avalanche of loose shale was already in motion and had no intention of stopping. A moment later, the landslide deposited her at the base of the slope, half buried in rocky debris and dust.

Shit. Sofia scanned the edge of the grove ahead, panting and paying no mind to the cuts and scrapes covering her body. There was no movement, but the singing was there, louder, inspiring her on.

She sprinted the kilometer or so to the outskirt of the oasis, ignoring the uneven terrain. Thirty meters from the brush, which she could see now was a tangle of dense scrub and thick trees, Sofia heard a sound that paralyzed her muscles. Terror struck the most primitive part of her brain. Her body had no response. It was something akin to a roar, a scream and a death cry all at once, combined in a dissonance that was grating and terrible. Her footing wavered, and she fell to her knees. A distinctly human shout, defiant and loud but beautiful in tone, cut through the haze like a splash of cold water. The sound somehow woke her muscles from stasis, and Sofia staggered through the undergrowth, darting through the maze of bushes that blocked her vision.

She reached a clearing and, unable to process what she was seeing, stopped.
Oh, my God.
The thing she'd seen from afar was indeed black, but slick like oil and covered with sharp quills. It stood taller than a man at the shoulder, with a stubby snout and a massively built jaw filled with irregular, yellow teeth. Deeply set in black sockets were two pinpoints of light that gave the indication of eyes, but not of life. It careened on all fours toward what she had thought was an oversized hawk—her second mistake. The beast's prey was not a giant bird as she had imagined. It was a man with the wings of a bird.

A man, with wings.

Sofia couldn't decide which of the two was more incredible. Even after all she'd seen in the past week, she could do little more than stand there, dumbfounded. But there they were: the black, oily creature snarling with rage and a winged man, clad in golden armor and robes of white, crimson and other bright hues. His armor plating was similar to Sofia's, only more ornate, fluted at the edges. Colored feathers—not of his wings—and complex woven embellishments layered so heavily on his body Sofia was surprised by his nimbleness. The man's face was obscured behind an embroidered mask.

Sofia's brain struggled for the word to define him. The feathered appendages seemed a perfect extension of the man, spread menacingly, like a game bird defending its clutch. They were painted in places with vibrant swaths of color, and the tips were alternating reds and other warm hues. The wings made his visage twice as large as a normal man, and in both hands he gripped a long spear inlaid with gold. Its tip trickled black gore that sizzled and steamed.

He was singing. It was a choral chant of some kind, and the stirring harmony pulled at her in ways she couldn't understand, but it was if she could feel and taste it. She wanted never to part from it.

The man caught sight of her. He stared right at her with golden eyes. Momentarily distracted, the singing stopped. The creature felt no such distraction, and charged forward, its bulky form shaking the ground as it did. The man with wings came to his senses in time to see the creature coming. A ring of light materialized around his head, obscuring his face like a glowing visor of fire. He thrust the butt of the shaft into the dirt, stepped on it with his foot, and angled the point of the spear at the beast as it barreled toward him. But the move was mistimed and too slow. The spear clipped the beast's flank, bowed and snapped, sending the parts of the weapon flying.

The creature howled again, this time so loudly it brought Sofia low. She covered her ears and screamed in terror. It was the sound of pure madness. In her mind was the horror of the mass grave, the screams, the hands all around her...

The winged man appeared immune to the effect. But he was now on the ground, the beast atop him—wounded, but by no means defeated. Even so, he began to sing again.

The creature snapped and clawed furiously as the man protected his face with one hand while trying to reach for something at his side with the other. Sofia regained her senses, the melody somehow focusing her attention back to the present moment. Amidst the song, she could hear the crumpling of metal as the creature tore at the winged man's armor. He unsheathed a small blade at his side and stabbed at the throat of the creature, which showed no sign of slowing.

Sofia reached for her sword, but there was nothing behind her. *Damn!* She must have lost it during her descent of the bluff. She desperately searched for something, anything. *There!* She spotted the broken spear lying a few meters away and dashed for it. The intricately carved shaft was incredibly heavy, but Sofia found the strength to heft the gilded lance into both hands. With a cry, she charged, aiming for the flank of the spined creature.

The black monster noticed her a split second before the spear plunged deep into its side, and it wheeled its massive skull toward her. Sofia met its eyes, paralyzed by what she saw. A darkness crept over her. The light dimmed and time crawled. It was like staring into the milky eyes of the man in the city. The same loneliness, the same sorrow. But this was magnified to such a degree that Sofia's very sanity stretched thin to the point of breaking.

The winged man used the moment to drive his blade deep into the beast's throat. With both hands, he wrenched the dagger across its neck and opened it from right to left. Hot gore poured from the wound, a boiling substance like molten ore, covering him. He grunted and moaned in pain. A hiss of steam. *He can burn.*

The beast slumped, gurgling, releasing Sofia from its spell. Stunned, she shook her head and breathed deeply to clear her sluggish mind.

She pushed with all her might to roll the creature off the man. The barbed quills tore at her flesh, and the creature's bulk was too great. The man moaned something she could not understand, gesturing to the shaft still protruding from the beast's side before slipping into unconsciousness.

Leverage. Sofia understood. She yanked the spear out of the wound with a sick, sizzling sound. Planting the shaft deep under the beast's head, Sofia pried upward with all her strength, but the thing would not move. She worked the spear in deeper and pulled instead, hanging her weight on the instrument. She grunted in frustration. A spark of anger flared up, and she thought of the brazier and her hands hovering over the fire. *It will not burn me.* Sofia tapped some hidden well for a surge of strength. To her surprise, the corpse moved just enough for her to heave its mass off the winged man and drag his heavy body free.

The golden plates of his armor sizzled and popped and would be brutally hot to the touch, but Sofia felt nothing as she removed the melted metal. She used the dagger to slice the connecting straps and peel the plates apart with the blade, prying the melted ones away from puckering flesh. The unconscious man's wings splayed in the dirt were blackened by the creature's inky filth.

Using what remained of the man's robes and what little water she had left, Sofia cleaned the gore from the man's flesh as quickly as she could. The black ichor left sickly burns upon his skin.

Sofia collapsed on the ground next to the man with the wings as shock set in. Nearby, the steaming corpse of the creature spewed hot blackness onto the earth.

As she lay there absently, the word she was looking for finally came to her.

Angel?

6

None of this makes sense.

Sofia eyed the carcass from a distance. It was an eerie thing, a black stain in the morning light.

She made her way down the cliff face, stepping over boulders and minding loose shale to the oasis below. The cave she had found, nestled between two great faces of stone, offered a good view of the area should any more...*things* approach.

It had taken nearly all night to drag the unconscious, winged man to safety, and still he slept. But restless curiosity urged her to move, and she wanted a closer look at the creature.

Noxious odor filled her senses long before she drew close to the scene of the battle. Sofia turned upwind, taking the long way to keep the acrid, sour smell from her lungs. They might become infected permanently otherwise. The winged man's woven headwrap she had tied across her face did little to keep the smell at bay, despite the strong incense smell that permeated the cloth.

Sofia noticed her mood darken in the presence of the hulking pile of dead flesh. She studied it in detail. It was animal, but it had an undeniably *unnatural* quality to it. The spines, for instance, seemed to have no other purpose but to make the thing look menacing. One set of limbs was oddly disproportionate, as if starvation had affected part of the body rather than the whole. The closer she got, the more feelings of sorrow, anger and hopelessness grew.

The beast's massive cranium lay in the dirt. The dim light that had glowed in its eyes had gone out, leaving only black pits in its skull. Curiously, on the side of the creature's head was what looked to be a human-like ear, sharpened to a point.

On the flesh not covered in spines, there were brands. Blocky, intricate symbols seared deep into the flesh in long, vertical patterns. Their edges, still slick with ichor, caught the light of the sun. The oily mass still radiated heat even after being dead for hours. The molten gore emptied from its body had seared the surrounding soil as it oozed forth, a dark stain on the earth. Sofia wondered if anything could grow there again.

Despite the grotesqueness, Sofia could not help but feel a sense of pride standing over it. *She* had helped slay the monster. The feeling was a mixture of terror and excitement. And there, too, the feeling of power.

She poked at the hide with the broken spear, burying the shaft between the tangle of quills, probing. No wonder the spear had shattered. The hide was a thick shell and would not give.

Sofia lingered near the body, and a bizarre impulse came over her. She drew the dagger from her belt to pry a serrated tooth from the creature's skull.

If asked, Sofia could not say why she wanted such a thing, and it did not come willingly. As she mutilated the maw to gain her prize, tearing with the blade to dislodge one of the fangs, a reservoir of emotion let loose. Angry, frustrated tears welled up in her eyes and mixed with sweat, burning more than fire ever could. Sofia sobbed as she hacked the tooth free with the tearing of flesh and the splintering of bone. *What's wrong with me?*

She knelt in the dirt, aimlessly rubbing the trophy clean, wondering what had caused her to retrieve it in the first place. The tooth was long, its root much longer than the exposed edge. Its shape reminded her of her own sharper canines, thick in the middle and honed to a squat point. It was the color of yellow marble and scalding to the touch, but she knew it would not burn her. It would forever remind her of that fact.

Sofia wiped her eyes clean with the back of her hand and left the carcass on the plain, feeling better the farther she got from it. She trekked back through the bush to her shelter in the cave.

She ran through it all again. The beach, the ruins on the cliff, the lighthouse—all shrouded in mist, all frozen in time. Scars of something terrible long ago.

And the people! What part did they play in everything? Herself, Alana and the others—strangers with no memories. *And now,* she thought as she approached the cave, *an angel and demon.* Never had she felt the lack of better words than she seemed to have. She palmed the tooth nervously.

Inside the cave, the winged man lay right where Sofia had left him with his head raised on a stone. His chest rose and fell at a steady pace.

The winged man did not wake but drank greedily. Sofia sat at his side. His wounds were healing fast. A quick inspection under the singed layers of embroidered silks revealed shrinking blisters and gashes that were stitching themselves up fast. *Angels don't bleed.*

Sofia was captivated by his appearance. The people at the lighthouse were attractive, no doubt, but the man with wings was altogether flawless, almost symbolic of a man. And yet, there was a woman's grace about him as he slept, his form somehow blending masculinity and femininity in perfect harmony. His gender almost seemed to shift with the light.

His face's symmetry was suspiciously perfect. His bronze complexion would hold up well to the sun. Deep-set eyes and a sharp brow gave him a stern look even at rest. But his cheeks were narrow and soft and descended to a pair of full lips; it was a contradiction of features that confused Sofia's primitive impulse to define man versus woman. His long, braided hair was the color of tobacco and littered with beads, feathers and decorative knots. Squarish geometric designs, either tattooed or drawn on his temples and neck, chased their way down his chest, arms and hands. Symbols of secret meaning, she guessed.

Sofia wondered what his name was.

Beside him lay the mangled armor remains Sofia had peeled from him after the battle. It was like the armor Sofia still wore, the visage of a lion the same as the one emblazoned on her chest now.

And then there were the wings. Sofia admittedly had scrutinized them closely more than once. They bore straight into the man's back, as one would expect but never *accept* unless seeing it firsthand. At the base of the wings, where they met the man's body, chiseled muscles took on bulky, unfamiliar forms to support and control the weight.

Sofia recalled the corpse of the warrior woman she'd found in the ruined city, the one whose armor and sword she'd taken before being chased through the tunnel. The man's armor had the same large openings, two notches to allow for the base of the wings to fit through after the armor was buckled together. But that didn't explain why the woman's wings were missing or what had taken them.

"Please wake up," she sighed.

Looking at him, a stray idea wormed its way into her brain. It wasn't the first time. And when it came, she dared not entertain it for long. She needed to stay calm, to think straight. But, she couldn't help but wonder.

Am I dead?

No. Sofia buried the thought and paced about. It wasn't possible. *There's another explanation. There must be.* People here breathed, they ate, slept and bled. Something else was going on, something *real*. But until the man with the wings woke up, there was little to do but wait.

Rather than pace around the cave, Sofia decided to try to find her sword, the damaged and melted one she'd lost during her descent from the ridge. It wasn't much, but it was enough of a distraction for the time being.

Sofia navigated holes and crevasses as she descended from the cave once more, carefully noticing the novelty of her shadow cast by the afternoon sun. So much time in the dull mist had had her thinking that shadows didn't exist. Hers followed her down onto the plain in lockstep. They walked together, Sofia and her shadow, skirting the edge of the tree line, past the corpse of the still-stinking creature to the open valley beyond.

The day was calm and quiet, though signs of life stood out more prominently now. She heard the buzzing of the living things. A few days ago, the fact would have amazed her, but now she swatted them away when they got too close and whined in her ear. *That's human nature for you.*

At the base of the scree slope nearly a kilometer from the cave, she found the blade jutting up from the pile of loose shale. She retrieved it, noting its imperfections in the light. The distorted steel was puckered and flaking in places with a blue-violet tint that faded to the colors of a sunset. Beautiful despite its flaws. Or rather, because of them. She thought of the sword's owner, the warrior who was still in that sad, gray place.

Sofia, lost in thought, her sword, and her shadow made their way back toward the oasis and through the thick brush to the water's edge. Seeing the dense cluster of life surrounding the tiny pool of water reminded Sofia of all the reasons why she couldn't be dead. She smelled the rich, earthy soil around the spring and felt the leaves of the surrounding plants between her fingers—some soft and some waxy, but all alive. She felt the wind on her face and the sun's warmth on her skin.

This is real, and I am real. Sofia was sure of it, at least enough to keep going until the man with the wings woke up. Then she would know for sure.

The temperature dropped near the shore. It was a hardly a shore, in fact, for the center of the oasis was a little more than a small pond, no more than a meter deep and perhaps fifty wide, but clear and cold. The bank was moist, and a ring of ancient trees and shrubs protected it. Kneeling in the soft earth, Sofia filled the nearly empty water vessels. Her task complete, the water calmed, and the surface smoothed.

For the first time in memory, Sofia saw the reflection of herself staring back at her. There it was. There *she* was. Were those green eyes staring back at her? It was hard to tell. They were cupped by sleepy creases below, the shadowed lids giving them even more contrast. She had the face of a young girl and mature woman in one. Youthful cheeks and a veteran jawline, a prominent chin and plump lips that always revealed some teeth when at rest. The dark curls on either side of her face framed her in a fierceness that felt appropriate. She flashed a smile and then a scowl and stuck her tongue out, watching how her face reacted. *My name is Sofia.*

Studying her appearance did not reveal any truths nor uncover any memories. She tossed a small stone into the pond, and her face broke into a thousand shimmering pieces.

It was nearing sundown when Sofia returned to the cave. She sat down next to her sleeping companion. None of the winged man's personal effects organized nearby proved particularly useful. Dried, pungent plants in a leather pouch, tiny scrolls encased in protective tubes, a collection of intricately carved trinkets and medallions, and a worn book in a leather binding were the sum of his belongings.

Sofia retrieved the book and what remained of her supply of bread, and sat propped against the cavern wall across from her silent companion. The embossed leather binding encased the pages with a circular design that spiraled toward the center. The spine was worn and opened obediently.

She expected similarities to the books she remembered seeing in the abandoned clothing shop, the squarish symbols all arranged in neat rows, but these shapes were different, more complex. They had the same, blocky look but were far more intricate, interwoven in a repeating rhythm like one undulating mass of shapes curling back on themselves.

As Sofia scanned the pages, a slip of parchment slid from the binding, something she must have missed before. On it was a circular glyph that contained smaller inscribed circles and symbols. It was strikingly similar to the inscription on the lighthouse floor. The feeling of something even vaguely familiar ignited a surge of excitement. A note jotted next to the glyph drew her attention to a specific intersection of the arched designs inscribed on the parchment.

It was the same point that Alana believed to have some significance, a time when something was going to happen. Sofia looked the man with the wings and wondered. He *does* know something about her situation. *Or,* she thought, *is the cause of it.*

Perhaps she shouldn't be so trusting. *Remember the lighthouse.* For all she knew, the black creature rotting near the pond below had turned on its master. Sofia's bias toward the man's beauty and her preconceptions might be her undoing. She had to be careful. *Hands in the fire...*

Sofia put the book aside and toyed with the fang. She probed the chips and grooves absentmindedly, feeling the heat but no pain, tracing the lines in her palm with its point. A breeze found its way into the cave from the valley down below.

The stink of sulfur lingered.

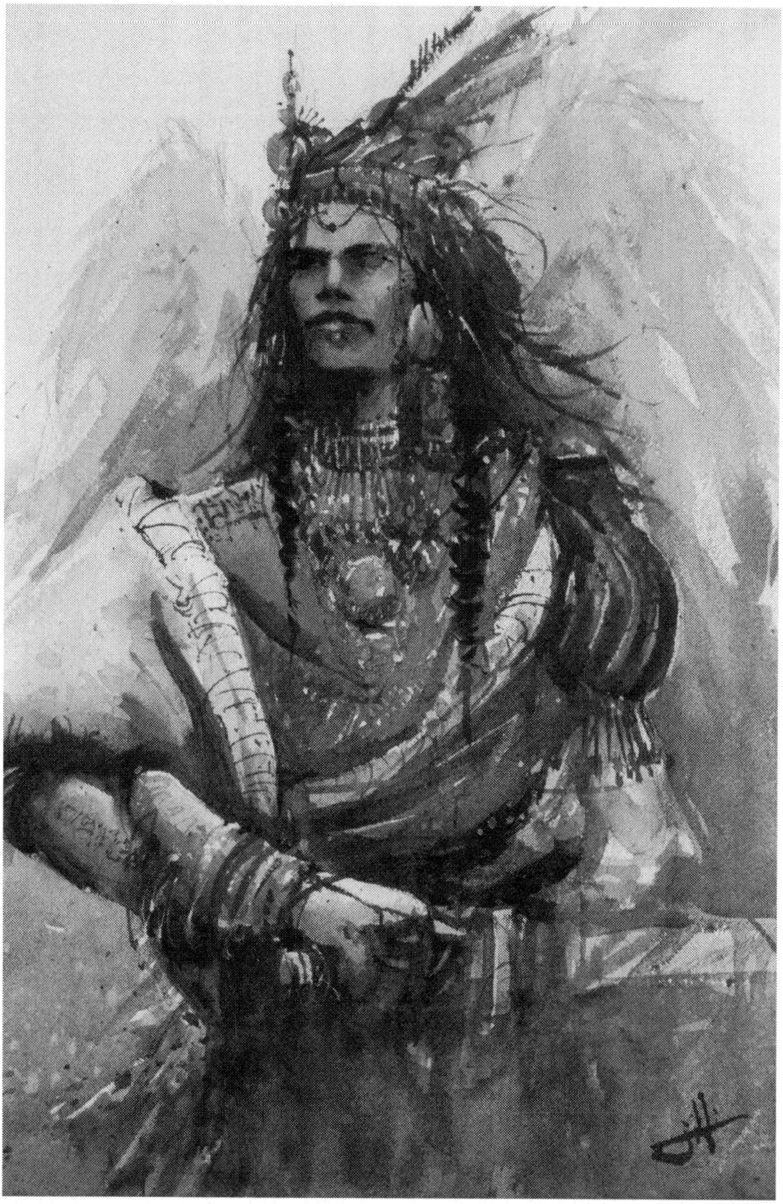

7

Sofia snapped awake, breathing hard and covered with sweat. The dream again. Each night was the same, always the same. The dingy apartment, the expectant mother—and Sofia's hands around her throat, crushing the life from her.

She sat up from her makeshift bedroll, stretching out the stiff muscles gifted to her from the hard cave floor. The inside of the cavern was warm, warmer than beyond its mouth, anyway, where the cold morning air waited to be warmed by the sun.

Sofia rolled over and squinted at the sun beginning to rise in the distance, using the light to reactivate her brain and shake the heavy gloom of the dreams. The walk down to the shore was crisp and still. The winged man had shown no sign of stirring before she left, so Sofia took her time.

She meandered through the morning fog, running her hands over the dew-covered plants as she descended and took in the sun's warmth. At the pond's edge, she splashed icy water on her face, shocking her senses back to the here and now. It made her feel alive.

After watching the sun fully rise, she headed back. Just before reaching the entrance, Sofia heard a voice echoing from inside the cave.

She paused. Excitement pounding in her ears. The voice didn't sound like a delirious fever rant, or a desperate call for help, but more like a...*conversation*. She couldn't understand the language. To her ears the words sounded old, a mix of dialects with harsh constants and a flowing rhythm. The voice was warm, melodic and heavily accented. She crept toward the mouth of the cave. The voice paused, began again, and then stopped once more, almost as if the speaker were giving someone else a chance to speak.

Sofia hid just below the entrance to the cave. She didn't know why—the man waking up was exactly what she had been waiting for. But now that the moment was here, it frightened her. Still, she had her sword, and she gripped it tightly.

"Hello?" Sofia finally called out. No answer, but she heard the rustling of movement inside.

The man stiffened as he saw her approach. It was strange to see him finally animated, sitting up, legs crossed. His folded wings arched a meter over his head and crossed neatly behind his back. His eyes were bright and gold in color, irises flashing like marbles of amber. There was feeling in the cave that drew her in and made her feel safe. It was not unlike the strange aura around the black creature, but instead of a melancholy and dreariness, Sofia felt a sense of harmony, of order.

The man nodded slightly, a simple and curt gesture. "Ciarros su te yainna" he said, his voice spilling forth like honey. He stared at her, unblinking, waiting. There was no sign of impatience or malice in his expression. He was simply *there*, looking at her.

Sofia had rehearsed how she would take charge as soon as the man awoke, how she'd demand answers and leverage her position as rescuer. But her plan fell by the wayside, dismantled by his gaze.

She sat down, sensing his eyes following her. "How are you feeling?" she asked finally, unable to think of something better. "I have water." The winged man cocked his head slightly. His eyes narrowed by a fraction.

"I am much improved," he said. He spoke the words Alana had taught her but with more dramatic flair on the *ar* sounds and a commanding use of consonants. Sofia stretched out and handed him the water. He winced. Sipping the water, his eyes stayed open, fixed upon her.

"I did what I could," Sofia said, nodding to his chest. She tossed her gaze toward the cave entrance. "That...*thing*, whatever it was, did a number on you. But you seem to heal fast. What should I call—"

"Ebrahym," he interrupted. "I am called Ebrahym."

Ee-bra-heem. She mentally repeated the syllables to herself. "I'm Sofia."

Ebrahym nodded once more. "So, tell me, Ebrahym," Sofia said, choosing her next words carefully. The questions whirled in her mind. *Where to even start?* "Where are we?" she asked.

Ebrahym stared at her for a few moments, past the point of being uncomfortable, as if testing her response. "The *Orvida*," he said, as a matter of fact. "in the great *Dominion di Esanya*."

"I see. And where is that, exactly?"

"From the water to the mountains and beyond. All that you can see lies within the Dominion," Ebrahym replied. "But the Orvida itself is vast beyond imagining."

"All right," Sofia said, trying to keep her composure. Ebrahym's calm demeanor poked at her temper. "Do you know why I am here? Or why I can't remember anything before a week ago other than my name?"

"Your name?" he asked intently, his eyes keener than ever. "You did not choose this name for yourself? It...came with you?"

"Yes!" Sofia exclaimed, her frustration rising. The peaceful aura of Ebrahym's presence waned. "Yes, I remember my name! Why is that so strange? What does it mean?" Ebrahym eyed her silently. Sofia pulled herself to her feet and paced about the cavern.

"Look," she continued. "I don't have any idea who or *what* you are. But this place—the things I've seen—I need to know what's happening here." Ebrahym said nothing and continued to stare at her with an unreadable expression. It was infuriating.

"Tell me, Sofia. How did you come by the armor that you wear and the blade that you carry?" Sofia glanced down at the breastplate still strapped to her chest. Her thoughts drifted back to the gray city in the mist.

"I. . .found them."

"In the city?"

Sofia wondered how much to reveal, but something about Ebrahym disarmed her. "Yes."

Ebrahym's eyes narrowed, two wide gems becoming slivers of amber. "I see. Did you find a lighthouse?"

"Yes," Sofia admitted, nodding. "But I didn't stay long. I left to look for help." He seemed to be weighing the truthfulness of her words as she spoke, testing her.

"We call it a *lúpero*," Ebrahym said after a moment. *He does know about this place.* "The creature you spoke of. You felt its effect upon you, yes?" Sofia shuddered. "*Noxurros,* the dark whisper. Our song keeps the aura at bay. When you surprised me on the field, I faltered," Ebrahym gestured to his injuries. "I found myself at a disadvantage, but you, it seems, did not." There was a suspicious quality to his tone.

"You're welcome," Sofia said with more than a hint of defiance.

"Indeed," said Ebrahym. He went on, "It is no easy thing for an *oulma* to slay one of their ilk. Most cannot even lay eyes on one so large and keep their wits, let alone face it in battle, untrained. It is most peculiar."

"Oulma?" Sofia asked.

"Yes. Your kind."

"And yours?"

Ebrahym stood shakily. "Different."

Sofia came to his side to catch his elbow to help him stand. He was nearly a half-meter taller than she, lean and strong. Together they limped to the mouth of the cave, and Ebrahym seemed to animate and glow from the light of the risen sun. He stretched his working wing wide; the injured one limped outward weakly. It was still a magnificent sight; one that Sofia's brain struggled to accept.

"What *are* you?" she asked. "What is going on, Ebrahym? Where am I, really?"

Ebrahym shook his head. "It is not my place to tell you. It is not the *Iriva*, the Way."

"Bullshit," Sofia said, staring up at him a few centimeters from his face. She poked his chest. "I saved your life, remember? I sat in this cave for two days watching over you—"

"Two days?" Ebrahym interrupted. Sofia nodded. "We may already be too late." He gestured for his book. Sofia handed it to him, and he retrieved the parchment scrap with the symbol on it. His face fell.

"Too late for what? What does that symbol mean?" Sofia cried. "Goddammit, I need some answers *right now*, or I'm gone and you can find your own way out of here." Sofia put on the hardest stare she could muster.

Ebrahym sat down, resting his wings against the stone wall. "I would not be here if not for you, that is true. But there are things in Orvida not meant to be seen by oulma such as you nor explained by one such as me. It is not the Way." Ebrahym's brow furrowed in thought. Sofia stood unmoving, fists firmly set on her hips. Ebrahym considered his options before sighing heavily.

"The lighthouse you found, in *Meridi,* I would guess, is one of many built to attract your kind and keep them safe. *Ilucenta*, the city you found on the cliffs, once served as a refuge for oulma who came from the sea. It was a beautiful place long ago. I will speak no more of that.

"There is a caravan that moves up and down the *Pasa di a Luvia,* the Light Road, to gather the oulma and take them to the capital, where they will be brought into the fold proper. That is the Way. The caravan has no doubt already reached the Meridi lighthouse and is en route to *Luminea,* even now."

Sofia's head spun trying to keep up. Nothing felt familiar. Ebrahym put a hand on his chest. "My kind is known as the *Sanguinir di Hestium*, the Host, The United Ones, charged with protection of the oulma. That is my duty."

"What do the oulma need protection from? More of those *things*?" Sofia imagined Alana and the others on some road far from here, surrounded by more of those obsidian monsters.

Ebrahym nodded. "I have been scouting their movements for days—a pack is near. They rarely come this far west, but something emboldens them. I fear their eyes are fixed on the caravan."

"Wait," Sofia said, confused. "Wouldn't I have seen a caravan on the road leading out of the lighthouse? Come to think of it, I don't remember any forks in the road, either. How did I miss them?" Her forehead wrinkled in thought.

"You traveled by way of the *Sepuselva*, the Grave Wood, I would guess," Ebrahym explained. Sofia could not hide her shudder. "That place is cursed and plays tricks on the mind. There, you can easily miss that which you were not looking for."

Sofia frowned. "But there are more of you, right? More, *angels* to protect the caravan?"

Ebrahym seemed almost offended at the word. "There are more of us, Sanguinir, yes. But there are too few swords among them for a pack this large. The pack will feed on the oulma's fear and overwhelm them. We must get a message to the caravan guard to prepare a defense and send a call for reinforcements from the capital." He looked at Sofia. "*You* must do this."

"Me?"

"Yes." Ebrahym flexed his injured wing as he spoke, wincing. "It will be days before I can travel again; the lúpero made sure of that. This is no wish of mine; it is a disgrace I allowed but one of their kind to best me. And I have already told you too much. But we have little choice, you and I. If you call any of those oulma from Meridi friend, you must go, for their sake."

The desperation in Ebrahym's melodic voice felt genuine. Worry wore on his brow, temporarily distorting his graceful features. They seemed more feminine now, somehow, perhaps the look of a worried mother.

Sofia thought about Alana and the other oulma, as Ebrahym called them, and felt a twinge of shame, even after everything that had happened at the lighthouse. If she had stayed, she'd be with the caravan right now, able to help. She thought about what Ebrahym had said. *I wouldn't be here if it weren't for you.* This was her doing, despite intentions. And she had told Alana she would find help and bring it back if she could.

But this...this was *insane*. What had she stumbled into? Even with no memories of a normal life to reference, the strangeness, the *incredibility* of it all was overwhelming. The more she learned of this place, the Orvida, the less she understood. But her answers would have to wait. The others needed her help.

"Tell me what I need to do," Sofia said.

She gathered her supplies and listened carefully as Ebrahym described the route to take to rendezvous with the caravan. Ebrahym instructed her to impart a simple message to the winged lieutenant in charge: *Hold and send for reinforcements. They are coming.*

Despite her frustration and lack of understanding the events in motion, Sofia felt a sense of purpose, or at least a feeling that she was moving in the right direction. Somehow, the fear of failure outweighed that of monsters waiting in the mist.

8

"You must climb fast," Ebrahym instructed. He had managed to hobble, with Sofia's help, to the base of a bluff on the far side of the oasis. It was a steep rise jutting abruptly from the valley floor, much steeper than the scree slope she'd descended days before.

She had asked about safer routes, or more specifically, ones that weren't quite so high, but Sofia had seen the urgency and worry hidden behind Ebrahym's golden eyes and conceded.

The climb, he assured her, was the fastest way out of the valley heading north. Now, standing at the foot of it, the ascent looked far more menacing than it had from the cave hideout. The setting sun cast long, lonely shadows across the jagged face of the crag.

Ebrahym's crimson sash crossed her chest like a swath of blood, standing out in vibrant contrast to the gold armor underneath. Ebrahym had told her it was a signal to the others like him, the Sanguinir, that she carried an official message. Sofia could smell incense and jasmine laced within the folds. At her back was the sword, and tucked neatly into the crook of her pocket, the fang of the lúpero. It throbbed with heat.

"It will be night soon," Ebrahym said. He supported himself on the broken spear shaft. "More lúpero will be coming." He looked off into the distance as the wind danced with the feathers in his hair. "The corpse of their kin is a beacon to which more evil will gather. But do not worry, I will make sure they notice me and not you."

Sofia nodded but felt little comfort as they past by the corpse of the lúpero. The scar upon the land around the carcass had grown even larger. Pungent fumes continued to pour from the still-sizzling mass. Sofia had nearly retched walking downwind of the thing, wondering how much fouler the smell could possibly get. It wasn't hard to imagine that its scent would be easy to detect, even kilometers away.

Looking up, she gripped the rock face, testing the holds. The *Plutilla*, Ebrahym called it, the Shelf.

Just beyond its precipice, stretching hundreds of kilometers in both directions, the *Lanuri di Lumbra*, the Plains of Lumbra. And due west from there, the caravan.

There was so much she didn't know. She sensed something bigger in motion, but it was beyond her understanding, just out of reach. Sofia wanted to trust Ebrahym, to believe in him. It was more than just his divine appearance. There was something familiar about him

"I really wished those wings of yours worked," said Sofia, gazing up.

"As do I," Ebrahym said, following her gaze.

"What if they come for you?"

Ebrahym chuckled grimly. "The lúpero have no love of water. It is too pure for their kind, irritates their flesh. If the worst comes, I will shelter there."

Sofia closed her eyes, trying not to think about the ground slipping away from under her feet. "Can you sing for me?"

"What?"

She turned to face him. "When I first saw you chasing after that thing, I heard you singing. That song...It made me feel, I don't know, *brave*. This is twice now I'll be climbing," She swallowed hard and looked up at the sheer rock wall once more. "Heights don't exactly agree with me."

A thin smile, the kind of modest men, crept across Ebrahym's face. He bowed slightly. "If you like. It is one of the ancient hymns, from the first *codixa*. It is called the "Oda di Halphyus," a song of valor and duty, commemorating one of our best leaders."

"And it's what, magic?"

"No, not magic," chuckled Ebrahym. His eyes shone with a flash. "The song stokes the flame that is already there. Nothing more."

"Ebrahym..." Sofia said. The thought they might never meet again stood out among all the other ones running through her head. She might be going to her doom above the wall, or leaving him to his. A nervous dread churned within, numbing her senses and eroding her resolve. There might not be another chance to know the truth. She swallowed hard.

"Am I dead?" she asked.

Ebrahym said nothing, staring right through her with a golden gaze. His expression was vacant, distant, as if hiding something. Like a parent withholding an ugly truth from a child.

For a moment, Sofia thought Ebrahym might give in and answer her, but as he opened his mouth, a delicate sound escaped from it. It was bright and clear as a star. Two distinct voices mingled in harmony, high and low, intertwined as the rhythm undulated on. Though she could not understand their meaning, the words penetrated and stirred her heart. Courage surged. Visions of glory flashed before her eyes. She slew monsters and climbed mountains, won battles and found love.

Ebrahym gave her a final nod as he sang.

Sofia set to it with the hymn burning in her ears. Its power was potent, but she did not lose herself to it. Not like before. Carefully choosing handholds and footholds, she began to inch up the face, cautious not to overreach. It was a long climb to the top. And with the help of Ebrahym's song, she left her fears on the ground below and began to ascend.

Sofia's fingers slid over bulging stones or inside cracks, searching the anchors by feel as her legs followed, slowly driving her farther and farther up. Bits of rock separated from their mother and tumbled down the face and stung her eyes. The handholds grew sparse. Sofia's muscles strained to hunt them out while keeping her close to the wall. Hot breath condensed on the stone staring back at her. She panted heavily, struggling to breathe. *I will not burn. I will not fall.*

The rock bit and tore at her hands and nails, grinding them, scraping them, wearing them down as she inched upward. Her muscles burned. *I'll never make it.* She looked desperately for someplace to recuperate her strength, craning her neck and scanning the rock face for signs of refuge.

There! Relief appeared in the form of a small outcropping a few meters above her. Separating her from it was a slab of sheer stone, split lengthwise by a jagged fracture. It was a long and difficult detour, but she needed rest. At her back, the sun began to slip behind the horizon. She studied the route in the dying light. Soon there would be none left to guide her.

Sofia pumped air into her lungs, reached to find the long crack and felt it cut deep into the rock. She anchored her hands into it tightly, shimmying toward the ledge where she might find rest. Her body revolted, and venom burned inside her forearms to the point of no sensation. When she could take no more, Sofia lunged at the ledge, hurling her upper body onto the jutting rock. Her chestplate crunched against the stone and her breast, rattling the air from her. Gasping, Sofia pulled herself to her knees and the sweaty hair from her eyes.

Ebrahym's song stopped. Sofia hadn't noticed it, and now the only sound was her own heavy breathing and the silence of the coming twilight. She shook some life back into her forearms and glanced below to take in the view.

Long shadows stretched across the plain, leeched of color, appearing as cold shades of charcoal. Whatever dam Ebrahym's chant had built up to keep the fear at bay was let loose, and the dread came crashing down upon her like a great wave.

Vertigo assailed her senses, and she clutched the rock, squinting tightly. The world dropped out beneath her. In its place, darkness, like the deep ocean. Her first memory. *There's no one here but me now.* She peered over the rim. It was hard to tell how far the fall would be from the ledge to the valley floor. Fifty meters? More? It didn't matter. The fall would crush bones. Her insides, splayed out on the plain, would appear little different than the remains of the lúpero.

No going back, she told herself. Alana and the rest of the amnesiacs, the oulma, needed her now. And so did Ebrahym. Sofia took the fang out of her pocket, feeling its warmth against her battered hands. She gripped it between two knuckles as if it were a claw and poked and slashed at the rock.

"You couldn't kill me," she said to the tooth. She stared up at the cliff. Darkness stole the warmth from the rock, and it towered over her like a tombstone. "You won't either." Sofia tucked the trophy away and rallied her muscles for another charge.

A guttural roar echoed through the darkened valley.

What Sofia thought was silence before—the soft, easily unnoticed ambient noises of the world—vanished. Replaced by oppressive silence. True nothingness. A shrill cry cut through it, a wail of death and agony and hunger that seemed meant for her ears and hers alone. It was the call of the lúpero, and more than one by the sound of it. The echoing yips and calls rippled down Sofia's spine. *Were they close to Ebrahym? Did they find him?*

She climbed on, feeling her way as her eyes adjusted to night. Her refreshed muscles found their pace, seeking the next hold, pulling, pressing with her legs, one after another. The crag separated from itself, fragmenting near the summit. Plenty of holds now.

The yips and growls floated all round her, driving Sofia hard up the rock face. Her hands found the makings of a channel, nearly a meter wide, and she wedged herself into it. Legs and arms suspended her as she climbed up the crevasse. It led her to a small outcropping, a deceptive false summit just before the true rim of the cliff.

The ledge was large enough to stand on and littered with stones and boulders. The howls of the lúpero below seemed agitated, excited. *Ebrahym.*

Sofia inched toward one of the larger stones with her back to the wall. The boulder rested precariously near the edge. After a few, powerful breaths Sofia braced against the cliff wall and put all the strength she could muster into it with her legs. The object resisted. Sofia pushed harder. Her limbs shook. She cried out in anger for a surge of strength. The boulder rocked, then slipped free from the ledge and tumbled to the ground below. As it struck, it sounded like the earth itself cracked open.

The yips and growls grew quiet for a moment, then erupted in horrible chatter. In the din, Sofia could almost hear voices speaking to one another.

The horrid shapes of the lúpero were a hundred meters below her. Their color was unnatural and stood out against even the darkest shadows of night, blacker than the rest. But she knew they were there and that the distraction had worked. Perhaps too well.

The pack howled and snarled at the base of the cliff, frustrated. The sound was that of breaking glass and the screams of dying things. And voices. Sofia could hear them now, even over her own labored gasps. Terrible, malefic tongues conspiring against her. A hint of sulfur danced in the air.

The boldest of their kind, a much larger lúpero than the rest, was not as easily dissuaded by the sheer stone wall as Sofia. It leaped onto the cliff face and charged fearlessly upward, slashing at the rock with talons that bore straight through the stone as easy as flesh. The grating sound echoed like a hammer against steel. The terrible rhythm grew louder. Faster. Sofia scrambled up the wall and pushed harder to the true summit until her muscles protested once more. A gnarled root clung to life between the rocks just above. She grabbed it and pulled herself up and over the edge.

Sofia gasped. The pinging of talons of steel sounded just over the edge. Exhausted, all she could do was wait for the beast. If the lúpero made it over the edge, she'd never outrun it on open ground. Her only chance was to attack when it was weakest—when it was surprised.

Sofia quickly disrobed her heavy outer layer and tossed one end of the fabric over the ledge—she needed to know exactly where the creature would be. She wedged the woven bait between two large stones and waited, gripping her sword tight and listening for the sound of claws. She wiped the sweat from her eyes. The rock itself shook as powerful talons punctured the cliff face, inching toward her. *It's close now.* Sofia crouched, still, heart thumping in her ears. She waited. The fabric lurched in her hands as the creature tore at it with a growl. It took the bait. One gnarled paw swiped over the edge, looking for purchase, its talons crushing smaller stones into dust. Then the other.

Between the paws, a giant head emerged, black as the night sky without stars.

Sofia met its gaze and plunged into despair. Time slowed to a painful pace, and moments became centuries. Whispers flooded her mind and confused her senses. She wanted to give up and give in to the darkness. To fall into silent oblivion and forever be free. A maw full of fangs reared up, hot and putrid, ready to oblige. Sofia was willing.

Then a spark ignited. It flared to life and became a wildfire. Within her, a great inferno blazed against the silhouette of a dark forest. Like primitive man, armed with the tool of fire to keep the dangers of the night at bay, she shouted at the blackness. It bought her a moment.

She drove her sword into the creature's eye socket, deep into the void. The creature howled like a storm. Her mind seized and convulsed at the pandemonium, unable to think. Unable to reason. The beast writhed and lashed and struggled to maintain its hold on the cliff face. Sofia blindly kicked and cursed and hacked at it. She didn't even feel the five talons rake across the flesh of her thigh.

A solid strike with both feet to the lúpero's throat was enough for it to lose its grip. Its claws dug into the stone, jaws snapping. Sofia cried out and came down hard with the sword, clean through one set of claws. The blade found rock underneath. Gore sizzled on the ground. The lúpero roared as it scrambled in vain before plummeting to its kin below.

Without pause, Sofia pulled herself to her feet and ran, ignoring the stream of blood escaping from her slashed leg.

She sprinted over the rocky plain until her legs began shaking and her head throbbed. Then she jogged, then walked, then finally stumbled, barely able to stand. Her lungs burned, and her leg was cold and numb and black with blood.

Stars rotated above her, and clouds passed by. She was unraveling, like those things she'd found in the ruined city of Ilucenta. She was running through that dark tunnel under the city once more. She was a shade. A shadow.

But she pushed on somehow, tending a fire within her that drove her through the night. She never looked back.

Hours later, Sofia's head hung as she willed her feet to move, fighting for each step. She limped until she might collapse, delirious, but long enough to see the first signs of sunrise. Then she felt grass underfoot, her boots completely worn through. *Grass*. Darkness finally gave way to the soft, warm hues of dawn. The light brought her back from the darkness.

And there, against the rising sun, Sofia saw smoke rising and brilliantly colored banners snapping in the wind.

PART II

—

HOPE

She beheld the seat of the Dominion,
And passed through its walls and its gates,
Set apart from the fold.

Nephahi Epoye IV 2:1

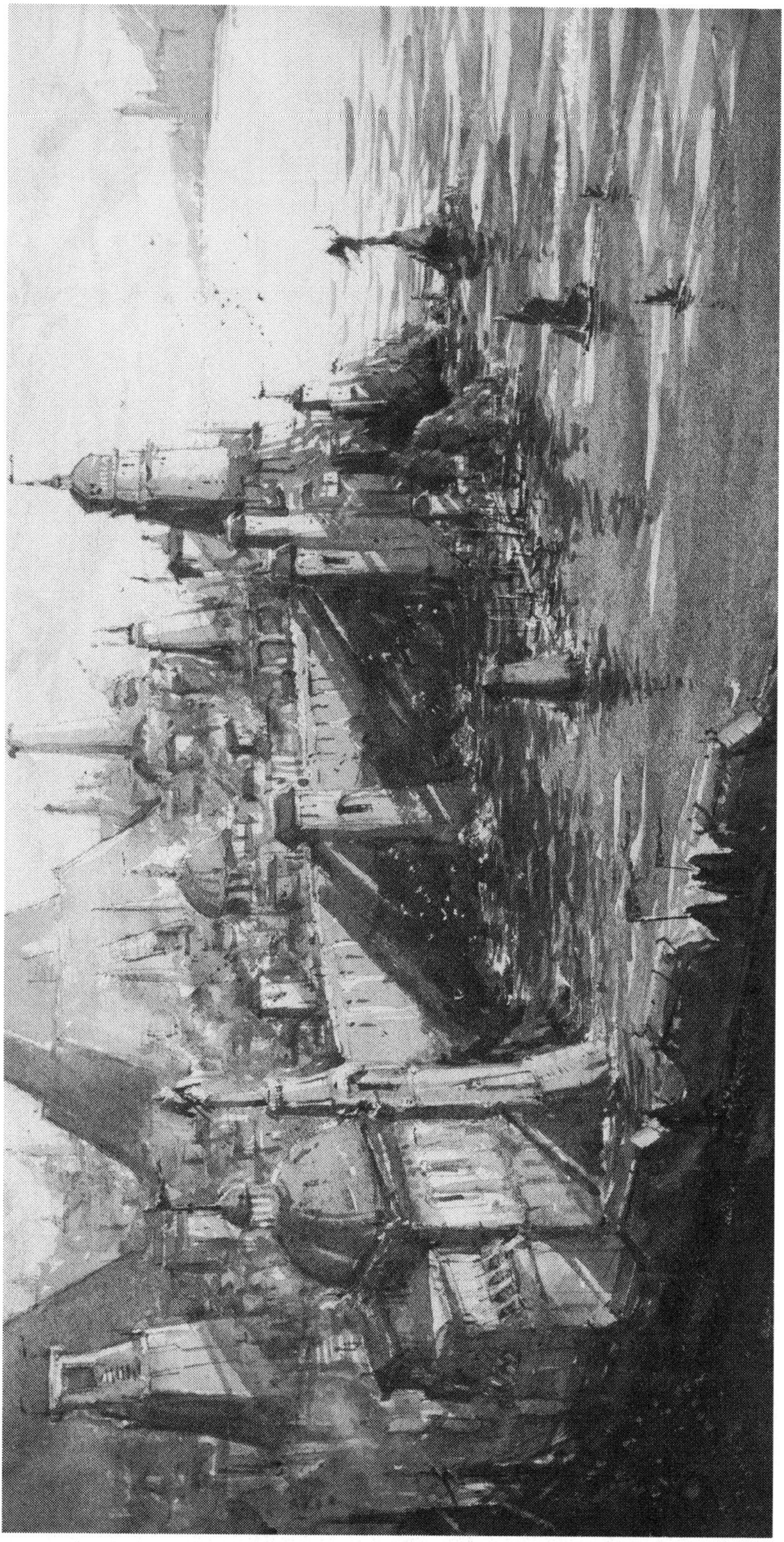

9

Dreamless sleep kept Sofia in the dark for days. There, the nightmare returned again and again. The same twisted memory ad nauseam. The choking of the woman's last breath terrified her, sickened her. Sofia would run through the woods. Monsters would chase her as she ran, always howling, always close. They would emerge, clawing their way up from the abyss to torment her, then fade away into nothingness. It was a cruel cycle that played out to the sound of screams.

Sofia found her way to her body and crawled back into herself. She woke with a start, covered in sweat, her body and mind reunited. *Where am I?* She blinked heavily. The world was a bright haze that stung her eyes. In the face of such brilliance, the dreams faded from view, back to whatever dark place they came from.

She wasn't in the cave. Overhead, a small, pitched tent, woven from wool and staked with wooden poles, shielded her from the outside world. Light burned through holes in the well-worn material like stars. The tent was a deep red color like the skin of an apple, like blood. She traced the heavy weave with her fingers. It felt like Ebrahym's robes.

Ebrahym! Sofia bolted upright, her body a knot of stiff fibers that obeyed the command, but not without protest. Her eyes fixated on a neat bandage wrapped around her right thigh. Black stains blotted through. *What the hell happened?*

The night returned to her in fragments. She was climbing through the dark and then...running. Farther than she'd ever imagined she could. *A shadow attacked me.* Her leg seized at the thought, and a stab of pain shot through her thigh, up her spine, to behind her eyes. She breathed deep, squeezing them tight to absorb the sensation and keep it at bay. *Then I was walking on grass. The sun rose. Colored flags? What was I looking for?* Her mind struggled to piece together the images floating in thoughts, trying to sift the real from the imaginary. Then she remembered Ebrahym's words: *They are coming.*

The message! The lúpero, the caravan! Purpose exploded into her mind. Did she tell someone before she passed out? The world outside began to filter in, and she became aware of it.

From where she sat, she could see pairs of legs crisscrossing the opening of the tent and hear a commotion outside; the indistinguishable murmurs of conversation, the sounds of people, of music, and metal striking metal.

Undeterred by her unwilling body and remembering her promise to Ebrahym, Sofia struggled to her ravaged feet—they, too, were bandaged—flipped up the wool flap and crawled out of the tent, her leg angry from the effort.

The sun overhead, in its full glory, blinded her for a moment, and the encampment took time to come into focus.

The caravan. More like a small city, the mass of travelers and supplies sat upon a hill covered in honey-colored grass that seemed to shine like a million shards of golden light rippling in the breeze. The camp extended down a gentle slope and half way up another, partly obscured by a looming purple shadow from a passing cloud. Rows of brightly colored tents were organized in a grid with space to walk between them like small neighborhoods. Hundreds of people milled about, and a mix of excitement and intoxicating energy filled the air. Sofia gawked at the overwhelming vibrancy. Colors screamed at her and poured in from every corner of her vision. She struggled to compare the drab, lifeless world of mist to this one, but her brain could barely recall it in the face of such brilliance. Even the oasis paled in comparison.

There were people all around. Oulma, Ebrahym had called them. But they were not the same people Sofia remembered from the lighthouse. They seemed so *alive.* They strolled through the makeshift paths in small groups, talking and laughing, with smiles that radiated such energy Sofia caught herself grinning just looking at them. Their skin glowed in every shade of earth imaginable, from the palest sand to the darkest onyx—all beautiful and striking. Sofia thought she recognized a few of them, but there were so many people it was hard to tell.

The camp swarmed. *What to do?* She noticed much larger, much more elaborate tents erected on the summit of a hill to the east. The tents stood two stories, staked with golden lines and covered with intricate patterns. Thick plumes of white smoke escaped from openings in the tops. Through squinted eyes, Sofia could make out figures with wings milling about. *What did Ebrahym call them? Sanguinir?* Sofia still didn't know exactly what they were. But right now, she needed to make sure she had delivered Ebrahym's message. *Everyone here is in danger.* She panned around the horizon searching for black forms silhouetted against the brilliant blue sky. As she scanned the distance, a heavily armored hand clamped down on her shoulder.

"So, you survived, after all," a woman's voice said.

Sofia turned to see that the woman's skin was dark as rich soil; the contrast between it and her bright, amber eyes made her all the more fierce. High cheeks, carved from stone, jutted out from her noble face. She was Sanguinir, one of them. Her hair was knotted and tied back in an intricate weave of braids that hung in heavy loops. Out of it, a plume of feathers exploded in a burst of color. Bands of pale ink striped her face and dotted beneath her full lips. The lines traced down her arms to the back of her hands, one of which sat upon a sword hilt. Strapped to her person was intricately inlaid armor, like Ebrahym's, but tailored for a woman's hips and narrower waist. Behind her, creamy wings speckled with brown spots arched backward, pinched neatly together.

And like Ebrahym, the woman seemed to be of two identities. Her body, her beauty, was woman. But Sofia sensed a masculine force under the surface. It flashed aggressively through the golden irises.

"I have a message," Sofia began. "Ebrahym told me—"

"Yes, we know. He is with the Host now," the woman's gaze was cold, alien.

"Is he all right? Can I talk to him? What about the attack?" Sofia lowered her voice as people passed by. "He said those creatures, the lúpero, are coming," she whispered.

"That is not your concern, *nuomen*," said the Sanguinir with a hint of disdain. *Nuomen?* "And it would be wise to speak of it no more."

"What is with you people?" Sofia asked defiantly, knocking the woman's hand away. "Ask Ebrahym what happened. I nearly died trying to get here."

The Sanguinir woman laughed, and Sofia's blood ran hot. "As you say. Now, be gone. You are free to be among the other oulma. But do not presume to know about matters far beyond you."

Anger stewed and simmered as Sofia limped through the caravan to clear her thoughts, with the Sanguinir following behind. Sofia wondered how long she'd been out. Days? Weeks? The landscape was so different now, so bright and full of life, so far from the desolate, foggy shores and gloomy wood. Much had changed since the beach. Even the cave felt like ages ago, and the lighthouse and before that had long passed into legend.

The clang of steel rang out across the camp as warriors sparred. The sound drew Sofia's focus back to the tents. But her chaperone, Jaziria, Sofia overheard her called, was always close. The other winged sentries and warriors all eyed Sofia with the same watchful, amber stares. None of the other oulma, the other *people*, seemed to pay much attention to the Sanguinir at all. It was as if Sofia alone recognized them for the curiosity they were. Nuomen, Jaziria had called her. *What did it mean?*

Jaziria kept her distance and, to her word, left Sofia free to wander the encampment. Music drew Sofia through the rows of tents. She overheard excited chatter about "the city" as she explored the grounds. *The capital Ebrahym spoke of?*

She wove through the crowds toward the rear of the traveling village. There, she passed groups of people deep in collective study, pouring over books. Each congregation was led by a Sanguinir, unarmored, wrapped in elegant robes of silver and white with sparkling glass gems woven into them. Some of the pupils seemed to recognize Sofia but shied away from her gaze. The books in their hands were akin to the one Ebrahym had tucked into her belt before sending her up the wall. Sofia reached for it instinctively and realized it was not there. Neither was her armor nor her sword nor...*the fang!* She felt around for the trophy and quickly realized it, too, was gone. *Dammit. They took everything.* She kicked a clod of dirt in frustration and grunted impotently as her injured foot throbbed. Jaziria eyed her dispassionately from a distance.

At the far end of the camp, a makeshift bathhouse of private stalls was erected in a star-shaped pattern. White sheets hung between small, wooden tubs filled with sweet-smelling water that bubbled and steamed. Strangely, there was no obvious way the water was being heated. But it didn't matter. It was a chance to escape the gazes of the Sanguinir. Sofia climbed into a stall and drew the shade closed, happy to shut out the world, if only for a moment. She gladly shed her ragged, bloody clothes. She eyed her body, covered in dirt and grime, cuts and bruises, and winced as she peeled away the bandage around her thigh. With it, clots of blood pulled away. Black, oily ooze seeped from the wound.

Everything melted away as Sofia submerged her aching limbs in the hot water. Her battered hands slowly worked the grime out from between her toes and other such places. She wrung out her thick curls. Steaming water trickled down her spine. Somewhere in the camp, music started up again. This time it was a slow, melodic chant that drifted over the bustle of ambient noise. Sofia let the sound carry her away, and by the end of the bath, she felt rejuvenated, alive. The cuts on her hands were almost healed, as well as her torn-up feet. Even her leg appeared less inflamed after only a short time in the water. A tingling sensation rippled across her skin. Sofia could feel the warmth of the sun on her face as if her flesh itself was new and experiencing sunlight for the first time.

Sofia snatched a fresh set of woven trousers and a tunic from a pile and threw them on. As she dressed, she eyed the tub of grimy water. It was black with filth, and it made her think of the lúpero corpse still rotting near the cave.

Sofia slid the curtain open, carrying her fouled and tattered clothes. "Feel better?" a handsome man with olive skin and sharp eyes asked. He waited for his turn.

"Oh," said Sofia, unsure if he was addressing her. "Much."

"It's something they put in the water. Feels good, doesn't it?"

Sofia offered a polite smile and nodded. "What's in it?"

"Bliss, of course." He flashed a wink. "And, I think, lavender."

The olive skinned man disappeared behind the curtain, and Sofia wandered off, caught off guard by the scent of cooking food that stirred her appetite. When was the last time she had eaten? Days? *How is that even possible?* Then she realized she had no memory of a cooked meal, *ever*, and only the taste of bread was familiar. Soon she was ravenous.

A team of cooks bustled about a ring of massive metal cauldrons, slicing vegetables and adding spices as they tended to the boiling pots. They sang as they did their work and called to one another, laughing. A round-faced cook, with a chest not unlike one of the giant pots, grinned and ladled a heavy pour of something earthy and savory into a bowl and handed it to Sofia when her turn came up. Strange aromas swirled around her.

"What do you see?" he asked her. Sofia shot the man a confused look, and he motioned for her to eat. She took a bite. The warm stew ignited not only taste sensations that were all together new—savory spices that were tangy and biting, yet sweet—but also more. Sofia saw things. A snowy mountain and a small dark cottage nestled in a drift with warm light emanating from the windows. Then she was by a fire, wrapped in a thick blanket as a heavy, gentle snow fell outside. A fire crackled in the hearth. The stew warmed her belly, and a sensation of perfect contentment enveloped her.

"Well?" the cook had an excited look of anticipation.

Sofia blinked back to reality. "I don't know…I saw a fireplace. And snow."

The cook's red cheeks creased as he grinned. "Ah! Yes! Exactly! It's the hickory. And iceweed, roasted over pine, of course. That's the key. I've been working on the recipe for some time. Lodge stew, I call it. Enjoy, please!"

The cook beamed with pride and ushered her along, and Sofia found a perch alone in the grass at the edge of the camp where she could gaze out at the rolling sea of golden hills. Almost alone, rather. Jaziria idly held her vigil a short distance away. As Sofia ate, visions of the cozy cabin mingled with the layered tastes of the meal. For an instant, she thought she could hear the winter wind as the food played tricks on her senses. After, she savored the feeling of a full, warm belly.

"Sofia?"

Sofia looked up to see Alana's wild hair haloed by the sun. The color and warmth of the place only added to her radiance. "Alana!" Sofia jumped to her feet. The women embraced and sat down together, backs to Jaziria, who pretended to be uninterested.

"What happened? Are you all right?" Alana asked, excitedly. "You were in rough shape when they found you. When I didn't see you in your tent, I figured you were wandering around. Do you know what's going on? The Sang are all on edge since you got back, and more are showing up every day."

"I'm fine, Alana, I'm fine. Wait, who?"

Alana nodded in Jaziria's direction. "*Them.* The guardians, whatever they are. Sanguinir is what they call themselves, I guess. They're here to protect us and lead us to the capital, Luminea."

"Yeah," Sofia said, her thoughts drifting back to the cave. "I know."

"What do you mean?"

Sofia lowered her voice. "I met one."

Alana looked at her intently. "What? Where? Tell me everything."

Sofia explained how she came to be at the caravan. The words flowed easy with Alana. Something about her made her so easy to trust. Sofia described the ghostly forest, wandering the plains and coming upon the lúpero and Ebrahym. A Sang, as Alana called him. Alana listened silently, unblinking, as Sofia recounted the battle and Ebrahym's recovery before sending her away with the message.

"Are we in danger?" Alana whispered.

"I don't know. Maybe. The Sanguinir are here to protect us, at least that's what Ebrahym says. But those things, the lúpero..." Sofia shuddered.

"There's something about the Sang, Sofia. They're more than just warriors. They've been teaching us things. Look." Alana dug into the earth and pulled up a handful of soil. She stared at the pile in her hands until a small, green vine appeared. It burst from the dirt pile and curled upward as tiny leaves sprouted from the stem.

"How—?"

Alana smiled. "They call it *Sphaera Divinia*. The Divine Sphere."

"I don't understand."

Alana smiled. "It's a kind of aura around us, but it feels more like music. If you listen for it, you can always hear it, even now. It's everywhere. It was hard to hear at first, but it's getting easier the more Sang there are around. And if I listen," she turned back to the tiny plant, "I can think of something and make it happen."

Sofia stared at her hands. *Fire will not burn me*. Was this Divine Sphere how she could resist fire? "What happened with Erado?" she asked, reminded.

The smile disappeared from Alana's face. "Well," she began. "We locked them in a shed after the fire since we weren't sure what else to do. They tried to *torture* you, after all. But the Sang showed up right on time, as the calendar on the floor predicted. The Sang took Erado and the others away after I explained what happened. I don't know what they did with them, but now they're...different."

"Different how?"

"I'm not sure, exactly. Better, calmer. They don't seem afraid anymore, or angry."

Sofia sighed an unsatisfied sigh. "I don't know, Alana. This place is maddening. The more I learn, the more lost I feel."

"Oh, Sofia..." Alana whispered. "The Sang you met, he didn't tell you? I thought he would have told you the truth. You don't know, do you?"

"Know what? What are you talking about?"

Alana nervously pulled a stray lock behind her ear and squinted at the sun. "We're dead, Sofia."

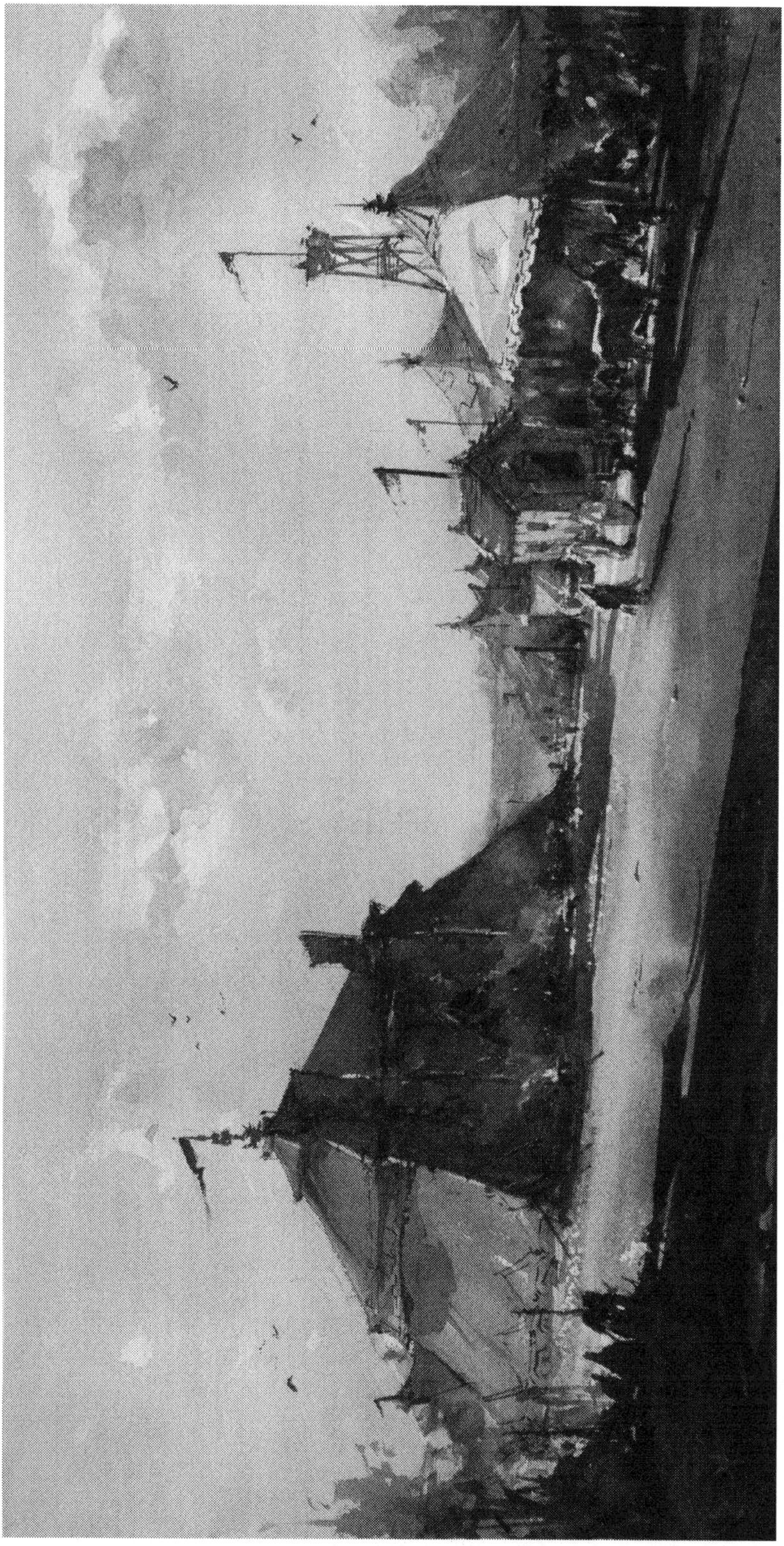

10

I'm dead. A ghost. A soul.

No matter how many times Sofia repeated the words, she couldn't believe it. She clenched her fists as she walked, feeling the muscles tighten and the blood in her veins quicken. She didn't feel like an apparition, but as she gazed at the caravan marching over the perfectly golden fields under the picturesque sky, surrounded by beautiful crowds of people led by strange, winged beings, it was hard to deny it all. But she did, anyway. She rebelled against the very idea, against the powerlessness of it. The Orvida, Ebrahym had called it. The afterlife. *Impossible.*

"Start from the beginning, Alana," Sofia asked skeptically, ready to hear more. They walked together next to an overburdened wagon, laden with supplies, as it hobbled across the uneven ground, away from most of the other oulma. It made its way through the tall grasses pulled by huge, horned beasts of burden that Sofia couldn't remember the name of. "What did the Sang tell you?"

"I was wondering when you were going to ask," Alana said. "In hindsight, I don't think I am supposed to tell you any of this."

"Because of this 'Way' the Sang talk about?" asked Sofia, recalling what Ebrahym had said to her.

Alana nodded. "But it didn't seem right to keep it from you."

"Well," Sofia said. "I already know the punch line. You might as well spill the rest." Sofia looked at Alana.

"You're right," Alana sighed. "The Iriva, the Way, is their code or belief system or something; I'm not exactly sure. But they take it *very* seriously. From what I gather, the truth of the *Afore*, that we all have died and moved on, should only be revealed by a Sanguinir. But not just any one. They are organized in different groups. The wisest ones are the *Sanguinir Corum di Aquila*, the Choir of the Eagle. They are the priests, so to speak." Alana gestured to one of the silver-robed Sang strolling nearby, his pearlescent wings glimmering in the light. His upturned hood made him appear more monk than warrior.

Sofia's brow furrowed. "I'm sure at some point everyone figures out we're, you know," Sofia struggled with the word. "*Dead.* Why all the secrecy?"

Alana continued. "It's more than just knowing the fact. It's the key to open the door to the Sphaera Divinia. Therein lies the truth of not just the Afore, but many secrets about this place. There is much more to the Orvida than it seems, and the Sang can teach us."

That's why Ebrahym wouldn't tell me. He couldn't, or wasn't supposed to, anyway. "So, they told you all this?" Sofia asked.

"Yes, when the Sang found us at the lighthouse, they offered us a choice: Know the truth and know peace."

Sofia scoffed. "Or what?"

Alana ignored her. "They didn't want to frighten us, Sofia," retorted Alana. "They offered us the *Riques di Experaro*. I think that's how you say it. The Rite of Awakening. It opened our ears to the music of the Divine Sphere. It's beautiful."

Sofia bristled at Alana's infatuation. "And that's when they told you that we're dead?"

"Not exactly. After the ritual, we just sort of knew it, along with everything else. The Afore is long past; I know that now. I am not the being I once was. Neither are you. But I also know now that it's very taboo to talk about it." Alana paused in thought. "I think that might be why your name is such a curiosity."

Nuomen. That was what Jaziria called her. Was there something about Sofia that was an affront to the Way and the Sanguinir? Could she, like the others, enter the Sphere? A strange pride kept her from wanting to, to avoid bending a knee and taking the same path as everyone else. But perhaps the Sphere was the key, as Alana suggested, to all her questions. "Did anyone refuse this Awakening?"

"Yes, a few. A man named Tiago was one of them." Alana described the man from the lighthouse, caramel-skinned with a finely trimmed beard that hid a toothy smile. Sofia vaguely recalled him.

The more Alana explained, the more Sofia's resistance eroded until she had no choice but to believe that she was indeed dead. And deep down, she'd probably always known it to be so. In the cave, staring at Ebrahym, an *angel*, covered in the wounds from a monster, she'd known. In the Sepuselva, near the mass burial pit and in the ruins of Ilucenta surrounded by the shades of men, she'd known. And it explained some of the oddities of this world: her strange immunity to fire, the little need to eat or sleep, why the world seemed impervious to change. And why there were angels and demons living in it.

Some things remained a mystery, though. Alana seemed to trust the Sanguinir wholeheartedly, but Sofia wasn't sure. The more she learned about the mysterious beings, the less they appeared divine. The Orvida might be the afterlife, but Sofia suspected the Sang weren't infallible agents. They seemed perfectly *mortal*. But colder, distant. Their amber eyes looked right through a person as if observing a different world entirely.

The dreams. It always came back to the dreams. Sofia considered what the revelation, what Alana called the Afore, meant for her nightmares. If she was dead, where did they come from? Could they be hidden memories from her previous life? The idea was disturbing. Like a weight slung from her neck, she felt its pull. She wished she were like the others, wiped clean of their past, both good and bad.

"More of them," said Alana after some time, stirring Sofia from her thoughts. She pointed to the horizon.

Sofia squinted to see them, tall banners first and wagons and figures next as they meandered over the rolling hills, headed toward them. As the days passed, more caravans appeared to join their own. Every time they did, Sofia felt a jolt of panic. *Have the lúpero found us?* But then the silhouettes of men and women would sharpen, followed by her sigh of relief. Trumpets would call out, and others would respond.

More and more oulma came to join the great caravan each passing day, each group accompanied by its own Sang escort. This one was no different. The newly arrived pack of oulma and Sang soon merged with their own, growing the number further. Sofia wondered if the attack Ebrahym feared would ever come.

Late in the afternoon, when the newcomers had met up and settled, the caravan halted and began to set up camp. The process was an elaborate, efficient ballet. Each of the participants knew their part in the production, and if not, followed another until they did. Hundreds of tents sprouted up across the plain in mere minutes, and within an hour, the cooking hearths were roaring and music was playing. The Sang took up their positions on the perimeter. Dusk soon descended, bringing with it a pleasant breeze.

Alana left to join a group of students to study the Sanguinir ways. Sofia followed and listened to the sermon from a distance, but soon took to the outskirts of the camp alone. Her hands traced the tops of the taller grass as she walked, the sun setting it ablaze with color. Jaziria, close behind, glanced in her direction, noting Sofia's heading, but focused her attention toward her conversation with another sentry rather than her duty. *She must be getting bored of me.*

Sofia found herself on a small hill overlooking the larger command tents. Their red peaks were in sharp contrast to the sea of green-gold around them. Sanguinir warriors paced about. Her gaze drifted up. Clouds shifted colors aimlessly, deepening into rosy hues.

Movement against the clouds.

The Sanguinir fell into a deep dive and picked up speed, swooping over Sofia toward the red tents. He wore a brightly colored sash across his waist and a flamboyant cape waving behind, something Sofia had not yet seen one wear. He pumped his wings a few meters above the ground to come to a stop and lightly touched down in the grass. The sentries gathered around him and followed the newcomer inside the largest tent.

The guards are inside, Sofia realized, noticing that Jaziria, too, was absent. Sofia didn't even stop to think. She was already on the move, creeping through the grasses toward the command tent.

At the perimeter, she paused like a predator waiting in the brush before slipping underneath the fabric of the massive tent. She found herself in an outer ring filled with supplies and storage, the perfect vantage point to observe the central room that was divided by yet another layer of thick fabric. Through a thin opening between two seams, Sofia could see the inner tent was packed with Sanguinir—two dozen at least. Ebrahym was among them.

It was the first time Sofia had seen him since the cave. Strength and color had returned to his face, and he appeared more regal than before but wore a look of grave concern. Despite his towering height, many of the Sanguinir were larger than even he. One of which was the newcomer who stood in the middle of the room on piled, woven carpets. He was not only taller than Ebrahym, but also broad and wide, a true giant with a pair of rust-colored wings. His head was shorn, and he carried his plumed helmet in one arm. On his skull were etched intricate designs that rose from his eyebrows over his head and down his neck.

"Seven *catans* have reported the same occurrence," the Sanguinir in the sash said. It was clear he was a kind of messenger, his voice sharp and clear with an official tone, "it appears the attacks are an organized effort." Murmurs filtered through the tent.

The messenger continued. "The lúpero are only the initial threat, a scouting force to test our defenses. A caravan to the east was attacked last night. It sustained the most casualties as of late, with reports of *impès* and *hestrago* among the *imuertes*, united in force."

Imuertes? Sofia wondered. *More kinds of monsters?*

"It is long since we have seen a united horde," one of Sanguinir noted.

"Losses?" a Sanguinir woman asked. She was the only seated one among them, arched nobly, her legs delicately crossed. Her bronze skin glowed in the candlelight. Red paint covered her eyes and forehead like a fearsome mask. It made her pupils shine like two tiny flames of their own. Piles of medals and sigils dangled from her armor, and it was clear she was the one in charge.

"The caravan held, Catan Madadhi, but three of the Host fell, including Catan Lorus. Their *aurolas* were recovered, thankfully. But it might not have been so without Ebrahym's warning." More murmurs, and the warriors glanced at him. Sofia wondered what casualties could mean in a world of presumably immortal oulma. Then she remembered the lúpero and the wicked gash on her thigh.

The decorated woman, Catan Madadhi, raised her hand, quieting the others. "It seems Ebrahym's decision to trust the oulma woman, a nuomen, no less, was fortunate. Against the Way as it was." Sofia caught smirks and grins among the Sanguinir faces. "It matters not. We are ten days from the outskirts of Luminea. We can reach it in seven if we do not stop to make camp."

"Catan?" Ebrahym ventured. "We will be defenseless should the imuertes attack after dark whilst we are on the move." There were few nods in agreement.

"Do you underestimate the Host, Ebrahym? Do you think we are incapable of fulfilling our duties?" Sofia sensed politics were at play here, and angels did not play at politics. Human beings did.

Ebrahym conceded. "No, *ser*."

Her point made, Catan Madadhi continued. "The *Quato Eros* has sent word: The Host is to stay in the capital. We cannot wait for reinforcements, for there are none coming. Given the possibility of a coordinated horde, a defensive perimeter with so few of us will only make us an easier target. No. We must move, and move fast." Nods and murmurs of agreement filtered through the ranks.

"Do not cause panic among the oulma," Catan Madadhi warned. "I trust you all understand what is at stake."

Ebrahym's gaze met Sofia's as Catan Madadhi spoke. Though she was well hidden, his golden stare pierced through her concealment. Panic rushed over her, but he did not move to call her out. Perhaps he understood that Sofia now knew more than she should but trusted she would do the right thing with the information: nothing.

Catan Madadhi stood up, and the other Sanguinir stiffened to attention, "Remember the Way and let us see it done."

As the Sanguinir filed out of the command tent, Sofia shuddered as she envisioned hordes of monsters, these imuertes, lurking just beyond the camp. They were coming after all.

The tent emptied. Sofia noticed on a nearby table, carved and inlaid with gold, the battered chest piece and sword she'd taken from the corpse in Ilucenta. And the lúpero fang. Sofia stared at the trophy and wanted it. She felt its pull and missed its warmth against her skin.

She waited for the Sanguinir to file out before slipping under the flap and darting to the table. She grabbed the fang, feeling its familiar hot sting against her skin. As she turned, a giant map that lay sprawled across the table caught her eye. Marble figurines sat on it, some pale with wings, others dark with tangled limbs. She didn't know most of the places the map described, but she recognized a few: Ilucenta, the Meridi lighthouse, and the road. Neatly depicted in the center of the map was Luminea, the capital.

Sofia wanted to study it further, but caution forced her to move. She considered taking the sword and armor, too, but there would be no way to hide it from Jaziria, who was likely already suspicious of her absence.

Sofia stuffed the fang into her pocket and slipped through the back of the tent, careful to retrace her steps and avoid the Sanguinir sentries milling about. The long way back, around the camp perimeter, led her to where she'd started. Jaziria was waiting for her in the early darkness of the evening, the sentry's cold stare clearly communicating her disapproval.

"Sorry," Sofia feigned. "Nature called."

11

Sofia's dreams continued. But she noticed details began to change. She strangled her victim night after night, but sometimes, the fabric of the curtains would be different. Or the hue of the carpet shifted. One night the woman's hair was pulled back to reveal her face, tear-stained and beautiful, and other times thick curls of black obscured it.

This time, the hair was up, and Sofia could feel it brush against the back of her hands as she crushed the life out of her. The woman's olive skin turned a deep crimson, eyes bulging and streaming with desperate tears until Sofia finished her work and left her slumped lifelessly in the corner.

Sofia didn't wake. She lingered in the dingy room. Turning away from the body offered her a vantage point she hadn't experienced before.

On the opposite wall, a cheap, oval mirror dangling on a wire caught her reflection. But it was not her face she saw staring back at her, only a shadow. It moved with an unnatural, inhuman quality, as if many shadows layered on top of one another moved independently, bound together by some purpose.

Sofia wanted to look away, but the reflection pulled at her. She and it approached one another in unison. A dark, withered limb reached out from the mirror's surface. Sofia mouthed a silent scream. Huge horns spiraled from the shade as it drew itself into the room, towering over her. The thing studied her with invisible, probing eyes. She could not see them, but she could feel their violating gaze upon her. Then the shadow took her, enveloping her in a shroud of darkness.

Screaming and thrashing on a makeshift cot hanging off the side of a wagon, Sofia awoke. And for a moment, she didn't notice the screams in the distance over her own.

The caravan had stopped. People were running in every direction as Sanguinir warriors shouted orders to one another. Spears pointed toward the front of the caravan, presumably leading the oulma to safety. Horns trumpeted wildly.

The lúpero. The imuertes. They're here.

Sofia rolled off the wagon, stumbling groggily to fall in line with a group of people rushing toward the head of the caravan. She felt rain on her face for the first time. The clouds above were bruised and unnaturally dark; a storm was upon them. Sanguinir warriors spiraled overhead like raptors on the hunt.

Falling in line, Sofia scanned the faces of the oulma next to her, searching for Alana, but she was nowhere in sight. Dawn had not yet broken, but in the growing light, Sofia saw grounded Sanguinir stationed around a makeshift bulwark of upturned wagons. They led the oulma through a small opening in the perimeter toward the center. Like sheep, they huddled together by instinct, their all-too-human curiosity compelling them to peer over the wagons to see what was coming. Sofia thought of the mass grave in the Sepuselva and hoped there would not be another.

Then, she saw what was coming.

Silhouetted against the eastern horizon, through the sheets of rain, a black mass undulated and squirmed like a pack of flies on a carcass. It moved as one organism across the plain toward them. Sofia was one of the last to slip inside the defenses. Catan Madadhi, clad in polished armor, pointed toward the makeshift gate with the tip of her spear. A pair of Sanguinir obeyed and heaved a wagon into place to block the entrance.

Sofia spied Ebrahym near the far side of the bulwark and ran to him.

"What can I do?" Sofia shouted. Ebrahym glanced at Catan Madadhi. His wet hair hung tightly against his face, and his amber eyes burned.

He faced her. "Stay away! This is not the time, Sofia. You know not of what approaches." He called to a nearby Sang. Rings of light appeared around the heads of the warriors as they prepared for battle.

"Yes, I do!" Sofia shouted back, meeting his golden stare with a fierceness of her own.

So, you know, his eyes told her. "Stay here!" he ordered. Ebrahym's eyes vanished behind the glowing ring that ignited as it encircled his head, as he, too, prepared for war.

Sofia wheeled in anger. Across the way, she saw an armored Sang in blue robes leap onto the bulwark with the help of her wings. The slender bow she carried let three arrows loose in a matter of seconds. There were no more than a few dozen Sanguinir in all surrounding the huddled mass of oulma. Wings spread wide, swords and spears drawn, they stood at the ready to face what approached.

Sofia heard them now. The sounds of trampling feet, snarls and yips and screams carried through the air, a thundering mass of chaos. It was like the call of a single lúpero but much denser, deeper and more maddening.

Through openings in the makeshift fortification, she saw them circling the encampment at speed. Large and small forms made up the dark pack, a writhing tangle of claws and spines, teeth, and slick, black flesh. The darkness began to creep in and unsettle her courage. The dark whisper, Ebrahym had called it. The noxurros. She hoped the Sang's power would be enough to keep it at bay.

"Sofia!"

She heard Alana's voice before she saw her appear from the crowd. She wore a hard expression on her delicate features, a thin mask covering the dread beneath.

"What do we do?"

"I don't know," said Sofia, looking around for a sign. She couldn't think with all the chaos. But she wouldn't sit idle and wait. Not for Ebrahym, not for anyone.

Just as she couldn't sit at the lighthouse and wait for something to happen, she was compelled to act, for better or worse.

Sofia caught a glint of steel and discovered a wagon laden with war gear, upturned and used to bolster the wall. She recognized the fabrics from the command tent and knew her stolen gear would be there.

"Alana, help me!" called Sofia as she ran to the supplies. There, she found her armor, the golden breastplate and tarnished sword. Seeing them gave her fresh courage. *The fire will not burn me.* She threw the armor on, clamping the pieces to her body, straps dangling.

Alana helped cinched the straps tight. "This is crazy, Sofia. You're not like them. You're going to get yourself killed!"

Alana didn't understand. Standing over the corpse of the lúpero she'd slain had awoken something within Sofia. A power. And a desire to use it. "I have to try." Sofia said, feigning a smile. "Besides, we're already dead."

Beyond the paltry wooden wall encircling the frightened oulma, the battle had begun. The metallic thud of swords finding flesh, the shouting, snarling, and the cry of a silvery horn echoed through the air. The Sanguinir were singing. United, their hymn somehow filtered above the roar of battle. It found Sofia, and the creeping darkness faded away, at least for the moment. A calm descended on the oulma.

"Do you feel it, Alana?" Sofia asked looking up.

"It's the Sphere," called Alana, grasping the shaft of a pike for herself. "Be careful, Sofia."

Sofia nodded and scrambled up the ramparts to join the front. From the top of the wagons, she could see other oulma following her lead, brave souls who would not lie down. Alana acted as makeshift quartermaster, arming the rest of the volunteers, inspired by Sofia's courage. *Or foolishness*, she thought.

The horde of monsters hit the weakest part of the defenses first: just between two overturned wagons. The opening formed a choke point, a death trap. Sanguinir held it on foot with sword and shield. Sofia had never seen anything like it. The brutality of the carnage was matched only by the grace of the Sanguinir. They moved with perfect balance, their blades finding the throats and skulls of monsters with every swing.

Empowered by their battle hymn, the Sanguinir cut the imuertes down in droves. One Sang ignited into a living being of fire, almost as terrifying as the monsters he fought. Above, an archer loosed arrows and shouted to her comrades fighting on the ground.

Sofia looked for an opportunity to help amidst the carnage. The noise was near deafening, shocking her nerves. It was difficult to think. She could feel the evil aura pushing against the hymn, a battle being forged in her mind. For now, the song kept the madness at bay. But for how long it would, she did not know.

To the right, the wagons bulged and splintered. The imuertes were trying to find another way in.

Sofia rushed to protect the flank, running along the top of the defenses, stabbing wildly at the madness on the other side. She couldn't look too closely, lest the darkness take her. Brave shouts called out from behind. She turned to see the few oulma following her lead and, from their perches upon the wagons, hacking at the monsters, occasionally finding their mark.

A lúpero lunged at one defender, pulling the man from the top of the wagon. He was torn apart a moment later. Seeing one of their own savaged caused the oulma militia to nearly collapse in terror, overwhelmed by the chaos. They covered their ears and screamed.

Sofia leaped from the rampart. It splintered apart a second later as the monsters spilled in. Her feet hit the ground. Something came at her, and she swung her sword wildly. The blade cleaved through a flat, round face with an unnatural number of eyes. More teeth and talons came at her. She hacked at them. Again and again. Each time her sword bit into flesh, she felt stronger. *The fire will not burn me.*

Everything fell away. A heavy silence followed by darkness. She could no longer hear the music of the Sanguinir. Fear and panic rippled through her body and deep into her mind. She moved through mud and fog as more monsters approached from the blackness. Their forms morphed and twisted like inky shadows in front of her, illusions that multiplied and then fell away in black smoke. A living mass of death yawning for her, beckoning.

And in her mind, Sofia heard screams. An endless chorus of screams, a dissonant din so sorrowful it threatened to consume her entirely.

But Sofia would not let it take her. She held on to the only thing she could: her anger. Her rage. She twisted her panic into a hot ball of fury. It compressed and churned, like the hot core of the earth, the center of the sun. A power so intense it threatened to destroy her if not released.

Fury overtook every nerve. She cut through the ranks of evil limbs and twisted bodies not with grace, but with a wild brutality. She did not slay her foes. She annihilated them. One imp-like creature, wiry and gangly, lunged at Sofia's chest, its teeth puncturing the armor and meeting the flesh underneath. She threw an arm around the creature's thin neck, wrenching it until she heard bones snap.

Another pair rushed toward her, but a wide swing of her sword opened their gullets from left to right as they screeched. She cut her way through the darkness. Limbs fell and hot gore sprayed. She was lost in a fever dream. There were no fears or desires. No friends, no love. It was Sofia alone with her rage. Simple, pure, absolute...

Metal met metal with a harsh clang. The sound snapped Sofia from the trance of battle.

Under her blade was a man, an oulma. Not a monster, not an enemy. Just a man, covered in steaming, dark gore, eyes wide with terror. One of the few brave enough to follow her. And Ebrahym's sword had stopped her from cleaving him in two. *Oh God.*

Senses returning, Sofia dropped the blade in horror. Her armor sizzled with heat, and all around her were the smoldering, grotesque corpses of the enemy. She was thirty meters from the wagons, only now realizing how far she had plowed into the enemy ranks. She had not only survived the attack, but had decimated everything in her way.

She looked around in a daze. The corpses of the creatures, these imuertes, as varied as they were foul, lay still in the tall grass as their hot innards burned away anything nearby. Larger lúpero lay among them. Acrid steam from the rain hitting the ichor lingered. Sanguinir archers unceremoniously shot down any stragglers with keen bolts from above.

Below, the crowd of relieved oulma fought to get a clear view of the one whom they'd seen leap over the ramparts but never expected to return. Alana was one of them. She had a broken spear in one hand and a splattering of black gore across her clothing. She, too, had taken up arms and followed Sofia's lead. But now, a look of astonished horror hung on her face, having seen Sofia nearly kill one of their own.

The shame was sickening. She stumbled backward. Her rage had nearly taken the life of a man who'd been brave enough to follow her. And how she had relished the violence! The thought terrified her. The Sanguinir looked at her with silent, burning stares. Their armor and wings, blackened with the residue of battle, hissed in the rain.

Ebrahym said nothing, but in his golden eyes, Sofia saw something she hadn't before.

Fear.

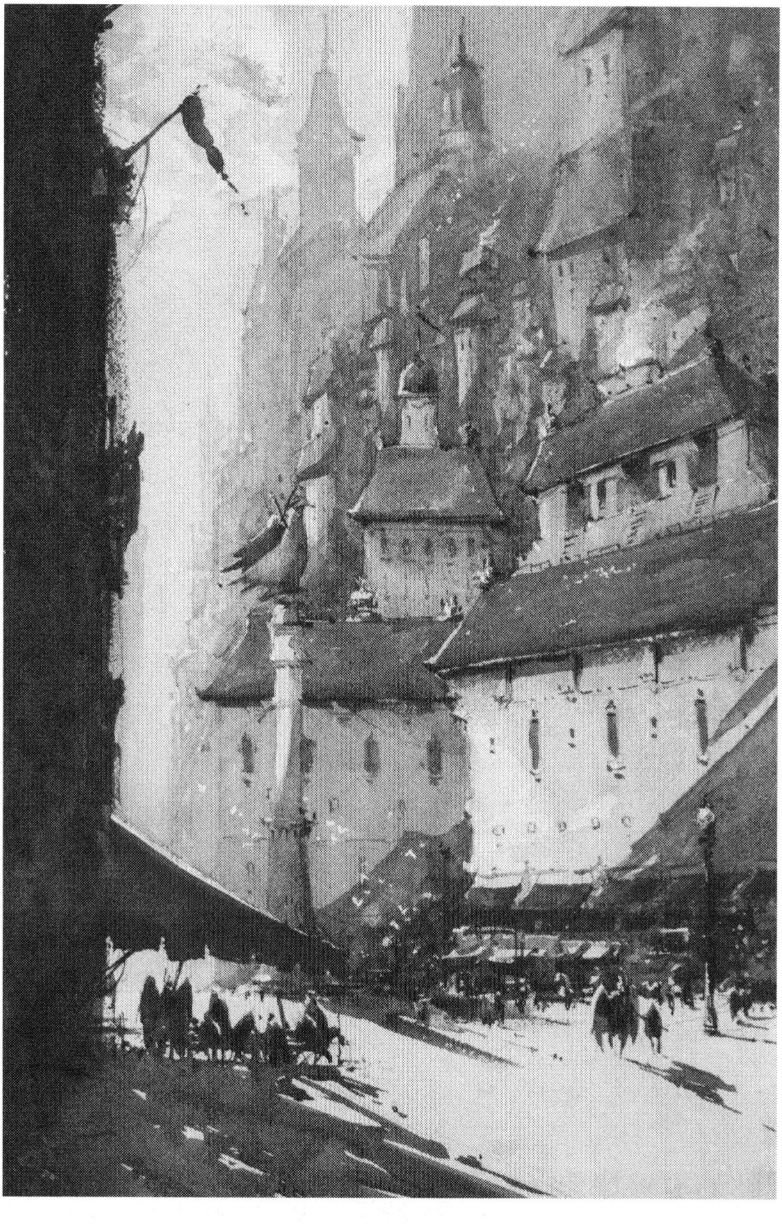

12

The magnificence of Luminea was difficult to comprehend, let alone describe. Even if Sofia could remember every moment from the Afore in perfect detail, she knew nothing would compare to the golden city in the sea. It gleamed on the horizon like a sparkling gem floating on a shimmering disk. From the center of the mass of civilization, arcs of light reached from the horizon to the sky above, twisting like vapor in the breeze. They eventually faded to a haze behind layers of thick clouds.

Towers and pyramids huddled upon an island in the center of a vast inland sea that the Sang called the *Aecuna,* the Cradle Sea. Clusters of atolls surrounded the main isle, all densely packed with civilization and connected by a web of bridges. They led inland, toward the sloping, tiered walls of earth from which the towers grew. The flat tiers stacked on one another and grew ever smaller toward the summit. There, the spires were most concentrated and elaborate. Tendrils of light emanated from the center of the island as if the city itself was built around them.

After days of hard travel since the battle, it was a reassuring sight.

As the caravan lumbered toward Luminea, Sofia found it hard to take her eyes off the skyline. The caravan had not stopped since the attack, and the people were tired, afraid. A melancholy had settled upon them, a dreariness that came from witnessing death. Only now, with Luminea in sight, did it lessen. The wagons and travelers picked up their pace.

But the sickening feeling Sofia carried did not fade. The shame of nearly killing an innocent man clung to her like a bad stink. The sound of swords meeting echoed in her thoughts.

"Beautiful, is it not?" Ebrahym asked. He'd rarely let Sofia out of his sight since the battle, and even now, as the caravan trudged along toward the city, he was at her side. Sofia couldn't yet tell where she stood in the amber eyes of the Sanguinir since the battle. *Is he watching me or watching out for me?*

"It is," Sofia agreed, thinking of the bodies of the oulma they'd recovered after the battle and wrapped in sheets. Hereafter or not, they were gone. The only thing left of them was gruesome, ravaged corpses, like the wandering people of Ilucenta. The dead eyes were the same. "I wish everyone could have seen it."

Ebrahym did not look at her. "Indeed. Their journey continues, as does ours. But along a different path." There was sadness in his voice, a distinctly feminine lament, like a mother's pain for a lost child.

"Ebrahym," Sofia began. "What happened to me?" It had taken days to find the courage to ask. She wasn't sure she really wanted to know. "One minute I was there, and the next I was...gone. It was like being near the lúpero, but different. I wasn't afraid. I was...angry. All I wanted was to destroy them all. Every last one." She struggled to get the words out. "I almost killed that man."

"Force of the mind is a powerful thing," he explained in a low voice. "We call it *Serrá,* your volition. Will. Understand, Sofia, the Orvida is not partial to change; entropy is not its natural state. Will is what remakes the world. It is what grants the imuertes the ability to inflict such suffering, such malice. We use it to give the Divine Sphere its strength. *Iriva ay Serrá,* Sofia. The Will and the Way. Together they let us work stone and metal, create music and art that transcend emotion, and change the nature of ourselves. Through it, we are united in common purpose, in order. In harmony."

"So where does my power come from? My dreams—" Sofia caught herself from saying any more and looked away.

Ebrahym raised an eyebrow, studying her. "Serrá can manifest in...mysterious ways, especially for the nuomen."

Sofia looked at him, too tired to press. "It means 'the named,'" Ebrahym said. "Those who remember."

"There are others?"

"Rarely," Ebrahym said. "Each carries something different from the Afore." His tone marked the end of the conversation.

They walked awhile together in silence, the clunking and creaking of wagons and the murmurs of conversation around them. One of the beasts, the word for it was *bull,* let out a funny bellow. A few oulma nearby laughed. Life was returning to the caravan.

The train of people and wagons snaked through the outlying fields onward toward Luminea as the sun climbed. The rolling amber hills opened to a vast valley, and the caravan made its way down the gentle slope. Enormous fields divided the landscape, and ancient-looking towns and villages appeared along the winding road. The buildings there were densely packed and old, layers representing millenia of growth with some of the plaster structures housing hundreds of oulma each. Draped across the avenues, colored banners spanned from building to building as Sofia and the caravan passed underneath. Smiling faces called down from terraced balconies covered in flowers. Sofia waved back.

The road meandered through the farmlands and townships until terminating at the shore of the Aecuna. Sofia saw no sign of the sea's other side, and it could have easily been another ocean.

A massive stone arch, topped with statues depicting Sanguinir warriors, loomed a hundred meters above the water, a tightly woven orchestra of cables and stone pylons stretching out across the bay. Suspended from it was a wide, stone bridge that connected the mainland to the city of Luminea. A fleet of boats bobbed just offshore, with hundreds more bustling about the island, propelled by wind and sail.

The oulma—tired, dirty and anxious, gathered at the arch as the caravan came to a halt. All necks craned skywards, taking in the towering Luminea skyline. Even in the growing daylight, the beams of light at the heart of the metropolis glowed brighter than the sun.

Sofia, too, was tired. She'd avoided sleep since the battle. She slumped against a wagon and drank greedily from a water skin.

"Hello, Sofia." She knew the voice belonged to Erado before she saw him. Her stomach tightened. He was thin as ever, his pale, blue eyes almost translucent in the sunlight. He carried himself differently than she remembered: quieter, less proud.

"What do you want?" she demanded. Her hand reached behind for a sword that wasn't there. It sat in a wagon somewhere.

Erado took a step forward. "I told myself if I ever saw you again, I would ask your forgiveness."

Sofia snorted. "For trying to set me on fire, you sick bastard?" Her blood was up now. That familiar ember seethed.

"Yes." There was sincerity in his eyes. Sofia hated it. "It was cruel what I did to you, and cowardly." Erado hung his head, and she caught herself momentarily falling for the act. "After the Sang found us at the lighthouse and welcomed us into the Sphere, I realized how wrong I was. I am sorry for what I did; I truly am. Fearful men do desperate and terrible things."

"But?" Sofia challenged.

"But," Erado continued, "that doesn't mean my fear was not justified."

Sofia gritted her teeth as her heart quickened. "What the hell does that mean?"

"I saw what happened during the battle," Erado explained. "You would have cut that oulma in half if that Sang hadn't stopped you. So, yes, I came to tell you I am sorry for what I did," he paused, "but I was right to fear you. I hope you find peace." He left without a word, leaving Sofia alone and seething with anger.

"What was that about?" Alana asked, appearing from nowhere. Sofia hadn't spoken to her since the battle. She didn't want to see the disappointment in Alana's eyes.

"Nothing, forget it."

"Hmm." Alana blocked the sun with one hand and gazed out across the water. "Amazing, isn't it?"

"Yeah, it is," said Sofia, taking in the view. She couldn't imagine a more beautiful scene. She turned to Alana. "I'm sorry we haven't had a chance to talk. I— "

"It's okay, Sofia," Alana said with a reassuring arm around her. "I'm just glad you're all right."

Sofia smiled, but she knew deep down she wasn't all right. Not really. But maybe she'd find out the reason why in Luminea.

Alana pointed. "Look."

An official-looking procession of Sanguinir of the Choir of the Eagle, draped in silver robes, marched across the bridge and into view. Though beautiful and proud, they seemed modest compared to the other Sang that flanked them. Sofia did not recognize the other Choir. Their garb was almost iridescent—a living tapestry of blues and violets and turquoises, gilded with colorful gems and bright feathers. They played an inspiring march with stringed instruments, horns and drums that announced their presence, dancing as they did. A group of uniformed oulma, carrying banners and supplies, followed close behind.

"What happens now?" Alana asked. Sofia shrugged.

The oulma from the caravan milled about, curious what was to come next. As the procession approached, the caravan guard, led by Catan Madadhi, embraced their kin, and soon, the uniformed oulma dismantled the caravan. They welcomed the newcomers across the bridge. Sofia and Alana moved to join them, but Ebrahym appeared and motioned for her.

"Follow me," he said. Sofia nodded and gave a weak wave to Alana. Alana waved back with a curious look on her face and turned to fall in line with the others. Sofia grabbed her pack from the wagon and ran to catch Ebrahym.

She followed him down a series of stone steps off the bridge leading to the waterline below where a boat was waiting. Several vessels were lashed to a stone pier, waiting to ferry travelers to and from the city. The vessel had three large masts and a crew of oulma tending to its rigging.

Sofia followed Ebrahym and stepped on board. A few shouts and choreography of movements by the crew let the sails unfurl, and the boat pulled away from the pier. A crisp breeze off the water filled the canvas, and the boat skirted under the bridge toward the atolls ahead.

"You won't be joining the others," Ebrahym said. The boat carved through the water, spraying mist on the deck.

The words stung. "Because of what happened? Because I'm *named*?"

"Yes."

Fresh guilt spilled over her. "I'm sorry! I don't remember anything. I just—"

"I know," interrupted Ebrahym. "Do you recall what you saw in Ilucenta, Sofia?"

Sofia nodded. *How could I forget?*

"They are the *umbra*, the fallen ones. Once oulma, like you. Many of them nuomen, with memories of the Afore. They cling to them like a sickness. Distant memories of loved ones long past, of failures, of sins."

Sofia's gut tightened. "What happened to them?"

"One must set aside the past to find stillness, to move on. The umbra are endlessly haunted, living in a darkness they create for themselves. Eventually, their memories eat away at them and destroy their minds. Their own Serrá, their Will, creates the hell they live in. Because of this, they exist outside of the Divine Sphere. We cannot let them influence others, nor will they ever accept the

Sphere's grace. So, they seek out dark places to hide with their grief and sorrow. Ilucenta was a great city once. Now it is but a tomb for the unfortunate to gather in."

"There was one that chased me," Sofia said. "Imuertes?"

"No," said Ebrahym, shaking his head. "Not yet our enemy, by way of your description. But on the path to becoming one."

Sofia glanced out over the water as the boat tacked over. An atoll was fast approaching to the east as the boat zigzagged upwind. Gulls soared past the sunbaked plaster buildings and tiled roofs. Overhead, the true scale of the towers manifested itself as the structures punctured clouds above. Sofia's thoughts returned to her recurring nightmare. *How can I let go of so many questions?*

"Will I become like them?" she asked. A silence hung in the air.

"I hope that will not be so," said Ebrahym. "But what to do next is for the *Altuma Councilia*, the High Council to decide. Among them are the oulma leaders and the *Quato Eros*, the four Archlords of the Host, the Sanguinir leaders. They will decide what your fate shall be. You must understand, Sofia, the nuomen represent a threat toward our entire civilization. Their power," he paused, clearly choosing his words carefully, "can be unpredictable."

"But they are people, aren't they?" Sofia whispered.

"It is unfortunate, yes. But we cannot take the risk. Not again."

Again? "I don't understand."

"Fear not," Ebrahym smiled, and for a moment, Sofia saw something familiar there. "You honored your word, Sofia, and I will honor mine. But you must trust me," his smile faded away, "for a hard road lies ahead."

As the boat made its way through the waterways between individual atolls, the conversation lightened. Ebrahym described the various districts of Luminea to Sofia, pointing them out as they skirted the shoreline. At the eastern edge of the city was the First District, an ancient quarter where the city had begun. The warm, patchwork facades of its buildings topped with tile roofs rose from the sea. Some of the founders of Luminea still lived there.

Closer to the water's edge was the Shorefront, a snaking wall of structures that followed the curves of the island. The district spanned multiple atolls connected by bridges and was littered with orchards and gardens that clung to the walls. The structures extended to the water's edge in the form of long piers and jetties supported by a latticework of pylons.

Beyond the Shorefront lay the great tiers of Luminea. Man-made plateaus supported spires that loomed like giants. There, Ebrahym explained, was the Market Strand, a line of vendors trading wares that wound through the city. Farther away still were the various artisan quarters, the Observatory and the Parish Grounds, in which the temples dedicated to the disciplines were located, as well as the Forgeward. Sofia listened to Ebrahym describe his home and imagined majestic locales nestled between the bases of the towers.

The yacht depowered its sails and drifted lazily to a massive causeway of boats and moorings on the main island. The docks buzzed with activity as oulma called to one another. The gulls overhead did the same. Their silhouettes, and those of the occasional Sanguinir in flight, darted above the city.

Sofia stepped off the boat and, gazing up, soaked in her surroundings. The enormity and grace of the vista was overwhelming. This was a city of gods. As Ebrahym led her up the stone avenue, away from the shore, Sofia found marvel in every detail. Every direction she looked provided some form of architectural miracle, crafted with such precision as to inspire tears.

Statues that likely represented decades, even hundreds of years of effort casually littered the streets and corners, almost mundane amidst all the remarkable beauty. Flowers and trees lined the cobbled streets, and everywhere there was color splashed upon the buildings. Sofia wondered if Ilucenta had once been this beautiful.

She followed Ebrahym to a massive ramp carved into the stone tiers. At its base was an enormous gate. The lighthous of Meridi would have easily fit inside, stacked multiple times. The ancient arch framed a passage through the defensive wall to the city interior. It was so wide that a dozen caravans could easily pass through without ever touching one another.

"Who built all of this?" Sofia asked, her neck craned as they passed by an elaborately carved fountain. The street bustled with people moving opposite them, smiling and laughing.

"The *Corum di Torru*, the Choir of the Bull. They are the makers," Ebrahym said, nodding to another passing Sanguinir garbed in embroidered, green robes covered in geometric symbols. She was a thick woman, voluptuous and strong with a pair of speckled wings that draped behind her.

The pair made their way to a small cafe on the outskirts of a large public square. A week ago, Sofia had been searching for water in a desert and running from monsters. Now she took tea in the sun. It tasted of laughter and mint, and she resisted the urge to giggle. How far away the smell of sulfur seemed.

As she sipped, Sofia wondered idly why anyone would bother with something as trivial as running a cafe for all eternity. When the proprietor—a refined sort with hawkish features and a wide, warm grin—returned, Sofia asked him.

"Everyone must do *something*, my dear. Bliss comes in many forms," he said. "I'm happy to have found mine."

Sofia eyed Ebrahym. His character continued to prove elusive. Sometimes she felt she was speaking to a powerful man; other times, she found herself sitting across from a graceful woman. Not only physically, but in voice and mannerisms as well. The transitions flowed so seamlessly they were easy to miss.

"Back in the cave," Sofia said, finally breaking the silence, "after you woke up, I heard you talking to yourself in a different language. Is that a prayer or something?"

Ebrahym eyed his tea. "Let us say I was asking for advice."

"From whom?"

He laughed for once. It wasn't quite natural, as if it was a long-forgotten impulse, rarely used. "A friend."

The carefree moment passed. "What will happen when I meet this High Council?" she asked, looking up at the walled city beyond. A flock of birds flew in the distance, their tiny forms giving scale to the huge structures behind.

He eyed her with a hint curiosity. "Try not to worry. What comes will come."

Sofia fiddled with her cup. "You are here to watch me, aren't you? Because I'm nuomen."

Ebrahym nodded. "It is the Way."

"I wish I could see more of it," Sofia said, taking in the view.

Ebrahym's eyes softened. "I can delay the summons for a day. You have earned that much. But I cannot let you roam the city alone."

13

Sofia rose early, hoping the morning light would burn away the shadows that came with sleep.

Even here in Luminea, the very definition of beauty, darkness found her. She remembered what Ebrahym said about letting go, about moving on. But how could she when the dreams returned night after night?

The streets woke up with her. Ebrahym was waiting nearby, but she took her time, enjoying the solitude.

Awnings like swaths of paint and elaborate signs lit up as the sun crept over the stone rooftops and between the massive towers and flooded into the streets. Sofia poked her head into shops and stalls, getting a feel for the place. She was amazed to see people going about *business*. A strange thing in a city full of people that would never run out of time. But as she exchanged words with the tailors, bakers, jewel smiths and artists, seeing the love and care they put into their crafts, she saw it wasn't work at all to them. This was their heaven. Sofia envied them in a way, envied their bliss. It shed light on her restlessness.

A sweet odor drew her into a corner bakery, an ancient-looking establishment that looked as if carved out of a single block of stone by a master sculptor. Each window was chiseled individually to perfection and inlaid with colorful glass. Inside, an array of glazed pastries glowed. The place was bustling, full of oulma in all manner of attire—intricate robes, oversized trousers with long capes, corsets, and always feathers and jeweled accents. Sofia overheard them talking about the caravan attack. Apparently, it was news.

She grabbed a sticky morsel covered in cinnamon and spotted familiar faces, oulma from the caravan. They too had meandered from the temporary dwellings for transplants, but they turned away from her as she approached. There was a man she recognized: Tiago, the one Alana described to her while they were still on the road. He was one who'd denied the Sanguinir's offer to accept the Divine Sphere. He gave her a nod.

"You're Tiago?" Sofia asked, approaching him.

"I am. And you are Sofia." He motioned for her to sit. "I've heard your name many times after what happened on the road. A brave thing, I hear. Me? I was huddled up with the rest."

"Consider yourself lucky," Sofia said. She shifted in her chair. "So, I hear you weren't keen on the Sang's offer about their Divine Sphere." He cocked his head, anticipating a question. "Why not?"

Tiago stroked his manicured beard. "It's funny what constitutes a memory, don't you think? I can't recall my name, where I was born, if I had children. You might call those things memories, but they could be considered merely facts. But what about the feeling of a sunset? The touch of a lover? Are these not memories too? We may not remember *facts,* but I think we *know* more than it seems." Tiago took a sip of what smelled like spiced coffee. "When the Sanguinir appeared, I felt something. It wasn't a memory, but it was familiar."

Sofia recalled her own awe at the first sight of Ebrahym. "What did you feel? What was it?"

"Suspicion." Tiago said. "I had no idea why at the time, of course. I had no grounds on which to base my opinion, but there it was. It was like a truth only a lifetime of experience could teach. You might call that wisdom. Perhaps I am an old man who finds himself in a young man's body." He laughed.

"What truth are you talking about? About the Sang?"

"About power, dear. *Power,*" he clenched his fist for effect. "Power corrupts, and you don't become powerful peacefully. Even if you have a pair of wings." Sofia nodded, conscious of her scowl. She too felt there was something less than divine about the Sang.

Tiago waved his hand. "Bah, I don't know. Perhaps, I once lived under the bootheel of some king or tyrant. Maybe I just lived long enough to not trust anyone anymore. But something inside of me resists all this." He gestured to Luminea outside. "And fears the ones that made it. It's too—"

"Perfect?" Sofia ventured. Tiago nodded.

Tiago's words lingered in her mind as Sofia said her goodbye and left to meet Ebrahym. *Power corrupts.* If not for Ebrahym, Sofia might be inclined to share Tiago's opinion. After all, Jaziria and the other Sang had not been particularly welcoming. But there was something about Ebrahym that disarmed her fears. Perhaps they weren't all alike.

She emerged from a crooked, cobblestone alley to find Ebrahym waiting near a well-kept garden that sprouted in the midst of beautiful stone structures the color of fresh butter. He wore robes of white and red, his wings lightly dragging across the stone as he walked.

"Good morning," said Sofia.

"It is," he said, closing his eyes for a moment to enjoy the sun. "Shall we? There is much to see, if you wish, before our summons tomorrow."

Ebrahym escorted Sofia through the massive gate at the foot of the First Tier, the outermost ring of the concentric districts. Within the wall, shimmering spires reached toward the heavens. Between the trunks of the great stone forest, Sofia caught glimpses of the plumes of light emanating from the heart of the city and watched them dance in the wind.

She was closer now to the strange light than ever before, and it tugged at her. Like the hymns of the Sanguinir, it warmed her heart in a way difficult to describe. Her anxiety waned in its presence.

"The *Sanctu Arcam*," Ebrahym said, noticing her gaze. He pointed toward the center of the city, made a gesture and murmured something to himself. "Some call it the Dawnlight. It is the most sacred part of all Luminea, the heart of the Sanguinir Host."

"What is it?" Sofia asked, still staring.

"It was discovered long ago, eons before my time. Luminea was built around it." As he spoke, Ebrahym led Sofia up hundreds of steps through the dark tunnel to the first of the tiered districts. "It is both the beginning and the end, the sacred path that leads from the Orvida to…the Æfter."

"Æfter? Is that like this place?"

"No one knows for certain, not even the wisest of the Host."

They wove between growing streams of people. "So, this Dawnlight…it's some kind of door?" Sofia asked. Ebrahym nodded. "Hm. Don't doors open both ways?"

"Indeed."

"And the oulma, they…*we* go through it?"

"Some do. That is why my kind exist, Sofia. To shepherd the worthy onward. And to…" his voice lowered as a crowd of oulma passed by, "keep the imuertes far from it."

She thought of the monsters on the road and felt her gut twist. "Why? What do they want with the Dawnlight?"

His gaze was far away. "An escape. Come"

Sofia wondered what the demonic imuertes wished to escape from. *Were they not content as they were, horrible as it may be?*

The tunnel connecting the Lower City and the First Tier was a small neighborhood in and of itself, with structures and dwellings carved into the tunnel wall. They flickered with luminescent spheres, and above, holes bored through the rock let beams of light cut through the shadows like golden shafts. When they finally passed through the other side, Sofia and Ebrahym found themselves in a great plaza that was a least two kilometers long on every side. The square was littered with statues that only giants could have carved.

But no mist nor madmen here, Sofia reminded herself. Ilucenta was far away.

She turned her attention skyward. Above, Sanguinir darted between the spires and bulbous skyships, *aeronavès*, Ebrahym called them. But the courtyard square was only the beginning of Luminea's true beauty.

They wound through corridors and libraries that surrounded the Observatory, a huge dome with carved outlets for massive bronze optics to poke through. Vast, hanging gardens and conservatories were everywhere, nurtured by ancient aqueducts. Their facades were adorned with ornate stone columns, elaborate buttresses and carved details Sofia had difficulty taking in. The plants that clung to the structures were unnaturally gorgeous, oversized and saturated with pigment. Their pollen hung heavy in the hair, sweetening it.

"Why are there no children here?" Sofia asked, finally noticing every oulma she passed was the same age, more or less. They wove through a crowded street, a side avenue of the Market Strand.

"It is rare, but some do wash ashore as such," Ebrahym explained. "But soon they change. Remember the Serrá, Sofia. The *Will*. They choose to become something different. Few choose to remain children forever."

Musicians played stringed guitars and brass horns on every corner, enlivening every street. Sofia and Ebrahym wound through them, and occasionally his feathered wings would brush her face as she followed. As they explored Luminea, smiling oulma nodded and bowed in Ebrahym's presence. Everywhere, people buzzed with activity. Sofia witnessed a performance of actors for a laughing and cheering audience of thousands. Canals with boats carrying singing ferrymen carved through the districts. Around each corner, Ebrahym revealed new wonders. Part of Sofia wished to become lost here, to be like the oulma around her. Content and happy.

But despite the beauty of the city, Tiago's words of suspicion lingered. Tomorrow she would face the High Council. Ebrahym had spared her a day. Her thoughts careened back into the shadow realm of the imuertes, of dreams and horrors waiting in the mist. *Tomorrow will come,* told herself, fighting the sense of dread brooding below the surface.

"Why are you doing this for me?" Sofia asked. Afternoon turned to evening and cooled the stone city from brilliant golds to gentle shades of violet.

"You ask more questions than not." Ebrahym's smile faded as he met her hard eyes. "As I said, I owe you a debt. No one should be denied the beauty of Luminea."

"It is beautiful," Sofia admitted. "But what I want is to *know,* Ebrahym. I want to understand this world, not just accept it blindly. There is a curtain over it. You let me peek through it but not see."

"And if what lay on other side was frightening? Would you still want to see?"

Sofia thought for a moment. "Yes."

Ebrahym shook his head. "That is why the nuomen are feared."

Night descended. Colored paper lanterns lined the streets, and performers and music replaced the vendor stalls and markets. Parades sparked to life, marching down alleys as people laughed and sang together. Wine and spirits flowed, and people danced in the streets. Joy radiated infectiously from every person.

Sofia, her mood slowly lifting, watched from the edge of the street as a striking man with pale skin and fine golden curls approached her. He smiled with chiseled features, bowing deeply before her. Sofia took his hand with a silly curtsy, playing along. He twirled her to the music, pulled her close and pressed his lips to hers. Caught off guard by the taste of sweet fruits, Sofia gave in to the excitement of the moment and returned the kiss. Urges stirred inside of her. Her fingers slid behind his neck and got lost in his hair. The man pulled away with a roguish laugh and rejoined the parade, blowing her a final kiss as he did. A stunned Sofia pulled her hair behind her ears sheepishly as her heart beat in her chest.

Ebrahym chuckled. "Here, you will find that love is more...universal in nature."

Even the occasional Sanguinir, stoic and conspicuous, mingled among the blissful oulma. Ebrahym was right: affection seemed indiscriminate and completely normal in Luminea. Was this the work of the Divine Sphere? Whatever the cause, Sofia nearly lost herself in the revelry.

Later, upon a rooftop overlooking a sea of lighted windows, Sofia and Ebrahym stretched out upon feathered cushions and watched the stars slowly revolve above. The Dawnlight in the center of the city undulated like a living being and cast a pale glow between the towers, giving them each a silvery halo in the night. Filled with wine and food that conjured up visions and sensations of pure joy, Sofia listened to the melodies echoing throughout the streets. It was like a trance, brimming with life and quite the opposite of the nightmare she experienced each night. It tempted her into a blissful escape, but she resisted. The reality of her situation cut through the music and wine.

"I've been having dreams," Sofia said. "Nightmares, really. Or memories...I don't know." She breathed heavily, reaching for the courage to say the words. "I think I may have done something terrible during my life. Something unforgivable. I don't feel capable of it, but it seems so real. Every night—"

"We cannot change the Afore, Sofia." Ebrahym's voice was cold, his features hardening. "Clinging to it leads down a dark road. Remember Ilucenta. You have seen where it can lead." Ebrahym put a hand on Sofia's shoulder, and it buzzed with energy.

Inside her pocket, the lúpero fang she carried burned hot. She held it tightly and watched the stars. She would not sleep tonight.14

14

Sofia and Ebrahym made the march up what seemed to be thousands of steps toward the High Council chancel in the Fifth Tier. They were deep in the city. Street music and parades had long faded. The Seat of the Host, the smallest and highest of the tiered districts, was solemn and quiet.

As Sofia summited the steep climb, the most isolated part of Luminea came into view: a city within a city. The tallest towers and finest temples of pale stone were neatly arranged in quadrants around the Temple of the Sanctu Arcam. At the base of each of the four slopes of the structure sat the quarters divided among the Host, where the Sang lived and trained under the glow of the Dawnlight.

The Dawnlight itself emerged from the central temple's apex, where a massive ring of stone, laying horizontally, hovered just above the temple peak. Sofia could finally see it clearly now. Huge, wispy arcs of light pulsated from an unseen source within the temple, twisting up through the ring of stone toward the sky. The tendrils of light churned slowly, hypnotically, and bathed the surroundings in a pure, strange, cold light, like that of a pale star.

This close, Sofia felt the Dawnlight's energy humming through the air. Her hands were moist with sweat. She and Ebrahym walked in silence down one of the four main avenues toward the corner of the great pyramid.

To her left, buildings of warm stone were splashed with red and marked with crimson standards. All around, great ceremonial braziers burned, and their white smoke filtered off into the distance. This was the Choir of the Lion's dominion, facing east toward the sun, prepared to meet any new enemy. Sofia could sense a more militaristic quality to the structures there—barracks, a kind of arena, and tall, watchful towers where skyships docked. It seemed organized for (and in celebration of) battle.

"Home," Ebrahym said as they walked.

In sharp contrast to the east, the shrines and towers of the south were covered in cerulean tiles that shifted in iridescent color, from deep turquoise to violet. It was the home of the *Sanguinir Corum di Servus*, Ebrahym explained, the Choir of the Stag. They were the artists, musicians, painters and poets of the Host, searching for the ultimate expression in form and beauty. Theirs was the work of divine joy, of love.

Even at a distance, their dwellings reflected their craft, erected around impossibly elaborate waterfalls. The Sanguinir there would describe it as the water of life, Ebrahym explained, and it represented their virtue, essential and ever changing.

Although the Sanguinir's part of the city was as beautiful as the rest of Luminea, there was a tension in the air that Sofia found hard to describe. A formal setting where she knew none of the customs. Where she was an outsider. And as a nuomen, an outsider with a reputation she didn't really understand. She fiddled with the fang in her pocket and tried to keep a steady breath.

They approached the central pyramid, and Ebrahym bowed his head and murmured to himself in the Sanguinirian tongue, holy words Sofia could not understand.

They entered the base of an obelisk, one of four such towers flanking the Temple of the Dawnlight, through a pair of wooden gates too massive to be considered doors. Inside, Sofia followed Ebrahym through a solemn gallery of sorts, past massive panoramas of breathtaking landscapes or scenes of battle. Ebrahym ignored the masterpieces. Whatever he was bound to do, he seemed conflicted about it. Or, at least, Sofia hoped he was.

Polished marble and colored glass formed the chancel innards. It was a round structure reaching hundreds of meters high, punctured by rays of light that streamed through vibrant filters, casting lively, colored mosaics onto the walls and floors. All was still and silent within the chamber.

A flash of the grungy apartment and the makeshift stained glass from Sofia's dreams careened into her thoughts, and with it, dread. Then the memory passed back into the darkness, but the feeling lingered. *Fire will not burn me*, she reminded herself. *I can take whatever comes.*

Through a pair of intricately carved doors, Ebrahym led Sofia to a mezzanine that overlooked the circular High Council chamber below. There, her eyes found what appeared to be a living god of war.

"Eros Terafiq," Ebrahym whispered. "Archlord of the Lion, one of the *Quato Eros*. Though I do not see the others—Halphyus, Verivryn or Rahazad."

The Archlord Terafiq paced gracefully back and forth, like one of those armored lions, metal greaves echoing off the marble. She addressed in the Sanguinirian tongue a wingless congregation of finely dressed nobles. Terafiq was tall and wide and awe-inspiring, like a violent storm, mysterious and powerful. Her hair was braided close and tight to her scalp and lacked the lavishness and opulence of the other Sang's hair. It pulled her features taut, and her face looked like a mask of hammered bronze. She held her chin high. Creamy wings with black tips twitched and flexed as she paced.

"And them?" Sofia whispered, gesturing to Terafiq's wingless audience. "The High Council?"

Ebrahym nodded. "The Altuma Concilia. Wisest of the oulma and the leaders of Luminea. This one has convened since..." he trailed off. "We Sanguinir are bound to serve them, and the High Council need the Host to enact their rule. It is a balance of power, and we do not always meet eye to eye. Come."

The pair descended yet another staircase to the chancel floor, inlaid with complex, interlocking symbols, like those on the floor of the lighthouse but dizzyingly more intricate. Sofia paused behind Ebrahym's wings after he stopped, and they waited under the shadow of the mezzanine.

Terafiq noticed them and beckoned with a nod. There were two small, low seats prepared in the middle of the room, carved with wood and topped with cushions. Ebrahym took one and Sofia the other.

The High Council sat perched high upon a curved stone bench that half encircled Sofia and Ebrahym. There were twelve of them in all, and each had an elaborate and different style of garb that hinted at unique cultural origins, but none Sofia could recognize. She had half expected them to be bearded men and refined, silver-haired women, aged elders who wore their wisdom on the outside. This was not the case. These oulma were perfect specimens of humanity, and from their positions on the elevated rostrum, they exuded a powerful, calm authority.

To the flanks of the dozen High Council members, oulma of presumably lesser status scribbled onto parchment while seated at carved wooden desks. They did not look up from their work.

A councilman with a shaved skull looked up from his podium and peered down at them. "I am Amadis, *Legatè Prima* of the Altuma Concilia," he began before turning his attention to Ebrahym. "It has been some time since you were last summoned before us, ser Ebrahym." The Sang bowed slightly. "It is a shame it is always under unfortunate circumstances. I believe we all know why we are here." His eyes turned toward Sofia with a hint of sadness.

"First Legatè, may I—"

"Thank you, Eros Terafiq, we have heard your testimony," First Legatè Amadis interrupted. Sofia studied the coolness of the Archlord; it seemed impenetrable. *Who was in charge here?*

"Now then, ser Ebrahym," the First Legatè continued. "We've read disturbing reports from the frontier about the caravan attacks. The Eros has already given us her...interpretation of this news." He let the words hang. "As I was saying, the reason why we are convened is to discover the truth of things."

Whatever the Archlord had told them, Sofia thought, the High Council clearly wasn't buying it.

A councilwoman, a round-faced cherub whose skin was painted into a mask, leaned forward. "Pray, tell us of the incident with the imuertes, ser Ebrahym."

"Of course, Legatè Idoya," Ebrahym replied formally. He described the battle with the imuertes, truthfully and without embellishment. As he did, Sofia found herself transported back to the battlefield again. The screams echoed in her mind, and her senses recalled the taste of sulfur. The images of bodies strewn across the golden fields refused to fade. She squeezed the fang inside of her pocket as Ebrahym went on. Her heart pounded.

"Dreadful," said Legatè Idoya, as Ebrahym finished his account.

A thin, hawkish councilman with long hair framing his face cocked his head. "Yet, is this not typical?" He paused. "Albeit unfortunate, of course. The imuertes are known to plague the caravans, are they not?"

"With respect, Legatè Vidal, not like this." Ebrahym stood to his feet. "I have been observing the enemy on the frontier for some time. I feel a threat is growing," he said, then took a breath. "The attacks seem highly coordinated, High Council. *Planned*."

"Planned?" echoed a Legatè Idoya, skeptically.

Legatè Vidal scoffed under his breath. "Are you implying that—"

"Yes, High Council," Terafiq interjected, her voice booming. "A *Fierno* has returned. A Hell Lord, from the very pit of...*Tolatni*." The word was strange, and it struck a chord. The High Council fell silent for a moment.

"We will not suffer *that* tongue, here, Eros," Legatè Idoya retorted, scowling. "And to make the claim of a newly risen lord of the *Inferna* without evidence is a bold one, Eros, and not your first attempt." The councilwoman regained her composure, softening. "We are, of course, saddened by the loss of so many oulma and Sanguinir, may they continue on the path, but Legatè Vidal is correct. Attacks on the frontier are not unheard of and do not mean a Fierno has emerged."

"May I remind the High Council that I did not say 'emerged?'" Terafiq asked with a sharp tongue. "I said *returned*."

"And may we remind *you*," First Legatè Amadis added, now hot, "that the propensity toward aggression is precisely why this High Council was created in the first place, and why the Sanguinir now serve it. Your duty is to protect the Dawnlight and safeguard the oulma. Penance for an old sin."

"I am aware of my duty," Terafiq replied coolly.

"We digress," said a deep, thunderous voice. The councilman, a dark-skinned man with a braided beard filled with beads stared ahead coldly, his fingers arched in front of his face.

First Legatè Amadis nodded. "Of course, Legatè Leoncio. Summon the Seer!" Two oulma quickly shuffled off into a nearby hall. "Ser Ebrahym, while the attacks on the frontier are concerning, you know the real reason you are here."

Ebrahym nodded once more. The First Legatè went on, "Your reports say you met this oulma, Sofia, after she abandoned the Meridi lighthouse and took to the road alone. There, she aided you against a lúpero."

"Yes, she could...withstand its presence," Ebrahym said. The High Council glanced at one another.

"And she is a nuomen, is she not?"

Ebrahym paused. "Yes, she remembers."

"And at the battle on the road," First Legatè Amadis pressed, "you indicated she, quote, 'dove into the enemy line without fear, putting twenty of them to the sword at least, unscathed...'"

"I did. But I go on to say—"

"That is all," First Legatè Amadis said, turning to Sofia. "Understand, *mes* Sofia, we twelve are responsible for the security of all oulma in the Orvida, across the Dominion of Esanya, and beyond. That burden weighs heavily upon us. All we have built as a people balances on the tip of a spear, and we must sacrifice to protect it. Our unfortunate duty is to defend against those who may threaten this.

"You, nuomen, come to us tainted, with memory and a name you bear from the Afore. I wish this were not so. But Divine Sphere cannot tolerate possible...insurgency."

A Sang unlike any Sofia had seen appeared from behind the rostrum, flanked by two aides. Her wings were arched behind and bound by silver rings, splaying them out in the shape of a star. A jeweled ring, a kind of standard, pierced by rods hovered above her crowned head. She was blind, and where the eyes and brows should have been was smooth skin, as if they had never been there before. She was beautiful and terrifying. Paint marked her chin, and she glided in front of Sofia, cocking her head as if listening for Sofia in the darkness.

"Close your eyes, nuomen," the Seer instructed. Her soft voice rippled through the room like a cold wind. Sofia closed her eyes, her heart threatening to escape her chest. "Look into the dark, dear. Fall into it. Do you remember?"

"No," Sofia said softly. *I don't want to look.*

"Ah, but do you dream? Do you dream of the Afore, dear? Does it call to you from the blackness?" The Seer's voice pierced her mind like needles through her eyes, twisting, searching. It was like a blinding light, like the Dawnlight, like the lighthouse, like fire, a hot beam to sear all the impurities from her.

Fight back. Fire will not burn me. She clenched her fist but tried to remain calm. "I am Sofia. That is all." The fang burned hot in her pocket.

"But you are not," cackled the Seer. "No! You are much more than that. I can see it. You cannot hide from me." The Seer began to hum and dove deeper inside of Sofia, clawing at her thoughts, exposing her darkest insides to the outside. Sofia collapsed to her knees, shaking, unable to stand the assault. Ebrahym knelt beside her, taking her arm.

"*Ex castigio,*" the Seer whispered with her hand on Sofia's head. The Seer kissed her forehead. Sofia felt a sudden release as the Seer's presence left her mind. The Sang turned and drifted out of the chamber without a word.

"No!" protested Ebrahym. "She is not lost. She does not deserve banishment."

"I am sorry," First Legatè Amadis said. "It is the Way. We all must pay for our sins, eventually." Sofia looked up to see the rest of the High Council with bowed heads. Sofia wanted nothing more than to slink back into the dark they accused her of, to curl up in the blackness and never return.

Sofia could take it no longer. The Seer's probing made her feel exposed and violated, and she could not stand by while her fate was decided for her. "Don't I have a say in any of this?" she shouted, staggering to her feet. The High Council looked surprised. Sofia pointed at them. "Who are *you* to judge me? Who are any of you? You talk of Will, well, let me prove I have it."

"High Council," Terafiq said, intervening with a hand raised. She concealed a thin smile and calmly paced before the rostrum. "Let us not also forget the service this oulma willingly offered to ser Ebrahym and the Host. Are these not the qualities we celebrate? Sacrifice? Bravery? Redemption? She has proven to be capable and is clearly spirited. What Serrá! The people have seen it. I hear tell there is talk in the streets of this *Sofia*."

As Terafiq spoke, all Sofia could see was the fear in the man's eyes on the battlefield before Ebrahym had stopped her from cutting him in half.

"If the oulma believe that the Sanguinir cannot protect them," Terafiq continued, "fear will devour this city. The Divine Sphere will erode from the inside, and the Sanctu Arcam, the Dawnlight, will be lost."

"What do you propose, Eros?" asked First Legatè Amadis, frustrated.

"Send her to the *Conventa*. Let her test her word."

"The trials?" asked Legatè Vidal, mocking. "Are you mad, Eros Terafiq? Her very presence may poison everything."

"She has potential, High Council, and we will need strong wings for what may come next. Fear not, between the regimen and the watchful eye of the Raven, darkness cannot hide for long."

First Legatè rubbed his chin. "You take a terrible risk, Eros Terafiq."

"Perhaps. But as Archlord, it is in my power to recruit *any* oulma I wish into the Conventa. Henceforth, she falls under the jurisdiction of the Host, so it is *my* risk to take. But do not worry, High Council," Terafiq turned her powerful gaze toward Sofia, the Sanguinir's cold stare betraying the warm glow of her irises. "If there is darkness within her, we will know it soon enough. And if she has not the Will to endure it, then we shall know that as well."

First Legatè Amadis nodded gravely. "So be it."

PART III

JUDGMENT

*So, she was set upon the Way,
Where the worthy, blessed to serve,
Endure wrath and woe.*

Nephahi Epoye XII 6:13

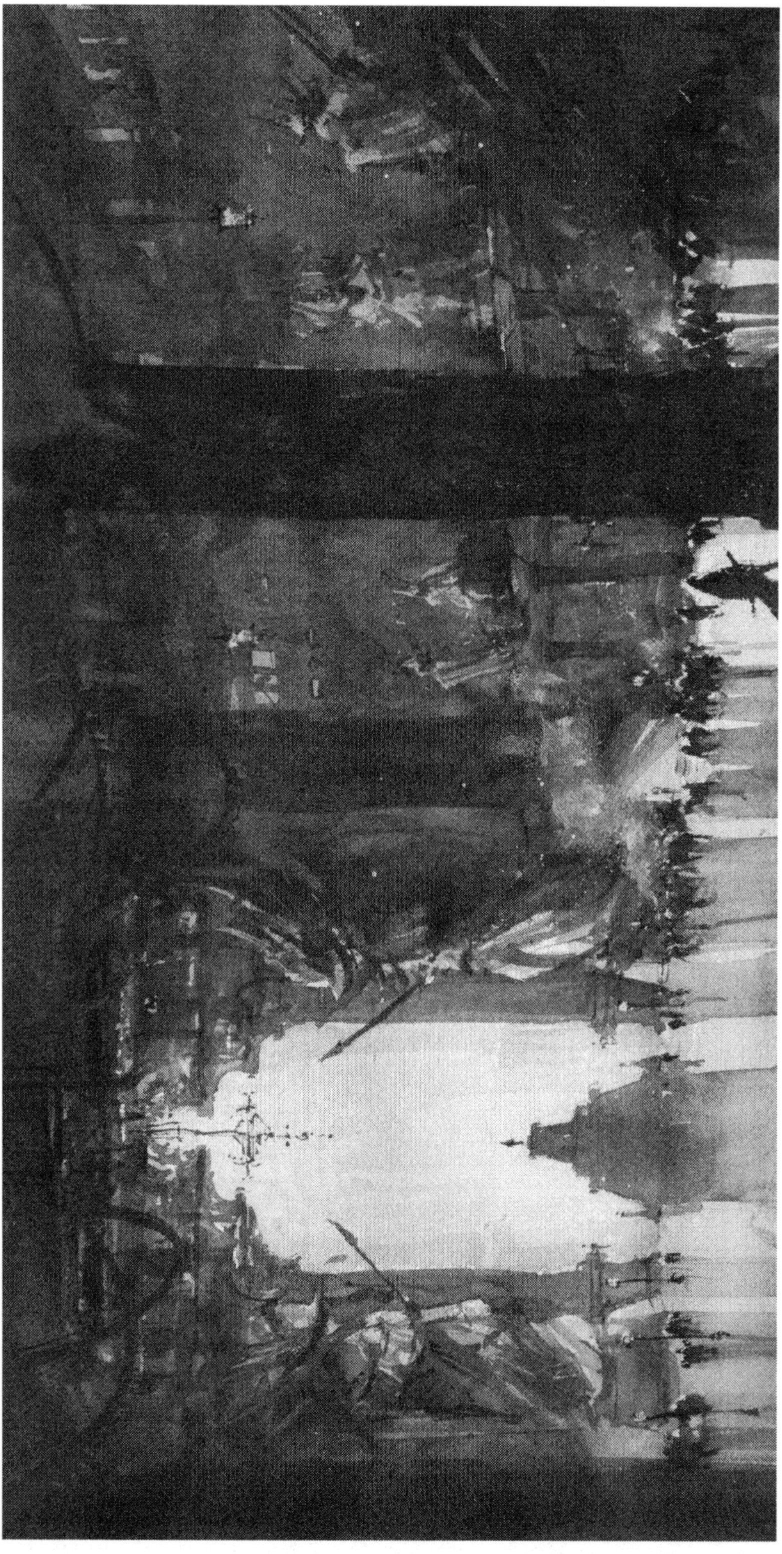

15

"What happens now?" Sofia asked. The heavy gates of the Conventa loomed overhead. The carved reliefs showed a mass of writhing figures and winged beings of fire standing triumphantly above them, flanked by other wingless warriors.

The night was still. Sofia hefted the pack to her other shoulder, adjusting the weight of armor and other small effects inside.

Ebrahym handed her a scroll signed with the wax seal of the lion's head. "Now you will have the honor of joining the other recruits, the *alumna,* as I once did. Many wait centuries for a chance to train at the Conventa. I fear what would have happened otherwise if the Council had let the Seer have her way." Sofia shuddered at the thought of the blind Sang poking around her mind again.

"Thank you for standing up for me in there," Sofia said. She sighed and looked up at the wooden gate once more. It was held firm by thick iron straps as wide as she. "I'm not sure what kind of soldier I will make. I don't much like taking orders." She paused for a moment, thinking. "What's stopping me from leaving, right now? I could slip out, be on the road and no one would know. Banishment doesn't sound so bad." She imagined exploring the Orvida and finding a little house on a hill in the sun and living there, in peace. A nice fantasy.

Ebrahym shook his head. "Your dreams will follow you, and the darkness soon after. Remember the umbra, Sofia. But their fate does not have to be your own."

"So what then?" Sofia asked. "Just roll over and do what I'm told? Say 'Yes, ser'?"

Ebrahym took her firmly by the shoulders. "Embrace this chance, Sofia. Most nuomen are not so lucky. Endure the training. Learn. Prove to them you are not what they think you are. Prove it to yourself."

"I trusted you once before," she said. Sofia smiled and placed a hand on Ebrahym's cheek and felt the familiar buzz of energy. "So, I'll try." His visage was womanly again, kind and familiar. He smiled, almost as if he was trying to be comforting but not sure how. He pulled her hand away.

Ebrahym pushed open the heavy gate with surprising ease. It groaned and opened up to a dark hall lit with candles. "Do not let the fire burn you," he warned as Sofia slipped inside.

I won't let it burn me.
I won't.

***

The would-be warriors mustered before dawn, nervously piling into some semblance of a formation in the courtyard. Sofia shook off the effects of another nightmare. The sick feeling lingered longer and longer as each day passed. She was beginning to see the face of the murdered woman everywhere.

Sofia noticed that with the brilliant light of Luminea came the darkest of shadows. Swaths of dark violet under the canopies, in the alleys, at her feet now. Even in a place such as this, darkness was all around, tempting her, as if the shadows pulled at her like the noxurros, the dark whisper of the imuertes. How easy it would be to slip into it...

The Conventa itself was in the quarter of the Choir of the Lion. It was a long, rectangular structure with an open, sandy courtyard. The students, the alumna, called the courtyard the *dustfield*, nearly three hundred meters long and two hundred wide. It was a sand-filled pit where the alumna, under the tutelage of the Sang, would become warriors.

High walls topped with flags flanked the perimeter. Other than the occasional banner, the Conventa was adorned plainly; this was no place for celebration. It was sparse and functional. There were no sculptures, no works of art here. No distractions. On one end of the giant courtyard were the barracks, a cluster of tall buildings with small windows and flat roofs where Sofia would return each night to rest. On the opposite side of the courtyard, a steep-sloped temple topped with a rust-colored dome leered over the sand. There, the Sang trainers made their home.

The two hundred alumna, Sofia's fellow recruits, stood on the dustfield, called to attention before dawn by trumpets. Their eagerness was palpable. Sofia, on the other hand, did not belong among them. They *wanted* to be here. They were chosen. Sofia wondered if any of them had seen the imuertes in the flesh before. They might not be so eager if they had.

At the head of the column of fresh recruits, a hawk of a Sang gracefully perused the ranks, flanked by two winged guards that followed close behind. His face, like porcelain, was long and regal. His brow sat close to his eyes and shadowed them like a bandit's mask in the sun. Inlaid bronze armor wrapped tightly around his frame, the intricate plates held in place with green silk. His raven-black hair was long and free-flowing in the morning breeze, as were the wings that sprouted from his back, black as ash. On his chestplate, a pair of bulls locked horns with a raven hovering above, its wings as black as its master's.

"I am Bethuel, sixth of my name, and this," he said, gesturing to the high walls around them, his voice carrying unnaturally well, "this, is my home. You are in the Raven's nest now. You will find no comfort here. But that is precisely why you have come to me, is it not?" He paused for someone to challenge him. No one did.

The Raven went on. "You few have had your fill of wine and prettiness and indulgences. You are not *meant* for eternity and are restless, eager for purpose." Backs stiffened in response.

"*That*," the Raven said, pointing to the wispy arcs of the Dawnlight, "is why you are here, why we all are here. To serve, to sacrifice, to endure so that others might be free to find their own path. But have no illusions! We are *not* the same, you and I, for I am not your tutor, your mentor nor your friend.

"I am the *blacksmith*," he grinned with a hint of menace. "You are my steel, filled with impurities and—possibly—strength. My charge is to hammer it out of each one of you, to temper your minds and bodies and your Will against our foe and free you from weakness. And make no mistake," Bethuel paused, peering out among the crowd through strands of black hair whipped by the wind, "after a thousand years, I am very, very good at it."

Across the dustfield, a pair of large doors opened as a procession of Sanguinir entered, the Quato Eros, the four Archlords, the leaders of the four Choirs. Even at a distance, Sofia identified their allegiances by the coloring of their accents: green, red, white and blue, each of them uniquely armored and adorned with symbols representing their virtues. The Archlord Terafiq and her entourage, including Ebrahym, made their way to Bethuel, who greeted them with an elaborate bow and offered a row of seats to his guests.

Terafiq herself wore full battle plate, fashioned with gold, and a long crimson cape and tabard inscribed with the visage of a lion. She gleamed like a small sun, hard to look at directly. If Ebrahym had an unseen feminine side to his being, Terafiq was the opposite. She strode with a distinctly masculine confidence.

To her left was a woman so graceful she seemed to float on air, delicately wrapped in opalescent armor and blue silks that curved around her voluptuous form like water. Verivryn, she was called, and more beautiful than Ebrahym had described. Bright plumes of feathers fanned out from her form in every direction, and her skin was marked with elaborate jewelry adorning each of her features. A mighty bow was slung over her spotted wings.

At Terafiq's right sat a man, small by comparison, his legs crossed beneath him and his wings crossed behind. Halphyus, the Eros of the Eagles. Silver chain over white robes covered with inscriptions tightly bound his small frame in a complex weave. His shaved head was a deep bronze and covered with white markings. He appeared almost as a statue, one of the many pale stone figures in Luminea.

Finally, at the far right of Terafiq was a mountain of a Sanguinir, Rahazad. The warrior stood a full meter higher than Sofia at least, if she had to guess. A dark head topped with thick knots of hair protruded from a giant body clad in heavy layers of bronze armor. His wings were massive, black and brown like that of a vulture. Thick chains of jade hung ceremonially from the builder, as Ebrahym called his kind. The Choir of the Bull. The Eros embodied his sigil completely. Power exuded from him.

The Quato Eros took their seats, observing the new crop of would-be protectors. Terafiq nodded at Bethuel, and he proceeded to walk between the ranks, arms folded behind. The alumna straightened at his approach, showing their best.

"I know some of you have waited centuries for this day. You," Bethuel called out an alumna standing before him, a woman with thick muscles and a pile of fiery red hair. He eyed her like a crow. "Do you think yourself worthy of the mantle? Of the aurola?" The redheaded alumna let out a resounding "Yes ser."

"Such enthusiasm!" Bethuel cackled, striding past the woman. "But I wonder if you are meant for such greatness? We shall see. The ranks of the Prime Auxilia always need filling."

Aurola? Mantle? Then it hit Sofia. This lot wasn't training to be a militia. The Raven was a Builder, a maker of things, Ebrahym had said. Not only temples and armor, Sofia realized, but the Sanguinir themselves.

The Sang were not born, they were *made*.

"But others," Bethuel said, appearing before Sofia as if from nowhere, "It would seem, have found their way here by...special request." His pupils were gold like the other Sang's, but mixed with black like the coals from a fire.

"You, alumna," Bethuel said, turning to Sofia, "you are known to me." He raised his voice so all in the square could hear. The others turned to look at her. "The name of Sofia is being whispered in the streets. A wingless Sanguinir, they say! Ha. A slayer of imuertes! A killer of—"

"Yes," Sofia said through gritted teeth. "I'm Sofia."

Bethuel bowed deeply. Her fists tightened. "Oh, my Lord!" he mocked, "You honor the Conventa, my humble nest, with your presence. Perhaps you would do us the pleasure of a demonstration of your prowess, since your reputation has preceded you so?"

The recruits moved in unison as if directed by some unseen force, and a moment later Sofia found herself encircled, with the four lords watching at the far end. All eyes bore down on her, golden and otherwise, and she wanted nothing more than to slink away to anywhere but the dustfield. A Sanguinir sentry approached with a handful of weapons and gestured curtly: *choose*. Sofia clasped the hilt of a small sword, feeling its weight. It felt like the one she'd taken from Ilucenta, but this one was clean and polished.

"Battle," Bethuel cried, arms and wings spread wide, "is not for the undisciplined." He slashed at Sofia so quickly she barely had time to raise her sword to meet the blow. The vibration numbed her hand as she tried to regain her footing. "For how can one control an enemy if they cannot control themselves?"

Another blow sent Sofia reeling, the clang of metal upon metal echoing in the square. She swung and found nothing but air, Bethuel easily dancing around her wild strike. He countered, delicately slicing her tunic without touching the skin as if to make a point. Anger boiled in Sofia, making her hands shake with rage.

"Anger does not make you powerful." Bethuel trapped Sofia's next blow in one smooth movement. The Raven smiled. "It makes you slow. And predictable."

Sofia let go of the sword with her right hand and jabbed, connecting with Bethuel's hard face. He barely moved, his hawkish grin widening. Sofia would never know what happened next. She eventually opened her eyes again to find herself face down, dirt clinging to her lips and nose, ears ringing and eyes blurry.

In the distance, Terafiq and Bethuel were speaking to one another. Ebrahym looked at her and nodded.

Prove them wrong.

16

Sofia glanced down. She shouldn't have. The narrow stone outcropping dropped away to the Luminean streets hundreds of meters below. The bodies of oulma going about their business there were merely colored specs scurrying about. Indistinct and terrifyingly small. The world spun, and Sofia felt the familiar sensation of reality toppling over, falling farther and farther away. She struggled to rein her panic. But there was no soothing Sang hymn, at least not for her.

She was outside of the Divine Sphere and on her own. As a noumen, she was outside of it, divided from its power. She was a threat, or so the High Council had said. It was like staring at a warm hearth through a cold pane of glass.

The small group of alumna huddled together on the small terrace. Baby chicks ready to be pushed from the nest. A gusty breeze snapped between the spires of the city. Thick cabling spanned the distance between the spires in a vast web. She had an idea what they were for but sincerely hoped she was wrong.

"I can't believe you volunteered for this," said Sofia, averting her eyes from the ground. Alana hung over the railing to get a better view, and Sofia's stomach turned. "A month ago, you had the choice to live like everyone else."

"And miss all this?" Alana asked with a smile and a deep breath. "Besides, it's your fault. If you hadn't gone all hero when the caravan—" Sofia shot her a look.

"Sorry," said Alana. "But if you hadn't, well, *inspired* the others to fight, the Sanguinir wouldn't have noticed me. I would have had to wait until the next century at least."

"Is that the real reason?"

"I want to help them if I can," Alana said, eyeing the oulma below. Sofia once again found herself in envy of her friend. Alana's compassion seemed to flow freely, like a spring and just as pure.

"Speaking of," called Matías, one of the other alumna, within earshot. He was built like a tree, with ruddy skin and thick black hair that hung unkempt around his sharply cut jaw. Sofia might have thought him attractive if he hadn't quickly proven to be an insufferable bastard. "What really happened that day the imuertes attacked? I heard you nearly split some poor fool in half after the battle." The other alumna looked at her.

The terrified eyes of the man she'd nearly killed rushed back. And with it, the shame. She could hear the clang of metal, of Ebrahym's sword stopping her from becoming what she feared. *How many more would I have killed?* She swallowed hard.

Matías went on. "It's supposedly impossible, you know? An oulma slaying another? *Desipar,* that's the old word for it. But no matter how strong the Will, it's never enough to destroy another oulma. Unless you're imuertes, that is. They certainly have a talent for it." He was inches from her face now. "So, which are you?"

Matías singled her out every chance he could, and though he was arrogant and obnoxious, it was hard to blame him. He and others like him had waited a long time for their chance to prove themselves. They resented Sofia for the special treatment in her Conventa placement, sentence or not.

"The next time we're on the dustfield," Sofia fired back. "I'll show you." Her hand had found its way into her pocket, and she squeezed the lúpero fang she carried until her hand trembled.

Matías flashed a smug grin as his bulky form towered over her. "Just say the word, newborn." *Newborn.* Everyone without a few centuries under their belt.

A whoosh followed by a hard thump saved Sofia from making a terrible decision. Bethuel swooped down to the terrace from above, his wings a black blur until coming to folded rest.

"Balance," the Raven began with the bravado of an actor, "is paramount in combat. You cannot hope to thrust with a spear without control of its weight. You cannot move with speed between foes without your feet beneath you. Balance is steadiness of mind, of body, of *will*. This is the prime tenet of Serrá. Perfect suspension, peace amidst the chaos around. Without balance, we fall." Bethuel savored the moment, clearly enjoying the irony of their precarious position on the edge of the tower.

"Your task is simple," he continued. "Cross the cables to the other side with speed." He motioned for the alumna to begin. "Or...don't."

Matías stepped up first, confidently hefting his large frame over the terrace ledge to where the cables anchored to the building face. They were less than half a meter in width and bowed deep in the middle—they spanned a long way. Too long.

Without hesitation, Matías dashed down the cable, his powerful form surprisingly surefooted on the narrow path. Sofia's palms sweat just watching him. She caught herself wishing he would fall.

"We can do this," Alana said with a nod, stepping up for her turn. Sofia followed suit a moment after.

"The fall from grace is easier than one might think," Bethuel called from behind. Sofia tried to ignore him, focusing her eyes ahead and willing her legs to keep from trembling.

The alumna had learned much of the Divine Sphere in these few weeks. It was a source of strength, a power, willed into existence by the Sanguinir. Their Serrá, their collective Will, made it strong. Their songs made it heard. But unlike the other students, Sofia could not hear it. So, she turned inward instead. She poked at that smoldering fire of anger to bring it back to life. That was *her* power and the only thing she could count on.

Staring out across the void between the two towers, she summoned it, taking a few deep breaths to calm her pounding heart. Her first step found the twisted metal cable, and she wavered. She fought to maintain her balance. The giant metal strands were warm on her bare feet. Gnarled and easy to grip. She focused inward, ignoring the spinning streets below and the skyship drifting nearby. Matías' jeers from across the way faded into nothing. She thought of her hands in the fire. She took another step. Then another. Then she began to walk with confidence. Then she ran, picking up speed until she was flying down the cable toward the other side. Everything slipped away.

And then, she fell.

Fear seized her muscles as she toppled off the line, screaming. The beautiful vista of Luminea rushed past her on all sides. Up and down lost all meaning. The roar of the wind drowned out any rational thought. Pure, ancient terror strangled her. Every cell in her body screamed in vain. She thrashed impotently at the air, with the frustration of dying pointlessly and filled with regret.

A strong hand grabbed her wrist. Sofia inhaled sharply, blinked, and looked up to see a pair of wings blocking out the sun. The Sanguinir carrying her pumped hard to gain altitude and dropped her on the opposite spire like a bag of refuse. She breathed heavily, trying to catch her breath and avoid the pairs of eyes she knew were upon her.

Matías reached out his hand to help her up, grinning.

***

After the first meal in days, eaten in relative silence, Sofia and the other alumna filed out of the mess chamber. More ritual than requirement, meals were a moment of rest. A Sanguinir in white robes led them up a winding staircase to the precipice of a flat, turreted spire. *More heights.* The skyline of Luminea stretched out under the midday sun, which was so bright Sofia had to shield her eyes. No one else seemed to mind much. Sofia found a red cushion along with the other recruits and kneeled.

Meditating was a part of everyday life now, but Sofia found it one of the most difficult challenges. With the other aspects of the training, she could more easily focus. She found no peace in the stillness. Instead, she smelled sulfur and filth. Heard screams. Saw monsters. The face of the murdered woman from her dream, frozen in terror. When she was alone with only her thoughts, with nothing distracting her, there was no escape.

The Sanguinir monks seated at the head of the class chanted in harmony. Their voices intertwined to become not voices at all, but a kind of all-encompassing force of sound Sofia could feel in her bones. It was the Divine

Sphere made physical, made real. It was only at these times that she felt it at all, like the Sang battle hymns. It was a lonely feeling to be surrounded by it yet so far away.

She struggled to simply keep her eyes closed. The war raged inside of her, and the images came faster now. The shadows lashed out at her from all directions. The figure of living darkness, the horned creature that haunted her, congealed from the blackness to devour her. Its lonely, grating call drowned out the world and beckoned her to the abyss.

Sofia could resist no longer. Her eyes snapped open. Breathing hard and covered in sweat, she met Bethuel's cold gaze from behind the chanting Sanguinir. The Raven said nothing, a cruel smile splitting his porcelain veneer.

Prove them wrong.

***

It was the fifth time today the alumna had ascended to 'kiss the dawn.' Four times since the sun had risen, they had been ordered to sprint up the hundreds of steep steps of the Temple of the Dawnlight by the call of a deep, bellowing horn. Whenever it summoned them, day or night, the alumna answered. They dashed from the dustfield or the meditation chambers toward the stone monument. Sofia cursed the pleasant soft arcs of the light dancing overhead. They mocked her as she gasped, pressing on her knee with both hands to will her body up another step.

Bethuel bellowed a triumphant song from on high as they toiled toward the top. He greeted each aluma as they crested the summit, eying them dispassionately as they stumbled past. Barely able to stand, the alumna hobbled to the doors of the temple interior to touch them before descending once again. In Bethuel's hand was a sword. A gift, he called it, for the last alumna to reach the top. The gift of pain.

The Raven delicately tamed a strand of black hair behind his ear and handed the sword to Sofia yet again. "Try to stay on your feet a bit longer this time."

She didn't.

***

The punishment continued. The Sang turned the world against the recruits to harden their bodies to pain. Such was their way, to separate the recruits' minds from their bodies in the most brutal ways possible.

The elements were turned against them. Tied to great stones, the alumna plunged deep into the Aecuna. The darkness and the pressure would build as

Sofia and the others sank into the blackness. Her lungs would scream for air, and she'd will them to be still. Several times she lost herself to the dark before being dredged up like some creature from the deep.

She was tested by air. First, across the cables and then with leaps between skyships as they passed through the city. Each time she failed, Matías and the others shouted "Wingless!" And laughed as she screamed in terror.

Sofia was falling behind.

The alumna found themselves facing the south wall of the Conventa, with the Raven striding upon it, looming like a black vulture over them. There, Sofia struck the stone until her knuckles cracked and bled. A trial by earth. Her fists found the grooves of a thousand alumna before her, worn down not by erosion or time, but by Will. Sofia bludgeoned away the nightmares, the imuertes, the fear. For hours, striking the unforgiving stone, she could lose herself in a sea of anger.

The growing cracks in the earth where Sofia pounded did not go unnoticed by the other alumna in the weeks that passed. The wall was beginning to fear her more than she feared it.

It was when they were tested with fire that Sofia showed her true power. As Sanguinir warriors, they all might be one day tested in the *Inferna*, the Below, the place of fire where the imuertes reigned. Their bodies and minds could have no fear of it.

First their flesh was subjected to the nearby torch, then boiling water, then coals and oil after. Most of the alumna could not contain their screams of pain, nor could they hide their envy when Sofia's turn came. Even Matías begrudgingly acknowledged her after a Sang placed a molten blade, fresh from the forge, across her back. Sofia concealed her smile as her rage boiled within like a shell of armor. The moisture from her skin hissed as it evaporated. She never screamed.

And always, Bethuel watched from the shadows, the light flickering upon his expressionless face.

***

Sofia dried the sweat from her palms with sand from her pockets, the dull training sword tucked under her arm. The Sanguinir before her was of the Choir of the Bull, lightly armored with links of chain and emerald cloak. A curved helmet hid his golden eyes.

Sofia kneaded the hilt tightly and planted her feet. She thrust her sword forward. The Sanguinir deflected it with ease and laid the back of his fist across Sofia's face. She kissed the dustfield, the sting bringing with it unintentional tears.

She came to her feet and thrust again, and once more met the ground. She looked inside for that spark, that power, that caged animal pacing in anticipation needing only to be unlocked. It came easier now. She and the Sanguinir circled one another, his wings splayed open.

She lunged, her sudden burst of speed surprising the Sang who raised his own blade barely in time to deflect the blow. The harsh clang of metal shattering cut through the air as the two sparring weapons met. Sofia's had broken in half. The sound echoed across the training square, and the other alumna paused their training to investigate the source.

Undeterred, Sofia slashed the Sang's face with the broken handle of her sword, opening a thin wound across his chin, marring his otherwise flawless features. Emotionless, amber eyes stared at Sofia as he removed his plumed helmet before tossing it away.

A few of the alumna hooted and called as an armored boot connected with her stomach and sent her spilling over backward, choking. She pulled herself to her knees, clutching her ribs and gasping for air. She stained the dust with bloody spit before summoning the strength to stand.

Prove them wrong.

***

She was not last this time. Now, Sofia was toward the front of the column as the alumna climbed the steps once more. It was night. They slept in heavy plate armor, yet bounded like nimble mountain sheep up the steps, undeterred. She jogged past Bethuel, who nodded ever so slightly.

Days bled into weeks and weeks into months. From brutal training at arms to the study of the ancient Sanguinir language, Bethuel pushed the alumna far beyond normal human capacity. And surprisingly, they adapted. It was as if matter was more malleable here, more easily reshaped than in the Afore. But it was not an easy process. For every step forward, there were dozens of painful steps back. The sparring was endless. The conditioning merciless.

Though the physical punishment was brutal, the psychological suffering was worse. The alumna spent days navigating the dark labyrinths beneath the Conventa, winding caverns that played tricks on the mind. Potent herbs and tonics let their imaginations run wild, and Sofia saw her dreams, her nightmares, come to life before her. The potions simulated the dark whisper of the imuertes and turned the mind against itself. The alumna closely treaded the line between light and darkness. It was the risk they took to understand the enemy and what drove the imuertes mad.

Many of the alumna could not withstand the torture. Over half quit and returned to Luminea, back to music and drink and the sun. Others simply disappeared. Each day, Sofia wavered on the knife's edge, one slip from tumbling into the darkness, one mistake from becoming what everyone believed her to be.

Yet the stronger she became, the more she feared becoming the thing that haunted her dreams.

A monster, a shadow.

No.

I will prove them wrong.

17

The moon was high, its soft light filtering through the barracks windows. The warm summer wind tried and failed to penetrate the cold stone of the structure. It was always cool inside the barracks.

Sofia stared at the ceiling, trying to perfect her technique of resting without sleeping. Eight days and counting, although she knew she must sleep eventually.

Two hundred and forty-two days had passed since she'd been sentenced to the Conventa and the Raven's brutal tutelage. The Sanguinir way of life was beginning to become her own. She often wondered if this was the kind of life she'd once lived, in the Afore. Perhaps the memories were there. Not in her conscious mind, but deep within.

Of all the disciplines involved, the art of war, martial combat, particularly with the short sword, came most naturally to her. Over time, upon the dustfield and after hundreds of hours of drills, the blade began to feel like an extension of herself.

Even now, the beaten sword that had traveled with her from the depths of Ilucenta lay beside her. Sofia's hand rested gently on the bound leather. In her other hand was the comforting warmth of the lúpero fang. Nearby, an ancient-looking book lay opened, heavy with wisdom and age, revealing a handwritten page:

"...The precise transformation process from umbra to full imuertes remains a mystery. Observations (see Explicacio Imuertes, *vol. XIX) suggest an unnatural progression, and that intervention from an outside source is essential for complete modification. Strong imuertes Serrá contributes heavily to the extent and severity of the final genus, often barely recognizable as human."*

Sofia took inventory of herself as a different method of staying awake, reliving each recent injury to mentally learn from her many mistakes: two cracked ribs, a broken finger, a lacerated quadriceps on the left side, torn ligaments in her right knee and a wicked black eye.

The shiner, courtesy of Matías, was a reminder of when he'd found his revenge after an unarmed sparring match was over. Sofia's heart quickened in anger just thinking about it.

She put the thought aside and took a moment to thank the Conventa healers, Sang from the Choir of the Stag, whose music cured a weary heart as much as their balms tended a gash. They were quite good at keeping up with the brutal punishment of training, but the human body, such as it was in this place, could only be pushed so far.

Sofia was approaching the limit. Her muscles were cut close to the bone now, defined and honed with use. Her skin had deepened in color, now a warm copper shell covering wide shoulders and muscled hips. Somehow all the alumna seemed a bit taller, too. Maybe it was just an illusion.

Her thoughts turned toward Ebrahym. He had not shown his face since that day on the dustfield months ago. *Had Terafiq ordered him to stay away?* She often wondered where he was in the wild—escorting oulma newborns like herself along the road? Did the imuertes attacks continue? There were whispers around the Conventa, but no one knew for sure.

Restless, Sofia sat up, taking stock of everywhere that wasn't sore—it was easier than the reverse—and slipped out of the barracks, sword in hand. Like a shadow, Sofia wove through the cloister's columns and corridors to the main training yard.

"You shouldn't be awake. You need to rest. Especially if you want that to heal," Matías said, touching his temple. He was propped against a railing, basking in the moonlight and munching on dried fruit.

"Can you not sleep either? Or is it because you know that *I know* where you sleep?" Sofia said. The posturing had become typical.

Matías laughed. "What do you really think will happen here? Even if you do everything right, pass every test the old Raven can throw at us, do you think they'll give *you* a mantle? You're either a fool or mad. I'm not even sure the Pax would take you."

The Pax, the Prime Auxilia. They were the army of oulma that supported the Sang on campaign. Otherwise known as second place. "We'll see," Sofia said. But secretly, she knew Matías likely spoke the truth.

Matías nodded out the window. "Do you know why you'll never be worthy? You don't care about any of those oulma out there. I thought it was an act at first, but now I see. You fight only for yourself; that's all you care about. The fact that you're the Eros' pet experiment doesn't change anything." Sofia could not summon a reply. The wound cut her deep. He was right, to some extent. She did not have Alana's selfless resolve.

He continued, his voice softer now, more distant. "Do you know of Tolaga? It's east of here, in the hills. A small town, for oulma who wish a quieter life. I found myself there, learning the metal trade from a Sanguinir, a builder. Orthuel was his name. For years, I watched him defend our tiny settlement single-handedly." The memory seemed to pain the giant man.

"Then, he fell. I watched, powerless to help as a pack of imuertes did their work. How glorious was his stand! But it was luck there was anything left of him at all. I carried his remains to Luminea and petitioned for two centuries to be accepted to the Conventa while learning the blade, the spear and the shield. Now that I am here, I fight for my fellow oulma. Every one of us here would sacrifice ourselves, as Orthuel did, to protect them." His look was hard. There was no sarcasm or arrogance there. "Would you?"

Matías' words and his surprising softness caught Sofia off guard. Shame from the memory of the caravan welled up, fresh and potent, more than she could bear. *I don't want to be what I am.* Sofia dashed down the stairs so Matías could not see the tears in her eyes. She headed to the dustfield, yearning to unleash on something.

Wooden dummies with intricate gearings flanked each side of the dustfield, and Sofia squared off with one in the moonlight. The air was silent and still. Matías' words lingered in her mind. *Would I give up the hereafter for someone else? For Alana? Ebrahym? What about for a stranger, or for nothing at all?* She wished she could say yes truthfully. But she *was* here for herself. To prove them wrong, to prove she wasn't what they said she was.

Sofia screwed the pads of her bare feet into the sand and lashed out, hips first, slicing the blade down upon one of the dummy's many armor-covered limbs. The blow landed true, and the mechanism reacted with a mechanically programmed counter of its own. Springs and gears squeaked and groaned.

Back and forth, Sofia and the wooden opponent exchanged strikes in a rhythmic pattern, and she fell into a trance, letting her thoughts fall away. It was the only thing she could do to settle a mind that never wanted to be still. The training apparatus spun and whirred, designed to keep pace with its attacker. The goal was to be fast enough to beat the dummy's reaction time for a killing blow.

She had never managed it; not yet.

Eventually, Sofia's footwork failed her, and her strike was late. She caught a wooden rod right in her already-fractured ribs. A white flash of pain brought her to her knees, gasping.

"If that thing can bring you down, what's going to happen with phalanx drills tomorrow?" Alana chirped behind her.

Always in good spirits. Her friend had physically changed since their time together at the lighthouse. Though still smaller than Sofia, Alana had shed much of her nymph-like qualities for strong, hearty limbs wound with muscle. A thick braid hung on one shoulder. She was made for this life.

"You're always full of useful observations," Sofia said, regaining her footing.

"Can't sleep again?" Alana asked as she worked an unarmed flow with a training dummy of her own. Sofia marveled at Alana's speed. She struck the wooden dummy quickly, her pale limbs like bolts of lightning in the silvery moonlight.

"No." For so long, she'd wanted to tell Alana about the dreams, her fears, all the things that ate away at her mind. So many times, she'd wanted to let it all out, but something always stopped her. Whether it was fear or pride or something else, Sofia didn't know. But the pain she felt was chronic.

"Sofia, listen," Alana said, coming in close. "I learned something. About the aurolas, the halos."

The mantle. The aurolas. The mysterious halos that gave the Sang their power. Even for those in the Conventa, there were still secrets behind closed doors.

"What? How?" The mantle was one of the most closely-guarded secrets of the Sanguinir. She and Alana had theorized for months what the aurolas might be.

"Another alumna, Jensia. Do you know her? Scholarly type. She's been here a long time, and she's taken a shine to me."

"I know her. So, what are they?"

"Not what! *Who*, Sofia," said Alana, her eyes wide. "They are *beings*. The Sang are like their *hosts* or something. Two minds living as one, sharing all thoughts. Imagine what the Will of *two* could achieve."

"Like growing wings," Sofia puzzled. *That's why Ebrahym sometimes spoke to himself aloud.* "Where do they come from?"

"The Dawnlight, of course," Alana said, staring up at the undulating arcs of energy wafting above them. Sofia remembered, too, what Ebrahym had alluded to about the phenomenon. He'd said that the Sanctu Arcam was a door. And doors open both ways.

"Imagine it," Alana said. "Sharing your mind with someone...something, all the time. I wonder what mine will find in there."

"I wonder, too," Sofia said, feigning a laugh. She already knew what a halo would find in her mind. But perhaps with it would come answers, wisdom. Perhaps then she could be free. But then again, if there were two minds that opposed one another, which one would win out?

"Well, come on then," Alana said, picking up a training sword. "Let's see if we can improve our chances." As the women squared off, Bethuel appeared from the darkness like a ghost, his black wings shrouding all but his pale face. Sofia wondered how long he had been watching.

"It appears that you alumna are in no need of rest," Bethuel said calmly. The two recruits stiffened, to attention.

"No, ser," Alana and Sofia responded in unison.

"You," Bethuel nodded to Alana, "wake the others. I doubt they need rest either. Make sure they know they have Sofia here to thank for it." Alana bowed her head and departed.

"Ah," Bethuel continued as he circled Sofia like a cat. "Diligently training, honing your skills, to one day be honored with a mantle. Such optimism. Such spirit. Do you know how many try, nuomen? Thousands. *Hundreds* of thousands. I know, for I train them all. With purer spirits and stronger hearts than yours, I can promise." Sofia let no reaction show.

"Let me speak plainly," the Raven continued, "for our time together draws to an end. There is no amount of pain that can drive out what lurks within you. You may believe me, for I have tried. I've come face to face with it. Do you know what

I have learned?" His face was inches from hers. The scrutiny was unbearable, like when the Seer dug through her mind.

"It *never* goes away," Bethuel whispered. "It grows like a weed, unable to be stamped out."

"Weeds don't grow in the Orvida," Sofia dared, still at attention. "Unless the Sphere wills it."

Sofia met Bethuel's eyes, his amber irises glowing like hot coals. He chuckled dryly. "Indeed."

Without a word, Bethuel turned on his heels and began his morning chant, calling his recruits to the dustfield.

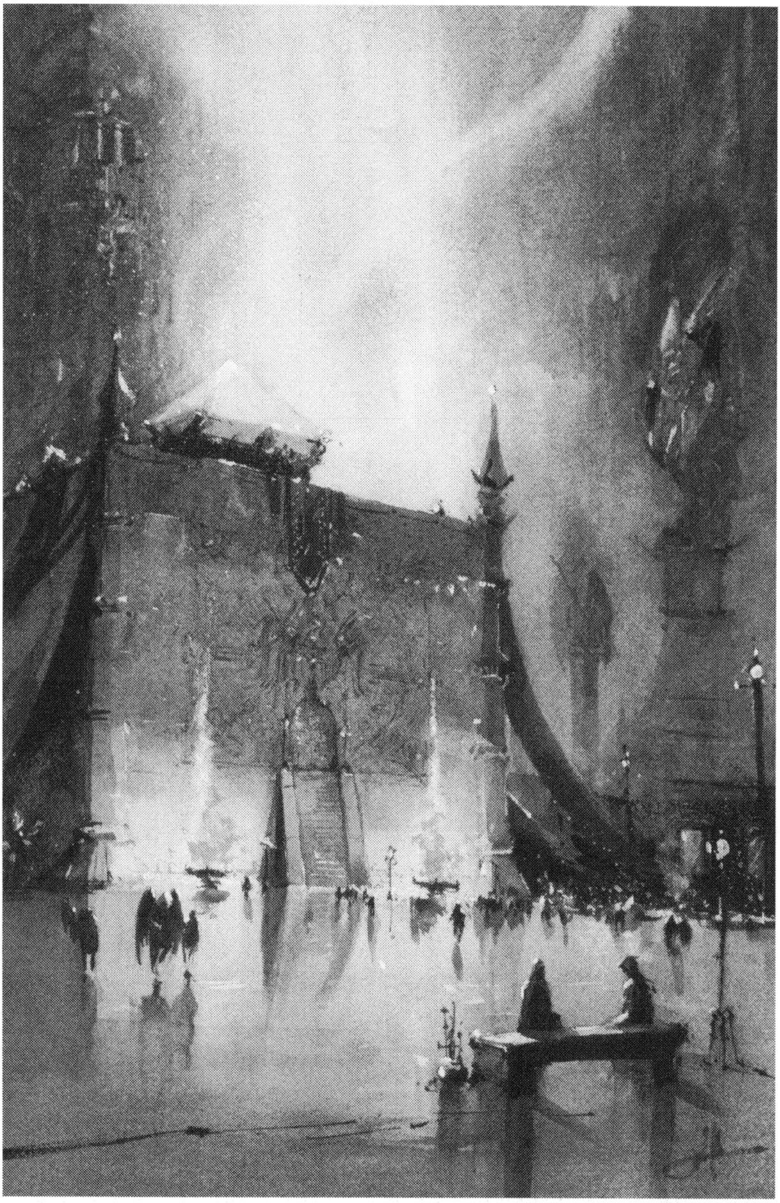

18

Incense hung heavy in the air. Sofia stepped off the mechanical lift, hundreds of meters below the city. Gilded gates groaned behind her.

The soft tapping of her footsteps echoed through the voluminous space. The arcs of light that flared above the city came from here, erupting up through a long shaft and through the temple. The exit point above was as bright as the sun itself.

Here, directly between the heavens and the earth, was the Sanctu Arcam, the Dawnlight itself.

What it looked like exactly, Sofia could not say, for its true nature was concealed within a thick cube of stone. She traced its perimeter but did not touch it. It seemed the thing to do.

The marble cube, more than a hundred meters on each face, held the Dawnlight within. The only way to penetrate the cube was through an enormous, circular stone slab covered with symbols and inscriptions, the Great Seal.

Sofia had read about it, and supposedly, it took the entire Host, every Sanguinir in existence, to move it. A flight of gradual steps led up to the Seal, for it was perfectly centered upon the face of the cube. At the top of the cube was a pyramid—not of glass or stone but formed from a single, massive crystal, willed into existence by the Sang of old. It was honed to a point. From the translucent prism, the intense, crescent-shaped beams of light emerged from the cube and filtered up through the temple's atrium. It was so bright so close to the source that Sofia could barely lay eyes on it.

The chamber surrounding the cube was a multi-tiered atrium with a vast, domed ceiling. The Dawnlight provided all the illumination required, but ceremonial fires littered the terraces and connecting pathways. Around the cube, carved canals lined with turquoise stones wound fresh water in intricate, geometric designs.

"Thank you for accepting my invitation," a woman's voice said from behind.

Her eye color was the similar to the Sang's but not as brilliant, and she had no wings. There was a sad weariness to her, though most of her face was obscured by a jeweled veil. White robes wove around her body, and large, elaborately decorated hairpins delicately restrained her auburn locks. A wall of perfume followed her and flooded over Sofia, overwhelming her senses.

Sofia bowed slightly. The woman returned the gesture and moved next to her, gazing out at the atrium. "Most oulma never have the opportunity to see the Sanctu Arcam this close. It is unfortunate, but it is the Way."

"You summoned me, but I don't know who you are." said Sofia. "You are Sanguinir, but— "

"Not anymore," the woman gently interrupted. "Not as I was, anyway. I am merely Nesta, now."

Her hands were hidden, tucked between folds of finely embroidered cloth. "I have been following your progress at the Conventa."

Are they spying on me? "And?"

"You continue to surprise the Raven, that I can tell you."

"So, why am I here?" Sofia asked, unwilling to tolerate more games. "Another test?"

"No," Nesta said. "No tests. No games. This is a warning from someone that *knows* you, Sofia. Who knows the darkness inside of you, the fire..." Nesta looked at Sofia, her eyes saying everything. They were not predatory or probing like those of the Seer or Bethuel. They were pleading. Flecks of gold mingled with dark patches in her irises that shifted in the light. She was different from the rest.

"Tell me of your dreams," Nesta said.

Sofia flushed. "What do you mean?" *How did she know?*

"Why else would I have summoned you? I thought you clever, Sofia. Did you think you were the first oulma with memories of the Afore to step foot inside the Conventa, to bleed upon the dustfield? There have been many nuomen. Always alike. Always the same questions. Always chasing shadows." Nesta sighed.

"But the High Council," Sofia thought aloud, "they made it seem like someone like me would never be allowed in the Conventa."

"Our kind is not allowed. Not anymore."

"*Our* kind?" Sofia asked. Nesta nodded. "I don't understand. You're a Sang. You communed with the aurola, the halo." Nesta nodded once again.

"So it can be done..." Sofia whispered. Newfound motivation surged within her. If it was possible, she could do it. She *would* do it.

"Yes, it can be done. But why do you seek the mantle?" Nesta asked.

"Answers. Why else?"

Nesta laughed with a sweet and sad tone. "If only it were so simple. I once thought the same as you. Alas, the aurola does not suffer selfish crusades. Follow me."

Sofia followed Nesta through a series of twisting corridors. They left the atrium and found a narrower hall lined with stone columns and an arched ceiling. Here and there, between the columns, brightly colored cushions lay scattered about. Nesta motioned for her to sit, and Sofia tried to remain relaxed as the Sanguinir paced around her.

"How long can you go without sleep now?" Nesta asked.

"Eight days."

Nesta nodded casually. "My best was three weeks and a day."

"What do you remember, Nesta? From the Afore."

"Oh, many things," said Nesta. She sat in front of Sofia and closed her eyes as if dredging the thoughts up from the deep. "I recall my tiny home thatched with leaves. A village in the mountains, surrounded by green. And my parents' faces, round and warm like leather. Do you remember such things, Sofia? Youth? Family?" Nesta's eyes opened and drifted upward as if watching scenes from her life play out above.

"My father," she continued, "was not an honorable man. He would hurt my mother. One day, he went too far, and I ran him through with his own blade made of stone. It was the rainy season, and I can still smell the forest as we fled into the hills." Nesta looked down at her concealed hands. "But the rain would not wash the blood from my hands. We ran for days after that, hunted by men. They found us shortly after. I was killed that day, Sofia, along with my mother. I was sixteen summers."

Sofia felt sick. Her own story had no such nobility, only savagery. "I-I have done the same," Sofia whispered, after a moment. "Worse. I don't know why or who she was. But I see it in my mind, every time I close my eyes. I'm a murderer; that's who I am."

There was no judgment in Nesta's eyes. Sofia almost wished there were; she deserved it. "Memories are mysterious things, Sofia. Like reflections in water, they often change the more we try to see them clearly."

She continued. "I once asked one of my brethren in the Choir of the Eagle why nuomen exist. The scholars there say that some pains are too great to be left behind. They are *part of us,* and we carry them with us, even after death. You feel that makes us weak." Nesta stared ahead, lost in thought. "And it does. So very weak."

"But you made it." Sofia protested. "You controlled it."

Nesta shrugged. "That is what I believed for a long time. I concealed the truth from everyone, even from myself. But here, in the Orvida, you cannot run from it."

Sofia cut to the heart of it. "After the communion, what did the halo tell you?"

Nesta shook her head. "The communion is our most sacred secret, Sofia. We share a bond, you and me, but this is something you cannot know. Besides, it is very difficult to put into words. For now, let us say the aurola did its best to protect me from myself. But I was not worthy."

"What happened?"

Nesta reluctantly continued, "I fought in the battle as Ilucenta fell. I was called Yasbrahi, then, eleventh of my name..."

"*You* are Yasbrahi? Yasbrahi, as in the *Mornshield*?" Sofia exclaimed, recalling the story. Nesta bowed humbly. "I read about you, how you fought during the siege. They say you held the west gate single-handedly for a month. They say you were a living wall of fire that could not be quenched."

Sadness exuded from Nesta's eyes. "That was many centuries ago. After the city was lost, I was not myself. My dreams became worse, twisted. Past blended with present, real with fantasy. I began traveling back to the ruins of Ilucenta, over and over for reasons I could not explain. I wandered the streets with umbra who were left behind. Then I searched deeper into the caves beneath the city..." she trailed off.

"I've seen the umbra," said Sofia. "Ebrahym told me about them. He said they turn their Serrá inward and...*change*." A tear escaped from Nesta's eye and disappeared behind the veil.

"So that's what happened to you," Sofia whispered. "You fell."

Nesta, the once proud warrior Yasbrahi, blinked back the tears. "Yes, I fell. To my unending shame, I fell. I betrayed the sacred trust of the Host, abandoned the Way and led my sacred mantle into the Inferna itself. It was only by the Dawnlight's blessing I was rescued."

"How?"

The signs of a smile emerged around her eyes. "My love," Nesta said. "Bethuel."

Sofia wore her shock plainly across her face. "You...and the Raven?"

"It took him a century to find me," she explained. "He was different then. A great catan and a leader within the Host. The Way was his very existence, a devotion only surpassed by his love for me. When he found me in the dark, I was nearly too far gone. Twisted, mad. Scarred. The healers did all they could, but I would never be the same." Nesta took a breath and unfolded her robe. Her limbs were tightly bound with wraps of cloth, but her scarred, blackened midsection was exposed. It glistened as if fresh. Sofia nearly gagged at the stench.

"These wounds will never heal," Nesta said, concealing herself once more. "Nor should they. Bethuel was sentenced to steward the Conventa, and my mantle passed to another, someone more worthy. Since then, no nuomen has been allowed to take the mantle again, for the risk to the Divine Sphere was too great. They—*we*, can never be controlled."

Sofia balled her fists and shook her head in frustration. "So, this training is what, torture? Punishment? Why did Terafiq bother putting me here at all?"

"Because there is nowhere else to go." Nesta said softly. The beads of her veil jingled as she shook her head. "Here you can be watched, but you cannot *win*, Sofia. Survive the Conventa as best you can. When you are done, put down the sword and forget your dreams. Both will lead you astray, as they did me."

Sofia felt the pressure closing in from all sides. She palmed the fang in her pocket instinctively. Was she truly a selfish martyr, a monster, as Matías suggested, or a lost cause like Nesta, destined to destroy herself?

No, I can't believe that. I won't. Will shapes the Orvida, and Sofia's Will was strong. It was not the Sanguinir's Will, but it was strong nonetheless. She was proving that every day in the Conventa. *The fire will not burn me.* If she couldn't believe in that, at least, then there was nothing else.

"You don't know me. None of you do." She thought of Ebrahym and the last words he spoke to her. *Prove them wrong*. "I'll make my own Way."

Nesta sighed heavily. "Do not let your ego destroy you, Sofia. The Host is uncompromising, the Divine Sphere unalterable. There is too much at stake for the Sanguinir to be benevolent in this." Nesta's eyes were hard with resolve, like shards of gold-colored glass.

"Heed my words, nuomen. If you lose yourself to the darkness, no one will be coming to save you."

19

The spirit singed Sofia's throat going down. It was a different kind of burn, not like fire, not hot. If it were, she wouldn't have felt it. But she felt this.

The alcohol came with an aftertaste of fruit and a warm sensation that bled through her body, starting from her gut and moving through her fingertips. She hadn't tasted it since that night when Ebrahym showed her the city. That was nearly a year ago, a mere blink in the eternity of the Orvida, but to her, a lifetime.

The celebration was well underway. *Viesto di Centigalo* it was called, the Festival of Century's End. In the past month, Luminea had transformed like a spring flower coming into bloom after a long winter.

Strings of colored flags and banners spanned between the great towers in every direction. The already elaborate spires and buildings were freshly painted with dizzying murals and vibrant designs depicting large animals and battles and other scenes. Vibrant mobiles hung from the skyships hovering over the streets, and ribbons ceaselessly flew this way and that, willed to never touch the ground.

The Sanguinir had established the Viesto di Centigalo thousands of years ago, and it had been observed with eagerness each century since. Each week of the festival was dedicated to one Choir of the Host. During that week, the hue of the city's adornments would shift, magically taking on the sigils and color of the honored Choir. The music and chants would change—thundering drums for the Choir of the Bull or the sharp brass horns of the Lions. And at the culmination of each week's celebration, the honored Choir would provide a gift back to the city, an offering. The Sang referred to it as *atonement*, but Sofia had no idea why.

The Choir of the Eagle's Century's End offering came, as always, in the form of a book. It represented a century of philosophical debate between the Sang monks. It was their typical gift to the oulma, though how well it was received, Sofia could only guess.

Next, the Choir of the Bull, the master builders, unveiled a new multi-tiered garden. It was said the structure miraculously stretched out over the Aecuna so far that it seemed to be floating on air. The Choir of the Stag, as was tradition, put on the most magnificent performance, with dancers who contorted the elements themselves and hymns that conjured visions in the minds of the audience.

Sofia saw none of these things. Until today, she hadn't laid eyes on anything outside of the Conventa for months. She and the other alumna had been sequestered in solitary training during that time. The isolation had been the last phase of their conditioning. A lonely, dark endurance test of survival. No one had spoken. There'd been no light. Sofia wondered if she'd dreamed the whole affair. She'd been blind for an hour when she'd finally seen the sun this morning.

They, the alumna, were the Choir of the Lion's atonement; the gift of hardened warriors, ready to serve. But before they took their oaths, the lions were released from their cages and allowed a night of welcomed respite.

"Another, my dear?" someone called out to her.

What the crowd didn't drown out, the musicians nearly did. The man was dashing, with narrow, devilish eyes. His hair was oddly piled high and cut short on the sides, and jewelry studded his ears. Not like the adornment of the stoic Sang, though. The man was intentionally more flamboyant in garb. Candles covered in red and orange paper lanterns littered the tavern and turned his skin a deep crimson.

"Why not?" Sofia asked, masking a slight slur. The numbness was sinking in, and she didn't fight it. After her conditioning to eat and drink once a week and sleep even less, the stuff hit her hard. She wanted it to, glad to be rid of her thoughts for a while and drown out the nightmares and dull aches that never went away.

The man poured the honey-colored liquor into Sofia's glass, did the same for himself, and sat down across from her. They saluted one another. Sofia defeated the drink in one fell swoop, making a weird face at the sting.

"Are you with them?" he asked, motioning to the center of the tavern. Alana and the majority of the alumna were there, dancing as if they did not know what was coming in two days' time. They were easily spotted in the simple, red jerkins of the Conventa. Sofia stared at her fellow students, realizing she had hardly spoken to any of them these last few months, even Alana. The solitary training had been all encompassing. She felt kilometers apart from them.

Sofia glanced down. "Is it that obvious?"

The man grinned and shook his head. "You don't strike me as a wing-chaser, darling. They always seem so dull. I'll never understand all the infatuation with the Sang, personally. Why waste of all this?" he gestured to the raucous setting. "So, they've let you out for your last hurrah, eh? To enjoy a night of freedom before the joust?"

Sofia pointed at him and winked, signaling he was right. "Something about bidding farewell to the material," she said. The music picked up in pace and volume.

"Shame, that. Waste of a perfectly good eternity if you ask me. I'm Benaro, by the way," he called over the tune.

"Sofia." She downed what little was left in the glass. Benaro refilled it for her.

"May I ask you something? Why choose that life? Honestly, I've never understood the appeal. Heroism, sacrifice and all that. All due respect, of course." Benaro flashed a grin and took another sip.

"I didn't choose it. Not exactly." Reality began to creep back it. "It chose me."

"I see. Well, that's unfortunate but not entirely unexpected."

"How's that?"

"When you've been around for a few centuries, you get a feel for the place. Do you know what I've learned?" Sofia shrugged. "In the Orvida, everything that *will* happen to you eventually *does*. Take your friend over there, the one with the sandy hair dancing with that large fellow. I take it she is brave, courageous, compassionate, etcetera?" Benaro pointed to Alana with the finger of a hand that was adorned with rings on every digit.

"More than you know."

"Of course. Now, consider a time a thousand years from now. If she hadn't been accepted to the Conventa now, she would have been eventually. No matter the twists and turns, her tendencies would have driven her toward some semblance of self-sacrifice and service."

"So, you believe in fate, Benaro?" The room was starting to spin.

"Not exactly. Only that we are who we are. One's true course seems inevitable here, given enough time."

"What's mine?" Sofia asked, leaning in. She studied Benaro's face, noticing the delicately drawn lines and makeup that decorated his skin. He peered at her, comically studying her features in return, like an actor hamming it up for the crowd.

"Loneliness, I'm afraid. Destitution," said Benaro with all seriousness. Sofia recoiled, suddenly drawn out of her pleasant haze. He laughed. "That is, unless you dance with me this instant."

Benaro grabbed her hand and led Sofia to the center of the tavern. The ceiling was low, lined with polished metal tiles. Flavored smoke lingered overhead in a thick haze. The drums pounded a primal rhythm into her chest like a blunt spear. A shoulder found its way into her throat as Matías shoved past her.

"Careful, with that one," he called out, clearly addressing Benaro with a wink. "Sleep with an eye open." All the time in isolation had made Matías no less of a bastard. Sofia felt the rage course through her like the warmth of the alcohol, but much more potent. It came faster now, and summoning it was as easy as breathing. Her fists clenched in anticipation, their faces inches apart.

"Careful, Sofia," Matías grinned down at her. "We wouldn't want to bring dishonor to the Conventa, would we?"

"No, I suppose you wouldn't." Her fist connected just under Matías' hardened jaw. It was like punching a piece of stone, but Sofia didn't let it show. Through the pain, she found satisfaction.

She threw another punch toward his gut, but the experienced warrior trapped the blow, yanked hard and found Sofia's head with his knee. The room spun out of control, and a moment later, the scene looked like hell.

Brawling figures bathed in bloody red light flailed wildly, the spirits eroding their discipline and training. *Was this the point of letting them out of the cage in the first place? To watch what happened?*

Sofia was atop Matías' back, maneuvering for a chokehold. Alana and the other alumna were trying to pull her off as Matías' spun wildly. The crowd cheered and hollered, and the music went on as the warriors drunkenly stumbled about.

***

The morning air was cold as Sofia and Alana walked along the waterfront at sunrise, making the trek back to the Conventa. The arching plumes of the Dawnlight danced overhead. Gulls squawked and split Sofia's head open with their cries.

"I wish I had your Serrá," Sofia groaned. "My head feels worse than when they tied us to rocks and sunk us in the sea."

Alana winced. "It's not helping as much as you think."

Boats heading out for a day of fishing listed out of their moorings to the singing of loyal crews. Sofia watched them work. The fishermen were not compelled to do what many would consider hard and awful work, but this was their craft, their calling. To each oulma, the entire Orvida was open to them. These few chose simply to fish, and Sofia admired them for that.

Like the boats bobbing along with furled sails, her thoughts drifted. Tomorrow was the final test. Their grueling stint at the Conventa was over, and soon they would no longer call the Raven their master. The Choir of the Lion's atonement, their gift, was the new brood of warriors. But they were not to be given over to the Sang or the Pax before it was decided who among them were most worthy. Rumor had it they vied for the honor of a single aurola. One halo.

Nesta had told Sofia not to pursue it, that it would only destroy her. *But I will be different,* Sofia told herself. *The fire cannot burn me.*

As they walked, Sofia realized how long it had been since she and Alana had spoken to one another. They knew each other intimately, of course, as only budding warriors could. They'd fought together. They'd learned together. Bled together. Sofia could spot Alana's feints coming, knew she favored her left leg in swordplay, knew to keep her at a distance. Alana, in turn, knew Sofia was like a hammer that drove forward with power until her opponent, the nail, was buried in the wood.

But Bethuel's methods these last few months had kept them far apart, intentionally breaking down dependencies, relationships. Such things could be used against the warriors, their fear of loss becoming the imuertes' greatest weapon. So, Sofia kept her secrets to herself.

The warriors walked for a while in silence, nursing their throbbing heads as they navigated the winding wooden planks of the piers. Sofia felt the tension between them. The Raven had done his work. The wedge between her and Alana widened day by day. She wanted to tell her friend how proud she was of her and to wish her luck. That she wanted to be like Alana: selfless, noble and righteous. But none of those things came out.

"Don't hold back tomorrow," Sofia finally said.

"What?"

"If we face each other, don't hold back."

"I won't." Alana squinted her eyes against the fierce sunrise that bathed the Aecuna in orange light. It looked made of fire.

Sofia struggled for the words. "Do you think I'm one of them, Alana?"

"One of what?"

"I know what the others say about me. About waking up screaming, not sleeping. And about what happened on the road." Sofia struggled to say the words aloud. "They think of me like those monsters."

"No, Sofia," Alana interrupted with authority. "No, I don't. But I do fear for you. I know there are things you keep from me, despite everything we've been through. I know you have your reasons."

Sofia kept her eyes on the horizon. "I can't. I just—"

"I know. Whatever it is, you'll have to learn to let it go in time." Alana stared intently at the water lapping the pier beneath them. She made a twirling motion with the flick of her wrist, and a plume of water rose in a spiral before falling back down.

"Not until I understand what it all means," Sofia said. "That's why I need the aurola. It's my only chance to be free of this. I think my life depends on it."

Alana's voice dipped into a whisper. "I've heard rumors in the Conventa, Sofia. There is talk of the imuertes uniting against us under a single Fierno, a Hell Lord. I've heard the stories, just as you have. How the hordes descend like flies, countless in number. And how the last time a Fierno emerged to the lead the imuertes, Ilucenta fell."

Sofia knew the stories. Hell Lords, so the tomes said, were unlike the common imuertes. They were not like the umbra, either, lost in a fog of self-pity and memory. The Fierno embraced what they were completely, and through their own Will, they remade themselves into visions of terror. Into gods, into demon generals.

"If it's true, Luminea will need defenders," said Alana. She hesitated, twisting the end of her braid. "Someone willing to die for that should bear the mantle."

"Someone not like me, you mean?" Sofia asked.

"I know you're a fighter, Sofia. You're probably the bravest of us all." Alana placed a hand on her forearm. "But I fear you live for yourself. Not for others, but in spite of them. If you were forced to choose, I'm not sure you'd choose wisely. And that could make you dangerous."

Alana's honesty hit home, a perfect feint Sofia didn't see coming. She felt a surge of guilt rise from deep within, an admission to herself that Alana was right. There was no judgment in Alana's voice. Only concern, and love.

Nesta's warning resurfaced in her mind, the scarred Sang's words shining through Alana's. *But what choice do I have?* If Sofia couldn't unravel the mystery, she feared it would consume her entirely.

"I got you something," said Sofia, easing the tension. Sanguinir tradition, despite its reputation for austerity, dictated the giving of gifts before a battle. A tribute to the moment before destiny, or so it was said.

The small trinket was a knot woven of gold around a lion. Heavily inlaid with red stones, it shimmered in the warm light of the sunset. "I found it in the Market Strand. All the jeweler wanted in return was a story she hadn't heard before, so I told her about meeting Ebrahym." Sofia tried to mask the loneliness in her voice. She missed him.

"It's beautiful," said Alana. She looped the gold chain around her neck and it rested atop her leather armor.

"And this is for you." Alana clasped a small, simple bracelet on Sofia's wrist. It was forged in bright silver, the name *Sofia* inscribed on its face. Sofia looked at her, quizzically. Alana smiled. "To help you remember who you are."

The friends held each other and, for a moment, forgot they were to be enemies tomorrow. The tournament at dawn would determine the recipient of a single halo. Until then, the two women walked as friends and allies once again, along the stone avenues of Luminea, ascending the great tiers toward the Conventa. They talked strategy and tactics, anticipation and nerves weighing heavy on their minds. Around them, the sleepy streets came to life, and the revelry of Century's End began anew.

It was quiet inside the Conventa when they finally returned A thick air of apprehension hung heavy in the halls. The alumna hardly spoke to one another. All were foes now. Sofia found her bunk inside of the individual quarters the alumna now occupied. On it, a small folded piece of parchment. It smelled familiar. She handled it carefully, her heartbeat quickening. The script was flowing and in the language of the Sang.

Remember yourself tomorrow. Swing true.

There was no signature, but Ebrahym's words were plain enough. Sofia thumbed the parchment, staring out the window. This was her chance.

Prove them wrong.

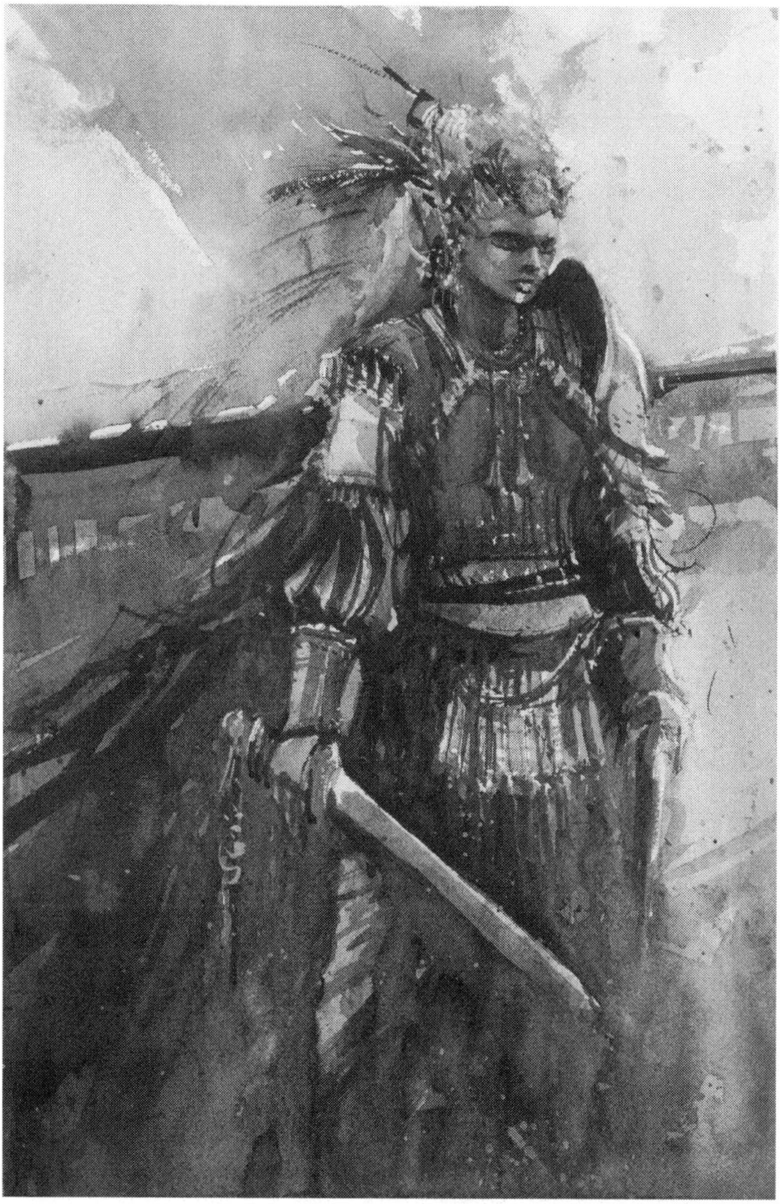

20

Sofia twisted the leather grip of her sword. It was hot in the arena, a colossal stone amphitheater that, on this day, overflowed with spectators. It was made of two massive stone wedges flanking a rectangular patch of dirt, like the dustfield but not as large. The sloping stone steps rose hundreds of meters into the air, and upon them, thousands of oulma sat in anticipation.

It was a tradition that Century's End culminated with the would-be Sanguinir warriors displaying their merit for the crowd of cheering oulma. Banners heralding each Sanguinir Choir snapped in the breeze, and flowers aligning with their colors littered the sand.

The alumna, 32 in all, anxiously lined the perimeter of the sandy battlefield, sweating in full armor, awaiting their turn in the ring. A volunteer attendant brought Sofia water, which she gulped greedily and then poured the rest over her head. Though the well-trained alumna were normally immune to such physical needs, the anxiety-inducing setting, the blazing sun and the hope for the honor of a halo was too much for their bodies to handle. So, they sweat.

Sofia rechecked the straps and buckles holding her armor together. She wore the same breastplate she'd found in Ilucenta, proudly polished to a mirror finish. Her sword, too, was the same heat-warped blade she'd carried from the ruins, across the plain and along the road to Luminea. And in her pocket, safely tucked away, was the lúpero fang, blazing hot. A fluted helmet sat in the dust at her feet, fitted with a crest of brightly colored feathers.

A short distance away, two of Sofia's fellow recruits rang metal against metal, each pressuring the other to yield. At one end of the great arena, a sloped pyramid overlooked the field where the leaders of the Sanguinir, clothed in fabrics and dress robes that reflected each Host, keenly watched and evaluated the performances. Ebrahym sat at Eros Terafiq's side. It was the first time Sofia had seen him in almost a year, but their attention was on something else—a conversation that took their eyes away from the contest before them.

Dust wafted across the arena. Colored bits of paper and flower petals drifted in the breeze, and the crowd gasped and cheered with each blow. Sofia's muscles twitched as she watched the bout.

Alana's words turned over in her head. They were all vying for a single aurola without a host. One Sanguinir would emerge from among them.

A rebirth, the emergence of a new halo was a rare thing. Eons ago, the *Hierarca Prima*, the First Hierarch, appeared. That first aurola emerged from the Dawnlight and bonded with an oulma who bore witness to the event. *Maestra*, he was also called, Teacher, the First of the Mantled. The first Sanguinir.

Since that time, scholars had spent eons trying to predict the next rebirth, but whatever dictated the arrival of new aurolas was far beyond their divination.

The sound of metal biting metal brought her attention back to the duel. It was a standoff. Sofia easily recognized the signs. Each warrior's shoulders were spent to the point of not being able to raise a sword. Both fighters were sluggish. They slowly circled one another, attempting to maintain their guard and regain their wind. Their plumage and adornments sparkled in the sun.

A desperate strike by one of the warriors, a sprite of a woman called Leira, left her wide open for a counter, which her much larger foe, the lithe and cunning Rafe, countered.

He dodged the swipe of her sword and followed through with his spear. A blow across the ribs sent Leira face first into the dirt with a crack that echoed across the field like thunder. Leira could not go on, exhausted and defeated. Rafe had won.

The crowd erupted with a cheer. Drums and horns announced another victory and signaled another defeat. Rafe helped Leira to her feet, each warrior saluting the other with grace and honor, the Sanguinir way. The Quato Eros and their entourage bowed from atop their altar, a sign of their approval.

One step closer. Sofia surveyed the board of names that marked their standings. Rafe's moved up in position. Leira's card now lay in the dirt with the rest. Sofia saw her own name, emblazoned in red paint near the bottom, but it had steadily worked toward the top of the pyramid. But so, too, had Alana's.

Sofia feared their names converging at the summit—like they had when they used to race up the Temple steps—not only because she didn't wish to harm her friend, but because she wasn't sure she could win.

The bouts continued as the sun began to descend. Sofia's power and skill kept her on her feet, and she moved up three positions. Alana did the same, proving to be leagues beyond her peers on the field. Sofia admired her grace and speed. It was no wonder she quickly became a crowd favorite.

Sofia was called to fight again, and once again slumped on to the bench afterward, victorious. Dust stuck to her moist skin. The bout had devolved into an inelegant scramble in the dirt, but her grappling skills had prevailed. She'd felt the pumping blood of her fellow warrior against her forearm as she squeezed. She'd heard her opponent's gasps and tried not to think of choking the woman from her dreams.

A bucket of cool water doused the rage to a simmer. In the arena, Alana took field once more, looking the part of a demigod of war in the setting sun.

Sofia pulled the wet hair from her eyes and glanced at the standings. If Alana won, they would face one another, as she had feared. Her gut churned. By the time her brain worked through the alternate scenarios, Alana had already won.

The cheering and drums signaling victory roared once more as Bethuel strode out into the arena, fully adorned in bronze battle armor edged with the green glint of aged copper and thick, emerald robes. His black wings and hair stood out against the bleached sand.

"Another Century's End comes to a close!" he announced with a booming voice. The crowd was silent, waiting. "The Conventa has given unto you the finest, has it not?" The stands let out a unanimous sound of approval. The Raven calmed them with a wave. "And now, the final joust."

Hushed whispers rippled through the crowd as it was announced their favored warrior of the day, Alana, would face the notorious Sofia. Her reputation outside of the Conventa had grown lately. Stories of her bravery on the road inspired her fame with a few, but the story of her nearly cleaving an oulma in two left most feeling suspicious and afraid of her. Was she a hero or a monster training to become Sanguinir, an imuertes spy? Every oulma seemed to have a different version of the story. She pushed it from her mind.

She hefted her sword and shield up as she walked into the ring, leaving her helmet behind. Alana was fast, and Sofia needed to see clearly. Anxiety mixed with adrenaline buzzed through her numb body.

Alana's eyes were barely visible through her polished gold helmet, but Sofia could still see them. They were full of ferocity, a practiced glare that concealed the love Sofia knew was there.

This was not her friend, now. This was her enemy.

"The honored victor of this trial," Bethuel continued as the warriors squared off, "will join the ranks of the Sanguinir in the eternal defense of our great city, Luminea. The vanquished will not." He glanced in Sofia's direction as he finished the sentence.

She looked in Ebrahym's direction. *Prove them wrong.*

A trumpet blew; the crowd erupted.

Alana dashed out of the gate with a flurry of quick strikes, testing Sofia's defense. More cheers.

Sofia anticipated the opener and defended with her shield, conserving her energy. The clang of steel reverberated through her arm. Trained as they were and capable of inhuman endurance, if she could tire Alana out, a few powerful blows could bring her down.

Again and again, Alana struck, trying to penetrate Sofia's guard, but Sofia held firm. Alana was a blur of steel and gold, of feathers and silk. Alana feigned a high blow with one of her swords. Sofia ducked but missed the second low attack that slammed into her shin, weakening her stance. A shove put her off-balance even more. Alana came down hard with both blades. Sofia caught them with her shield just in time, but the force drove her into the dirt and sent the shield flying.

Sofia desperately defended from her prone position, slashing wildly as Alana looked for an opening.

I will not let them win. I will not be defeated on my back.

The anger was starting to overtake her. She tried to keep it at bay, keep it under control, but she was losing ground to it. Alana had the Divine Sphere as her ally, focusing and enhancing her Will. Ebrahym's instruction to remember herself ran through her thoughts, but she needed the rage now. This was her only chance.

Sofia roared as she let the darkness overtake her. Anger surged through every nerve, every cell. The image of the inky shadow figure appeared in her mind. But she did not fear it. She *was* it. Her vision narrowed. Her heart thundered. Alana swung again. Sofia's blade caught Alana's sword and it screeched down to the hilt, momentarily trapped. Sofia crashed hard into Alana's forearm with her armored elbow and heard the bones give underneath.

Alana sprang back, clutching her arm in disbelief. Sofia regained her footing and charged. Blows descended from on high like lightning bolts, and Alana was forced to deflect, rather than absorb the powerful strikes.

Sofia pressed harder, driving her opponent to her knees with blow after blow. Sofia couldn't see anymore. A single goal consumed her mind and pressed her body; the utter destruction of whatever lay in her way.

With a desperate cry, Sofia came down hard onto Alana's weaker sword, fracturing the blade in half. The crowd gasped as Sofia poised to strike a killing blow.

Sofia's eyes met Alana's once again, this time seeing nothing but fear reflected back at her. *She fears me.* They were the eyes of someone gazing at a monster. Sofia fought to regain her senses, but it was like running through a dark fog, trying to find the light. Part of her savored the fear, the other part was sickened by it.

The moment lasted just long enough for Alana to regain her footing. Sofia let loose her sword too late.

The blade fell toward Alana's helmet, but Alana danced aside at the last instant, letting the sword crash into the dirt. Alana snaked her hands around Sofia's wrist and used her momentum to hurl Sofia to the ground. Alana rolled on top of her, quickly drawing a dagger. The cold steel pressed against Sofia's throat. The rage drew back like a tide pulling back to sea.

On her back, Sofia noticed how beautiful the sky was. The last light of the sun lit the underbellies of the clouds aflame. A few stars had already appeared.

It was over.

Alana helped Sofia to her feet, pulling her from the dark trance as the crowd cheered. "I thought you were lost. I saw it in your eyes." Alana gasped. "But you came back."

Sofia couldn't face her. The crowd and horns and drums echoed around them, drowning the arena in a ruckus. Bits of paper filled the sky like colored snow.

She would never forget the look in Alana's eyes. It was one of disgust, horror and sadness. The look was the same as the man had after the battle on the road.

Same as the umbra in Ilucenta. Same as the woman whom Sofia murdered each time she slept. It was the look of one staring into the face of evil.

"It's all right," Alana said, embracing her sister-at-arms. "It's over." Sofia said nothing and pulled her friend closer and fought back the tears.

Alana was right; it was over. Sofia couldn't help feeling that even though Alana had stayed her hand, she may have been tempted not to.

The tears came, and Sofia wondered if would have been better that way.

21

The entirety of the Sanguinir Host assembled in formal attire to witness Alana's communion. Soon, she and the aurola would be one. Hundreds of Sang had gathered, each elegant and powerful. Sofia scanned their faces for a sign of Ebrahym, but there were too many to count.

Sofia watched anxiously from her place in the back of the great hall, a cathedral-like structure filled with terraces and balconies, packed with winged figures. This was the Temple of the Mantle, whose only purpose was to observe this ritual.

Above, the ceilings of the temple were so vast it was difficult to make out the detailed murals painted upon them. Arched supports intersected in repeating patterns to support a massive glass dome, a dizzying display of architectural miracle. Light streamed in from every angle, filling the space with crisscrossing beams of gold, and a steady hymn of anticipation echoed throughout.

Sofia felt the core of the temple pulling her and everyone else toward it like the gravity of a star, as if the structure itself sought to compress everyone inside into a single point.

The alumna who had since completed their training but were not chosen to be haloed, Sofia included, sat together. Witnesses worthy of observing the communion. That much she had earned, at least. On their chests, a sigil of the Conventa, the single token of recognition from their time at the trials. Many of them had taken vows and were bound to serve the Prime Auxilia.

Scores of alumna from centuries past made up the volunteer legion, which outnumbered the Sanguinir tenfold at least. Their vast numbers filled the rear of the cathedral and spilled out through the arches to the exterior terraces and courtyards. They wore fine tunics decorated with medals and sashes and golden braids.

Being part of the Prime Auxilia, Sofia was told, was a great honor and noble cause, but she had trouble accepting second place. She had refused the oath, for now. She needed time to think.

I was so close, Sofia kept repeating. The key to her answers had been within her grasp. She'd spent the days since the tournament reliving the bout with Alana, blow for blow, wishing she could go back and change things, to gain an advantage. It was all Sofia could think about until she saw her friend, and then jealousy mixed with pride.

Alana looked like fresh snow, washed clean for the first time in months. No caked dirt mixed with sweat from the dustfield, no knotted, haphazardly tied-back hair to keep the sweat from her eyes. She walked proudly down the aisle parted through the crowd, like an eager bride. Only instead of a husband, Alana would join a halo in holy symbiosis. Sacred symbols marked her hands and face. With bare feet, Alana made her way down the long stretch to the altar flanked by two Sanguinir dressed in silvery robes. As she passed, the Sang and Pax warriors in attendance bowed their respect. She kept her keen eyes forward and still. Sofia wondered if she was afraid.

Alana made her way to the altar and climbed the steps. It made Sofia think of all those times they'd kissed the dawn, struggling up the steps of the Temple of the Dawnlight together.

Now, Alana scaled the altar steps with grace and ease. She knelt within the carved stone circle at the summit and waited. Behind her, the four Eros of the Sanguinir ascended the steps. At the summit, they stood like gods, shimmering and proud, their wings pointed high in salute.

The hymn that had lingered in the background began to intensify, echoing through the enormous cavity of the cathedral. There were no words needed for this ceremony; Sofia could feel the weight of the hymn's power vibrating through her body. It reminded her of Ebrahym's song, but much more potent. The harmonies and complexity of the melody were too much to comprehend. It seemed to intertwine and blend in such ways that Sofia could barely perceive anything beyond a single, omnipresent sound.

Another Sanguinir, one Sofia had never seen before, walked down the aisle carrying a small chest covered with inscriptions and elaborate filigree. *The aurola.* How and where it had been kept while awaiting a host, Sofia could only guess. The bearer wore a white hood that masked his face, as if the identity of the one who carried such a treasure was not to be trusted, even by their brethren. All in observance of the mantle knelt as the chest passed by, until it finally came to rest before Alana, who was still kneeling upon the stone altar. There was a pause in the hymn, a single note held in elaborate harmony.

Alana opened the chest before her.

The light emanating from the box glowed softly at first, like the gentle arcs of the Dawnlight. Then, Alana herself began to glow. She pulsed with energy as her features slipped away and only vaguely resembled something human. The radiant figure of pure light, the being that once was Alana, rose to her feet, craning her neck toward the sky, arms outstretched.

Oh my God, Sofia whispered to herself. The sight was overwhelming. Tears blurred her view as her brain struggled to process the sensation.

The light from what used to be Alana intensified, so much so that Sofia averted her eyes from the small star blazing in the center of the temple.

The Sang's voices swelled, bringing the hymn to a thundering crescendo. The melodies and harmonies wove together toward resolution that a primitive, very human part of Sofia's brain begged for. The beautiful song drowned out all else, a symphony that threatened to split Sofia's mind apart. Something inside of her began to vibrate dissonantly, off time, preventing her from completely embracing it.

United in song, the Sanguinir quickened the rhythm to drive the mystical process onward. Wings began to emerge from behind the glowing figure as she hovered above the altar. The newly formed appendages reached out like glowing fingertips toward the sky. As the song reached its climax, all harmonies converged and came crashing down in a moment of pure resolution that sent a wave of gooseflesh across Sofia's skin.

The hymn faded. The entire cathedral went silent, save for two voices that held the last note of the song suspended in two octaves. Both voices were Alana's. But she was no longer the woman Sofia knew.

Now, Alana was Sanguinir, and Alana no more.

***

"Hello, Sofia."

Ebrahym was dressed in formal attire, prepared to attend the celebration in Alana's honor. His eyes were as piercing as ever.

"Hey," Sofia said. Now that he was here, after all this time, she wasn't sure how she felt. *Why do I feel like hating him?* Maybe it was herself she hated. Her failure. "I got your note. It's been a while."

"Indeed," he said, in his familiar, detached way. "You look strong."

Sofia scoffed. "Not strong enough. I failed. I tried to do what you said. But after all this time—a year of fighting, bleeding, training, studying, I failed. It almost happened again, Ebrahym. I almost lost control in the arena with Alana. Just like the caravan," Sofia sighed wearily. "Nothing's changed, only now I'm more dangerous than before."

"I spoke to Nesta." Sofia shot him a surprised look. "She believes in you, Sofia, even after seeing what happened. So do I."

Sofia blinked. "Why?"

"Anyone can build the strength to swing a sword. I sense your strength is much more than that, but to what end I do not know. We both sense it."

"We? You mean Nesta?"

"No." Ebrahym touched two fingers to his temple. *The aurola.*

Sofia ran her hands through her hair, pulling it tight, a habit to release stress. "Where have you been for the last year?"

"Hell and back," he said, his angular face darkening. "After the summons with the High Council, Eros Terafiq ordered a few warriors to take the wing far into the frontier to see if the threat is real. If an army must be raised, we need more proof to convince the High Council. We've been tracking across the plains, rooting out dens and burrows, searching for signs that there is darkness on the horizon. Something is coming, Sofia."

"The Fierno," she whispered.

Ebrahym arched an eyebrow, momentarily surprised that Sofia knew of it. "Yes," he said. "The first one in millennia." They stood there for a while as the gravity of the news hung in the air. The Sang cleared his throat after a moment. "Are you joining the feast?"

"No," Sofia said, looking out from the terrace to the stream of Sanguinir leaving the temple below. "I don't think so." Trumpets and cheers echoed through the streets. Beneath them, Sofia could see a parade of Pax, Sang and oulma alike following Alana as she meandered through the street, smiling radiantly and shaking hands with each person she met. Her wings were brown with white tips. Sofia wondered if they were different by choice or a random luck of the draw.

"I see," Ebrahym said, sensing the deeper meaning of her words. "And the Prime Auxilia? Have you considered taking the oath?"

"I don't know yet. I thought all *this* was going to give me some answers," she said, gesturing to Ebrahym's wings and beyond. "But I feel more in the dark than when I first arrived. Now I understand. I'm going to have to find the answers myself."

Ebrahym stared off toward the horizon in his all-knowing way. "It is possible there are no answers to be found at all, Sofia. Perhaps what you seek is something unknowable." Ebrahym paused, glancing at Alana below. "In truth, part of me wished the mantle had passed to you. What a Sanguinir you would have made."

"And the other part?"

Ebrahym sighed. "Relieved that it did not. The aurola are wise, yes, but they are powerful, potent. What you fear, losing control, is real. If the power of an aurola were...compromised, there is no telling what terrible things might come next."

"I have it under control."

"I have no doubt you believe you do," Ebrahym said, smiling. "But do not mistake the mantle as your only path to salvation. They are guides, yes, but not gods. Not prophets. Each of us must still follow the Way on our own." Sofia laughed. Confusion wore plainly on Ebrahym's face. "What is it?"

"Nothing, just something someone said to me," she said, remembering Benaro's words, the only thing that stood out in the hazy memory of two nights ago. "That everything that should happen in the Orvida eventually will."

"Be wary, Sofia," Ebrahym cautioned. "Take Nesta's story to heart. Should you get lost in your search, there may be no turning back."

"Thank you," she said. She embraced the Sanguinir, pulling his massive frame to hers as her fingers wove through the smooth feathers and clutched them tightly. She took in the familiar smell of incense and flowers as if it were the last time. "Goodbye, Ebrahym."

His eyes poured over her like honey, but he did not stir. Still distant, still more Sanguinir than human. "Farewell, Sofia."

Sofia retreated to the Conventa, away from the music and the dancing, away from everything. She needed somewhere quiet. Somewhere familiar. Ironically, the place she longed to be free of now felt like the closest thing to home.

Ebrahym's words stayed with her as she packed her few belongings. The barracks were barren and quiet now, all the alumna enjoying the celebration for their once-fellow student, now a Sanguinir warrior.

Sofia wished she could join them, wished she could accept her place and just live, like other oulma in the Orvida, but she couldn't. *What is wrong with me?* Doubts and questions gnawed at her mind. And as much as she was proud of her friend, Alana's glory only made things worse. The familiar urge to just start walking reminded her of the beach and the lighthouse from so long ago. *Maybe I should see what is out there.* Sofia needed to get as far away from anything Sanguinirian as possible, at least for a while. At least, until she figured out what to do next.

Her head hit the bunk after packing, exhaustion catching up to her. The empty silence was a relief. No sounds of swords clanging or cries of pain. No horn summoning them to kiss the dawn.

Weariness washed over her. Sofia dreaded the thought of sleep and the dreams that would follow, but she was so very tired. Not her body, but her mind. Her *soul*, whatever that was. But the darkness came for her, and she slipped into a deep sleep, alone.

PART IV

RUIN

Ally and foe bore witness to her fury,
And the price of blood was paid, a heavy toll.

Liba di Halphyus 16:9

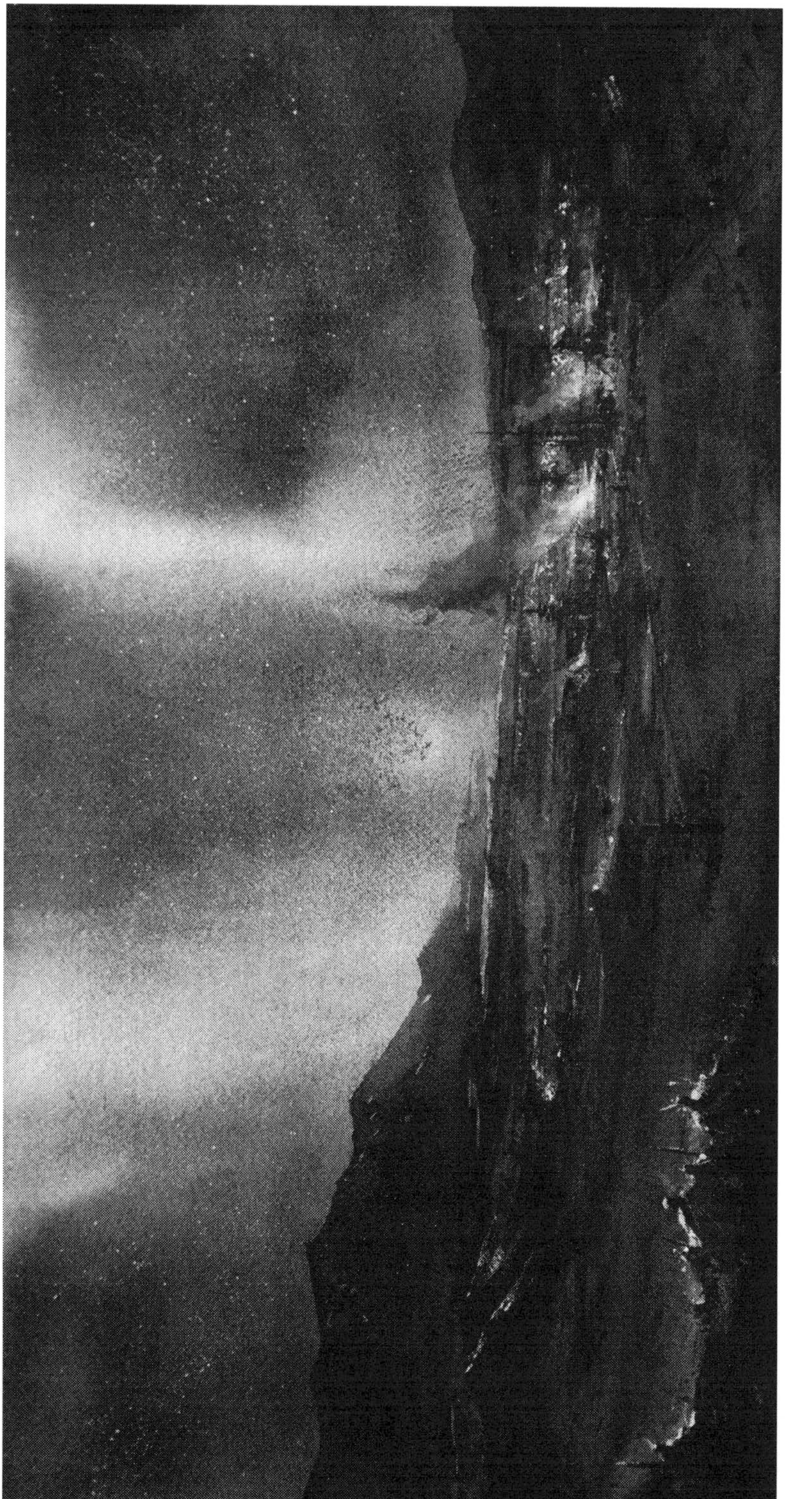

22

Something caught Sofia's eye as she scribbled. She looked up from the piles of scrolls and worn books sprawled across the table and peered into the gloom. There were no windows of colored glass here to burn away the shadows. It was a tomb of a place.

Around her, hearty stone walls encased the endless rows of shelves and books unmoved for centuries. A congregation of candles surrounded Sofia's makeshift desk, an ancient slab of wood hewn to seat twenty. Now, it sat only one.

Is someone here?

She pulled her stiff limbs from the wooden chair, setting the quill down on the open page of the book. Candle in hand, she relit the nearby sconces that had long gone cold. Her Serrá helped coax them to life. The weak, amber light was little match for the overwhelming dark, though it did its best to keep the shadows at bay. She kept meaning to retrieve one of those autonomous orbs of light that lined the streets above, like the one she'd found in Ilucenta, but it always seemed to slip her mind.

"I thought I might find you here."

Sofia jumped. Eyes flashed to life, staring at her from the black like shards of amber. The voice was familiar—one of them, at least. It was a pair of voices now, entwined in harmony.

"Alana?" Sofia rasped, startled.

"No, not Alana," the Sanguinir said, stepping into the light. She used the Sanguinirian tongue now. "I am *Anayah*, now."

It was true. The Alana that Sofia once knew was gone, replaced by something even more striking, beautiful and powerful. Anayah looked the pinnacle of humanity and, at the same time, appeared devoid of it. She had the detached, absent quality of the Sang. Eyes once blue blazed like embers, studying her. Sofia could no longer read them. Alana was Anayah now, winged and glorious.

The gulf formed in the Conventa between the women was now very wide indeed. *I'll miss your smile, Alana.*

The Sang floated into the light. Despite the gloom, her long hair shone like strands of curled gold. It was laced with red beads. There was more red about her, too, and it made her allegiance clear. The crimson robes inlaid with golden designs marked her as a true warrior of the Host, of the Choir of the Lion, from now until eternity. The warrior choir suited her.

Sofia slumped back into her chair and pinched the bridge of her nose to bring herself back to the world. She stared blankly at the empty wine bottles and stained glasses strewn about. *How long have I been down here?* Her plan had been to take to the road to see what answers she could find. The need for a map or two had led her here, to the most ancient parts of the city, and here she had stayed.

Anayah eyed the sprawled books and papers. "I see you are keeping busy."

Sofia nodded. Heavy, ancient tomes lay across the table. Treatises on the demon, histories from long ago, and accounts of other Orvidian cities and kingdoms: Calèdia, the Vijas Protectorate and the States of Laèn, and the remote lamaseries of the east, where the *Monte di Iyar,* the Monks of the Sand, called home. There were maps, too, and etchings of Luminea itself from a time when the towers were small and the temples modest.

"May I sit?" the Sang asked. Sofia gestured to the chair nearby. A thought came to her, and she whipped up the quill and began to write again.

"I hear tell you may be leaving Luminea," Anayah said. Her voice rippled with an undercurrent of melody.

"I'm thinking about it," Sofia said, burying her head in her books. In the margin, she crudely scratched a likeness of the apartment she returned to each night in her dreams.

She had spent the last few weeks cataloging each detail as the dreams came, looking for clues. The visions were intensifying, as if her failure in the arena had inflamed some infection that her mind continued to battle day and night. She was so tired.

"I want to offer my apologies," the Sang said. Sofia paused her scribbling, but her eyes stayed low, fixed on the parchment before her.

"Did you hold back in the arena?" Sofia asked as she resumed writing.

Anayah's answer came slowly. Sofia knew she couldn't lie. *None of their kind can. The aurolas won't let them.* "No, I did not hold back," Anayah said.

"Hmm. Then there's nothing to be sorry about." Sofia sighed, regretting the jab at once, and tossed the quill aside. She pulled her dark curls back until her scalp stretched. "I'm sorry, I don't know why I said that."

But she did. Her failure in the arena was still an open wound where envy festered. Embarrassed, she swallowed hard and met the Sang's eyes.

"I am proud of you Ala—Anayah. You were worthy. *Are* worthy. I wasn't. That's that."

"That is not why I am here, Sofia." Anayah took Sofia's hand in hers. She could feel the hum of energy between them. Anayah's wings twitched to avoid the back of the chair, and she noticed Sofia's gaze drifting toward them with curiosity.

"They were strange at first," Anayah said, smiling. "Dressing has taken some getting used to."

"I'll bet," said Sofa, eyeing the feathers. She reached out to touch them and hesitated. Anayah nodded her permission. "Can you fly yet?" The feathers felt like strands of stiff silk.

"I am still...practicing." Anayah's porcelain face opened into a thin smile, a pale reflection of what it once was. The two laughed. Sofia heard three voices echo in the chamber, one being her own. The laughter faded away to a stillness that hung in the air, unresolved.

I might as well come out and ask it. "You can't tell me anything, can you?" whispered Sofia. "About what it's like now. Communion. Sanguinir secrets and all that."

Anayah shook her head. "Even if I was able, I am not sure I could find the words. Perhaps it is not something *for* words. But if it helps, it is not like any of these books describe. All is not revealed to me. Things appear in waves and visions, in songs and light and feelings. I can *sense* it inside...Almost as if I were someone else, body and mind, but also myself, simultaneously looking inward. I am sorry, I should not—"

"It's ok," said Sofia, trying not to let her envy show. "You obviously didn't come to tease me with things you're not supposed to talk about."

"No, I did not."

Sofia drained the only wine glass left standing watch over her work. "Ok, *mes* Anayah, then tell me why you're really here."

***

Anayah led Sofia from the dim halls of the library's innards into the brilliant midday sun outside. The blinding light stung Sofia's retinas, like when the alumna recruits first emerged from their isolation at the Conventa. She shielded her eyes.

The blurry mess resolved to the familiar, picturesque Luminea metropolis of stacked buildings with terraces and warm roofs and busy winding streets beneath them.

Down the hundreds of sloping steps, the two women, one winged and the other not, made their way to the winding, stone streets below. They turned east, toward the hanging gardens that flanked the Third Tier.

Sofia felt as if awoken from a dream. As they walked, she wondered how it was she had lost herself in the archives for so long.

The gardens were thick with perfume as the women strolled through the eaves. Stone aqueducts propelled water overhead, underfoot and all around the lanes, flowing life to an assortment of bizarre and brightly colored flora.

But despite the serene surroundings, Sofia sensed tension within her friend. They made small talk, but even with her newly found poise, Sofia saw through Anayah's divine veneer.

Anayah paused before speaking, choosing her words carefully. "There are things in motion out there, Sofia."

"What do you mean?"

"Past the shores of the Aecuna, to the west. Beyond even the Divine Sphere's reach, the imuertes gather. Larger and larger packs have been spotted moving with purpose. Caravan attacks have increased, and villages and towns to the west have been sieged and raided, yet not destroyed."

Sofia shuddered; the dusty memories of battle suddenly shone bright and terrible again. "What do they want?"

"To sow fear. To erode our Serrá and enfeeble the Sphere," Anayah sighed. "Despite this, the High Council still does not believe Eros Terafiq's claims of a newly risen Hell Lord, even after these many months."

"Anayah," Sofia said, the name still strange on her tongue. "Has a Fierno come?"

Anayah nodded with a grim look upon her face. "Some of us believe so. Though the High Council knows the Eros' words to be truthful and honest, our kind cab still be susceptible to *exaggeration*. Being truthful does not necessarily preclude one from being *wrong*. The Legatès want proof. The Archlord has called for an incursion, far from our borders, to find it. Ebrahym and the others are already far awing, scouting."

Sofia waved her hands in frustration. "I don't understand. Why not muster the entire Host? Everyone keeps whispering and wondering, but why wait? Rally the army and meet them head on."

"No wonder Eros Terafiq has an interest in you," chuckled Anayah. "You are like her in many ways. I wonder now if that is why she defended you. But the Council, however, sees it as their duty to avoid a full-scale war. After what happened—"

"Ilucenta?" Sofia offered. Anayah's eyes revealed nothing. "I've read about the final battle, about how the Hierarch fell during the siege. Terafiq was the last Sanguinir the High Council appointed to command the army," Sofia said, recalling the ancient texts still fresh in her mind.

"All true. But not the source of our fear. Something worse..." Anayah caught herself before continuing. "It does not matter; we have our orders. I will be commanding the *leta*, the wing of Prime Auxilia under Catan Ebrahym," said Anayah. The formality sounded strange. She had snapped into duty, and with it, her charm had vanished. A distinctly masculine tone emerged in her voice. It was a regal, disciplined tone and to the point.

Anayah continued. "It is customary for a new Sanguinir to command a detachment of oulma. I can choose the warriors I wish to fight with, and I want one of those to be you. That is why I have come."

Sofia's heart quickened at the thought. Not the rational part of her, but the primal part, the angry part, the part that had hacked the tooth from the lúpero's carcass. But she held her reason; this was a dangerous game to play.

"I'm not Pax, Anayah. There are whole legions to choose from."

"Yes, I know, but—"

Sofia's temper flared. "Alana!" Other oulma treading the garden jumped. Sofia steadied herself, voice low. "You *saw* what happened in the arena and...on the road. I can't be trusted with a sword."

"I did, Sofia. But I am...scared." Anayah flinched at the words as if her other half was wounded by them. Sofia could see fear in the molten pools of copper staring back at her. *She can tell no lie.*

"I know what you are capable of, Sofia, yet I trust no one else. I am not sure what we will face out there or what will happen. But I know I will have a better chance if you are with me."

Sofia kneaded the stone railing overlooking a manicured grove. She knew she should say no and walk away. Heed Nesta's warning. She'd tried to do right thing from the moment she'd washed up on the beach. She fiddled with the silver bracelet still on her wrist, the one Alana had given her. *To remind her who she was...*

I'm trying. But at each turn, Sofia seemed to drift further and further into the shadows no matter what she did.

Perhaps it was the same force willing her to agree now, pulling her away from Luminea. Sofia saw the desperation in Anayah's eyes. Despite the Sang's strength and power and the halo she carried, she was afraid. *Do I really have a choice?* If she could help Anayah, she would. She had to. And in the process of doing so, she prayed she might save herself.

"What the hell?" Sofia said, forcing a smile to ease the tension.

"Thank you." Anayah squeezed her shoulder.

"On one condition," Sofia interrupted. Her voice was low and stern, her words deliberate. "If I lose control again, you won't let me hurt anyone. Whatever you have to do. Promise me."

Anayah stared at her, the golden eyes drinking in her resolve. She nodded faintly, sadly. "I swear it."

23

"Do you think we'll see any?" Matías asked, securing his tarnished, well-worn breastplate. It was simple steel with little ornamentation, but he wore it with pride. No vibrant colors marked his helm, no sigils or plumes of feathers. The dark trousers and an earthy colored jerkin beneath the plates of steel were unusually modest.

This was not a mission of glory. Matías rubbed thick, dark grease over the metal surfaces to dull their shine and did the same to his face. Thick stripes slashed across his nose and cheeks like claw marks.

"I'm counting on it," said Hektor, within earshot of Sofia. He looked equally grim in his dark camouflage, smaller than Matías, with a long mane of wild hair pulled tightly back. A manicured beard showed his fastidiousness. "I want a taste of the real thing."

"Agreed, brother." The two clanged their vambraces together in a sign of respect.

Matías hefted a heavy spear. "But let us not forget to watch our backs," he called as he skewered the air toward Sofia. The words carried clearly for everyone to hear. The eyes of the other warriors drifted toward her. *Remember, you're here for Anayah.*

Sofia remained silent as she honed the edge of her sword into oblivion. *Fools. They have no idea what's out there.* The grinding wheel whirred, and she focused intently on its work, willing the metal to subject to it. Most of the sword still wore the bruise-colored signs of heat damage, but the edge was clean and sharp.

Dozens of Prime Auxilia warriors tended to their weapons and armor in a similar fashion and prepared for war in their own way. Many of them wore scars about their faces, a tradition. They wanted their scars to show. Tattoos and markings covered their arms, dedicated to their respective units: The Horns of Valor, the Right Hands, Sunlancers, the Gold Pride and others. Some of their kind, like Matías and Hektor, were new to the ranks.

"Sofia!" Matías jeered. "Do the imuertes know we're coming?"

"How would I know?" Sofia asked through gritted teeth, knowing his meaning. She ground the stone harder against the blade of her sword. Sparks flew as she willed the blade to a razor's edge.

"Don't they come to you while you sleep? What do they say to you?" He knelt, his dark eyes meeting her own. Sofia's rage clawed from the dark hole toward the surface. She could feel the other eyes of the Pax upon her.

Sofia whirled around to Matías, her sword finding his throat in a flash of steel. She dug a fist into his kidneys. "Next time you find *yourself* asleep, I'll show you."

There was something dark hidden in the undercurrent of her voice. It felt all too satisfying.

"You only prove my point," Matías said, chuckling through a strained throat. "You're not one of us."

"Thankfully not," Sofia said, shoving him away.

The sounds of heavy footsteps echoed through the armory. Ebrahym, Anayah and other Sang filed in, returning nods to the respectful Prime Auxilia troops who bowed before them. They wore full battle attire, but like the Pax, they, too, had shed their ornamentation. Their armor was grim, a metal of soot-like color that was flat and dull.

"I am Catan Ebrahym," he said, his dual voices deep and commanding. Sofia remembered him in the tent with Catan Madadhi on the road. Ebrahym had not been senior then, nor as cold.

He went on, "As you know, our aim is to discover the intent of the imuertes to the north. A small wing of *lenientès*—Gawayn, Tufayl and our new sister Anayah, will lead you to the border under my command."

Ebrahym nodded, and Anayah removed a rolled parchment from the folds of her armor. She unfurled it onto the heavy oak table with her black-gloved hands. The Pax soldiers crowded around.

The map had similar landmarks and features Sofia had seen in books, but also small marks and notations with dates—the movement across the land of the dark imuertes packs. There were hundreds of such marks surrounding the expanse to the north, south and east of Luminea.

"I will lead the advance wing with Anayah," Ebrahym explained, "while Lenientè Gawayn and Lenientè Tufayl follow with second and third wings shortly behind. We will approach by skyship, traveling far to the northwest where we have reports of imuertes activity. Scouts have been unable to survey closer by wing; the skies swarm with their kind. So, we will descend by glider to have a closer look on foot."

Sofia recalled her training, such as it was, with the gliders at the Conventa. More theory than practice, the extent of it constituted basic operation of the contraptions on the ground, during the day. Their purpose was, of course, to mimic the capabilities of Sanguinir flight so that Pax soldiers could follow them into battle. She had always been skeptical of their reliability.

Likewise, Sofia had never spent much time on *aeronaves*, the skyships that dotted the Luminea skyline. They were strange things: hulls like those of a sailing ship suspended from long, air-filled bags that curled at the ends like pea pods. Special oulma pilots and crews steered the vessels, keeping them aloft with concentrated Serrá, their combined effort heating the air inside of the bags so that they never needed fuel.

"For many of you," Ebrahym said, golden eyes surveying the troops, "this will be your first encounter with the enemy. But under no circumstances are you to engage. Our task is to gather information and remain undetected. I expect no losses upon our return." A unified "Yes, ser" rang out. Sofia caught a hateful glance from Matías.

"Lenientè," Ebrahym said and motioned for Anayah.

The Sang woman nodded, her radiance and power emanated, filling the space. "The lead wing will land *here,* in the central *Basquio,* the North Steppe," Anayah said, pointing to the map. The area was swarming with references to imuerte movement. Anayah's voice showed no sign of apprehension, though Sofia knew it was there. "Once we confirm signs of organized activity or should we meet resistance, all wings shall retreat to *this* ridge and fall back to Luminea."

"How will we make our way home?" asked a particularly grizzled Pax soldier.

"We have a hidden harbor in a cave near the Borra River," Anayah replied, pointing again. "We will traverse by foot and sail the river until it meets the Aecuna, then onward toward Luminea."

Ebrahym nodded, taking control of the room once more. "I do not have to tell to you be cautious. It has been many centuries since we have seen imuerte activity on this scale. New evil may await us, conjured up from the Inferna. But trust the sword and spear next to you, and we will find victory. *Ey esen Serrá Iriva bes hefecto.*"

By our Will the Way be done.

"*Ivá!*" Anayah called out the Sanguinir cheer in response, as if on cue.

"*Ivá, ivá, ivá!*" the mass of soldiers replied in unison, save for Sofia. Distracted, she tried to read Ebrahym's sharp features. He avoided her eyes. *Does he, too, wish I wasn't here?* She could sense sadness, perhaps dread in him.

Sofia glanced at the map as the Pax filed out. Her eyes followed the lines to the north until there we no more lines to follow, and she wondered what they would find there.

* * *

The dream again. There would be no rest for the mission ahead.

Sofia found herself in the grungy apartment. The same yellowing walls, the same threadbare carpet. The scenario played out as it had time and time again. There were tears; there were screams. Once again, Sofia's hands found their way around the woman's neck to crush the life from her.

But the details were different this time. There were strange markings covering Sofia's hands. *Were they carved into her?* Through the haze, Sofia could not be sure nor make out their meaning.

After the deed was done and the woman lay dead in the corner, Sofia's body turned to face the mirror, slowly. Patiently.

She saw herself, naked and pale, with a strange symbol branded upon her chest. The glyph smoldered and cracked and sent hot embers flying. With horror, Sofia stared into eyes that were not her own, but black pits that gleamed like oil. And behind, lurking in the darkness, the horned creature loomed over her. Its clawed hands clasped her shoulders as a wicked grin split the face of her reflection.

Sofia awoke in her bunk, seizing back to life, covered in sweat. She scrambled to find something to write with and scrawled the symbol onto the nearest piece of parchment she could find. But the dream was so palpable she would never forget the strange sign. Two arcs descended to meet a point like a V, with a line slashing through them to form an inverted triangle.

The symbol didn't seem to have any special significance, but Sofia could barely look at it without feeling a choking fear. It was like the sickly aura of the lúpero, a feeling of hopeless dread and weariness. She clawed at her chest, telling herself it was just a dream.

Sofia lay there for hours, staring at the symbol until the trumpets of battle called her to arms.

24

It was *cold*.

The sensation perplexed Sofia, who had long forgotten the feeling. Her time at the Conventa was designed, among other things, to make her immune to the common complaints of the body. Regardless, it was damn cold. Something powerful here willed it to be so. Something more powerful than the Sphere was at work, more powerful than Sofia's hidden rage.

She rubbed her hands and blew hot breath on them, and rechecked the myriad of straps and buckles that held the glider frame firmly upon her back. It was a clunky thing.

The nearby Pax soldiers looked similarly awkward, waddling around the cramped deck of the skyship. The veterans didn't seem to mind. They kept to themselves and stood at the deck's edge smoking pipes.

Sofia avoided peering over the railing, even though the gloom of the night obscured the earth below. Indigo clouds broke up the dark mass below through which she and the other members of her squad would descend, any minute, toward the ground. With this contraption on her back.

The familiar pit in her stomach tightened.

"Shit," Sofia muttered to herself. She shuffled away from the edge to take shelter in the middle of the skyship's deck, as equidistant as possible from any gilded railing.

In the distance, the first signs of strange, greenish light, *northfire*, it was called, began to dance. It had the look of glowing serpents slithering through the sky, and it reminded Sofia of the Dawnlight, but somehow more sinister.

Crimson Wind, the vessel that carried them, was no more than a few dozen meters in length and a few wide, and it was packed with warriors. Above, the air-filled bags were like inflated reeds lashed together, bulbous in the middle and thin at the ends.

"Not nervous, are you?" asked Matías, testing the wing flaps of his own glider. He and the other darkly dressed figures nearby chuckled. "Don't worry, Sofia. It's only three thousand meters between you and the ground. It'll be quick."

Don't let it show. Sofia ignored him and continued her prep, pretending she wasn't nervous. But she was. Despite her time with Bethuel, traversing between the towers of Luminea on cables, leaping from one to another, Sofia had never managed to shake the fear of heights. It was the falling. It was the fear that at any moment all she knew and all she was could be over.

She clenched the mechanical levers that extended from the glider. As she squeezed, tensioned cables attached to the crude, stiff wings pulled them tight and changed their shape to better adapt to the airflow. Everything appeared to be in order.

Or it wasn't, and she would be dead within the next five minutes.

"Form up," Ebrahym ordered as he appeared from belowdecks. Anayah followed, both the Sanguinir in the same black armor. They looked like shadows or some cosmic distortion that swallowed up all the surrounding light.

The squad of Pax warriors lined up, dragging their awkward rigs behind them like flightless birds trying to imitate more capable cousins.

Anayah touched Sofia's shoulder as she passed, a welcomed surge of warmth in the cold night. Anayah did the same for each soldier, a sign of good luck. Ebrahym nodded to her, and they dived off the deck into the blackness below.

Shit.

The Pax soldiers followed suit, one after another. Sofia hesitated when her turn came, frozen at the edge, her feet standing partly on the deck and partly on nothing at all. She sucked cold air in quick breaths. Below, the pale forms of the Sanguinir descended with the gliding Pax close behind like a flock of baby birds.

Sofia noticed her iron grip on the rigging. Her hands went numb. She wondered idly what the ropes were made of. Then she felt a boot heel impact her spine and heard Matías laugh from above.

The rush of the wind around her was deafening. A thunderous void swirled around her. Her guts revolted. She squeezed her eyes tight, reining in her terror enough to not scream. Ground and sky were indistinguishable and gave the illusion Sofia wasn't falling at all, but suspended and unmoving.

It was, of course, an illusion. She *was* falling. And fast.

Sofia scrambled to gain control of the glider and right herself toward the wind. The contraption strapped to her back pulled her every which way. It spiraled and careened like a leaf in the wind, dragging her with it. She reached behind her for the right-hand control, stretched awkwardly as she tumbled. The cable and handle whipped wildly above her. Tears streamed from her eyes, pulled away by the wind. The control was still attached to the rig for the moment, thankfully, but whipping wildly and threatening to break free.

Sofia rolled slightly, blindly swinging her arm backward to feel for the handle. Clouds kissed her face as she fell through the mist, thrashing and contorting her arm until her joint screamed in protest.

Topographic details below sharpened fast, providing a much better look at what was going to kill her.

She rolled hard once more and threw her arm back simultaneously, catching the cable in the crook of her elbow. She returned it to its rightful hand and pulled hard on the controls.

The artificial wings groaned apart, jerking her hard against the harness.

Smaller and smaller adjustments helped her regain control. In a moment, Sofia stabilized the rig. Her speed now matched that of the wind that carried her aloft, and the roar of air past her ears vanished. It became eerily silent, almost peaceful.

She laughed the desperate, hysterical laugh that comes when the body is stressed to its limit and has no idea what else do. Eager to touch the earth once more, she slipped into a spiraling descent and followed the others into the blackness below.

***

Her feet found the rocky terrain as she touched down upon cold tundra. Landing in a run to compensate for her speed, she hit the release mechanism to send her glider skidding across the ice-encrusted ground. It scraped to a halt a few meters away.

Shit.

Gasping, fighting back the adrenalin that had done its work to prime her muscles for anything, it took Sofia a moment to realize she was, in fact, safely on the ground once more. She stamped at it to confirm its certainty.

After a vow to avoid any future endeavors that involved her leaping off perfectly good skyships, Sofia took a deep, cold breath.

Ebrahym and Anayah were already on the ground watching clumsy Prime Auxilia struggle with their contraptions as they landed.

The air was still, the tundra in every direction a frozen expanse of some alien wasteland. Countless stars scattered the sky, congregating in thick masses of light where there were no clouds to obscure them. The strange viridian bands of light had intensified during her descent. They danced above in long trails with a mind of their own, and the entire landscape was bathed in a sickly green glow. It was oddly beautiful but terribly lonely.

Sofia unbuckled her harness and reaffirmed her sword still hung at her side, strapped to her hip. The chill bit deep like icy fangs.

Sofia pulled her hood over her head to block the sting and warmed her hands around the lúpero fang nestled in her belt. So far so good. She glanced up for a sign of the retreating skyships, but the blackness hid their otherwise easily distinguishable shapes.

"All well?" Anayah said as she came into view. On her waist were strapped two short blades, her pale skin a bluish glow against the darkness. Only her eyes betrayed the coldness of their surroundings.

Sofia nodded, her breath pluming into a puff of steam. "I can't feel my face."

Anayah seemed unfazed by the chill. She threw Sofia a leather flask of spiced wine, and Sofia took a long draw. It poured down her throat like warm honey and spread to her stinging limbs. "I am glad you are here," Anayah said.

Sofia smiled grimly. "Not sure I can say the same."

Anayah scanned the horizon. "I know. I feel it, too. There is something strange at work here."

"All accounted for?" Ebrahym asked as Sofia and Anayah joined the huddle of Pax gathered in a low depression. Silent nods returned. "Good. I will scout ahead to ensure the way is clear. Anayah is in command." Ebrahym departed into the darkness, his keen eyes piercing through the veil.

"Map," Anayah ordered. A tall, soft-spoken Pax warrior named Camila produced a parchment and a thin tube of brass. She unscrewed the tube, extending its length to reveal a small but brilliant torch. Anayah wrapped her wings around the huddle of troops to block the light. A mother goose protecting her goslings.

"There is a valley to the north," Anayah said, tracing the sketch of a ridge. "We need to make it there unseen before dawn. If the imuertes are near, they will return to their lairs before the sun rises, so we will have a better chance of observing their activities and their number. But remember, we are not to engage under any circumstances." Anayah collapsed the torch device and looked up at the mats of densely clustered stars, calculating the time based on their positions in the sky.

"We have less than two hours. Move quickly."

The wing of troops ran at a good pace, in full armor, over the uneven terrain. Bits of leather between the metal plates of Sofia's armor masked the normal clanking noise. Instead of greaves, she wore hide boots that were softer and navigated the rocky ground silently.

The warriors, led by Anayah, formed a wide diamond as they covered the icy ground. Each of them willed their bodies to sprint hard, taking in sharp, cold breaths to keep up. Even with all their training, they struggled. This place was working against them.

Anayah appeared to dance over the hard-to-see depressions and obstacles. She occasionally pumped her wings to gain a few meters of altitude before drifting down to continue on foot.

The Sang froze ahead of them, signaling to take cover. Sofia dropped to the cold ground. The ice crunched underfoot. She listened. The stillness remained unbroken, and she could hear nothing but the blood pumping in her ears. Sofia squirmed across the ground up to Anayah's position.

"Anayah?" Sofia whispered as loud as she could. There was no answer. She crept up farther until she and Anayah were face to face. The Sang's eyes were pale, empty discs, the amber irises rolled up and behind her lids. They shuddered as if processing something.

"Anayah?" Sofia repeated, shaking her friend by the shoulder. Anayah's eyes snapped straight, the golden light sparking to life once more.

"Sofia?"

"What are you doing? Are you all right?" whispered Sofia.

Anayah nodded. "Ebrahym is a few hundred meters ahead. I was asking him if the road ahead is clear. Hold fast, there is something out there." Anayah darted away. I didn't know they could speak to each other like that.

Sofia focused on the darkness ahead of her, straining to detect signs of movement or faint sounds on the breeze. Then she heard it; a slow, prodding thumping.

The Pax soldiers popped their heads up from their prone positions as the sound reached their ears in turn. Sofia scanned the horizon from her hide until, out of the corner of her eye, she thought she saw a mountain move.

It was no mountain, but something else, something she knew only from books. It was an ogorantè, a herald giant, a monstrous imuerte of legend.

And it was coming.

The behemoth lumbered directly toward them, slowly coming into focus as its heavy footfalls impacted the ground like falling trees and reverberated through the tundra. Sofia felt the vibrations in her chest.

The thing was equally massive in every direction, a gnarled form of iron interwoven with charred flesh that creaked and grated as it moved. A pair of massive arms pulled the giant forward on two proportionally smaller legs like some great ape. Its skull protruded from the mound of muscle and metal with more eyes than seemed natural, bound by a crude, makeshift bridle.

The groaning of metal grinding against metal echoed. The sound threw uncontrollable chills up Sofia's spine. Hanging from its bulk, gleaming in the pale light, a pair of massive metal discs larger than a Sanguinir's wingspan and hollow in the center, were lashed to the creature with chains through the opening.

Anayah signaled silently to take cover. The squad dug to any lowland, crack or gully they could, hopefully out of the path of the lumbering giant.

As it approached in full view, Sofia could smell the burning, rotten flesh and taste metallic, sulfur rust in the air.

Then, she felt it. It was not like the aura of the dark whisper, that mournful aura of despair. This was different. The giant's essence pulled her toward it.

Suddenly, Sofia felt compelled to follow the thing to the ends of the earth. Through fire, through storms, through battle, she would follow it and be content. It tempted her with the promise of a dark pilgrimage. As it approached to within a stone's throw, Sofia could see the other Pax feeling the same agitation and temptation to move.

And then, the great gongs rang out.

Small, gangly creatures, like parasites scuttling atop the ogorantè, struck the metal discs with huge mallets on chains. A shockwave of sound echoed across the frozen landscape.

The sound penetrated Sofia's eyes, bones, organs and whatever lay at the core of her being. It was an old sound, older than time and deeper than the center of the earth. It was a sound to break barriers, shatter the Divine Sphere and whatever Serrá dared to resist it.

Sofia felt her muscles spasm, threatening to make her break cover. In the bushes beside her, a Pax soldier shook uncontrollably as if fighting a fever. He lurched forward, then rose to one knee, preparing to run.

The herald giant and its crew were nearly on top of the squad, the looming mountain of metal and meat a few massive paces from their position.

The nearby warrior broke. Sofia had enough of her faculties about her to lunge and grab him as he tried to run and embrace the call of the ogorantè. Estan was his name, and Sofia had him by the ankle as he clawed at the tundra, trying to crawl toward the herald in a trance.

Sofia felt it too, as the gongs sounded again, promising blissful peace if she were only to follow the sound. She closed her eyes, fighting every urge her muscles had to let go and follow Estan into the dark oblivion, but she held him firm with both hands. Inside, she clung to her rage, the only thing she could count on. She squeezed her eyes tight as the gongs thundered above them once again, cracking the air like lightning. She wanted to scream, to cry, to laugh, to give in entirely and be one with the glorious sound. If she'd just let go, she could march in the wake of the giant forever.

Estan thrashed and kicked violently, but to his credit, held his tongue. He was not lost yet. Sofia opened her eyes to see Anayah had joined to helped hold Estan down, fighting to keep him quiet.

Then, the moment passed. Just as the light returns after an eclipse wanes, the siren call of the herald giant faded along with the ogorantè form as it lumbered on into the darkness.

"I'm sorry, I'm sorry, I'm sorry…" Estan said, panting, after the creature was long out of sight. "I. . .I don't know what happened. I'd never felt anything like that before. It was calling to me, promising me—"

"It's all right," Sofia said, glancing at Anayah. Was it?

"It will pass, Estan. Listen for the Sphaera Divinia. Hear its song and find your way back." Anayah squeezed his shoulder and came to her feet.

"Sound off," she ordered. The Pax obeyed, though groggy and stumbling as if waking from a heavy sleep. They said their names one by one and regained their faculties. Even Matías took heavy breaths with his hands on his knees before coming to attention.

"I did not expect to see an ogorantè here," Anayah said to Sofia in a low voice. "Heralds are a rare sight and only found in the greatest of hordes, summoning all nearby imuertes for greater purpose. It has been centuries since the last one was felled. They are dark omens for even fouler things."

"Fierno," Sofia whispered. Anayah said nothing and ordered the warriors to get moving.

The squad resumed their formation and their pace, running with speed across the tundra. Although uninjured, they were on the backfoot, less confident than before. This was not at all like the magnificent frescoes of Luminea depicting glorious battle in the sun. This was not what the Choirs of the Host sang hymns about.

Here, hundreds of kilometers from nowhere, in a cold land filled with monsters, there was nothing to sing about. This was a deadly game of hiding in the shadows and hoping not to be found by the things that called the darkness home.

25

The sun rose, but no warmth followed. The squad, led by the two Sang warriors, made their way toward the precipice of a gentle valley covered in snow. The tundra descended into a shallow bowl stretching kilometers into the distance where, to the north, jagged peaks of ice loomed.

The beginning of the valley was marked by a craggy rise of outcroppings that overlooked the expanse. Ebrahym wormed his way, quite ingloriously, to the edge. Sofia had never seen a Sang in the dirt. His outstretched wings lay flat on the ground, almost blending into the earth.

A few hundred meters away from Ebrahym, at the edge of the valley, Anayah led the Pax toward the catan's position. Though tempered like bars of iron, the Pax soldiers were still breathing hard after their non-stop run through the night.

Ebrahym signaled, and they approached with caution. Once again, Sofia found herself on her belly, crawling and crunching across the frosty earth. Her breath billowed up in front of her.

Four of the Prime Auxilia—Matías, Hektor and two others—nodded at Anayah's hand signal and took vanguard positions behind the squad in the lowland scrub, while Sofia, Anayah and the other Pax soldiers dragged their weary bodies up to the edge of the valley, spyglasses in hand. Sofia and Estan slid next to Ebrahym, under his wings.

"Anayah, tell me what you see," said Ebrahym as the warriors took up position. His eyes remained fixed on the scene ahead.

Anayah scanned the horizon, unaided. Sofia did the same with her scope, panning across the valley below. "Burrows," said Anayah.

Gaping holes punctured the valley floor below, pits that led to places Sofia didn't want to imagine. They seemed to swallow up what little light the dawn offered.

"*Freshly made* burrows," confirmed Ebrahym.

"How can you tell?" Sofia whispered to Anayah.

"Heat," Ebrahym said as if the question had been directed at him. "They bore the tunnels using the domesticated *igdracio*. These are still warm, which means the imuertes are not only here, but they are also close and on the move. Strange, though," he hesitated. "I have never seen them so numerous."

Even in the dim light, Sofia could see the distortion caused by the heat around the diameter of each pit. She imagined the igdracio, the fire serpent she had read about, harnessed to chew through solid stone, erupting from the surface like a stream of magma.

Are they still here, even now, slithering their way through the earth? Her mind wandered back to the sea, to her first memory of waking in this strange place and the fear of something terrible lurking in the dark water beneath her. How little things had changed.

Each pit was connected by black trails of scorched earth. Training the spyglass, Sofia could make out the silhouettes of tiny, patchwork structures near the rims of each hole. Ropes and cables crisscrossed the openings to suspend what almost looked like crude umbrellas.

"Down there," said Sofia, pointing out the structures. "Near the edge of the burrows."

"The work of lesser demon, the laborer *impès*, the death children," Ebrahym explained. "They build such things to mask the burrows from light of the day. Their ilk is not formidable, but they are deft and clever. Something has set them to good use."

One of the veteran Pax spoke up. "*Lots* of them, by the looks of it. There must be a hundred hellholes out there."

There were, scattered across the tundra like deep, infected pores, blights upon the otherwise cold and tranquil surroundings.

"But where are their owners?" asked Anayah, her eyes turning to the east. "The light is almost upon us. They should be retreating to their lairs by now."

"Indeed," agreed Ebrahym with a rare wavering in his voice. "This is beyond my experience."

To the east, light inched its way across the valley floor. The great shadow covering the earth receded, drawn back like a massive curtain draped across the landscape.

A bellowing roar startled the soldiers. It conjured up memories of the lúpero attacks, and even centuries of training couldn't keep it from worming its way into Sofia's mind. It thundered from deep within the unseen network of caves, echoing up through the depths and spilling forth across the silent tundra. *A call.*

She focused her mind against it. *I will not bow to this,* she told herself as the swelling terror eased. *Imuerte fire is nothing to me.*

The other oulma were similarly distracted, recalling their training and using the Sanguinir chants, accessing the Divine Sphere, to keep the evil at bay.

Then, like flies descending upon a corpse, the imuertes appeared.

Their numbers were hard to guess. The hordes funneled toward the pits like filthy water in a drain. From every horizon, the writhing mass of chaos charged across the plain to its collective sanctuary in the earth. In the skies above, huge swarms of winged creatures, wicked imitations of the Sang, appeared from nowhere. They blacked out large parts of the sky and formed eerie silhouettes against the fading green lights above.

Now she understood why they'd approached on foot. At least on the ground, they had some cover. In the air, even a wing of Sanguinir would have been torn apart by the flying monsters that outnumbered them a hundred to one at least.

More rumbling, this time from behind. Sofia looked to see the oil-slicked hide of monsters glinting in the morning light approaching at their backs. The stampeding horde thundered in the squad's direction and to their dark hovels beyond. Whether the imuertes sensed their presence or not, she could not tell, but it was clear the pack wasn't slowing down.

A hundred meters away, Sofia glanced at the four Pax soldiers, the vanguard. They dropped to the ground for cover, making the best of their limited options. Even if Sofia and the rest of the warriors could reach their brothers and sisters in arms, the stampede would already be upon them.

Sofia glanced desperately at Ebrahym as the clamor of the approaching horde built like superseding thunderclaps. The other warriors, too, looked to the Sanguinir for orders. He shook his head, as if sensing her urge to do something.

"We cannot help them now," the Sang catan said. The veterans nodded solemnly. The younger ones glanced back in desperation.

"We can't just leave them!" hissed Sofia.

"We are surrounded! There is no choice but to hold fast, or we all are lost." Ebrahym ordered. "Quickly!"

Ebrahym rolled over the edge of the stone outcropping, gripping firmly with one hand. The other found his sword, and with a strength Sofia had never seen, he plunged the steel into the rock face with a grating *clang*. Anayah followed his lead, driving both her swords into the stone. "Anchor yourselves!" Ebrahym called over the ledge.

The Pax soldiers slid over the precipice and, using any strap of leather or makeshift rope they could find, cinched it to the handle of the blades embedded in the rock.

The helpless squad sat suspended like bags of fruits at a stall in the Market Strand, dangling just below the precipice. The ground below was not far underfoot and flattened generously to the valley below, but the outcropping might be just enough to hide them as the horde thundered past.

When Sofia's turn came, she looked back at her comrades and the black tide rearing up to swallow them. The ground began to shake beneath her feet. Matías was out there. She could see his bulky frame trying to disappear into some lowland cover with the other members of the vanguard. How she loathed him at that moment. He represented the rest of them to her. All the suspicion and doubt the oulma of Luminea felt toward her, the Raven's distrust, Terafiq's manipulations—if it could all be personified, it would be the man called Matías. How easy it would be to follow Ebrahym's command and let him and the others die. Even if she didn't desire it, she knew it was the logical decision, to let the imuertes trample and pound their flesh into the earth and carry on.

Then she remembered Matías' words to her that night in the Conventa. *Would you sacrifice yourself to protect them?* he once had asked her.

"I can't," Sofia said to Ebrahym, who hung beneath the edge of the small crag with his hand outstretched. *I must do something,* her eyes said. *No,* his protested, but she was already moving.

Sofia sprang to her feet and sprinted along the edge of the outcropping, away from Ebrahym, Anayah and the other Pax. Anayah called after her as she bolted, yelling and clanging her sword against her armor.

The black, writhing tangle of imuertes fast approached. Sofia's primitive instincts told her to flee. Her Will fought hard now to keep moving.

Before she could take another step, the horde stopped dead, skidding to a halt on the frosted ground a stone's throw away.

As they did, a noxious wave of sulfur, dust and filth that followed with the pack caught up and kept moving at speed. It washed over Sofia like a putrid wave, and she fought the urge to retch. The familiar, infectious aura seeped into her mind, distorting her sense of the world. But the aura, that deathly shadow that followed the imuertes was not there. All was still.

The rumbling of their hooves and claws fell silent and, like a line of refined cavalry, the imuertes pack stood motionless and silent. In the wretched tangle of forms, Sofia recognized their shapes, knew the names but could not find the words.

There were parts of animals among the creatures, a perverse combination of the visage of men and women with black horns and the beaks of carrion eaters, with molting scales and bloody, broken hooves. They were somehow nobler than the rest and stood above them like wicked masters. Other shapes in the mass were simply indescribable distortions of the human form—distended, swollen, contorted or exaggerated in the most disturbing and unnatural ways. Mouths mixed with teeth and eyes in incomprehensible combinations. Among the horde, flesh rotted off the bone or smoldered. Some were hosts to mats of wriggling parasites and insects. A flash of beauty appeared occasionally in the ranks, high atop aberrant mounts—a pale, feminine shape here and there with exposed breasts, yet each of them marred by missing bowels, eyes or jaws.

It was as if a catalog of nightmares from every human to have ever lived stood before her. Sofia's eyes could barely contend with the insanity of the sight.

She gripped her sword by instinct, for it was the only thing she knew to do. Hot steam burst from the maws of the creatures as they panted the cold air, but they did not approach. Something kept them at bay.

She took a step toward them. And then another, testing their intent. Hundreds of eyes watched her.

The horde remained there, frozen, like one of the frescos in the temples of Luminea. Sofia crept forward, her boots crunching the snow. The air was still and quiet. Soon, the four separated members of the squad lay at her feet.

"What are they doing? What's happening?" said Matías, his voice at the edge of madness. He peered out from his cover in a thicket covered in frost, trembling. Hektor lay at his side. The other two Pax soldiers were wedged in a small gully not far beyond.

"I don't know," whispered Sofia.

Matías glanced at the imuertes and shook his head in disbelief. Realizing the futility of the situation, or noting Sofia's apparent fearlessness regarding it, the warrior came to his feet. The others followed his lead, the five oulma not fifty meters away from the imuertes horde that still would not attack.

There was a look about Matías, a pale expression of fear, his eyes wide and searching.

"I—I can hear them. In my head," Matías said, rubbing his temples and banging at his helmet. "They are speaking, showing me things...Oh! No! Get out! By the light, they are coming to devour us! And Luminea! The city will fall, and the Dawnlight will fall to the darkness."

Tears streamed down Matías' face as he rambled on. Finally, his face showed a sign of realization. His fear-ridden face contorted into a mask of malice.

"*You*," Matías said as he turned to Sofia. His red eyes were cold and pitiless, barely visible under his heavy brow. "You've betrayed us! Bringing us here to be slaughtered by the enemy. You are in league with them!"

Nearby, a dark scowl overcame Hektor's face as he hefted his spear into his hand. From behind, the two other Prime Auxilia, Marta and Osias, skulked toward her, unsheathing their blades.

Before Sofia could protest Matías' insanity, he was on her. Ignoring the imuertes that watched from a distance, Matías slashed wildly, forcing Sofia to defend. It was like being in the arena again.

Sofia didn't want to hurt him; this was not the man she knew. But he left her little choice. Matías thrust toward Sofia's midsection, but his timing was slow, and she countered with a fist to the jaw. Hektor jabbed with his spear, searching for an opening. Their grunts and gasps filled the air.

"Matías!" Sofia screamed. He pressed on like a madman, landing a slash to the inside of Sofia's leg that dropped her to the ground, followed by a crushing blow to her shield that brought her to her knees.

Matías swung wildly, raining blow after blow on her crumpled form. It was all she could do to remember he was not the enemy and this was the work of the monsters watching, but he would not stop. He would not stop.

Please, Matías. Stop. And then, the anger came.

The rage wasn't the slow, controlled rise she was accustomed to, the kind she could see coming. The kind she could control. Unrestrained fury smashed into her consciousness like a falling star. The impact sent shockwaves through her system that made her hands shake and her vision narrow.

Sofia spat as she sprang back to her feet with newly found strength, and in a blur of anger and power, struck back. Matías was slow, disoriented by his delusions, and her attacks blasted through his guard. She slashed across his midsection, opening a deep wound across his flank.

Someone shouted her name in the distance. She was in the fog again, naked and lost, trying to find her way out of the darkness. Her eyes barely recognized the man in front of her. Matías inspected the blood spilling over his hand, a sad look of profound disbelief splayed across his face. It transformed into a hateful snarl before he lunged again.

Sofia screamed as plunged her sword through Matías' chest. The blade exploded with hot flames that belched a forge's heat. It was her Will, her Serrá, made real.

Blood dribbled and gurgled from his mouth as Matías' face relaxed as if released by some force that drove him on. The fire from Sofia's sword licked at his clothing and caught. He seemed to regain his senses for a moment, if only to witness his final one. Anger gripped him again, a raw look of betrayal as he swung wildly at Sofia's face. She cried out and drove her blade deeper into him, to the hilt, with a sickening, wet crunch.

Sofia watched the life leave Matías' eyes and saw the face of the murdered woman from her dreams before her. It was the familiar look of disbelief and betrayal, of fear and anger. She had killed him, as she had killed the woman in her dreams so many times before. *Desipar* was the word for it. The destruction of another oulma was thought to be impossible within the Divine Sphere. But Sofia was an outsider and had a Will of her own. One of a killer. She was the shadow in the mirror that haunted her, no different than the horde that stood watch nearby. *Are they to calling me? Testing me?*

"What do you want?!"

Singing came from somewhere in the fog. A hymn beckoned her out of that dark place, back to the real, but time slowed to mud.

Matías' slumped body lay on the ground, and Hektor, Osias and Marta shook their heads in horror. Whether aghast at what they were about to do to Sofia, or at what she had just done, she could not say. But inside, the rage burned, and so too did her blade.

She teetered on the edge of the abyss, struggling to maintain control, shaking with terrible purpose. Clenching tight, she followed the song, its pace quickening, bringing her back to the present moment.

It was then Sofia realized the imuertes had broken ranks. Their collective limbs spun to life in slow motion as they mounted a charge toward her. She closed her eyes, following the rhythm of the battle hymn, planting herself firmly in the here and now.

Opening her eyes, Sofia pulled her flaming blade from Matías' corpse, gently cradling his neck as she did so and turned to face the wave of terror descending upon them.

Warriors formed up around her, Ebrahym taking the place by her side. He continued his song, a loud and vibrant hymn that spurred Sofia's muscles to action, and pushed away the grief and shock. Time crawled back to normal pace. The darkness melted away like a spring thaw. Anayah added her own harmony to the sound, a high-pitched and silver set of chords made the chorus even brighter. The Prime Auxilia joined in the song as they formed up around the Sanguinir, knowing no better way to spend their last few moments.

Sofia, too, began to sing. She looked in amazement as the blade wreathed in flames danced before her eyes. Just beyond, the imuertes horde was coming fast.

This fire is for them.

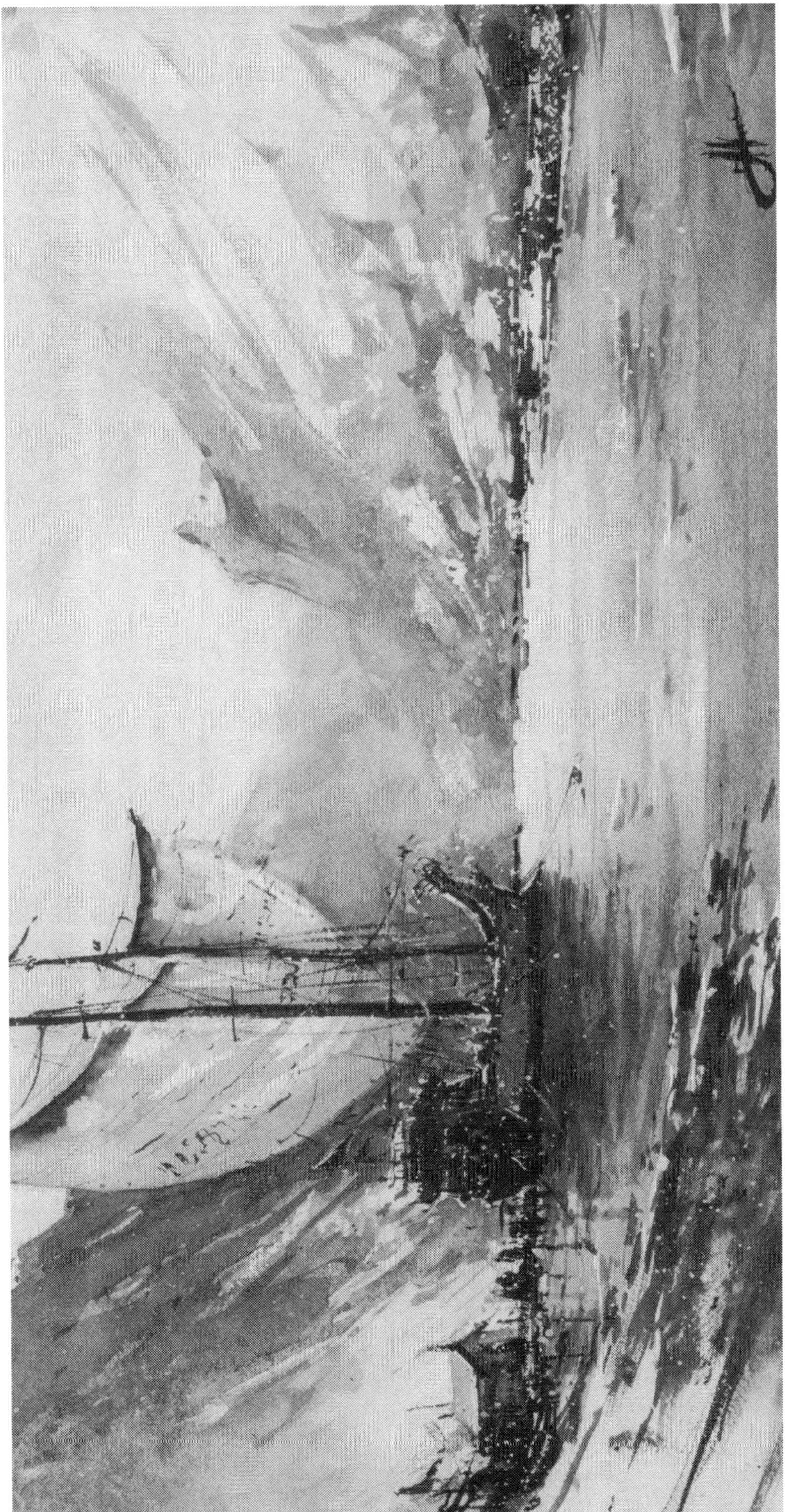

26

There was no time to mourn. Not yet.

Ebrahym formed the point of the wedge as the imuertes crashed into the defenders, talons and teeth clattering. Armed with a massive shield, the Sang pierced the wall of carnage coming at them, parting the wave of monsters like a plow through the field.

Sofia could not comprehend the force that struck him nor how he remained standing. Ebrahym was an extension of the earth itself, unmovable. Wings splayed back, bellowing a loud chorus and shielding the soldiers from the brunt of the impact, he held the line like a defiant stone in a raging river.

His aurola flared to life, calling forth the ring of light that appeared around his helmed skull.

Sofia and the others dug in behind. Shields and swords at the ready, their heels ground the cold earth beneath their boots. Through gaps in the layers of feathers that separated Sofia from the evil rushing by, she saw slavering maws, contorted, rotting limbs, fangs, claws and dead, lifeless eyes.

She focused her mind on the ground beneath her feet and the shield in her hand. Hot blood still raced through her veins after killing Matías. The grief began to seep through the battle hymn and mixed with primitive, ancient terror, the kind that lurks deep within every human being.

Sofia wanted to scream, to curl up in a ball and let the wave devour her. Then it would be over. But the others held, and so long as they did, so would she.

A spindly, spidery creature darted from the flank and crashed into the squad's flank, buckling it. One Pax soldier fell to his knees as the others filled in to protect him. Blood stained the snow.

A monster lumbered toward them, hissing from the slashed mouths scattered across its twisted form. It was a disgusting combination of mouths and teeth. Perhaps a man once, it now appeared more insect-like and gruesome. Pit lurker, or *ilsecte,* in the Sanguinirian tongue.

At the lurker's many heels, lúpero hounds yipped and snarled, waiting for their chance to strike. Smaller creatures filled the ranks between them—death children, pale and dwarfish with no eyes and plenty of fangs. They chittered and clamored over their larger brethren with anticipation.

Ebrahym shouted to Anayah, and the pair of Sang squared off against the spider beast. Anayah's eyes, too, disappeared behind a glowing disk of light. Together they were two lanterns in the early dawn.

As the Pax huddled with their backs to one another, Ebrahym pumped his wings to gain altitude and used gravity to propel him, shield first, toward the ilsecte's swollen abdomen. The oulma desperately hacked at the swarming fiends.

Nearby, Anayah was a blur, her swords singing as they slashed apart mutated limbs.

A lúpero lunged at her from behind, but the Sang summoned the earth itself to come to her aid. A stone wall emerged from the ground, called forth by Anayah's Will. The lúpero crashed through it, dazed. Anayah was on top of it a moment later, severing its head with a single strike as the spined carcass skidded into the snow, sizzling.

Ebrahym moved so fast he seemed to be in multiple places at once. As he struck, single notes of pure sound rang out like cathedral bells, a beautiful song of battle.

Below, Anayah wove through the pit lurker's spindly legs, hacking them down like reeds. A disgusting mass of flesh nearby, more mouth than not, sensed an opportunity. It dove after her, jaws snapping, ichor flying. Sofia called out, and Anayah spun to meet it.

Her wings, willed from their normal silkiness to hardened shards of steel, sliced the thing open long ways and sent a spray of hot filth flying.

The Pax were wearing down. Though hearty, they were not Sang. Three had fallen already as they struggled to hold their ground. The remaining were wounded in one way or another and smoldering with steaming imuerte blood.

Sofia found herself facing two more lúpero hounds, their spines slick with filth and their maws pouring forth hot stench. They came at her at once.

A fellow warrior, a stout woman with a thick, black mane, dove bravely into their path but could not raise her defense in time. A set of talons slashed across her face, opening it up and spraying a mist of blood into the cool morning air. Sofia felt the warm splatter on her cheek.

The lúpero charged on, its lust for blood unsatiated. Sofia dropped to one knee, raising her shield at the last second to absorb its bite. As she did, the flank of the other lúpero revealed itself. She punctured it with a cry, skewering its gut from below. It howled and careened toward Anayah who finished it off with brutal efficiency. Estan, the soldier who'd nearly succumbed to the siren song of the herald giant, crushed with an ax the head of the lúpero still snapping at Sofia's shield. The lúpero slumped to the ground in a heap.

The two warriors exchanged nods, panting for air, searching for their next opponents.

They came from above. Winged imuertes, drawn away from the burrows by the sound of battle, screeched and barreled toward Ebrahym. Sofia looked in time to see them strike home, plowing into the catan from behind, the tumbling mass of wings and bodies crashing to the ice and dirt.

"To Ebrahym!" she cried.

The defensive ball of Pax soldiers hollered and cut their way toward the downed Sang. Suddenly, a sphere of light erupted, surrounding Ebrahym's body.

Huge plumes of light burst forth. Ebrahym glowed so hotly Sofia had to look away. The imuertes clamoring over him screeched in agony, recoiling. Ebrahym cut them down as they retreated. His golden eyes burned behind the halo. His blade sang with fury.

It was a gamble, of course. The Sang were powerful, but even their Serrá had limits. Taxed too greatly, their power would be exhausted. Sofia hoped Ebrahym had enough strength remaining as he took to the air once more.

The gamble paid off. Imuertes fled in all directions toward the sanctuary of their burrows, and the wounded pit lurker stood alone. Cut off from its foul kin and sensing its disadvantage, it skittered back on its remaining limbs, lashing out defensively.

Sofia and the remaining Prime Auxilia charged. They roared as one, barreling toward the wicked thing with blades at the ready.

Overhead, Ebrahym called for a spear as he banked wide, gaining speed and altitude before swooping over the Pax toward the last foe standing. He was no longer ablaze, but his voice was deep, a thunderous harmony, beautiful and terrible.

Hektor launched his spear into the air. The Sang caught it as he screamed past. Anayah glanced back and, piecing together the plan, let out a beautiful and terrifying shriek. It was loud and sharp, enough to split a mountain in two.

The sound dazed Sofia as much as it did the pit lurker. Sofia regained her senses in time to see Ebrahym plow into it with the spear, clean through to the earth underneath. Pinned, it hissed and spit as it thrashed violently until seizing up, contorting in agony. Then it was still, whatever foul substance that kept it alive now soaking into the earth.

The tundra was silent once more, disturbed only by the sound of the warriors gasping for air. *We're alive.*

Sofia felt more disbelief than anything. Steam billowed from the scattered corpses, imuerte and oulma alike. The surviving Pax looked at each other, their armor and feathered mantles caked in gore. They exchanged handshakes and solemn gestures of respect and honor. The veterans merely nodded to one another knowingly. The newer Pax laughed with delirious relief, not knowing what else to do.

Among the dead were six of the bravest oulma warriors Sofia knew. In the empty grief, she was proud of them and thankful for what they had done. But it saddened her that she did not know their names.

Save for one.

***

Sofia, Ebrahym, Anayah and the five remaining Prime Auxilia soldiers ran for three days straight before the strength of the oulma gave out.

There was no time to mourn nor tend to the dead. They fled with haste, stripping themselves of heavy armor and supplies. Blades and boots they kept. Each of them carried a new burden that could not be so easily cast aside. Sofia's heaviest of all.

They continued to retreat. The imuertes inched closer, sheltering in unseen refuges during the day as they pursued. It was the only thing that kept them from catching up. But they were close. Sofia smelled them in the air. Their calls echoed in the night.

So, the exhausted and disheartened squad pushed harder each following day to gain ground until collapsing, utterly exhausted. Every Will had a point at which it could push no longer.

The Sanguinir, however, empowered by their halos, endured. They carried on and shuttled the oulma the remainder of the journey by air, while the rest stumbled on as best they could. On the edge of the river where their secret harbor lay, the oulma regrouped and waited for the rest of the squad to join them.

Sofia did not sleep as Anayah carried her. Gliding over the tundra, neither said a word as the icy ground rolled by underwing. There would be a time for words, but it was not now. Sofia could barely look at her. *But I had no choice. I had to kill him.*

She and Anayah were the last to reach the harbor. "Harbor" was a generous word, for the inlet was little more than a small lagoon that held an ancient-looking skiff nestled against a rocky cliff face.

The anchored ship was similar in design to the hulls of the Sang skyships, though this one looked more at home in the still, icy water. Pale canvas sails hung from slanted masts and billowed as the crew set them free. Around the hull, patches of ice covered the turquoise water in places and clung to the mooring lines and railings of the small vessel.

As Anayah descended, Sofia caught sight of the other Pax already on board, tending the rigging and making preparations to leave. Anayah landed on the nearby shore. Sofia's aching body found the earth, her legs enjoying the feeling.

"Are you well?" Anayah asked.

"I'm okay," Sofia said, not knowing what else to say. The guilt hung in her throat. She would be forever different now, though in what way exactly, she didn't know.

Anayah's gold irises revealed nothing, still pools of amber that spared no warmth. The two women said no more to one another and climbed aboard.

On deck, Sofia wondered who looked worse, the other Pax or her. Hektor nursed a vicious slash across his leg. Marta was still standing, along with Estan. His face bore puckered burns of scalding imuertes innards.

Two other veterans, Renato and Tierra, tended to the rigging. Bandages clung tightly to their limbs, but their features were hard and determined—they were no strangers to war.

In all, they left six comrades behind in the frozen mud. The image of Matías' face lingered in Sofia's mind. She recalled the last moment, his face full of hate changing to the desperate look of a lost child. Whatever evil spell had infected him, it had vanished just in time for him to realize his end. To see Sofia was responsible for it. She wished she had said she was sorry, said something. But she hadn't. She'd simply driven the blade deeper.

And so Matías would lie there still, among the dead. For there were no processes in the Orvida for the earth to reclaim flesh. No decay. So, he would remain.

Sofia collapsed on the deck. Hektor looked at her. He wore hate plainly on his face. She'd killed his friend. And no matter what had come over Matías, imuertes spell or otherwise, it was Sofia who had laid him down. Hektor would not forget.

Ebrahym took the helm and cut loose the anchor. He spoke little and only to give orders to the crew as they unfurled the sails and the skiff drifted from the lagoon. The wind picked up and pushed them along toward Luminea.

Days passed without incident. Sofia watched the stillness of the tundra pass by. The boat tacked south toward warmer lands. She turned the fang in her palm absently and waded through her thoughts. Why had the imuertes ceased their charge? Why had Matías gone mad?

Sofia could not shake the feeling of being watched as she'd run him through. Something had wanted to see what she would do, and she had obliged.

27

The funeral was brief and private. Sofia couldn't help but notice the grim irony of attending a memorial ceremony in the afterlife. But here she was, in the presence of the winged Sanguinir, mourning the deaths of the six Prime Auxilia who did not return from the north. It might only have been five, if not for her. Maybe none.

Death, presumably, is what had brought her to the Orvida in the first place. She saw its signs everywhere in the dark corners of the otherwise perfect world. Shadows of mortality left over from the Afore. Even in her own mind, death surrounded her. She seemed incapable of escaping it. She wondered, as the ceremony continued, if Matías and the others somehow found themselves in a better place. But what was left after this? Was there anything?

It was said fallen oulma traveled beyond, to the realm where the Sanctu Arcam led, the mysterious *other side*. The Æfter. But even the wisest of the Sanguinir philosophers did not know for sure. For all they knew, this second chance was the last one anyone ever got.

Sofia brought herself back to the eulogy. A barrel-chested man, thick as an old tree, recited practiced words with reverence. He had recited them many times before. The man was oulma, not Sanguinir, a Prime Auxilia veteran of many centuries and, by the look of him, no stranger to war. He carried his scars with pride.

Castor was his name and he, along with Legatès from the *Altuma Concilia* presided over the ceremony. Other officers and high-ranking veterans of the Pax, adorned with the sigils and medallions of many battles, came to show their respect as well. They wore dress uniforms, brightly embroidered robes marked with plumes of feathers and tassels of rank, and sandals. The finest jewelry adorned their ears and throats. On their faces, two vertical streaks of white paint beneath the eyes—tear stains to honor the fallen.

There were few Sang in attendance. This was a human affair. A soft chorus drifted in the background.

The tombs, such as they were, for no remains resided in them, lay below the streets of Luminea within the Temple of the Dawnlight. The mausoleum was a massive cylinder constructed around the open shaft that connected the inner chamber, where the Dawnlight emerged, to the temple and the heavens above. The concentric rings, intricately carved from stone, encircled the undulating arcs of light. Each ring measured several times Sofia's height. Elaborate railings traced the circumference, and battle standards and flags, swords and honor sashes, and other offerings of memory littered the space.

Then there were the names. On the walls were the names of the dead, etched in the stone over millennia by dedicated masons. There were tens of thousands of names on a single level. Hundreds of thousands, perhaps.

Sofia found the scale of time overwhelming. There were hundreds of centuries of war remembered here. So many names, so much death lying just under the surface of the beautiful streets above. So much for the idea of heaven.

The ceremony concluded. Hands were clasped, knowing nods exchanged. The procession of oulma ascended back to the city proper for a feast to honor the sacrifice of those they bid farewell. Each of the presiding warriors touched the freshly carved names of the fallen, as was tradition. *Ey tolla Serrá, Iriva bes hefecto*, they would say. By their Will, the Way be done.

Sofia lingered behind, kneeling to examine the freshly carved names: *Osias, Andres, Gael, Luna, Julio*—she read them slowly, trying to imagine their faces in her mind.

Matías. She read the name with care. The memory of him came easily. She was back on the frozen tundra once more, grasping the sword of fire in her hands, Matías' look of terror staring back at her. "I'm sorry," Sofia whispered to the stone, gently tracing the letters with her finger.

"Are you?" Hektor said from behind. His eyes were red beneath the unkempt mane of hair that hung about his face. White streaks adorned his face as well, though they looked as if they were smeared by the real thing.

"What?" said Sofia, startled.

"You heard me."

She scowled. "Of course I'm sorry. How could anyone want this?"

"You are clever," Hektor said with a sarcastic grunt. "But while the act might fool the others, even the Sang, it won't fool me. I was *there*. I know what I saw. You have some power over the imuertes, some connection. Matías knew it, and you killed him for it," he choked. "You killed my friend."

Sofia's gut churned. "They poisoned his thoughts," she said, returning her attention to the names. "And *yours*. I tried to…I did what I could. If I hadn't, your name would be on this wall, too, along with the others."

Hektor closed the distance between them, and Sofia stood to meet him face to face. She hadn't meant it as a threat but as a sad fact. Hektor was visibly trembling. She couldn't help but pity him, but she couldn't disagree, either. It *was* her fault, intentional or not.

Even so, wild, forbidden thoughts had plagued her since. *What if I do have some power over the imuertes? Some connection?* Sofia did not linger on the idea for long, not wanting to consider the consequences.

"You don't belong here," Hektor said, pointing at her chest. "Matías saw you for what you really are."

"You have no idea what I really am," Sofia said with a flash of menace. The words came out in a sinister tone and did not feel like her own, but they felt good.

Her skin began to prickle with anger. Hektor stood firm, though Sofia could see the hesitation in his eyes. *Fear.*

"Sofia," Ebrahym interrupted, appearing from deeper within the tomb. The Sang wore a red tunic and an empty expression. "It is time." Sofia nodded and left Hektor standing by the memorial, fists clenched, alone.

***

"That is all?" the Sanguinir scribe asked as she scribbled into a thick tome. Faelyrn was her name, an Eagle, a lorekeeper. A white hood covered her head and face, and an intricate tattoo decorated her chin. Her slender fingers were a blur as she transcribed without peering down. Occasionally her wings twitched in time to match her pace.

"Yes, for the third time," said Sofia, recounting the details of the mission again. Reliving the pain over and over left her numb, and the words were losing meaning. Matías was becoming less of a person. Just a thing that happened, a name etched on a wall.

Sofia sighed heavily, gazing out the open windows nearby as the afternoon transformed into evening.

After the service, Ebrahym had led her back to the Sanguinir quarter of the city where her fellow soldiers were already recounting the events to the official scribes. Sofia gathered there were bigger things in motion now. She'd heard the rumors floating around the marble halls like incense since their return. The threat was real.

The Choir of the Lion, the warrior sect of the Sanguinir, were petitioning for Eros Terafiq to be elected *Hierarca*, Hierarch.

Not since the siege of Ilucenta had there been a Hierarch, for only in desperate times was a Sang appointed to control both the entire Host and the Prime Auxilia. The High Council was wary. They would not hand over power lightly. *But why not trust the Sang?* Sofia often wondered. The reasons were deeper than the fall of Ilucenta. Something else had happened long ago, something terrible to cause such paranoia. Anayah had almost let it slip once. And Ebrahym, too, always cautious not to reveal too much. Whatever it was, there was no record of it.

"Let us return to the moment when you disobeyed Catan Ebrahym's orders," said Faelyrn. If there was an ulterior motive to her question, her dark complexion and regal features did not reveal it.

Sofia shifted in her stiff chair. "I told you already. I thought if I distracted the imuertes, the vanguard would have a chance to link up with the rest of us. I wanted to save them. I had to try."

The emotion was lost on the Sang. "By your account, the imuertes ceased their assault. They held back, quote, 'as if something was controlling them,'" Faelyrn said.

"Yes."

The Sanguinir scribbled again. "And you know not the reason for this?"

"No."

"I see. And that is when," said Faelyrn, referring to her meticulous notes, "Matías, of the Prime Auxilia, took up arms against you, supposedly under some kind of imuertes influence."

"I'm not sure what caused it," Sofia admitted. Her hands kneaded one another. "One minute he was himself, the next, completely mad. I was forced to defend myself. I had no choice."

"And thus, you ended his life, committing desipar." Faelyrn seemed to struggle even uttering the phrase. Sofia affirmed with a nod. "And the imuertes did not...interfere with this?" Sofia shook her head.

"What does it mean?"

The Sang place her quill on the table. Her dark skin gleamed like oil, her eyes a brilliant shade of autumn leaves, narrow and searching.

"*Desipar* has long been thought impossible. The Orvida does not easily change, as you know. It takes Serrá to achieve the simplest aims: plow the field, fell the tree, forge the sword. Slaying the imuertes requires much more. Such is the Way of things. But for one oulma to destroy another," the Sang paused, choosing her words. "*That* takes incredible conviction. To violate the fundamental laws of the Divine Sphere is to counter our entire way of life. Since the Divine Sphere was created, there has been only one other time..." She let the words hang and watched Sofia, gauging her reaction.

Sofia fought to keep her temper in check. "Matías was *not* oulma then," she said. "Somehow, he became like them. I can't explain it, but the man we knew was gone. I did the only thing I could."

"Did you ever threaten him?" Faelyrn asked sharply. Sofia eyed her interrogator and considered her words. The animosity between her and Matías was no secret. She wondered what they were really trying to get at.

"We often disagreed," Sofia said, finally. The Sanguinir studied her for a moment, her golden gaze seeking signs of falsehood. Appearing satisfied, Faelyrn dismissed her, compiling her notes as Sofia left.

Ebrahym was waiting for her outside of the small, stone room. The two walked through the columned corridors, their bodies breaking up the last rays of light from the setting sun that flooded the halls. They kept their voices low.

"Have you slept?" Ebrahym asked.

"No." It had been fourteen days since her last nightmare. With everything that had happened, she was afraid what new evil might come to her in the darkness.

"I believe you, Sofia," Ebrahym said. "I told them as such that you are no murderer. I cannot explain what happened with the imuertes, for never in all my centuries have I experienced its like before. Matías was not himself, no longer the oulma we knew..."

"I disobeyed orders," Sofia said.

"Yes." Ebrahym hesitated, internal conflict showing plainly on his face. "But, perhaps...perhaps the Way is not always clear to us. Yours was a brave decision, Sofia, one I would admit I might have made myself if our positions were reversed. But when I saw you facing certain death..."

"Yes?"

"I, too, felt compelled to act, no matter the cost. Almost as if I had no control over it..." Ebrahym seemed to drift inward at the words. There was more confusion than affection in his voice, and Sofia wondered for the first time if Sanguinir could feel the same way oulma did.

"So what happens now?" Sofia asked after a moment's pause.

"The Host prepares for war. You have undoubtedly heard rumors of a new Hierarch. Terafiq will call, and we will answer. As for you," Ebrahym paused, "I cannot lie to you, Sofia."

"I know."

"There are growing suspicions about you, both within the Host and without." He hesitated. "I admit, I once had similar thoughts. But now I feel, I *know*, that you have an important role to play here and that you are not the enemy. I have not forgotten the debt I owe you." He squeezed her shoulder. "Whatever may come, I will honor my promise to help you."

Sofia smiled. Ebrahym did not have the look of the hardened warrior she'd seen in the field; his look was wise and soft. There was love there, though not the kind between lovers. More like family. It was somehow familiar, simple, like a memory of something experienced in a previous life. And for the first time since returning from the lonely north, Sofia was warm again.

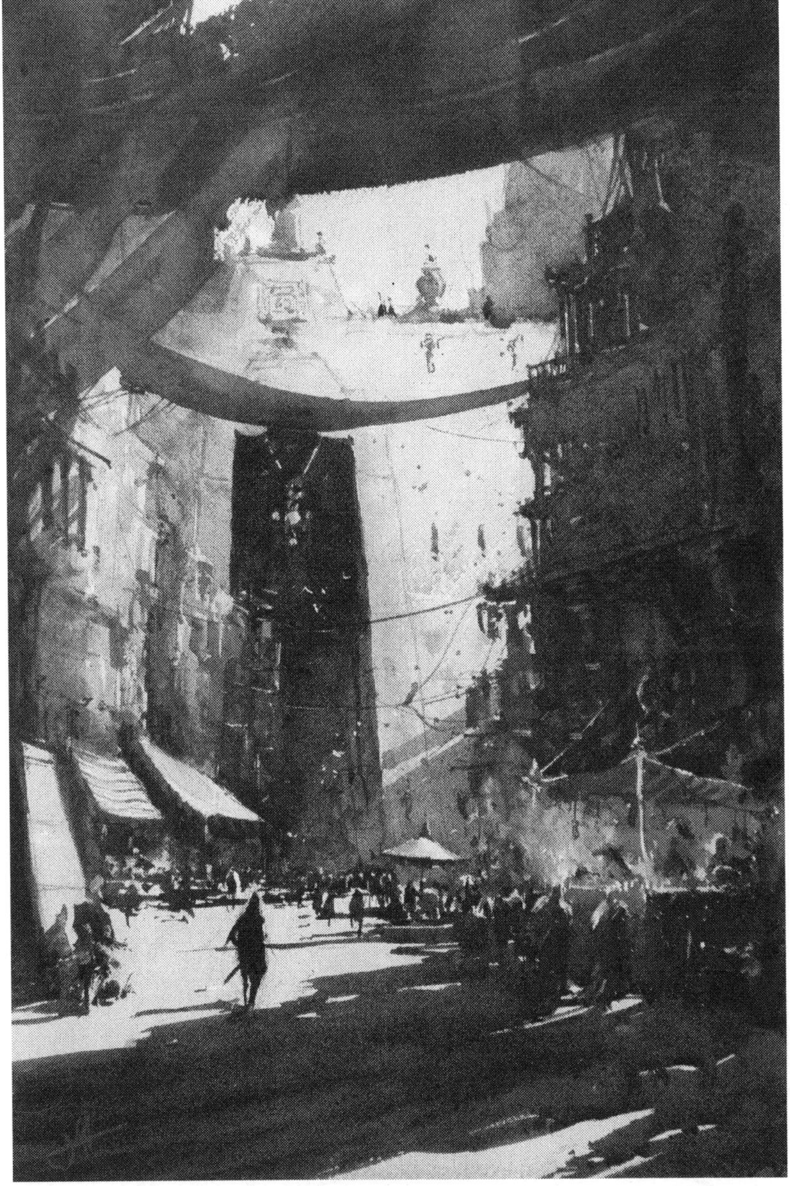

28

Sofia sat on the old mattress, gently caressing her swollen belly. There was a figure before her, but she dared not meet its eyes and kept her own fixed on the grungy floor.

It spoke to her. Cryptic whispers in a language she did not understand scolded her. Accused her. She said nothing, trying only to focus on the growing life within her.

The stranger in the room shouted and unleashed his rage on the cheap furniture. Candles stacked upon the nightstand shattered, and shards of glass scattered across the worn carpet. She prayed. She knew not the words, but the feeling was there, asking for help that would not come.

The thing was inches from her face now, urging Sofia to look at it, but she would not. She couldn't. She ran to the corner of the room, but the dark form was on top of her. Hands like hot iron clamps seized her throat. Oh, God, how they burned, even as her lungs began to scream for air and the smell of her own melting skin filled her senses. Darkness crept over her as she thrashed in angry desperation.

In her last moment, Sofia's eyes snapped open to meet her attacker. She had to see it, had to face it. She had to face *him*. Deep green eyes stared fiercely back at her. The eyes were like her own, brilliant emeralds in a pit of coal, yet they were surrounded by such grotesqueness Sofia could only describe it as more beast than man, with huge, adorned horns and skin like ash-covered embers.

Upon its forehead, the symbol—the V with a slash through it—burning red hot, like a fracture in the earth revealing the hot innards inside. The creature smiled, its cracked lips splitting fire and blood. It whispered one word from beyond the void.

Espen.

The word shuddered through her like a vile current. Darkness came, reality blurred to nothing, and the last ounce of life left her body. Sofia slumped to the floor.

She shot upright in her bed with a shriek, instinctively reaching for the blade under the pillow and slashing at the empty air. Blood smeared her sheets and covered her hands; her own nails had punctured the flesh of her palms as she'd slept, fists clenched in fear.

She put a bloody hand to her throat. It throbbed with heat. *It burned me. Nothing can burn me...* In panic, Sofia pulled her aching body to the edge of the bed where a small bowl sat next to the window. The shades were drawn tight. Cool water helped wash away the nightmares, and she soon returned to the world. Outside, it was not yet dawn along the waterfront.

She pulled her hair, damp with sweat, back behind her ears and clutched her knees. It had started a few days after returning from the mission, when she'd finally succumbed to sleep, the weariness of body and spirit too much to bear any longer.

Since then, the dreams had begun to change. Something was different since the encounter with the imuertes. Something inside. It was in the air and under her skin. The nightmares were increasingly slipping into the real world. Strange bruises scattered her body, and illegible nonsense was scratched onto the walls and table near her bed, written by her without her knowing.

At her bedside was a leather journal, bound with a strap. The lúpero fang was tucked beneath the cord.

She unraveled the binding and added another entry to describe the latest nightmare. Only recently had her role in the dream changed from attacker to victim. She was not the killer anymore. Now, she watched herself die, night after night, at the hands of a monster.

Perhaps they are just dreams after all? Maybe she was not the murderer she thought she was. Maybe the imuertes had some peculiar, previously unknown effect on the oulma: the power to manipulate dreams.

Her thoughts drifted back to the pregnant woman. *Me.* Sofia touched her abdomen, recalling the sensation of life growing inside of her. It seemed as real as the bed she sat on. *Did I have a child once?*

She felt as if she were the center of some cruel drama unfolding for a sick audience. She thumbed idly through the book, notes and scribbles covering the pages. Some were covered edge to edge with disturbing sketches of the dark form that haunted her. Drafted in dark, heavy lines, its crudely drawn figure glared from the page. She was no artist, but even the rough approximation of the thing that haunted her was enough to make her skin crawl and nausea creep into her throat.

She tossed the book aside in frustration, put on some clothes, including a scarf to conceal her burned neck, and closed the door to her room behind her. It was green and covered with gold-colored vines. She thudded down the winding stairs in her heavy boots, flight after flight, passing dozens of other doors as she did. Each was numbered and decorated differently, all personal reflections of the oulma who lived there. In every window, paper animals hung from string and danced as she passed. At the bottom of the stairs was the parlor, a small communal eating space packed with tables and chairs.

"Sleep well?" Paola asked. Like a mother hen, she cared for the building as if it were her own coop, the tenants her chicks. The parlor was small but covered in fresh flowers, even on the ceiling, and their aroma intermingled with the smell of coffee.

"Not particularly."

"Bad dream, I take it?" Paolo threw her thick, knotted locks over her shoulder. They jingled with beads and were littered with colored feathers like some kind of nest.

Sofia nodded, taking the steaming cup from Paola in both hands. It, too, was handmade and covered with intricate, square glyphs. She took a sip. Hot and bitter with a hint of cherries and childish wonder. Paolo had a knack for it. "Does the word Espen mean anything to you, Paola?" she asked, taking another drink.

Paola crinkled her caramel brow for a moment and waved a hand. "Not that I can remember. But I'm no good with names. Now faces," she beamed widely, "*faces* I can remember for a thousand years. I could recognize an oulma I met one time while drunk at a Century's End millennia ago but couldn't tell you half the names of the oulma living here," she waved above her head, laughing at the idea. "Espen, hmm? Man or woman?"

A weak smile escaped from Sofia's stony mask. She rubbed her eyes. "I'm not sure."

Paola shrugged. "Probably been hundreds of Espens at one time or another. Sounds like one of those names that might be common. Not like Sofia, a much rarer breed." She winked and forced another smile from Sofia.

Paola made her think of what mothers were like. She was a shepherd through and through, and had found her calling helping wayward oulma like Sofia find their way. It was strange how many ways the human mind dealt with forever.

"Chin up, Sofia," Paola said, refilling her cup. "If someone's worth knowing, you'll run into them eventually."

Sofia said goodbye and left Paola's place behind. It was a towering patchwork of windows and brightly painted balconies only now tasting the morning sun. Overhead, gulls were beginning their loud routine.

As Sofia meandered along the pier, navigating between the sailors and fisherman preparing for another day of doing what they loved to do, she thought again what the darkness had whispered to her. *Espen.* Frustrated, she stuffed her hands in her pockets and meandered aimlessly down the ancient wooden dock.

"Wind will be easterly today," one sailor said to another as Sofia passed behind them. The two men, willingly bronzed by the sun but heartily handsome, hunched over a map as cups of tea steamed into the cool morning air. Sweet pipe smoke filtered from their little conclave.

"Aye, let's stay clear of the channel. No sense fighting the current," said the other.

Sofia glanced at the map lying between the two men. On it were the names of hundreds of landmarks, villages, towns and other settlements of all different types. She wondered if Espen was not a person after all. *Could Espen be a place?*

"Excuse me," she asked. She feigned a sweet smile and asked where the fishing was best.

The fishermen, glad to talk trade, were all too happy to show off their vast knowledge of the Aecuna and its hidden gems. As they explained, Sofia scanned the map. A small, faded star marked a location on the map to the northeast with a scrawled label that caught her attention. *Espleña*. She had read the name before in passing, but only now recognized the similarity.

"This place," Sofia asked, pointing to name on the map. "Espleña. What is there?"

"What's that? Oh, Espleña. Nothing to catch there. No, you'd want to turn north for a few days..." one of the fishermen began as if telling a fable to a wide-eyed child. The wooden pipe hanging from his mouth worked fiercely.

"Tell me about Espleña," Sofia said, hiding her impatience. But the desperation in her eyes was true. "Please."

The fisherman dredged up the memory. "Espleña. Let's see. Not much of note, truth be told. A small town, if you could call it that, on the other far shore of the Aecuna. Many weeks by sail. We stop there sometimes to resupply or ferry visitors to Luminea proper. Small that it is, those who live there seem to like it that way. A little quieter than the hustle and bustle here," the sailor nodded upward toward the spires of Luminea.

Something didn't fit. "Was it always called Espleña? Was it ever known by any other name?" Sofia asked.

"Eh?" The man's tanned flesh furrowed under his leather cap. He tugged at his heavy, carved earrings. "Yes, come to think of it. Oh, what was it again—?"

"Espen," said the other. "It was called Espen, once. Long before our time. Forgive my comrade—he has the memory of minnow." The two men laughed.

"Espen," Sofia whispered. "Did something happen there?"

"Imuertes," the fisherman said soberly. He spat as he did. "During the last war, it was caught in the wake of the horde. But the Sang held it, they did, thank the Dawnlight. It was renamed after the victory. Now *that* was a party! Oh, it's been centuries since I've thought of that night. Those Sang put on this show where they flew in the air with colored fire in their hands. I met this beautiful red-haired woman —"

Sofia had stopped listening. Espen. Ilucenta. Even in the timeless hereafter, it seemed, history found ways to repeat itself.

Her mind raced as she thudded down the wooden pier, leaving the fishermen to their stories. Something wasn't right; she could feel it. If the imuertes were descending from the northwest, as reconnaissance indicated, then Espleña lay directly in their path. *Could the town be in danger?*

Sofia hadn't considered the possibility that her dreams might be *premonitions* of something coming. But then again, why would she? The visions seemed like memories, but perhaps she was looking at the whole thing sideways. Perhaps she was not as powerless in all of this as it seemed. Was she somehow seeing into the world of the enemy? If it was possible that she somehow intercepted information about the enemy's next move, she had to act.

Sofia sprinted through the streets of Luminea, dodging yawning oulma as they meandered sleepily through the avenues. She raced through the Market Strand as the shopkeepers set up their stalls for another day of barter, rushing by them with their occasional complaint.

Within half an hour, Sofia was climbing the steep steps to the Fifth Tier and the Sanguinir citadels. Above, Sanguinir forms darted between the towers. She wondered how she might explain the premonition in a way in which any Sang would believe her. Then again, she only needed to convince one.

"I cannot let you pass," said the female sentry, a beautiful Sanguinir warrior with silky blond hair and pale skin. Her cheeks were studded with blue gems. She and her counterpart stood watch at the entrance to the inner sanctum, a series of courtyards and chambers reserved only for the Sanguinir elite.

"I have a message for Terafiq," Sofia said.

"I know who you are," the guard replied. The dual harmonies of her voice vibrated with annoyance. "If you have a message for the *Eros* Terafiq, deliver it to me, and I will see that she gets it."

Though she could trust the Sang's word, there was no time to waste. "Forget it," Sofia said.

She followed the wall until it turned a corner, and she disappeared behind it, following the perimeter until finding a scalable scaffolding out of sight of the guards.

Sofia leaped onto scaffolding, moving fast up the rigging to a terrace above. Her hands began to sweat as she climbed higher, and the dizziness returned. Breathing slowly, Sofia focused on her objective. The holds were firm and plenty, thanks to the heavy ornamentation on the architecture, and within minutes, Sofia was up and over a terrace railing and inside.

It was a familiar sight. Stone columns supporting rotund, ornamented dome ceilings.

She slunk through the corridors of marble, hiding her form between columns as passing Sanguinir strolled the halls. She headed to the primary chambers, or at least, where she thought they might be.

As she turned the corner, however, Sofia came face to face with Ebrahym, his sudden appearance triggering Sofia's honed reflexes. She lashed out instinctively. The solitary Sanguinir deflected the strike with ease.

"Sofia? What are you doing here?" Ebrahym whispered, surprised. He glanced around and shuffled Sofia into a nearby antechamber that overlooked a courtyard teeming with bright foliage. The sun was just beginning to warm the buds, and they yawned open to collect its warmth.

"I need to talk to Terafiq," Sofia said, not knowing quite where to start. "I think an attack is coming."

"An attack? How can you know this? We have received no such warning."

"It was a dream. No, it was more than that. I saw...something," she shuddered. "It whispered something to me. Espen. I had never heard it before but saw it on a map this morning. Espleña. Ebrahym, it's directly south of burrows we discovered. They are coming."

"Sofia..." Ebrahym said.

"Listen to me!" She pulled her thick scarf down, revealing her burned and bruised neck. The Sang peered at her through narrow slits of amber. "These are not just dreams. I can't explain it, but I *know* something is happening soon, and it's happening at Espleña."

29

Drums echoed through the Fifth Tier. Trumpets blared, calling the congregation of Sanguinir warriors to present themselves for inspection. The expansive courtyards teemed with decorated, winged figures in swaths of red. Incense burned fiercely in the air.

Packs of oulma squires and attendants buzzed around each winged warrior, tending to their armor and preparing them for war. Over the finest robes of heavy silk, the oulma strapped thick layers of polished metal to the Sang's massive bodies, swords to their hips, and shields to their backs. By the end, there was little flesh left to be seen.

Sofia had never seen the Choirs fully mobilized. They were like gods making ready to descend to the mortal realm.

Their fellow Sang, artisans from the Choir of the Stag, were busy decorating the wings of their brothers and sisters with painted glyphs, adorning their battle gear with plumes of colored feathers, bejeweled garlands and ribbons. Heavy standards towered over each Sang warrior, banners that depicted their aurolas' legacies and deeds throughout the centuries.

Sofia helped strap the golden plates to Anayah's back, cinching the thick leather straps that held the gilded armor together. The flutes of her carapace curved gracefully toward the sky. The breastplate was narrow at the waist, accentuating Anayah's feminine form with exquisite adornments. At the joints, colored fabrics embroidered with gold showed through.

To say it was ornate was an understatement, but having nothing but time, craftsmen in Luminea achieved wondrous things. There was no thought of concealment or camouflage with this kind of battle gear. Such armor was designed to meet one's foe head on—and for them to see one coming.

Sofia sensed a distinct difference in the way Anayah carried herself. Even more of her youthful moxie had been replaced by a regal calmness. She was distant, almost in perpetual awe, like someone seeing a brilliant night sky for the first time. Sofia handed her the plumed helmet, and Anayah slid it over her head, her fierce eyes burning from the shadowed slit.

"You haven't spoken about it," said Anayah as she cinched a bracer to her forearm.

"About what?" Sofia feigned.

"About what happened in the north. With Matías. We have barely spoken since then. I know you blame yourself for what happened. And now," Anayah gestured to the mustering soldiers around them, "and now, we go to war."

"I'm fine," Sofia said, threading the line that held two leg pieces of armor together and drawing them tight. "What happened, happened. I can't change that. But maybe I can do something to help make it right."

"With these visions of yours?" Anayah asked.

Sofia tightened a strap harder than she needed to. "You don't believe me, either?"

Anayah took Sofia's hands in hers. "I did not say that. I have heard what some are saying about you, Sofia. Do not listen to them." Sofia nodded.

"You are one of the Host, wings or not." Anayah slid a sword into the scabbard, and it clicked, locking the hilt in place. "Without your warning, we might not have had time to assemble. Espleña is a few days away by wing, but we should get there in time."

"*If* I'm right. It's hard to be sure of anything anymore."

"In either case, make no mistake, Sofia. We will triumph." Anayah flashed a confident smile, a reflection of her former self.

"I know," said Sofia, securing the last piece of armor in place and clapping Anayah on the back. The Eagle priests clustered around Anayah, anointing her with the elemental offerings. Sprinkles of dust and water, smoke from the incense and fire from sacred torches signaled the completion of the ritual.

Sofia looked at her friend with pride as the hooded Eagles did their work. It was surprising how fast the Host had assembled after Ebrahym delivered Sofia's warning to Eros Terafiq. It was surprising that the Eros had listened to her at all. Whether Sofia was making it up seemed unimportant if it served Terafiq's ambition to rally the entire army to her call.

"Anayah?" Ebrahym called out. Sofia turned to see the catan fully adorned in elaborate armor of his own, though it was hewn with harder, masculine curves. A burst of plumage emanated from behind his helmet that gave the appearance of rays of light exploding forth from it. Bright-colored sashes flickered in the breeze, and his long red cloak kicked up dust as he walked.

Anayah nodded curtly. "Yes, Catan. I am prepared."

"Good," said Ebrahym. Sofia exchanged a knowing nod with Anayah as Ebrahym led Sofia by the arm away from the warriors, out of earshot. The heavy sound of his footsteps and the groaning of his armor made him seem like a giant. "I know you wish you were coming with us," he whispered.

"You know I can help."

"The High Council and Terafiq agreed that you should not be involved. They take great risk deploying so many of us away from the city. Given the unknown nature of your...connection with the imuertes, they thought it wise to keep you from the battle. If there is one."

"Because of what happened with Matías?"

"If you can indeed hear them, we cannot know for sure they cannot hear you. Even now, the enemy may know we are coming."

"But that's why you need me," said Sofia. "I'm not sure how or why the imuertes stopped the charge or how I know the things I do. But maybe I can help." She stared deep into his golden eyes and thought back to the cave when they'd first met. How long ago it seemed. "I'm not afraid."

"I know," he said with a heavy, armored hand on her shoulder. "But I am." Sofia could feel the energy pulsing between his fingers.

He turned away and called out to the Sanguinir warriors to assemble, and at his command, they formed in tight, orderly lines. Behind the ranks of winged figures, the Pax soldiers formed regiments prepared to ascend the rope ladders to the skyships tethered above.

"May the winds be with you on this day, my brothers and sisters. My lions!" Ebrahym called out to the warriors. The drums went silent and his powerful voice carried far.

"Ivá!" cried out the warriors in harmony.

Ebrahym struck his spear against the stone with a clang. Then again. The warriors soon followed suit, and the beating grew louder. The drums joined in the chorus and the hymn resumed. "Chance has given us an opportunity to strike at the enemy. No longer are we at their mercy, no longer in their shadow. By the Dawnlight, you will answer this call with fury!"

"Ivá!" The pounding din of metal upon stone continued. Louder now.

"Make no mistake. Our Serrá shall be tested today. The Sphaera Divinia challenged. But we will not let it yield."

"Ivá!"

"We will not let it falter."

"Ivá!"

"BY OUR WILL!" Ebrahym called out like a crack of thunder.

"THE WAY BE DONE!" the army called back.

Sofia watched as the Sanguinir catan snapped his wings open, and scores of Sanguinir warriors followed suit in perfect unison. They leaped from the ground and into the air as one, trumpets once again calling as they pumped their wings and took to the sky. Tears welled uncontrollably in Sofia's eyes at the sight.

The Pax soldiers, desperate to keep up with their Sanguinir comrades, scurried up the thick rope ladders to the skyships with the precision of an orchestra. The ladders retracted into the hulls soon after. One by one, the skyships caught the breeze and yawned northward in slow pursuit of the Sang flock heading to war.

Sofia imagined Ebrahym and Anayah soaring toward danger, a crusade based on nothing more than a dream. Perhaps a fantasy. Behind them, scores of Prime Auxilia soldiers, not unlike the ones left dead in the freezing mud to the north, followed faithfully.

So many lives, such as they were, hinged on Sofia's convictions. She wondered if she would see any of them again.

I can't sit here and do nothing. She paced around the dusty courtyard, hands on her hips, weighing the options. She eyed the last of the skyship fleet drifting lazily above, still tethered to the spiraling towers. Some were still tied to their anchors, wooden propellers not yet in motion.

There's still time.

Sofia blazed through the winding streets, up the many flights of stairs that spiraled up the great spires. The last of the skyships would depart any minute. She would not let them leave without her.

She dashed past robed figures and colored glass windows until emerging onto a small terrace, high above the streets below. Her nausea caught up to her at the sight, and she steadied herself with a few quick breaths.

Bridges made of wood planks and rope fanned out in every direction, each one attached to the belly of an unguarded skyship. A wave of relief washed over her. *I can make it.* But before she took a step onto the gangplank, a powerful voice stopped her cold.

"That would be a mistake." It was Terafiq. Sofia turned to face the Sang, who was more terrifyingly beautiful than Sofia remembered. The giant of a woman towered over her encased in a golden shell of colored fabrics and gems that reflected blinding sunlight. Her helmet rose to a graceful peak, with long braids exiting the back, woven with jewelry and fabrics.

"There is no place for you there." Terafiq nodded to the distance. "As much as you may want it to be so, you are not of the Host nor the Prime Auxilia."

Sofia clenched her fists in defiance. "No, I'm not."

Terafiq let out a boisterous cackle. "I like you, girl. Since first we met. You remind me of myself an eon ago. I told Bethuel such. Strong in spirit and decent with a blade, and a you have a hard head. But I have made mistakes before. Despite our likeness, there is a difference between you and me, is there not?"

Sofia avoided the hawkish glare. "I don't know."

"Of course, you do. The darkness. It calls to you, comforts you when you lay your head to rest. It is part of you. I can practically smell it." The Eros leaned in close. "You may think yourself noble, playing soldier, thinking you wish to protect the city, to serve, to sacrifice. But this is a lie." Sofia chewed on her lip and trembled. She felt the anger rising. "For your heart calls for something else, out there, in the shadows."

"If you think that, why keep me here? Why let me into the Conventa? Why not just kill me?"

"Kill you?" Terafiq laughed again. "Even if I could, I do not wish to kill you. The light needs a little darkness to shine all the brighter. Though your part in this crusade may be over soon enough, I suppose I owe you thanks."

"For what?" Sofia asked.

Terafiq waved an armored hand. "For *this*. Without your warning, I might not have swayed the Council to act. And you slaying an oulma while under an imuertes spell—fear is a powerful motivator, is it not? You may prove to be the one thing we needed to stir us from our complacency, enough to take the fight to the enemy."

"I thought the consensus was I was some kind of traitor," said Sofia.

Terafiq shrugged. "That does not mean you cannot be useful. Besides, when Ebrahym and the Host return, we shall know once and for all."

Sofia sensed the finality in Terafiq's tone, for the Sang could only tell the truth. "Know what?" Sofia asked.

"Whether we can trust you," Terafiq said, a smile creeping about her chiseled face. "Or not."

30

Wails of pain echoed through the corridors in both the common and Sanguinir tongues, the latter, melodies of agony.

The hymns of the Host, normally drifting through the Fifth Tier, filling the temples and monuments with uplifting harmonies, were absent. Screams replaced them.

Sofia stirred from her meditation. The small quarters she shared with several other Sanguinir servants and squires came to life, called to attention by the noise. The oulma, who had begun their service hundreds of years ago, scrambled to their feet. Sofia had wondered during her short stay among them if some were happy spending their existence serving others. Perhaps it suited them, or perhaps they simply didn't know what else to do.

In either case, the oulma roused and dressed in a flurry, and she followed them, hurrying down twisting stairs toward the source of the shouting.

Through carved portholes, she could see the shapes of Sanguinir warriors struggling to maintain flight against the backdrop of stars. Even at a distance, she could see that most of the warriors flew in pairs, carrying motionless forms between them, eagles clutching limp kills. A pit in her stomach tightened. *Could one of those lifeless forms be Anayah? Or Ebrahym?*

She scrambled down the stairs and followed the growing mob of oulma into the great courtyard, already transformed into both landing zone and field hospital.

Sanguinir were scattered across the square, having collapsed where they had landed. Some were still smoldering and slick with imuertes gore. Around the downed warriors, the oulma scrambled to erect torches and light braziers. They brought water and carted medical herbs, poultices and bandages from the deeper stores of the barracks.

Sofia was momentarily paralyzed by the scene, unable to see how she might be of use. The smell of sulfur overwhelmed her and made her guts revolt. She wandered aimlessly through the chaos, trying to decide what to do. In some ways, she feared battle far less than this.

The dissonant wails of the Sang disturbed her. She had always known the stoic warriors as unbreakable, noble and resolute as carved granite. Seeing their frailty, their *fear*... She scanned the injured and bleeding warriors, darting between them as groups of more capable oulma than she did their work, hoping none of their contorted, bloody forms were those of her friends.

A hand grasped her ankle as she walked by, startling her with its energy.

"Save us...save...us," the Sanguinir sputtered just before passing out. Half of his once-beautiful face was shredded, black and greasy in the torchlight. Sofia had to turn away as the light reflected off the bone of his cheek. His armor, polished and glistening not a day before, was now a twisted, scorched mass of slag, still sizzling with heat. All gallantry and glory burned away. What was left was a shadow of the Afore; pain, blood, suffering. These were the things they were supposed to be free from. Now it had found them here.

Instinct kicked in, and Sofia found her resolve. She grabbed a nearby knife. She recalled her first encounter with Ebrahym—how long ago that was. She knew the armor's attachments inside and out now, thanks to her training, and worked quickly to slice apart the straps and buckles. An oulma woman, her steaming arms covered in blood and black ichor, mirrored Sofia's movements. They nodded to one another as they pulled off the chest piece and the skin that would not be parted from it like the stubborn bark of a tree. The Sang wailed in terror once more. Tossing the armor aside, Sofia gaped in horror at the man's chest.

Burned into the skin was the symbol from her dreams; the V with a horizontal intersection across it, blackened and charred.

The brand was deep, somehow burned *under* the armor. A wave of sickness washed over Sofia, and she retched uncontrollably at the sight of it. A throng of oulma descended on the body in a flurry, applying salves and healing herbs as Sofia tried to gain control over herself. *What does it mean?*

She felt a weak hand reach out to find hers as she swallowed deep breaths to steady herself. The Sang clung desperately to consciousness, his one, good eye wide with fear as he pulled Sofia close, the flame of a single candle struggling against the darkness.

"He lives. He lives. He lives." Blood gurgled from the corner of his mouth as he spoke. His wings were splattered with it and partially obliterated by fire.

"Who?" Sofia whispered into the Sanguinir's ear. "Who did this?"

"Angorzhu," the warrior sputtered. "Angorzhu lives."

The name hit Sofia like a strike to the throat, stealing her breath. It was like the dark whisper of the imuertes was concentrated and shoved down her throat, into her nose, her eyes and ears.

She slumped as a pack of oulma carried the warrior away to the makeshift surgery tables nearby. Shock clouded her mind. Dizzy, she was trapped, like in one of her nightmares. Time slowed. Screams and pathetic wails drifted through the air. The Sanguinir had brought something back with them; she could feel its potent aura all around. It lingered on the bodies, living and still, and befouled the beautiful city with its presence.

She stumbled through the camp, intoxicated, trying to get clear air to breathe. But she couldn't escape the choking sensation. It was a symptom of some greater evil threatening to devour them all.

Out of the corner of one eye, Sofia saw Ebrahym touch down across the courtyard. In tow was another figure, and Sofia fought back tears as she recognized the helmetless warrior Ebrahym and his fellow Sang carried.

Anayah.

Sofia sprinted, bellowing for help, catching her friend in her arms as Ebrahym fell to his knees, exhausted. He appeared to have aged a century in the span of a week. Beautiful sigils and feathers were caked in mud and filth.

"Is she alive?" Sofia asked, desperately checking Anayah's body for hidden trauma. She stripped off the helmet, marred by claws or blades, to reveal Anayah's face, splattered with gore and burns. "Ebrahym! Is she alive?"

Ebrahym nodded heavily. Sofia found blood on her hands from Anayah's scalp, but her breathing was steady and deep. Sofia called for help until her voice cracked with grief. The oulma healers came and stripped off the Sang's armor, revealing more wounds underneath.

Sofia could do nothing but cradle Anayah's head and tend strands of damp hair from her face.

Ebrahym waved off the healers from buzzing around him, marshaling himself to his feet. Sofia understood that though weary beyond imagination, the catan needed to appear strong. Proud and defiant, Ebrahym began to shout orders and direct the aid efforts. Sofia could see the truth, however. A desperate sorrow wore on his face, deepening the shadows of his features.

"Ebrahym, what happened? What happened?" Sofia asked, tears still streaming down her face, still clutching Anayah's body in desperation.

"It was him," Ebrahym said, his look distant. "The Fierno has shown himself, Sofia. Angorzhuatli. Angorzhu, the Hell Lord, has risen. And he was waiting for us."

***

The High Council and its Legatès called for an emergency session in the wake of the Battle of Espleña—or massacre, as it was being called—and once again Sofia found herself in their presence.

The blood was still wet and the wounded were still arriving, and the High Council was already looking for someone to blame, someone to call traitor.

The twelve Legatès and the Quato Eros, stood in grim vigil over the hasty proceedings. Oulma and Sang alike wore garments that betrayed their station, unadorned and unceremonious. This was no time for ritual and protocol.

At their feet, Ebrahym sat in the chair Sofia had once occupied. White cotton and bandages had replaced golden armor plates. His wings were tattered and still bore the stains of battle. They hung heavy behind him, rising and falling with his breath.

Terafiq paced before him. The only sound was her heavy footsteps upon stone. Sofia could not remember seeing the Eros in anything less than full battle armor, but tonight she wore modest robes of cream and white.

Terafiq nodded to Ebrahym as he cleared his throat, shifted uncomfortably and described the mission in detail.

The Host had arrived at Espleña with no sign of the enemy, he explained. Defensive preparations made and scouts dispatched, the Sang warriors had searched for signs of the imuertes. It wasn't until the sun had set that the enemy had shown its face, and when it had, it'd crashed into the town like a tidal wave, drowning it in a deluge of nightmares and horror.

Sofia could barely contain herself as he spoke. *What have I done? I led them into a trap.*

"We were completely outnumbered," Ebrahym recalled. "Fifty to one at least. And the imuertes were clever, organized. Never have I seen them act in that way—anticipating our attacks, probing our defenses, taking advantage of our weakness. What we saw at Espleña was no random horde, it was an army."

"Go on," ordered Terafiq.

Ebrahym nodded. "Cavalry of beasts eroded our flanks, exposing us to assault from the front. Our only choice was to defend the town proper and try to funnel the enemy. We garrisoned as best we could, but their numbers overwhelmed us. The Pax were..." Ebrahym drifted back to the battle, Sofia could see it in his eyes.

He continued. "They were cut down like wheat to the scythe. We held as long as we could to allow the oulma to escape to the few boats and set sail as the city burned around us. But, to my shame, many were left behind." Ebrahym hung his head, and Sofia knew he carried the failure heavily upon himself.

Terafiq seemed unfazed by the recounting. "They were organized, you said, ser Ebrahym," asked Terafiq. "How?"

Ebrahym took a deep breath, raising his chin dutifully once more. "Angorzhuatli, he is called. Angorzhu. The Fierno." The Council members and the Sanguinir Eros whispered to one another. Terafiq raised a hand and silenced them. For once, the Legatès did not question her authority.

Ebrahym went on. "The horde was chanting his name in a dozen different tongues. The Hell Lord revealed himself and personally led the charge, then overwhelmed us. He is a myth no longer." Sofia's head began to swim.

Terafiq's eyebrow rose with interest. *Or was it excitement?* "Tell me of him." Sofia got the sense Terafiq already knew what he was about to tell her.

Ebrahym took a breath. "A man mixed with the visage of a grotesque ram, skin like smoldering coals. Black smoke follows him like death. Tall and broad, he is gilded pridefully from head to hoof and shakes the ground upon which he walks. Banners of a cloven chalice herald his name. Even now, I can still see the markings of the depraved carved into his flesh. The sight itself tested my Serrá like never before. He is destruction incarnate, my Eros," said Ebrahym. "And he is coming."

The dark figure from Sofia's dream. It was *he* who haunted her thoughts, this Angorzhu.

She'd known it in her bones, even before Ebrahym had described him. The threads tightened, somehow pulling the fragmented aspects of herself together into some terrible whole. She was connected to him somehow. With every cell of her being, she knew it was true and hated it. Her fate was inexorably tied to the Hell Lord. The only question now was, to what end.

Sofia's mind wandered as the Council debated their next move. Terafiq urged the rallying of the entire Sanguinir Host in preparation for the defense of the city. The High Council protested. Ebrahym said something. Their words became distant and muffled.

The light faded away from the room, and then she was alone in the dark space. The shadows before Sofia moved, lurking just out of focus. The lúpero fang in her pocket radiated heat to the point her clothes might ignite. On her wrist, the silver bracelet that wore her name began to sizzle and melt as the darkness whispered to her...

"So be it," said First Legatè Amadis with a heavy sigh. Sofia was present again. The Legatès were standing, Terafiq and Ebrahym keeling.

"We will make ready for the ordination. May you, Eros, protect the light with the power we bestow upon you."

Unanimously agreed, the High Council adjourned. Orders were passed between the rank and file oulma, and they dispersed from the chamber, imbued with purpose. She was alone with Terafiq and Ebrahym in the chamber. Terafiq looked even larger than before. *Was that pride?*

"So, it was a trap." Terafiq said to the empty room. She turned to Sofia. "I was there when the battle of Ilucenta began, did you know? It was a beautiful city, once." She paced as the story unfolded, her wings brushing gently across the stone floor, arms clasped behind like a wise giant.

"One day, a decade into the siege, a refugee appeared at the gates of Ilucenta. Understand, it was not uncommon for wayward oulma to appear as she did—they fled the countryside toward the cities every day. We took her in, and I, not even a catan at the time, was charged with her care. I saw something in her, something of myself. Zara was her name.

"Despite being under siege for years, the Host did not know what drove the imuertes toward our spears nor what their goal was. Zara, however, said she knew the cause and that visions had shown her. She told us in detail of the Fierno and what he had planned. Naturally, we were skeptical. How could an oulma know such things? But Zara knew things she could not possibly know, predicted things that would come to pass. Some thought her a spy, but I judged her to be true." For the first time Sofia saw a crack in Terafiq's prideful armor.

Terafiq sighed. "I was wrong. Zara foretold an attack on the eastern wall. The time, the place. She had not given us cause to doubt her, and our scouts confirmed the horde's movement. We made ready our defenses and prepared for the assault."

"What happened?" Sofia finally asked after a long pause.

Terafiq stared up at the frescos. "Zara sabotaged the north gate, and the imuertes streamed in. Thousands were killed that day. The city fell weeks later."

Her gaze turned toward Sofia, hardened once more into an impenetrable mask. "She was a spy, an agent of the enemy sent to infect us with her lies. I trusted her, and my mistake was costly. Zara disappeared that day, and my sword has longed to find her neck ever since," Terafiq said with heavy regret.

"But we must endure, for that is the Way. I understand your attachment to this oulma, Ebrahym; I do," Terafiq continued, nodding at Sofia. "For I feel it also. She has the spirit of a warrior, this one. But I will not be manipulated again. I have committed this sin before."

"But why, Eros?" Ebrahym asked. "If you suspected a trap, why did so many have to suffer in Espleña? Why the rouse?"

"We had to be sure." Terafiq said heavily.

"I am not a spy, or a demon, or anything else," Sofia cried, her mind unraveling. The fiery rage flared to life. "I follow no one's orders."

"And that is why you cannot be trusted," Terafiq said. "Sadly, I fear you may not even know the part you play. Angorzhu is clever and played me for a fool once. He has returned to finish what he started, but he is now revealed—within and without."

Terafiq pointed at the floor defiantly. "I know his tricks. I know his Way. And as Hierarch of the Sanguinir, steward of Sphaera Divinia, protector of Luminea, I will ensure *my* Host will never let history repeat itself."

PART V

—

DESCENT

And into utter darkness she fell,
Where the lost make pilgrimage,
To the kingdom there, ever burning.

Nephahi Epoye XVIII 12:2

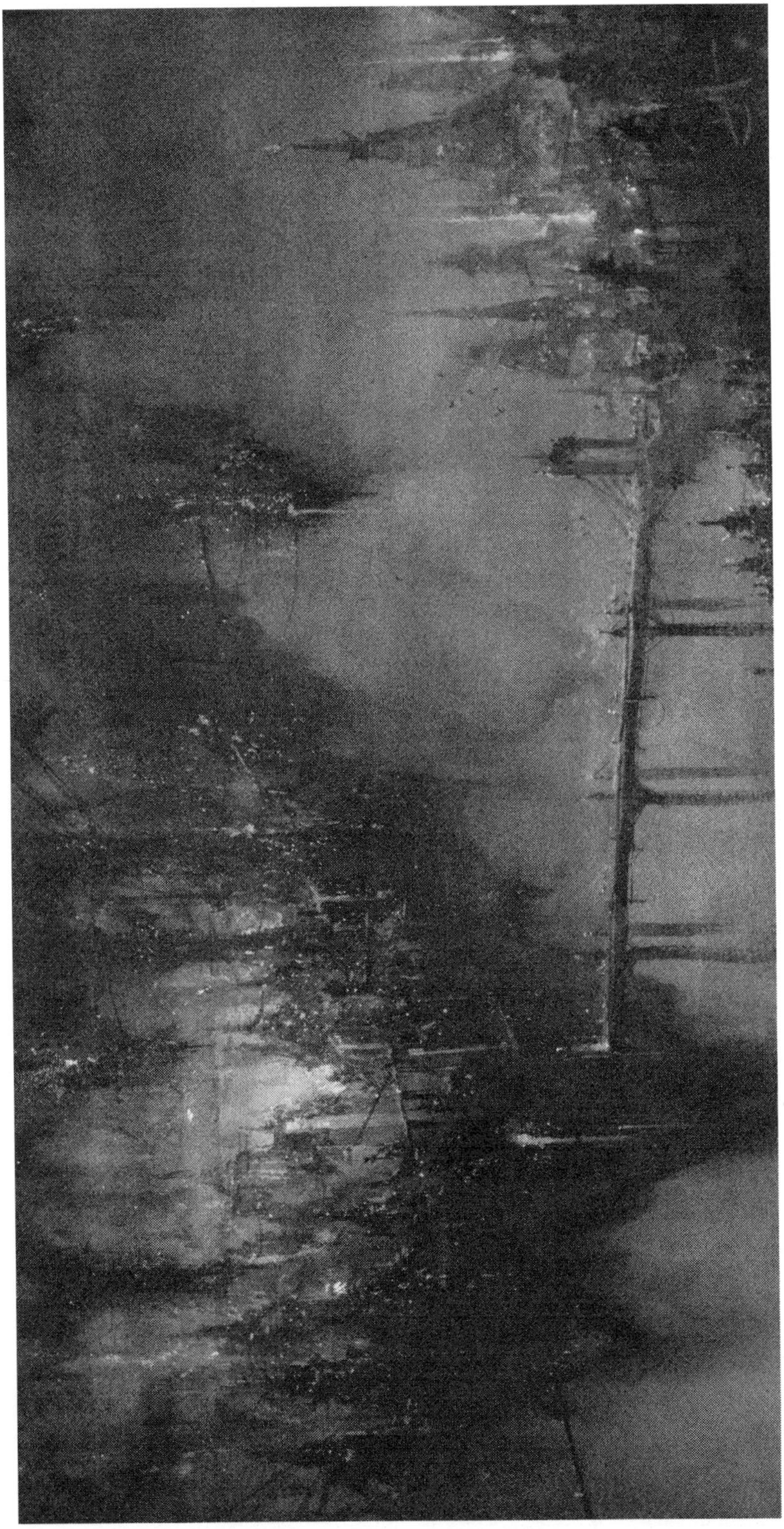

31

Sofia imagined a public trial. Not just a trial, a *spectacle*. A witch-hunt on the grandest of scales. Only one of Luminea's great amphitheaters would do as a setting. She pictured a vast arena filled with Sanguinir and oulma alike, sitting in righteous judgment above her.

They would denounce her. Call her imuertes; call her traitor. Witness after witness would stand to testify against her. Spouting rhetoric, they would twist and distort the truth to portray Sofia as the monster they imagined. These oulma would do what the Sanguinir would not. Or, rather, would not do publicly.

Sanguinir, though burdened with the truth and incapable of deceit, would testify to her *oddness*. It was the truth, after all. The Hierarch Terafiq would likely make an appearance, but Sofia imagined it would be a formality. Her station prevented her from any personal role in such a spectacle. The cruel trainer Bethuel would no doubt take center stage and expound on Sofia's many shortcomings. All that, she could take.

Anayah would be called to the stand. There, she would be forced to recount the incidents of Sofia's lack of control, her strangeness. Anayah would betray her. In her heart, Sofia knew her friend would take no pleasure in what was to come but would have no choice otherwise. But that wasn't the worst Sofia imagined. No, that would come next.

In the end, Ebrahym would take his place before the court. The Legatès would extract everything he knew of her, knowing his word to be infallible. From their time together in the wild to her strange— some would say *blasphemous*—dreams, to the death of Matìas and the grim details of the Battle of Espleña. They would poke and pry. He would endure it all, as Sanguinir do, with the same noble look upon him. He would do his duty.

Even so, it comforted her to imagine Ebrahym with sadness in his eyes as he helped seal her fate. That it would pain him to see the entire city of Luminea turn against her provided a little solace. But what would become of him? Of Anayah? She hoped the mob would not turn its hungry eyes toward them.

Hazy rays of sunlight cut through the tiny window of Sofia's cell. She'd watched their movements the past few days; the sweeping motion of the beams against the floor gave the illusion of time in a timeless place.

Kneeling, Sofia carved notches in the stone to mark their paths with a great deal of effort, for the ancient rock would not yield easily. Like the master masons of Luminea, she focused her intent, willing the stone to give way to her tooling. Sweat poured from her brow as she fought to make the faintest scratch in the surface so to leave some sign that she had been there at all.

The sound of iron grating against itself shook her from her tedious work. The heavy door of the cell creaked wide open, revealing the first souls she had seen in a week: two hooded Sanguinir wrapped in robes. It wasn't clear which Choir they came from, but maybe that was the point.

The Sang said nothing, but their stoic demeanor made it clear Sofia was to follow them. *This is it.*

She had expected that when they came for her, they'd bring some fresh clothes to make her presentable. The blood of those who'd returned from the Battle of Espleña was still on her trousers. It mixed with the sweat and dirt that came with life in a cell. But they didn't bring her clothes. They just started walking.

Sofia thought about running for a moment, then realized the ultimate futility and followed the Sanguinir in silence.

The sentries led her first underground, through a series of tunnels connecting the various temples and structures in the Fifth Tier. Then they ascended a flight of stairs and made their way through a large, empty dining hall, through a side door and up a long, spiraling staircase. Sofia and her guard finally emerged into a glassed rotunda overlooking Luminea.

Light enveloped the entire room, and it took a few moments for her eyes to adjust. What she saw was a neatly organized space, densely packed with strange artifacts, a kind of study or trophy room.

"Come," Terafiq said, waving off the guards.

She led Sofia through a pair of doors to a terrace shielded by billowing fabrics fastened with rope to carved wooden frames. Terafiq took a seat on a backless stool that allowed her wings room to rest on the ground. Sofia followed suit. The Sanguinir sipped from a steaming cup, for a long while saying nothing. Sofia wondered what terrible game the Eros was playing.

"I am sorry, Sofia," Terafiq said, breaking the silence. "I am not sure you deserve this, any of it," the Hierarch continued, putting her cup down. "Of course, you know I was honest when I said I saw myself in you. But not only was it true, I also meant it. You do what you must, what you feel is right."

"I suppose so," said Sofia.

"Yet, what you *are* and what you wish yourself to be are not the same," Terafiq's gaze hardened. "Angorzhu and that traitorous wretch, Zara, taught me a hard lesson at Ilucenta all those centuries ago. There is no room for chances in war, which is why I present you with a gift. It is all I can offer you."

Sofia stiffened. "What gift?"

"Exile," Terafiq said. "I am sorry."

That's it? No trial? No theatrics? Perhaps it was Sofia's pride talking, but she was almost disappointed in such an underwhelming verdict. She tried not to let her confusion, her anger, show.

"Do you really think I'm the enemy?" Sofia asked as calmly as she could. "Like this Zara who betrayed you?"

Terafiq shrugged her heavy shoulders. "When you first appeared, I had my doubts. That is why I sent you to the Raven. Now, I know you are not an agent of the enemy. At least, not a willing one. You are, however, an unknown variable and a risk that I cannot take."

The Hierarch stood, gesturing widely to the skyline beyond. "But consider what you *have* accomplished. You have united the Host and awoken the people to the facts in front of them; a Hell Lord draws near. Not even *I* could have convinced them of such until it was too late."

The Sang's wings twitched with anticipation. "Angorzhu will raise an army and descend upon Luminea like a swarm of flies. But now, we will be ready. We will be strong, thanks to you. You should be proud of that."

"And what happens to me? I just walk out of the gates, and that's it? After all of this?" Sofia paced in frustration. "The pain...all those deaths..."

"Sacrifice," Terafiq said, nodding. "War demands it from us all, and exile will be yours. We must endure. All of us."

"Exile," Sofia repeated. "Running away. I thought of it so many times, but I convinced myself to stay. To do the right thing, to help."

"Help who? Yourself?" Terafiq asked. Sofia said nothing.

"I believe in your heart you *think* you desire the righteous path," Terafiq continued, placing a heavy hand on Sofia's shoulder. "A hundred imuertes would not deter you from action. I can see it in your eyes, even now. They could come at you for days, and you would not yield until you were broken or destroyed.

"But this is not righteousness, and not the strength needed to win a war. A proud martyr is the selfish one who sacrifices for nothing more than their own glory." Terafiq sighed in an uncharacteristically human way, "Believe me, I know this better than most."

As much as it pained Sofia to admit it, Terafiq had a point. "So, what do you want me to do? Just slip out quietly in the night? Disappear?" Sofia asked.

The Sang shook her head, beads clinking softly. "No. Do the thing you wish you could; sacrifice. *Be* what they suspect you to be. Embrace the rumors. Play the part of the enemy within. Let them whisper as you walk the long road out of the city and wonder what fate will befall you. Have them believe in those who cast you out—that they are wise and just."

"Do you not see?" Terafiq exclaimed, arms wide. "Through this sacrifice, you will unite all Sanguinir and oulma in common purpose! Together, we make the Divine Sphere an impenetrable ally against the enemy. *You* have the chance to turn their fear into courage if you have enough of your own to take it."

Betrayal was one thing. Pretending to go along with it was another thing altogether. "I am not a traitor," gritted Sofia.

"I know, girl," Terafiq said. "But we all have our part to play, and this is yours. Go find some quiet corner of the wild to call your own and find your answers. Find your Way, if you can."

Terafiq revealed Sofia's sword, the heat-scarred blade she had carried as a newborn from Ilucenta. The Sang eyed it, caressing the edge with her fingers. She handed the blade handle first to Sofia.

"Do you know of the one who carried this sword?" Terafiq asked. Sofia shook her head, taking the blade as she would an infant. "I knew her well. She was my catan during the siege of Ilucenta. More than that, in truth. How strange it is you were the one to find her there."

"Why is that?"

"Her name was Nilayah, a great warrior of our Choir," Terafiq said. "It seems we both choose friends that temper our spirits. Friends, I think, much better than ourselves."

"I don't understand."

"Nilayah was once the steward of the aurola that your friend, Anayah, now protects. That sword belonged to her. Now, it shall return to the wild, with you. Use it well."

***

They allowed her to gather her meager belongings—a few items of clothing, her books and journal, the bracelet Anayah had given her. She wondered about the halo within her friend, imagining the warrior falling in that stairwell in Ilucenta. Nilayah's aurola became powerless when its host body breathed its last. Now, it rested in Anayah. *Strange.*

Sofia fiddled with the silver bracelet on her wrist. Anayah had told her the trinket was to remind her who she was. But the fang that hung on a cord around her neck, warming her chest, did the same. Both were part of her. The potential for glory and the prepotency of the darkness, always on the knife's edge.

"Sofia," a soft voice called from behind. "It is good to see you again." Nesta, the wingless Sang she had met deep within the Temple of the Dawnlight, appeared to hover like a pale spirit. She looked different in the light of the day. More fragile, weak. She still wore her veil. The masking odor of perfume permeated the room.

"I hear tell you are leaving us," Nesta said.

"Not exactly by choice."

"I see," Nesta said, head cocked slightly, her dim, golden eyes probing. "A blessing in disguise, perhaps? I heard the story of what happened in the north. And the battle."

"I'd rather not talk about it."

Nesta took a seat. "But leaving is what you wanted, is it not?"

Sofia sighed. "Yes. I mean, I don't know."

"Do you believe in destiny, Sofia? Fate?" Sofia shook her head. "Neither do I. Too much randomness in the universe. Yet when you exist as we do, for as long as we do, you begin to see the long patterns form. Not the day-to-day ones, but eons of history ebbing and flowing in a recognizable rhythm. Despite myself, sometimes I wonder if there is a thread tying it all together." Nesta paused, as if floating back from someplace else, and blinked slowly. "When I told you my Sanguinirian name—"

"Yasbrahi?"

"Yes. Do you know its meaning?"

"Tell me," Sofia said, curling up on the edge of the cot.

"Sanguinir titles are unique, yet are rooted in the name of their aurola as a sign of respect. *Marahi,* she was called, my halo. A powerful consciousness. Wise, patient. I took part of her name as my own, combined with our word, *yasabra.* It means 'messenger.' I was the eleventh of my name. Lasrahi before me and Ilrahym before her."

"Ilrahym?" Sofia asked in surprise, recognizing the sound. *It almost sounded like...*

"The masculine form used by male bearers. For them, Marahi is *Marahym.*"

"So that means—"

Nesta nodded deeply. "*Ebrahym,* yes. Twelfth of his name. It means 'protector.' It was he who took the mantle of Marahi after me."

"He carries your halo," Sofia echoed, her head spinning. "He knows what you know." Her brow furrowed. "The battle of Ilucenta, your descent into the dark. He knows all of it."

The Sang nodded. "That and more."

"But what does that mean? Why are you telling me this?"

Nesta smiled. "You will know soon enough. May you find your Way, Sofia. Goodbye." Nesta bowed once more, kissing Sofia's forehead through the sheer lace. She left, her veil jingling softly down the hall. Sofia wasn't sure what to make of the connection. Perhaps Nesta was right, maybe there *was* a thread tying all things together.

Sofia finished packing, slung the bag over her shoulder and gave the small room one last look, thoughts of ancient beings running through her head.

"I'm ready," Sofia murmured to herself. And she was.

Soon, it would be over.

The pair of Sanguinir guards followed her this time as she descended from the Fifth Tier, away from the billowing wisps of the Dawnlight, down hundreds of wide steps to the more densely populated areas below. She led the way through the bustling courtyards and narrow streets of Luminea with her escorts following behind.

The Market Strand was bustling, alive with shouts and laughter. Haggling, a sort of ritualized game (for there was no currency), so engrossed the surrounding oulma that few noticed as she passed. Her smile at the sight of the energetic crowd vanished as quickly as it came, and she wondered for a moment if she'd ever see Luminea again.

For the first time, though, she found it difficult to be angry. The smoldering fire within lay dormant and quiet. In a way, this *was* what she wanted. The chance to explore the Orvida and find her answers had always been her plan. But like most things lusted after, now that she had her freedom, she dreaded the thought of what to do with it.

She held her head high as the trio passed through gate after arched gate, descending from the highest of the Tiers and districts to the outer perimeter and subsequent boroughs of Luminea. She did her best to avoid curious glances from passing oulma, the ones that recognized her. But their numbers began to grow. Sofia imagined their thoughts as she passed. *Is that...? I think it is. Are they finally...? They are! Good riddance. I heard she was a traitor...*

More passersby seemed to realize something was happening and began to congregate and follow close behind, their curiosities piqued. The pack grew like a flock of birds in flight, each new individual following the previous by instinct, but perhaps not understanding why. They neither mocked nor taunted her. They pursued in silence, waiting. It almost made it worse.

Sofia crossed the smaller bridges connecting the lesser of Luminea's atolls to the main island as morning gulls called overhead. The patter of the crowd drifted close behind.

Along the waterfront and outlying neighborhoods of stacked, sunbaked structures, Sofia and her entourage came to the massive bridge that connected Luminea to the mainland. Stone pylons on either side, towers in and of themselves, were the first of dozens of such supports that dove through the turquoise waters of the Aecuna to the bedrock below. Banners and ever-burning lamps lined the edges and the manicured berm in the middle of it. Between alternating flows of early risers and cargo-laden wagons, Sofia saw a lone Sanguinir staring off into the distance.

Ebrahym. The warrior did not look the part now. He wore sensible, modest robes, and looked to be waiting for something. The light bounced off his milky wings in a glow.

The onlookers held at the bridge's edge as if they were afraid to pass any farther. They bunched up behind the two Sanguinir sentries, waiting to see Sofia's banishment, or whatever this was, to its conclusion. Even wandering Sanguinir had joined the crowd, aloof, but curious.

"You going to fight a war looking like that?" She came in close so the others would not hear. "Or just trying to leave me with a modest impression?"

"Neither." Ebrahym's hands rested on a heavy belt laden with pouches. Around his neck, a sling bearing a heavy pack hung low.

Sofia was glad to see her friend one last time, but she looked at the skies, searching for another. "Anayah wanted to be here," Ebrahym said, following her gaze. "But her duty called her to the front."

Sofia's chest tightened. She wondered if this, too, was part of Terafiq's design. To further isolate her. *But why would she allow Ebrahym to come?* "Can you reach her? With your, you know, telepathy?" Sofia asked.

"Not at this distance, I am afraid. I was supposed to go with her; many of us were. Eight divisions of Prime Auxilia and twelve Sanguinir wings were ordered to fly west and destroy an advancing horde. They likely are engaged with them now."

"It's happening," said Sofia, looking toward the horizon. "The war. It seems so far away." Ebrahym nodded, his eyes refusing to reveal anything more.

Sofia imagined it. A great battlefield. Rolling plains blackened by ash and fire. Hordes of imuerte monsters and shadows clashing with massive legions of Prime Auxilia soldiers and Sanguinir warriors. Darkness and blood and fire. Glorious, terrible. Sofia wondered why the Sang would leave one of their best behind.

"Why are you not with them? Isn't that against the Way?"

"I...declined the order."

For a Sang, such was equivalent of blasphemy. "What do you mean *declined*? Can you even do that?"

Ebrahym scowled in thought. "I informed the Hierarch the Way has shown me a...*different* path. I choose to follow you into exile." There was no real affection in his voice. Ebrahym simply stated the fact as something that was so.

Sofia struggled for the words. Although the idea of not being alone elated her, she knew it was a fantasy. "I can't ask you to do that. The imuertes are coming for Luminea. The oulma, the Host, Anayah—they will need you."

"You misunderstand," he said, with typical, Sanguinir frankness. "I do this *for* them. I will honor my oaths, but I must go by a different road. The High Council and the Eros can debate my actions, and my punishment. But I am free to do as the Divine Sphere and my aurola allows, so they must accept it. Our fates are intertwined now, Sofia, as is the fate of all Luminea. I know it. I *feel* it. Hierarch Terafiq believes your part in things is over, but I, *we* suspect it has only begun."

"We?"

Ebrahym softened, as he sometimes did, appearing more gentle, feminine. "My halo speaks to me more often as of late, guiding me as if I was aloft in a strong wind, toward you. Never have I felt its influence so potently, and never has it led me astray. So, I will have faith in the mantle, and in you, to wherever it leads."

"Nesta said—" Sofia blurted before catching herself. "I mean, I thought you weren't supposed to tell me Sang secrets."

"Hmm. Things sometimes change."

Sofia paced. "Not *here* they don't. Terafiq told me to find someplace quiet, far away. Her advice was to let it go. The dreams, fighting, all of it. Just fade away while the Host fights this war."

"And will you?" Ebrahym asked.

"I don't know," Sofia said, finally. "I'm not sure I could, even if I wanted to."

An impending dread deepened in her chest. If Ebrahym was right and the fate of Luminea was indeed tied to her own, it might not matter what she did to avoid it. The darkness would find her.

She felt as if she were back at the lighthouse so long ago, staring into the mist and the road leading to the unknown. Now, as then, she took a step. Then another. Ebrahym matched her pace, saying nothing, and the pair walked. Sofia stared at the horizon as they crossed the bridge and the sun ascended from the sea of grass to the east and beyond.

32

Days turned to weeks and the grass to sand. Sofia and Ebrahym chased the sun east, guided by an unknown force. Like birds in migration for the season, the two pilgrims followed an instinct into the deep desert. Sofia never once said which direction to go, and Ebrahym never asked. It was an understanding they felt in their bones.

The sun began to disappear once more behind the horizon at their backs, plunging like a stone into an endless sea of sand. Sofia's long shadow stretched out ahead of them as she crested the dune. It was a distorted version of herself, clawing across the sand.

Ebrahym was gone, scouting ahead once more, searching for a route or water. Alone, her thoughts often drifted back toward Luminea. Though there were times when she ached to be there again, the desert had its own beauty. It was lonely, yes, but beautiful.

Sometimes, the anger would come. It would sneak up behind her like a predator and pounce hard and fast. Flares of rage would erupt like wildfire. But there was no outlet for her anger here, no target for her rage. In the silence of the desert, the anger fizzled out as quickly as it came, diffused by the emptiness and heat.

She saw Matías sometimes, too, appearing as a phantom. His pale form would materialize out of the corner of her eye, pale and bloodied, run through by her sword. He'd reach for her, beckoning her to him. But he wasn't real. Matías was dead, still, and by her own hand.

She would never be able to escape that fact, no matter what desolate wasteland she ventured to. *I didn't have a choice*, she would remind herself. While that part was true, Sofia couldn't be sure that some part of her hadn't enjoyed it. Whenever the thought came to her, she'd shake her head vigorously, as if she could empty the thought from her skull.

The sun vanished completely as Ebrahym touched down. His face was wrapped in a headscarf like the one he'd worn when they'd first met. He nodded slightly northward, where the dunes became flatter and more easily navigable, and they headed in that direction. The nighttime chill began to creep over them.

They walked for a while before making camp and settling in. Sofia unrolled her thin blanket, brushing the sand from it. *When was the last time I slept?* She couldn't remember. She unpacked the rest of her gear and tried to recall. They had been traveling night and day for weeks now, and her last dream was long before that. The lack of sleep was starting to catch up with her. Her mind was fuzzy and sluggish.

"Maybe I could be a farmer one day," Sofia said as she worked on igniting a pile of kindling from their meager reserves with a piece of flint. She fumbled with the tool and sent sparks every which way. "You know, take care of a small piece of land, grow crops. Something simple."

"Perhaps," said Ebrahym, taking the flint. "Tending the earth takes much patience. I do not believe that is your strongest virtue." He scraped the shards of metal together, and sparks erupted, disappeared into the kindling and were replaced by flame. "No offense meant."

Sofia chuckled. "Did your halo tell you that?" The retort managed to produce a smile from Ebrahym, and then it vanished.

"I tended fields, long ago," he said with a hint of sadness. Sofia propped herself up in front of the burgeoning fire. The pair talked often, but rarely about the past. It was not the Sang's way. Sofia listened intently.

Ebrahym tended the fire with focused effort. "Before my communion, before I became Sanguinir, I once grew wheat so rich it looked as if gold itself sprouted from the ground."

"Tell me."

Ebrahym crossed his legs beneath him. "When I came to the Orvida, I was like most oulma. I washed ashore like any other, wandering through the fog. I had no memory of Afore, but I always wondered if perhaps I once was a man of the land. It seemed to come naturally—I would ask, and the earth would listen."

He stared at his open palms. "When you work the land, it is not a matter of *making* things grow. You cannot do that, just as you cannot make the rain. You simply remove all the obstacles in the way and let the earth do what it will."

He looked toward the west and made a Sanguinir gesture of reverence. "I spent time in Luminea, but the rolling hills and open sky called to me. And so, I traveled to the provinces and worked a small piece of land to grow my grain."

"Near Ilucenta," Sofia said. He nodded.

"What was your name, before your halo?" dared Sofia. She had never heard Ebrahym speak so much before. She pushed for more.

A look of confusion momentarily twisted his face. "Hmm. It has been many centuries since I have thought of it. The Way teaches us not to dwell on the past. Not the Afore, not even our self-illusions of memory in this place."

"No," he said with a curt nod. "For now, I am Ebrahym, twelfth of my name. And even *this* is transient, like the shape of the dunes. One day I will be nothing but light, and free." And just like that, he was Sanguinir again, distant and aloof.

Darkness fell in earnest, and a trillion weak stars revealed themselves. Sofia lay on her back near the fire and watched them slowly rotate past. They were not as brilliant here. Something pushed them away as if their light was an offense to the place.

Still, they were apparent enough. In their randomness, she looked for shapes of animals and objects formed by the points of light, a pastime as old as man itself. She thought about what Ebrahym had said about getting out of the earth's way to let things grow. Here in the desert, she had no obstacles, nothing stopping her save one thing: the question of what to do next.

"Why did you give up farming?" she asked, breaking the silence.

"The imuertes burned the fields," Ebrahym replied with no emotion. "Outside of Ilucenta." It came across as more of a factual statement than a memory.

"You never talk about it. The siege, I mean."

"I was there only for a short time. Some of us escaped before the last attack and the fall of the city. Many did not."

Sofia considered the coincidence, among all the others. Nesta believed there were no coincidences. Perhaps she was right.

Sofia had found the ruins of Ilucenta after washing ashore, the same place where Ebrahym had first met their common enemy, the Hell Lord, Angorzhu. There, she had also found the corpse of Terafiq's friend, the Sang, Nilayah, whose aurola would eventually pass to Anayah.

Nesta had been there, too. Her stripped mantle would make its way to Ebrahym, and her estranged lover, Bethuel, would teach Sofia the way of the sword.

So many coincidences. And most oddly—and perhaps most importantly—she'd met Ebrahym by chance. Thanks to a lone lúpero, they had been brought inexorably together by the enemy they'd fought against. Now, they found themselves together again as outcasts on a journey with no destination but likely an end. If there were deeper connections between the events, Sofia could not easily see the thread yet, but she was beginning to think it was there.

"And after the battle, you joined the Conventa," she said.

Ebrahym lay on his stomach, resting his head on his arms. "Hmm. When I was eventually chosen and entrusted with a mantle, I learned my halo, too, was there during the siege."

"Nesta told me. Her aurola passed to you." She chewed her lip. "You saw him there, didn't you? During the last battle? Angorzhu." It was hard to even say the word.

Ebrahym didn't answer. Sofia pressed. "Ebrahym, tell me."

"Yes. And I see him still." The heaviness in his voice hung in the air. He turned his head from the fire.

"As do I," Sofia whispered. She stared into the fire knowing the nightmare would soon come. But not tonight.

They lay in silence for a few hours next to the fire, the chirping sounds of the desert occasionally interrupting the silence.

***

Sofia soaked the headwrap in the still, silty water and wound it around her neck. Above, the sun was nearly at its zenith and merciless, beating down like a blacksmith's hammer. Whatever Serrá empowered the frigid night, it was equally potent during the day, igniting the desert into an inferno. And while Sofia's body remained resilient to its effects, she wasn't completely numb to the relief of cool water running down her spine and chest.

Months of travel now separated her from Luminea. She often wondered about the war and if Anayah was alive. How many Pax had fallen in the mud? How many new communions had ushered in new Sang?

Sofia strained to reach her arm down the opening and fill the water vessels, long dry. The small, natural well had been easy to find, for the desert had offered little else of interest over the past week. The stone slab shielding it from the sun the was color of rust or rich spices.

The last vessel filled, Sofia took refuge in the shade, eyeing the bleached, cloudless sky. Although the land was harsh, the time spent in the barren landscape had begun to change her. Sofia felt at peace in the surroundings. Or at least, more at peace. There was a simplicity to the desert, perhaps, she thought, due to the lack of living things complicating everything. But there was life here. When night fell and temperatures plummeted, a mysterious world was revealed. Creatures that lived their entire lives in the shadows emerged from the underworld to roam freely.

But Sofia most admired the time when day turned to night or night to day. As one transformed into the other, there was a moment of perfect balance. It was then Sofia felt truly at peace. She would forget the nightmares that plagued her. She would forget Matías' contorted face as he slowly bled to death, and the corpses of the other oulma who fell to the imuertes. The training, the shame, the pain—all of it would melt away. As darkness made way for light or as the light banished the dark, Sofia was content.

As she sat under the rock, the weeks without sleep snuck up on her.

This time, the uncontrollable urge to drift into slumber was too strong. She fought it at first, but her mind slipped away, falling from her body into the darkness. As the sun inched along its arc toward the horizon, Sofia fell asleep.

Once again, she found herself playing the part of the mysterious woman with dark hair, sitting on the old mattress in the worn-out box of an apartment. She kneaded the string of beads in her hand, the cross symbol dangling. She felt the impatient kicks of the life within.

There was something large next to her, yet she couldn't move to see what it was. But she felt it. She felt its weight sinking into the mattress and her body falling toward it.

A heavy arm draped over her small shoulders. It was at once comforting and formidable. Sofia's head fell to the thing next to her on its own volition, resting upon its massive bulk. A thick aroma of musk filled her senses. This was a powerful creature, strong and fierce. She knew it would protect her from everything outside. But there was fear, too. Even as she lay in the thing's arms, feeling its heat and the cozy weight of it enveloping her, she was frightened by it. She knew it was capable of horrible things.

She could not recall how she knew, but somehow, she did. Just as she knew the sun rose in the west and that rain fell from the sky, she knew the thing next to her was corrupt. Evil.

Layered in the masculine aroma lingering in the air, Sofia smelled sulfur, and a primitive part of her brain began to panic. She tried to pull away, but her body would not respond; it was a prison from which she could not break free.

Then the thing began to whisper and squeeze her tight. The whispers were too low to hear properly, lingering just outside of understanding. Dozens, hundreds, of voices, commanded to speak by some force. Sofia tried to close off her senses, to find silence, but the murmurs grew. The thing began to crush her with its presence. It engulfed her. The darkness found its way through her nose and mouth, through her eyes and ears until, choking, Sofia was at one with the emptiness...

Ebrahym stood over her as she roused and rejoined the world of light, gasping. Returned from his scouting errand, Ebrahym glistened with sweat and seemed to amplify the light around him. It was difficult for her to look at him directly, momentarily blinded by the brightness.

"The dreams again?" he asked. Sofia nodded, not entirely sure as to their meaning. "Come, we must go. Now," Ebrahym said, reaching for her hand.

Sofia shook off the grogginess and slung the water vessels over one shoulder. She grabbed Ebrahym's extended hand and found her feet. "What is it?"

"Smoke on the horizon. Less than a day's journey by wing."

Rather than carrying Sofia in Ebrahym's arms, which would have been uncomfortable for more than one reason, the two worked out a crude sling Sofia used to secure herself to Ebrahym's back. Between his massive wings, Sofia sat like a large pack, her arms draped over his neck as he rode the thermals.

Against her grumbling, they soared far above the desert floor, where the wind was stronger, though so was her urge to vomit. She kept her eyes closed most of the time and clutched the Sang's neck. As the wind rushed by them, so did the strangely comforting smell of sweet sweat and incense.

As they soared toward the billowing plume of smoke in the distance, Sofia wondered what this new vision meant and whether it, too, was a premonition of things to come.

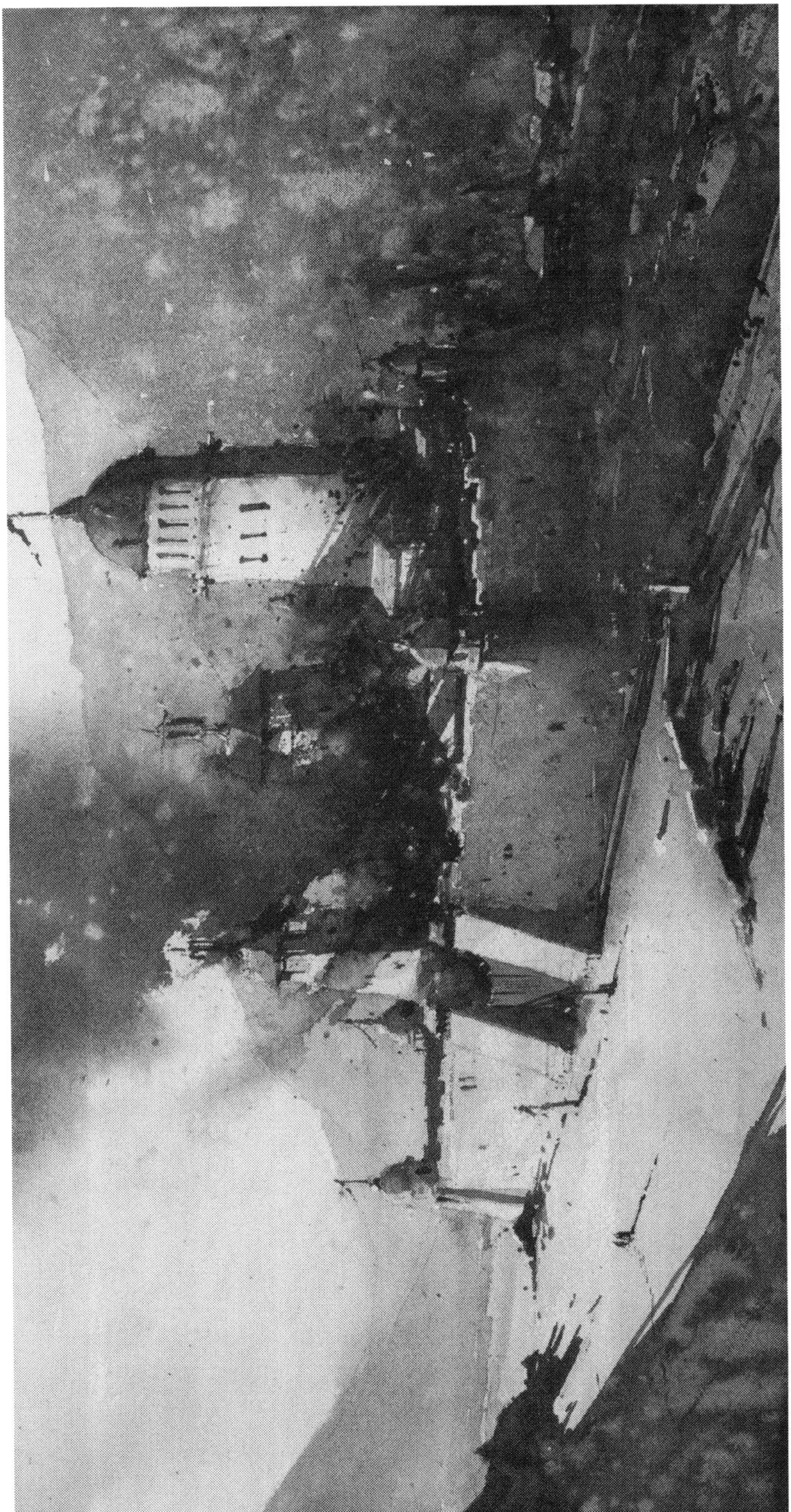

33

Parts of the monastery still burned as Sofia and Ebrahym approached it.

During the night, Sofia tracked the beacon through the dark desert, and they followed it like a star. Like the Meridi lighthouse that had once guided her out of the mist, the flames drew them forth until the sun rose once more.

Then, the plume of smoke led them onward.

From the air, Sofia couldn't tell if the complex was built from quarried stone or carved from the earth itself.

It had the look of an ancient artifact unearthed from the sand, mounds of which clung desperately to the walls as if trying to draw them back into the earth. Six walls in all encased a dusty courtyard. The sanctuary's heart was a green organ, a lush garden surviving beneath worn, stretched canopies. Sofia noted the irony. *Another oasis.* But this one was much smaller than the one she and Ebrahym had sheltered in so long ago.

A mismatched array of structures from different eras consumed every remaining inch of the compound. Six tall, thin turrets topped with crumbling domes marked the intersection of each wall along the perimeter. Narrow windows, all dark, dotted the towers.

As Ebrahym descended with Sofia on his back, gaping holes scattered across the walls appeared if some giant beast had taken bites from them.

They touched down outside of the perimeter, gliding through the hazy smoke, reintroduced to the sweltering heat at ground level. For once, Sofia would have preferred to have been up high. Between the fires that smoldered around them and the searing sun above, the conditions were choking. She wrapped the scarf around her face to keep the smoke at bay.

They walked the perimeter, weapons drawn. Crackling embers popped and hissed. One wall of the hexagon was completely leveled. The ten-meter barrier of stone had been caved in by immense force. Fragments, some twice Sofia's height, littered the courtyard compound.

She and Ebrahym moved about the debris with caution, using the Sanguinir hand gestures she'd learned in the Conventa to communicate silently. She climbed the piled rubble to enter the city proper and felt a distinct feeling she had done this before.

She had. She'd once climbed the broken wall of Ilucenta to gain entry to the main city. She pushed aside the feeling of dread the memory dragged up and followed Ebrahym into the smoking ruin.

They made their way through cramped, narrow alleys to the small courtyard at the heart of the structure. Fires still smoldered at their feet. Some of the green clung to life around the spring, a water source bubbling up from the earth and contained in a ring of stone. Scattered around the ancient-looking stone paths leading to the well lay the occasional sandal, a bucket for carrying water, a beaded sigil. But no owners, dead or otherwise.

"What is this place?" Sofia whispered as she picked up one of the beaded medallions. The beads were carved from wood, painted red, and on the silver disk was a glyph: the torso of a man whose lower half was a serpent consuming the man's head in a paradoxical cycle.

"A lamasery," Ebrahym said as he eyed the gouges in a block of nearby stone. "Home of the *Monte di Iyar,* the Monks of the Sand."

"Who are they?" she asked, eyeing the medallion.

Ebrahym sheathed his sword, satisfied for the moment. "Some believe that living in Luminea fosters a weakness in spirit. The *monte* seek to avoid attachment. After the founding of the Host, they sought a different path. That symbol in your hand is a warning—self-destruction from ego. The sand monks see it as an inevitable, given enough time. So, they live as modestly as possible. Eat as little as possible. *Sense* as little as possible.

"I have heard stories of monte masters spending centuries walled inside dark caves, meditating. Some use their Serrá for more extreme measures, to put out their eyes and close their ears or remove their ability to speak. They will spend a thousand years in contemplation before making a final pilgrimage back to Luminea to enter the Dawnlight."

Sofia pocketed the medallion. "They don't fear the imuertes?"

Ebrahym shook his head. "The entire Orvida is transitional in their eyes. A dream. War is just another distraction to avoid."

Sofia could see evidence of the monks' beliefs represented in the lamasery. There were no ornamentations like the grand architecture of Luminea. Ancient-looking, wooden tools leaned against the structures, waiting to be used by dedicated hands once more.

They made their way to the main structure of the compound, a long, multi-floor type of barracks. With the aid of a torch, Sofia saw that the dark interior rooms were as sparse and plain as the facade. The larger rooms featured communal tables, roughly hewn dishware and the occasional book; the only signs of inhabitants. These items, too, seemed ancient.

"Where are they?" Sofia asked. Torchlight flickered in Ebrahym's amber eyes. The Sang did not answer and continued through the interconnected rooms, searching.

Sofia came to a room that must have belonged to someone of note, perhaps a leader of the place. While still modest, the room was larger than others and filled with stacks of books and parchments. She navigated the waist-high maze of knowledge to a desk. An open book sat silently, waiting to be read. She struggled to discern the hastily written scribbles. The language was familiar, but the dialect and the handwriting made it difficult to make out. One sentence, however, stood out:

They walk among us.

The words sent a prickling chill across her flesh. *What happened here?* Sofia closed the book and searched for Ebrahym, finding him down a steep flight of wooden stairs in the lowest part of the structure: a dug-out cellar. Shelves full of dust-covered jars containing preserved foods and other provisions lined earthen walls. Dust drifted through the air, and with it, a sense of dread.

Sofia ran her fingers across the grime. "I thought erosion didn't exist here."

"It does not," Ebrahym said. "Unless one wants it to. The desert is entropy set in motion. A strong Will pushes the sand to the west."

"And what about the monks? There must have been dozens of them here," Sofia said, idly eyeing a jar full of pale preserves. What they were exactly, she could not tell. "What happened to them? Did they disappear?"

Ebrahym swept the dirt on the floor aside with his boot. "Perhaps not all of them." A cleverly concealed handle emerged from the grime like a fossil. Sofia found the seams with her fingers and grasped the iron handle. She looked at Ebrahym, sword at the ready. He nodded, and she flung the door open. He leaped down the dark tunnel as Sofia watched and waited.

A scream erupted from the dark hole. "Please! No! NO! Please don't hurt me! PLEASE!"

***

"Have some." Sofia set the cup of hot tea on the table in front of the woman.

Though haggard and filthy, she was stunning. The woman's head was shaved but in perfect proportion to the rest of her face. Slightly wide-set eyes and generous lips gave her an exotic, youthful look, though both features were marred. Heavy, bruise-colored circles marked the area around her smoky eyes, still wide and anxious, and her lips were cracked and bleeding. The woman gripped the cup with both hands and took a slow sip.

"What's your name? Can you tell us what happened here?" Sofia asked. Ebrahym stoked a fire in a hearth near the table. The woman said nothing, her eyes fixed on the table.

"You're safe now. He is Sanguinir," Sofia said, nodding to Ebrahym. "We can help you."

The woman eyed Ebrahym across the room. "You do not understand," the woman whispered. The words came slow and raspy, as if the woman's voice had not been used in an age. "They are everywhere. *He* is everywhere."

Sofia and Ebrahym exchanged concerned glances. *Angorzhu?* "Who? The imuertes?" Ebrahym asked, already knowing the answer.

The woman nodded. "They appeared from the sand and vanished soon after. We had no warning. There was so much screaming. I hid—"

"It's all right," said Sofia, placing her hand on the woman's arm. The woman was still cold from her hiding place in the earth. "Who are you?"

The woman thought for a moment. "We have no use for names. You may call me *Oro*. It means 'other.'"

Ebrahym put a hand on the woman's shoulder. "I am familiar with your ways, Oro. Tell us what happened here. Please."

The nameless woman held Ebrahym's gaze for a moment and nodded. "They were imuertes, that much I do know. It had been so long since we had seen any of their kind." She took another sip to steady herself. "That night was my turn to cook—every full moon—for those who still need to eat. I was in the kitchen preparing the meal when I heard the shouting. Then I heard the rumbling. I looked out the window, and I could see the imuertes flooding into the lamasery. I heard screaming and I...I..." Oro burst into sobs.

"Ran?" Sofia asked.

Tears escaped from Oro's eyes. "Yes, I ran. I left my brothers and sisters behind and hid in a hole while they were taken. I know am not supposed to lament for them. Cowardice is irrelevant, but I am not like the masters in this thinking. I still feel."

"It is not your fault," Ebrahym said softly. "There was little to be done."

"You said the others were taken," Sofia said. "Taken where?"

Oro wiped her tears away, streaking the dirt that caked her skin. "I do not know. There are caves to the east of here, very old. Ancient tunnels, supposedly, from the last war. If I were to guess, I would say the imuertes retreated there."

Ebrahym stroked his chin. "How many?"

"I cannot say for sure," said Oro. "Dozens of them, perhaps more."

Sofia pitied the sobbing woman in front of her. She saw herself in a way, a victim of circumstances beyond her control. A broken thing forced to witness the loss of her friends. But at the same time, she found a small part of herself repulsed by Oro's unwillingness to act. The weakness made Sofia ill and stirred the anger inside of her. She felt ashamed for it.

"Oro," Ebrahym said kneeling at the woman's feet. "You said you saw 'him.' Whom do you speak of?"

Oro laughed desperately, the kind of laugh when the body knows not what else to do. She stared into her mug. "I only saw him for a moment before I fled. He was one of them, but with wings. Wings like Sanguinir, like yours."

Oro soon slept near the fire, seemingly comfortable on the bare floor, though she asked for the table to be moved so she could sleep beneath it. There she lay, stiff on her back with entwined fingers resting gently on her belly. Every few minutes, she would take a new breath. Ebrahym and Sofia stood near the window, taking in the breeze. The pungent scent of sulfur somehow still hung in the air.

"Do you know what she is talking about?" Sofia asked quietly.

"No," Ebrahym glanced back toward Oro. "My thoughts went to Angorzhu at first, but this winged creature sounds different. A lieutenant in the ranks, perhaps? A vital target opportunity, though we are but two swords."

Sofia thought of her dream and the crushing darkness that came with it. It was another sign; she felt it.

"We have to find those caves," she said. "Whatever this thing is, it's connected to Angorzhu. Maybe this is why we traveled here in the first place. Exiled or not, it doesn't mean we are going to give up on Luminea. This is our war now."

Sofia expected Ebrahym to protest, but he simply nodded. "By *our* Will," he said.

Sofia smiled, nodding. "*Our* Way be done." She knew Ebrahym thought her plan unwise, but he didn't waver or try to convince her otherwise. Not once since stepping foot outside of Luminea had he doubted her, ever questioned her instinct. She hoped his faith in her was not misplaced. Ebrahym would follow her to the edge of the Orvida and beyond, even if it meant they would never come back.

34

"Be mindful," Ebrahym said as they surveyed the scene.

The desert had bottomed out, soft dunes replaced by hard, cracked earth that split open like a dried wound. Ahead, rock formations concealed the entrance to the caves Oro described. Jagged, bloody splinters of bone jutting from pale flesh.

Wind whipped at her eyes and mouth, and she tightened her headscarf to keep the sand out. The sun was beating down hard enough for any oulma to retreat from its glare.

An hour later, they reached the entrance; a narrow sliver of dark leading deeper into the canyons. Ebrahym knelt before it and pinched the dirt between his hands. It smelled sour. Tracks pounded into the hard earth led into the dark gully beyond.

"How many?" Sofia asked, checking her equipment as the Sang peered into the darkness with keener vision than hers. She drew her sword, her best friend, her survival, from the sheath, kneading the grip anxiously. It was long stained black with wear.

"It is hard to tell," said Ebrahym, smelling the earth. "A small pack. Mostly low imuertes kin, but something else along with them. Something larger."

"You want to turn back?" Sofia asked, staring into the canyon opening. "I'm not one to shy away from a fight, but who knows what we'll find down there. We're still only two."

"Do you remember the concept of *fastidio,* from your training?"

Fastidio. Infiltration. Hit and run. Small squads penetrating deep behind enemy lines, hunting the foulest of the imuertes ranks with the aim of destroying them and, it was hoped, escaping without a trace.

"Not preferred by the Choir, if I remember right," Sofia said. "No glory in it. Dirty work meant for the Pax." There was more bite to the words than she intended.

"Practicality confused for vanity, Sofia. It is a sound strategy, though dangerous. That kind of war puts an aurola at great risk of being lost, something we cannot afford with so few numbers against the enemy's many. But, imuertes hordes break without the lieutenants to lead the rest. Cut off the head, and the serpent withers. At times, it is worth the risk."

"We're snake hunting, then?" She asked rhetorically. Sofia pounded the earth with a fist. "Well, what does your halo say? Is this snake worth the risk?"

"It is," said Ebrahym solemnly. "Even though we put Luminea to our backs, we will not abandon her nor the oulma we are bound to protect. The war continues. *Our* war continues."

Sofia nodded. She wondered where Anayah might be, what kind of battle she was fighting. So far from the center of the Host's Dominion, if there were anything Sofia could do anything to help her friend, she would see it done.

"It's settled, then. Anything else?"

Ebrahym pulled the hood from his brow. "Be quick, be quiet and be ready to run."

***

Navigating the caves was like slithering through the veins of some long-dead giant. Sofia and Ebrahym had slipped under the skin and worked their way through the narrow crevasses to the flesh of the earth below.

Light became scarcer, the colored stone colder, with each step. The way was rough and uneven, natural, and did not have the same appearance as the burrows Sofia remembered scattered across the tundra. No igdracio carved this path.

The Sang stopped when the light vanished completely, giving her pause to let her eyes adjust.

I can do this. Their time in the desert together had helped her hone her Serrá. She turned inward, focusing her thoughts on the darkness. She imagined it dissipating like a fog burned away by morning light. *Breathe. Will it to be so.*

A moment later, hazy gray tones emerged from the blackness. They defined the contours of the rocks well enough. She took another breath and nodded toward the pair of glowing, golden eyes looking back at her. They pushed on.

The slope descended steeply to the point where Sofia was forced onto on all fours to avoid skidding uncontrollably toward the darkness below. Talon marks marred the stone, the grooves somehow more ominous in monotone shades of gray.

She felt the sharp edges of the stone and remembered her cliff ascent long ago. Ebrahym had given her a message then and told her to climb. The lúpero had followed. The sound of claws driving into rock pounded in her memory. Looking back, it hadn't been courage that'd helped her then. It'd been not knowing how much there was to fear. Now she knew.

Ebrahym held a sign to halt. Sofia nearly missed the signal, and feathers met face before she froze.

Scratching.

Something picked at the stone a few meters away. Sofia's heart responded in kind, preparing her for action.

Ebrahym motioned toward the wall, and the two warriors pressed themselves against it. Sofia squeezed her sword, tensing her muscles, awaiting the order. She stoked the fire within, coaxing that flame, her power, to life. It had saved her so many times; she prayed it wouldn't fail her now.

They floated there, pale eyes appearing like ghostly orbs. All six of them milky and dead. Sofia and Ebrahym ducked behind a nearby ledge, hoping they were out of sight.

The imuerte chattered as it skulked across the stone, claws ticking in the silence. It clamored down a boulder like a spider, sniffing the air. *Impès. Death child.* Ebrahym signaled to hold, waiting for the creature to approach. Sofia stilled her breath, trying hard not to let the sound of her armor, light as it was, betray her.

The thing inched forward, sensing something. Its labored wheezing stunk of rottenness.

Then Ebrahym was upon it, his sword striking like a whip. The impès' head slipped clean off its neck with one strike of the Sang's sword and fell to the cavern floor with a wet thud.

After a silent moment, Ebrahym probed the creature with his boot. It was pale and gnarled like a deformed child, its oversized mouth lined with fangs. Seared on its chest was a crude symbol of a feather or perhaps the fletching of an arrow. *A brand.* Sofia wondered if it symbolized this imuerte's allegiance to something fouler, the creature the terrified Oro described. The one with wings like a Sang...

They left the corpse bleeding out on the cavern floor and delved deeper into the darkness, emboldened by the lack of resistance. Sofia had barely noticed the imuertes aura hanging in the air, but the deeper the two lone warriors descended, the worse she began to feel. It was a like a humid cloud, and with every step they took, its power grew, as did the stink of sulfur.

The cavern opened into larger chambers fashioned into crude stone hovels. Horrific altars made of meat, bone, blood and feathers littered the filthy cavern, illuminated by smoldering torches. Sofia wondered where the feathers came from—there were no birds to speak of here.

A narrow passage led them into an even larger cave system lit by greenish, unnatural light. It seemed to come from all directions, conjured up from no particular source. Above, wicked stone spikes hung from the ceiling like petrified drips of gore. The ground was carved smooth, and a makeshift throne constructed of all manner of evil tidings sat empty in the center of it. It looked like something an insect would build, using whatever materials could be found, bound by organic fluids. Crude adornments of bone hung delicately from it. A disturbing amount of care had gone into the thing.

"Few enter *my* domain uninvited," a voice screeched in the darkness. The two warriors, startled, set their guard and scanned for their enemy.

"Ah!" the blackness said. "You have brought *her* with you, I see. My thanks. My Lord will be most pleased. Yes, most pleased, indeed." Ebrahym looked at her.

How does this thing know me? Instantly, whatever barrier was holding her courage together began to strain.

"Enough!" Ebrahym called out defiantly. "Show yourself!"

The thing obliged.

Though dimly lit, its grotesqueness was clear. A tall, spindly body rose from the shadows, pale in the green glow. It was adorned with elaborate armor, but it was hard to tell from all the heavy jewelry that lay atop it. Strings of beads and baubles strangled every limb and appendage. They almost looked like...Sanguinir and Pax sigils. The medallions of warriors long gone. Huge plumes of black feathers adorned a face whose very flesh had rotted away, revealing a wicked smile of bone. Dead eyes glistened from deep sockets as the creature bobbed gracefully toward them like a predatory bird. As it approached, Sofia could see the cloak now, the wings that Oro had spoken of.

Upon the creature's shoulders sat a bloody mass of gore-caked feathers. Wings severed from their bases, stitched together so they dragged behind like some morbid, kingly robe. It was tapestry woven of death, of trophies taken from Sanguinir warriors.

Sofia's mind raced with horror. Her stomach bottomed out within her. *Could any of those wings belong to Anayah?* The thought of this thing cutting the flesh from the corpses of Sang disgusted her. *The warrior in Ilucenta...Nilayah...her wings had been taken...*

Then another thought amidst the sporadic firing of neurons: her own hands cutting the fang from the lúpero, taking a trophy as this thing did. The disgust deepened. She hated this thing. She hated herself. An uncontrollable fury welled inside like a thunderhead cloud. It swelled and churned and wanted nothing more than to unleash itself upon the creature in front of her.

I will have this creature's head.

The skull-faced creature held a curved blade, a kind of scythe, and tapped its hilt on the stone in rhythmic patterns. It synced perfectly with her own beating heart and was getting faster. *How does it know me?* It was maddening. To each side of Ebrahym and her, dark shapes skulked from the darkness, flanking them. Sofia's heart threatened to burst through her armor at any second.

"Forgive me! My excitement overshadows manners. Allow me to introduce myself," hissed the creature, bowing deeply. "*Irazitlaminqui*. Grand *Micali* of the Seventh Circle. Royal Lash of the Eastern Horde. Irazi, some call me, the *Wingtaker*, at your service."

Irazi twirled his weapon flamboyantly, but with a deftness and speed unlike anything Sofia had seen before. The imuerte finished the display and stood erect as a schoolmaster would. "Welcome to my domain, painfully dull as it is. My *Achontli*, Glorious Master, bid me to this desert until my task is done, but I long to resume the hunt. And now that you are here," Irazi said, with a bony finger aimed at Ebrahym, "I shall begin again."

"You expected us? How?" called Sofia.

Irazi rattled with excitement. "Ha! Our spies knew you trespassed our desert the moment your feet touched the sand. But far and wide are the dunes. We needed you to come to us." The creature snapped his jaws with a pop. "Fortunately, *his* kind is so predictable. So noble. All it took was a little fire for you to come running."

Anger was bubbling over, causing Sofia's hands to shake. "What do you want?"

"Why, *you*! I'll take his wings, as matter of course. But my task is to take you *home*. What does your kind call it again? Inferna? Yes, that is the word. To us, it is *Tolatni*, the vast Nothingness. Oblivion. Bliss. Have you seen it, Sanguinir?" Irazi mocked, his spindly arms waving. "Our great city of Mictlani? The Seat of Fire to which all the lost gather to the welcoming arms of our Lord? No? A shame you will not have a chance."

"But you will, *Sofia*," Irazi hissed. "For my Achontli tires of dancing in dreams."

"Enough!" Ebrahym cried out and charged toward Irazi, blade held high.

He belted the first shining notes of a battle chorus. The disk of light materialized around the Sang's head and flames burst from his blade as he charged toward the creature. In the darkness, he looked like a meteor falling to earth from the heavens.

The lesser imuertes nearby unleashed, spilling upon Sofia, trying to drag her to the ground. Ebrahym swung from on high with his sword, but Irazi moved like smoke in the wind. He danced lightly about the rocks with inhuman agility. Ebrahym struggled to keep pace. Irazi laughed a shrill cry of glee, enjoying the dance. His screech echoed throughout the cavern, summoning more monsters to his call. Sofia shook off the pack of pale, chattering wretches and momentarily found her footing. They lunged at her again, biting blindly, hoping to clamp down on her limbs.

She whirled, slicing two of the creatures apart across their midsections, relieving their foul innards from their bodies.

Inside, a firestorm raged, like the kind that consumed forests. She was standing at the edge of it, marveling at its beauty and power. Then she threw herself into it, succumbing to the inferno. Unbearable heat and noise churned around her. But it would not burn her.

I am the fire.

The demons screeched and leaped wildly, clamoring at her limbs. But power surged through her. She flung the creatures aside with pathetic yelps. It felt good, powerful. She growled and landed a fist that caved in the skull of another death child and made her way toward Ebrahym.

"Yes! Yes! More!" Irazi cried with sick kind of ecstasy.

Ebrahym became a being of pale fire, bringing brilliance to a place that had never seen the light. It disoriented Irazi's minions, and even the lieutenant himself staggered.

Ebrahym moved to seize the moment. But Irazi's weakness was a clever feint. To Sofia's horror, Irazi sidestepped Ebrahym's blow, and with a deft stroke, used his blade to sever a wing clean from the Sang's back.

Foul minions dove on the bloody wing as it hit the ground, fighting to be the one to drag it back to the darkness.

Ebrahym cried out in pain, a scream drowned out a moment later by Irazi's cackle, gleeful and unsettling. The imuerte danced about, toying with the warrior, but Ebrahym held his ground and countered with a crushing kick against the creature's armor that sent him reeling. Irazi screeched again, louder this time. Rumbling sounded deeper in the caves.

Sofia saw an opening and charged toward Irazi, her sword held high. "Sofia! No!" she heard Ebrahym call from behind. Irazi simply stood, smiling wickedly, the glint of his eyes like bobbing orbs in the darkness.

As she closed the distance, Sofia felt the life leave her muscles, and she slowed as if trudging through mud. Suddenly, her fire was doused and all her power with it. The crushing weight of the imuertes aura, the dark whisper, broke the levies of her mind and swallowed her up. She dropped her sword and fell to her knees, powerless to resist. Ebrahym was calling, but everything was distant and muffled. Not even his song could reach her. There was only dark silence.

Irazi's face met hers, and she could smell the rotten flesh desperately clinging to the creature's skull. It was chipped and carved with miniature, explicit scenes of violence. Where flesh remained, insects feasted on the remnants and skittered between Irazi's exposed teeth, filed sharp. Abyssal sockets where eyes should be stared at her.

"Do not be afraid," Irazi whispered. In the heavy silence it sounded like stones grinding together. He kissed her forehead with cold teeth, for there were no lips. "He will set you free."

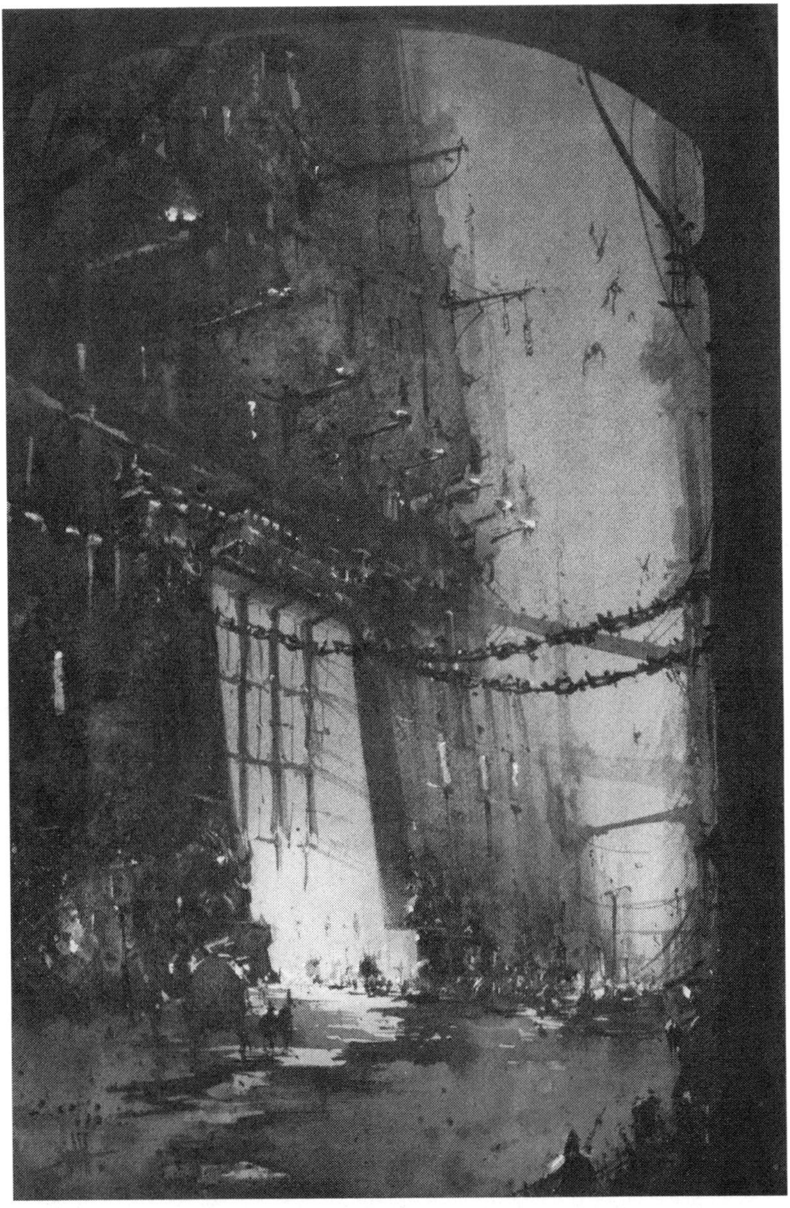

35

The sound of a hammer brought Sofia to consciousness.

The ping of iron against iron rang out as the spikes found purchase. The sensation of nails driving through flesh was enough to drag her mind up from the depths of nothingness back to the surface like a newborn, screaming.

A lesser imuerte scurried away into the darkness, its evil work done. Sofia was alone now, crucified against a metal wall, arms splayed out and bleeding.

The pain was unbearable and beyond her to describe, let alone face. Every movement, every breath, agony. Her body twisted itself in desperation to find relief. It only worsened the pain. She breathed quick and shallow and tried to see through the pain and sharpen her dull thoughts.

Where am I? Where is Ebrahym?

The scene replayed in her mind: Ebrahym's dismemberment, Irazi's wretched laugh. The Wingtaker. He'd lived up to his name.

Sofia flinched with white-hot rage, her anger stinging her muscles to action. Her limbs fought against the restraints, sending a searing acid of misery coursing through her. The intensity threatened to plunge her mind back into the darkness. She twisted and writhed and screamed in frustration until her voice broke. The echoes screamed back. Then, silence.

Breath returned slowly, enough to suppress the pain, giving her a moment to survey her surroundings. A jagged, twisted place bathed in crimson light. This was neither the cavern she and Ebrahym had entered nor a clawed-out imuertes burrow. It was beyond anything natural.

A lavishly carved chamber enveloped her, adorned with black obsidian furnishings, glistening wet. The room itself was a massive cage, an iron cube fashioned from thick metal bands, and heavy rivets the size of a human torso held the sections in place.

As her eyes adjusted; more of the space came into view. It was a kind of multi-tiered manor built within the cage. Furnished landings and rugs scattered the area along with foul machines of torture and ancient-looking weapons. Through openings in the serrated lattice of iron, Sofia could see the chains that suspended the enclosure above.

And then she realized where she was.

Mictlani.

The imuertes capital, the heart of the Inferna. She followed the chains upward where thousands of flickering lights made a crude simile of the night sky. *Fires.*

Sofia traced the silhouettes of an inverted cone of rock looming far above her, so huge she could not grasp its enormity from her restrained position. Mictlani was a mountain standing on its head. Dwellings scattered the face of it, bored straight into the rock. Thousands upon thousands of them, dark hovels for things much darker.

Spidery bridges spanned the chasm to the massive stalactite, giving it the unsettling look of a swollen egg sac suspended in a web. Streams of liquid fire bled from the mass and drew long, glowing lines before cooling and disappearing into the darkness below. The sight was a crude reflection of Luminea, a blasphemous mirror image of that beautiful place of pyramids reaching skyward.

It was said that as long as Luminea had stood, there had existed its counterpart in the darkness beneath the surface. Mictlani was supposedly the bottom of the world, beyond which an infinite abyss lay. Lost and troubled oulma, the umbra, gathered here like beads of water on the sides of a bowl, pooling toward the center. It was a place where the manifestation of agony and misery was made real by terrible Will.

And it was, indeed, real.

Below, Sofia watched the blood from her pierced feet slip through the grated metal floor to the nothingness beyond. There was only emptiness there. A featureless, silent maw that threatened to consume the tiny chamber suspended above it. Like one of the twinkling torches above, she was but a tiny flicker in a dark, dark place.

Sofia struggled between moments of panic, but there was little she could do. Against the strain of the iron pinning her in place, there was no fight to be had. She would either bleed out within the next few hours or succumb to exhaustion within the next few days, for soon she would be too weak to move.

Out of the corner of her eye, she caught movement in the shadows.

A massive, inky cloud pulsated as if the darkness itself was alive. Sofia felt a familiar feeling of dread infect her mind. She knew this thing. She knew it from her dreams.

"You are strong," the darkness said. **"I knew it would be so."** The voice was deep and harsh, like the sound of mountains grinding against one another. It was a whisper and a roar at once. Calm and menacing, like the looming blade of an executioner waiting to fall. And familiar. It belonged to whatever haunted her, the thing that came to her as she slept.

The Fierno. Angorzhu. The Hell Lord.

The imuertes leader of the horde that threatened every oulma in the hereafter stood a stone's throw from Sofia, speaking to her. There was no sickly aura about the creature, no effects that dulled her thoughts and conjured her fears. *Strange.*

"You know me," Sofia said through labored breaths.

"I know you," said the darkness, said Angorzhu.

"I've seen you in my dreams," said Sofia to the thing lurking in the shadows. "Are you going to kill me?"

The darkness laughed like the rumbling of a gathering storm. **"If that were my aim, I could have done so ten times over. I have watched."**

Sofia's mind raced. "It was *you*. In the north, when the imuertes just stood there."

"Yes. I stayed my children then. A shame about your companion," the darkness said without a hint of compassion.

"Matías," Sofia whispered. "His name was Matías."

The voice was devoid of pity. **"I was curious about your character. I saw his clearly enough. Weak. Easily manipulated. Afraid. But not you. Even then, I could tell you were different than those winged fools and the flock that follows them. I sensed you were special, but I had to be certain."**

"And?" she said, fearing the answer.

"His blood stained your hands, and here you are," the imuertes said, as a matter of fact. **"Did you feel it? The moment when you saw the life leave him, did you sense it?"** Sofia said nothing, turning away as the tears formed. **"I know you did. The blood warming your hands from the cold. The feeling of release, the purging of fear and pain, and the silence that follows. Peace."**

"No..." Sofia whispered.

"You will not find death here," Angorzhu said. **"On the contrary, this is a place of life and rebirth. Look around you!"**

Sofia sensed the imuertes moving in the shadows around her. **"Do you see signs of falsehoods or myths here? Systems of control, of *lies*? No. This place, my home, is a bastion of freedom. This is a place of truth. I was drawn to it long ago, and that same impulse is what brought you to me. You seek the truth, just as I did. Why else would you carry this?"**

The lúpero tooth she had carried with her, her trophy, landed at her feet. The creature knew too much about her. She felt naked again, exposed and vulnerable.

"You have yearned for this place, and now you are here, as my guest."

"You nail all your guests to the wall?" Sofia spat, summoning what courage she could.

"Pain is a blessing," the darkness replied. **"It transforms us."**

A hulking shape pooled from the shadows. The Hell Lord, in all his terrible and magnificent glory, stood before her.

Nearly twice her height, the Fierno was a communion between man and beast. But the edges of his form were indistinct and dissolved into thick, oily smoke. It was hard to tell where the darkness ended and he began. In her dreams, she had seen Angorzhu—a horned figure lurking in the shadows—but here, in the flesh, the sight of him inspired true terror. On cloven hooves, he moved toward her, shaking the elaborate cage as he did. Proud. Patient. Savoring the moment.

"**Beautiful,**" Angorzhu said, his face now a short distance from hers.

Now she saw him. He was broad and tall, with a prideful chest and thick, muscle-covered arms that had the look of burning logs. Carved inscriptions covered his body; foreign symbols and heretical script she could not read cut into his flesh. Embers still burned in the wounds. From his skull emerged a pair of massive horns like black steel, straight-like to either side, curled upward at the ends, adorned with golden trinkets. Heavy, circular earrings hung on either side of the Fierno's face, and everywhere that could be pierced and gilded was.

Sofia caught glimpses of the man he might have been once. But now, a monster. Face more akin to an expressionless mask; a visage carved from a blood-colored gem.

And upon his brow, gouged out of the flesh there, was the symbol from Sofia's dreams, the V with an intersecting line through it. The mark of Angorzhu. It burned like lava, as if he himself were made of liquid fire waiting to burst forth.

Angorzhu touched her face with his massive, clawed hand. He examined her profile; his touch should have seared her skin to the bone. She felt its heat, but there was no pain. The imuertes snorted with the hint of a smile. While there was no physical pain, the sensations from her dream welled up and surrounded her—an indescribable mix of terror, awe—and somehow, despite hanging crucified before the enemy of enemies, Sofia felt strangely comforted. The familiar nightmare. It sickened her.

"What do you want with me?" she whispered as two, clawed fingers caressed her chin.

"**To free you,**" Angorzhu said, still eying her like a doll.

"Then let me go."

Angorzhu laughed deeply, the way the earth would laugh if moved to it. "**True freedom requires pain. You will learn this, as did I.**" Angorzhu said. He craned his massive head upward, his ornamentations jingling. He dangled her silver bracelet, the one Anayah had given her inscribed with her name upon it, and eyed it curiously. "**I remembered things from Afore. Terrible things. A life of pain and suffering. I found no solace in the light, only lies. But in the darkness, I am free of it. Pain purged it from me. Now I am the master of it.**"

Angorzhu gestured toward the surface. "**The Sanguinir believe that the denial of self makes them worthy of ascension. They perpetuate the illusions of Afore. Morality, law, order—all artificial. All lies. They deny their true nature, as do you, Sofia. But here,**" Angorzhu said, "**is the natural order of things.**"

"What do you want, then?" asked Sofia. "Just stay here in your perfect kingdom. Leave the oulma at peace."

"I cannot. Once I become the master of the Orvida, my time of ascension will come. The Sanctu Arcam will lead me from this place. Once I lay waste to Luminea and stand before the light, I will do so without the bounds of morality. I will travel beyond and bring the darkness with me."

"And how many will you slaughter on the way?"

Angorzhu waved a heavy hand aimlessly. **"Meaningless. The universe is fueled by pitiless violence and fire. A cruel and dark place where light is but a reprieve from the eternal dark."** Angorzhu splayed his arms wide. **"Fire consumes the field so that it may grow anew. Stars burst, destroying entire worlds in an instant to give rise to new ones. So, too, am I a great and terrible force in the universe. A purging fire. A necessary evil. There is no right or wrong of it. I simply am."**

The imuertes slipped back into the shadows and left Sofia hanging there, bleeding. Reeling. There was no doubt in her mind Angorzhu was a monster and the creature of chaos he claimed to be. But he was not the mindless, primitive creature she'd imagined. She was drawn to him as one reveres an elder. Beneath his twisted logic, there was almost a charisma that seeped into her mind, tempting the darker parts of it.

Tears escaped from her eyes and fell silently into the abyss below. Here, her resilience to the fire would be put to the test. She hoped she could endure it.

And all the while, Nesta's warning repeated in her mind. *If you are lost in the dark, no one is going to come for you.*

Sofia squeezed her eyes tight and hoped against hope the Sang was wrong.

36

Months bled on. Deep in the torture pits of Mictlani, the time slipped away and never returned. Sofia spent most of it in a dark cell. The touch of jagged iron against her skin. The distant sound of screams. Her only company the lonely, maddening chorus of wails that seemed to shape her thoughts with an invisible hand. Malice. Cruelty. Suffering.

During long stretches alone in her cell, she tried to imagine the light of Luminea and the Dawnlight at its heart, and the songs of the Host and the color of the water, but the memories dimmed with each passing minute. Her Serrá had long faded. The only world she knew now was one of fire and blood and blackness.

And then there were the dreams. Before, the memory in the small bedroom would come to her each night and play itself out. And somehow, Angorzhu found her there, invaded her private thoughts.

She no longer dreamed the dream. Incoherent nightmares had taken its place. Visions of the torture chambers melded with the familiar aspects of the dream. Imuertes cackled on the fringes, in the corner of the apartment and in the shadows, as if the room itself was a mock set, a stage on which Sofia went through the motions for a clamoring audience. And Angorzhu was always with her in the dreams, a patient witness of the bizarre madness.

The city of Mictlani was hard to distinguish from her nightmares. The place was built in the pursuit of pain and suffering. The inhabitants relished it. Celebrated it. Built temples in honor of it. Primitive imuerte artisans and smiths made instruments of misery as their counterparts in Luminea forged jewelry or masterpieces of art. Newly formed imuerte monsters were pitted against one another to weed out the weak to the cheers of the onlookers. The winner was not the last standing but the one who endured the most suffering. It was a sweltering, bloody meat grinder that kept turning.

Sofia's side ached, and she turned mechanically to the other, her neck bent at an awkward angle. The endless din of screams and cries of agony echoed through the tunnels. But she was numb to them now. Their anguish became the buzzing of flies to her, an annoyance to be ignored.

She tried with all her Will not give in to callousness. So many times she thought of Ebrahym and Anayah as if they were by her side, watching the horror unfold. She wanted to make them proud.

But there were moments she caught herself staring at the horrific abuse she witnessed in the pits, even when she might have looked away. She had watched the skin flayed from a jabbering umbra—a death child had peeled it from him like softened onion. She told herself she would not cry out as the umbra did. She would not break as they did. They were weak. *Perhaps they deserved such punishment...*

No! She pounded her skull, reminding herself in erratic whispers that these umbra were lost oulma. *People*, like her, wandering in the dark, forgotten, consumed by their pasts. They deserved her pity, not her wrath. Not her hate.

Footsteps echoed close. *Are they real?* The cell door ground open. "Hello again, my sunshine," a sickly-sweet voice poured out. "Come now, Sofia. You should know the steps to this dance by now."

Zaniyoatli. Zani. The woman from the lamasery, the one called Oro who had played Ebrahym and her for fools. Sofia relived the feeling every time she heard the demon's saccharine voice, sugared to the point of nausea. Condescension and arrogance masked in a candy coating.

It had been she that had once betrayed Terafiq. Zara, she was called then, who infiltrated Ilucenta and blinded the Sang with misinformation. One of Angorzhu's most trusted spies, cunning and cruel.

Zani wore no clothes, as always, her milky complexion in ghostly contrast to her surroundings. Long white hair, willed to length by sinister pride since the lamasery, hung over her breasts and down her back. The locks framed the imuerte lieutenant's narrow eyes, daggers ringed with crimson. She tiptoed across the metal floor barefoot, gently caressing Sofia's head. Sofia trembled at the touch, jerking violently by reflex.

"I know, sunshine. But no bleeding today. I see you are still worn from last time. No matter; today we will just watch."

Sofia followed the pale hips leading her down the corridor. She had made the trek hundreds of times by now. Down through the maze of cages where fresh umbra newly descended to the Inferna sobbed in the shadows or raved and cursed as she passed.

Through the hive of stone, a catwalk led them over the Blood Market, a chaotic mob of all manner of imuerte trading in evil. It was anarchy that never seemed to ease, only intensify. Imuertes bought weaker ones as slaves, exchanging them like animals. They bartered for hunks of meat and limbs in exchange for other, fouler things, and in every stand were dangling talismans and other items Sofia recognized from the world above.

"Come now. We must not be late."

They passed through the great forges and armories, where the fires never cooled, by way of the temples—dark places Sofia had never seen the inside of. Choirs of unending wails and moans escaped from their carved stone mouths,.

Sofia barely raised her eyes from the ground, following Zani's pale feet across the black stone to their ultimate destination: the torture pits. The *schoolhouse*, Zani called it. There, human beings were transformed into something else, something terrible. The darkness of each of them pulled out through the navel and turned inside out. Zani, charged by Angorzhu with Sofia's education, was her teacher.

Nearby, the pale, shapely imuerte took her place and lounged sensuously on a leather sofa stitched from human flesh, including their faces. Distorted, they called out in silence. Her long white hair hung to the floor beneath her head, and the strange tentacles concealed within revealed themselves. Like something that ought to live and die in a cave, they emerged from Zani's spine, tendril servants that braided the hair of their master. They wove the strands of hair like the knowing fingers of an old woman.

"Remember what we discussed last time, my sunshine. If you look away, I will make you bleed." Sofia said nothing, trying hard to maintain some measure of composure, some honor, some pride. There was none to be had. She was filthy, with barely enough rags to cover herself. Skinny and weak. Hair in nasty clumps that smelled even to herself. She stood there as a student being disciplined.

"Now," Zani said as she absently picked at her nails. The tentacles continued to weave. "Pay attention. Today, our lesson is about the nature of compassion. This will be a hard lesson for you. After all, your weakness for it is what blinded you to my true nature when we first met and, well, here you are."

Sofia could not even clench a fist in protest. Her ragged fingers seized and shook with effort.

"Look there, sunshine, and tell me what you see."

Sofia approached the balcony overlooking the pits and the madness below. The torturers were at work, cleansing the sufferers from their false ideas of morality, identity, humanity. It was like an orchestra pit from one of Luminea's amphitheaters, only multiplied in scale. Huge pyres burned to illuminate the evil symphony of iron, blood and flesh. Cages, blades, fire, every manner of pain and suffering was represented in its cruelest form.

Below, humanity ripped itself apart in the cruelest, most disgraceful ways imaginable. It was a hell man made with his own hands.

When Sofia had first laid eyes on the carnage, she'd vomited and cried until there was nothing left. Now she just stared numbly.

"Well?"

"Misery."

"And what is compassion?" Zani asked.

"Helping people," Sofia managed.

Zani let out a disappointed sigh. "Rudimentary, but correct, I suppose. And do you see umbra helping one another down there?"

"No. They are hurting each other."

"My simple sunshine," Zani smacked, "have you learned nothing during our time together? What of the healer who removes the arrow to stitch up the wound? Does that not help the patient, despite the agony inflicted? Pain is but a tool that allows us to discover our *true* selves." She slid from the human sofa to come alongside Sofia, the tendrils floating as if suspended under water.

The madness was unbearable. It was all Sofia could do to resist the urge to tear her own eyes out. She watched a pack of imuertes in the process of creating a lúpero from the remnants of some poor oulma.

Like the Sang, the imuertes, too, were forged and willed into being and shaped into an ideal. This one was midway through the transformation. Stripped naked. Covered in strange markings. His legs, which had already been broken with mallets and set in reverse, were held in iron clamps. A cage surrounded the creature-to-be, bruised and bloody, suspended by chains lodged in its flesh. What was left of the man whimpered. Two hooks set into the top and bottom jaws pulled the mandibles forward with the help of grinding machinery to form a snout.

Sofia knew the rest of the process; she had seen it many times. As the jaws distended, carved fangs of stone would be hammered into the flesh, like the one she'd carried for so long. Skin blackened permanently by fire. The quilled hide would be sewn into the flesh later. Where it was harvested from, Sofia did not want to know.

"I never tire of the screams," cooed Zani as she slumped on the railing, eyes closed in bliss. "The songs of freedom." One of the milky tentacles probed outwards, pointing toward the transformation in progress. "The most responsibility lies with that one," Zani said.

There was a hooded figure next to the wretched creature-in-making, standing patiently, unmoving. But from it emanated a dissonant chorus that pushed the others around into absolute lunacy. "All of this work is for naught if the umbra does not want it. That is the lesson you fail to learn, sunshine. The *nechtolinia*, the painsinger, shows that one the way. Without their guidance, none of us would find peace."

"And why didn't you have a lúpero hide stitched onto your back?" Sofia asked, dredging up a fiber of courage. A tentacle lashed at her and bit deep with rows of hidden teeth. The wound added to her many others.

Zani grinned. "Some of us are destined for a higher purpose."

Sofia combed through the ashes of herself, searching for the spark inside of her. It flickered. Just for a moment; a flash of what she was appeared in the darkness. Her heart moved. "A higher purpose? What's yours? Bedding an imuerte when he calls for you?"

A flurry of tiny mouths lashed out in a swarm, biting deep into Sofia's flesh, holding firm. Zani followed them in a blur, her milky form suddenly appearing to block Sofia's view of the carnage below.

The imuerte was taller than she. But her tentacles lifted Sofia from the ground, the tiny razors gripping tight. Blood oozed from the wounds. Zaniyoatli pulled her close, so close Sofia could see her own reflection in the demon's eyes. She did not recognize the pair of tiny, gaunt skeletons staring back at her. Zani's hot breath washed over her. It stank of perfume struggling to mask the stench of decay.

"Do not test me." Zaniyoatli hissed. "If not for the wisdom and mercy of my Achontli, Angorzhu, I would split you lengthwise and send your pieces back to your precious Luminea myself."

"Go on then."

Zani cackled and was suddenly her sweet self again. "Oh, sunshine." She kissed Sofia deeply on the mouth, the sensation festering and hot. "There is hope for you yet. I will admit, you are more resilient than I thought. More than that Sanguinir companion of yours, anyway. Irazi so enjoys playing with his food."

Sofia's heart plummeted. For a moment, Sofia imagined the Wingtaker at work, mutilating Ebrahym's body bit by bit... *No! He made it out; I know he did.* Whether the truth or a lie, she convinced herself to believe it. It was all there was. All she had.

"I see we have more work to do," Zaniyoatli said with a wicked smile.

***

The tortured became the torturer.

Sofia knew well what the Hell Lord and his pet were trying to do. But there was no way to resist it, not even take her own life. *Life. What does it even mean now?* When she smashed her head against the walls of her cell into unconsciousness, they restrained her. When she refused to play along, they hurt her and ten more umbra as punishment. There was no escape. At least, not on her own.

Nesta's words were poison now, a warning that Sofia could not believe. *They will come for me.* She clung so tightly to the delusion it was the only thing keeping her sane. There was one condition though. To be rescued, she must survive. *Endure.* Whatever she had to do, Sofia would have to withstand whatever hell awaited her for any hope to escape. One day. But not now.

And so, she did as she was told.

She burned out the eyes of a helpless oulma, a gangly, pathetic creature lashed to a stretching rack. She peeled the skin from another as it screamed. *It.* She would catch herself thinking that. *These are people. Remember that.*

She stood at Zaniyoatli's side and hacked off the limbs of imuertes that had displeased Angorzhu and fed them to a lúpero, stroking its mangled snout as she did. She even sewed new feathers into the cloak of Irazi, handling with care the trophies of fallen Sanguinir warriors. As she embraced the insanity of it all, she could feel him, the Hell Lord, in the shadows, watching. Always watching.

Days passed without her knowledge. She would awake as if from a dream, once again herself and unaware of the atrocities she committed during her blackout. It was all slipping away.

One day, she caught herself adjusting a torture device so that it would work more efficiently. She vomited after coming to her senses and was whipped for hours after.

Pain and suffering became her very existence. Her world was misery, made less so by her willingness to inflict it upon others. She gave and received pain in a cycle of madness that threatened to consume every part of her.

Each night, if there was such a thing there, as they dragged Sofia back exhausted and broken to her cell, she would curl up in a corner and rock gently back and forth, trying to remember the reasons why she must not give up. They did not chain her anymore. They did not need to. There were no tears now. Her strength was wearing as thin as the meager clothes that clung to her.

For all the power and will she'd once commanded, the strength to walk through fire and face whatever lay on the other side meant nothing now. There was nothing to combat such insanity, such overwhelming hate and sorrow.

And no matter how hard she resisted, she knew there would come a time when her Serrá would exhaust completely and her spirit would crumble. She would fall to the darkness, and by that point, she would do it willingly. Gratefully. And that was what scared her the most.

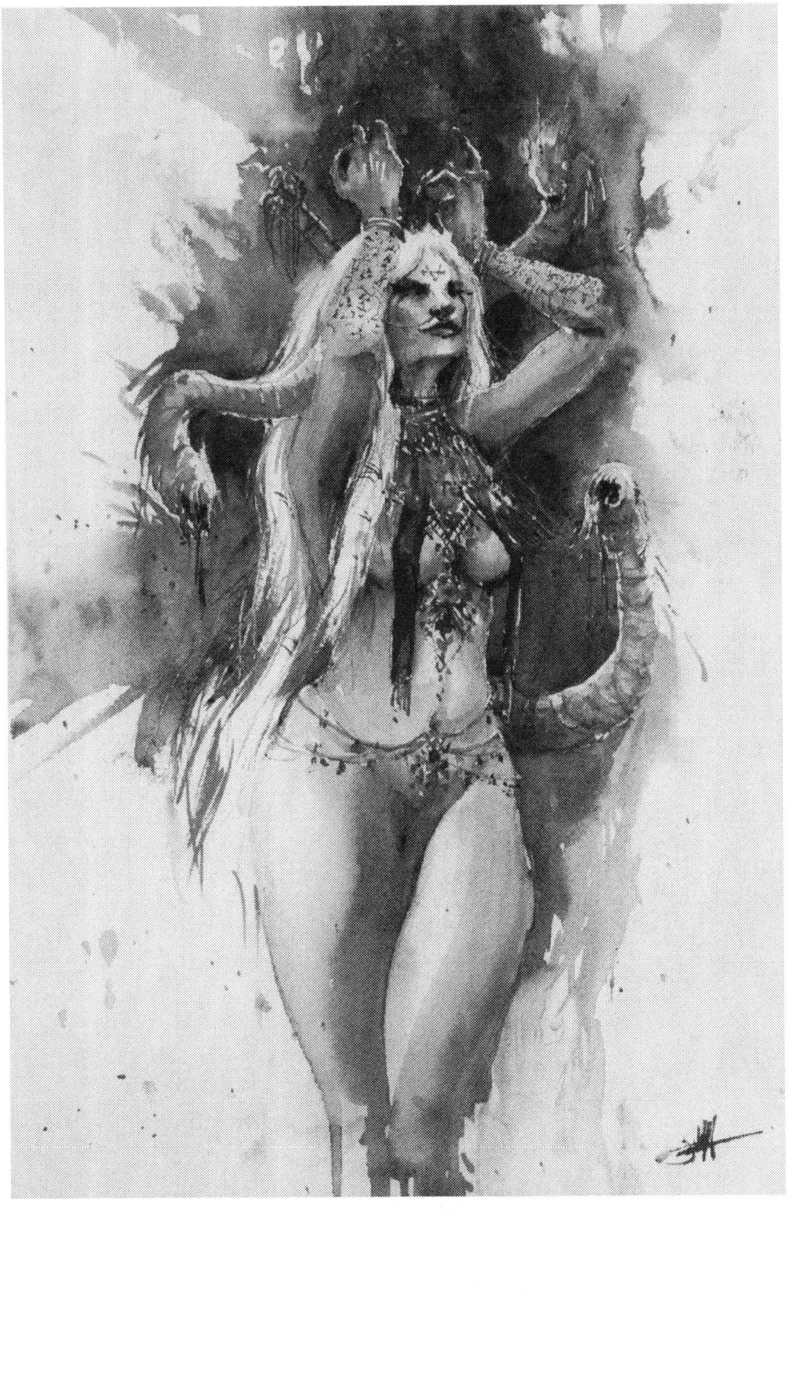

37

Crack. The snapping of a whip shattered the unusual silence. It had been so long since Sofia had experienced it—silence. Her imprisonment in Mictlani was never without the echoes of screams, the grind of metal and the sound of fire.

Now, in the darkest of the dark, this black womb of a cavern, the silence was menacing. It threatened her from the shadows, showing its dark teeth.

Crack. Crack. She tiptoed down the carved stone steps as instructed, and the whip sound grew louder. Zani pushed her down the hall and ordered her not to keep the Achontli waiting. She almost detected a hint of envy there. Sofia traced the side of the tunnel with a filthy hand to keep from tumbling down the stairs. Weariness clung to her.

Crack. She reached the bottom of the steps, and the still cavern expanded before her. A stone disk suspended between four perpendicular bridges hung over a black pit. Floating, fiery wisps of light cast a red glow upon the immense, carved tablet. It was inlaid with intricate engravings that moved and danced in the light.

Standing upon the stone platform, four imuerte did their work upon the fifth in the room. Angorzhu.

The Hell Lord knelt in the center of the stone dais, his face hidden from her. The minions surrounding their Lord were massive—swollen, fleshy creatures with engorged limbs poking through dark robes.

They were made for this work, using their muscle to deliver pain upon their master with wicked leather flails. *Crack.* One of the whips flashed in the darkness and split the silence open like thunder. Blood and embers sprayed in a fine mist as the lash opened up the Hell Lord's flesh. He did not move, frozen like one of the imuerte murals Sofia vaguely remembered hanging in halls of Luminea.

Crack. The last whip sounded, and the servants whispered their horrible blessing. Angorzhu stirred, refreshed as if waking from a slumber. The others took their cue, bowed, and made their way across the bridges backward, so as to not show their backsides to their lord.

As one passed her, Sofia caught a glimpse of the demon's face beneath the hood: devoid of eyes, nose or features of any kind, just a piece of solid skin stretched over a skull, split at the mouth.

The Hell Lord beckoned her forward with a growl, and Sofia crossed the bridge, each step intentional and slow. If this were to be her end, she would not run or cower from it, however much she wanted to.

Angorzhu's massive bulk stood before her. His wounds poured molten fire and popped with embers. The sight still terrified her, but by now she was numb and weak. Terror can only sustain itself for long before being replaced by a dull, resigned sorrow.

"*Quimhuat zah tiquiz que.* **The liturgy of the lash,**" he rumbled. "**The pain encompasses all thought until the moment it ceases. Then, all that is left is you.**" He shifted to one side and placed a hand on a pulpit rising from the center of the stone floor. She couldn't see it before, not behind Angorzhu's massive frame kneeling before it. Square on all sides, the pulpit was inlaid with writings and inscriptions. At its peak was a book, thick and old in appearance, its cover stained red and sealed with a heavy lock.

"**Zaniyoatli tells me you continue to resist,**" Angorzhu said. He turned to face her, the wispy aura of soot following like a ghost. The jewelry adorning his face and horns jingled. Embers burned beneath his heavy brow. The symbol seared on his forehead burned as brightly as ever. "**Why?**"

"I will not be like them." Sofia managed. "Like *you*. I'd rather not exist at all." It was not a challenge or a threat but a sad fact. Sofia fiddled with her fingers as she spoke. What nails she still had were cracked and bloody.

"**You already are like us.**"

Tears escaped her eyes, the first ones in recent memory.

"**I understand,**" the imuerte rumbled. "**Belief is a powerful thing. It is the very essence of what the Sanguinir call** *Serrá*. **I can smell it.**" he snorted, caressing the edge of the tome. "**Tell me, do you know the story of the Unspoken War?**"

"No."

"**Of course not. The Sanguinir wish it forgotten.**" Angorzhu paced, his claws clasped behind him with the measured delivery of an experienced storyteller.

"**There was a time when their kind was new to the Orvida. The oulma were primitive then, when the Sanctu Arcam first revealed itself. They were a reflection of a more brutal Afore when man was superstitious and fanatical. The first aurolas, in their arrogance, thought they could change mankind. They were mistaken.**" Angorzhu twisted the lock on the book's cover with his claw and snapped it open. The pages rustled like the distant memory of a tree's leaves in the wind.

"**Have you wondered why the Sanguinir take the forms they do?**" Sofia stared ahead. "**The first of the Host became the manifestations of beliefs they could not remember, not consciously. But they were weak and susceptible to power's seduction. Armed with the halos, they controlled the passage to the beyond, what you call the Dawnlight. They formed their cult so the oulma would worship them as gods. But the oulma rebelled.**"

"You're lying."

"Desipar." Angorzhu growled. **"To slay an oulma. A sin invented by the Sanguinir and covered up, masked by their precious Sphere. Look around you,"** Angorzhu gestured. ***"We are the aftermath of that war. The Sanguinir believed our kind to be monsters, and in the fires of that war, they Willed it to be so. Those who did not perish became *tilcah*, what you call imuerte. Tilcah means forgotten ones."***

No! It can't be.

"Evil begets evil."

"I don't believe you," Sofia whispered. Betrayal rose in the back of her throat to choke her. "They would have told me."

"See the truth for yourself, as I once did," Angorzhu paged the tome to a bookmarked passage. Sofia scanned the writings, tracing with her gnarled fingers the ancient Sanguinirian verses describing the story. Handwritten notes lined the margins. Sources, dates, references to the names of authors she recognized from her own time in the library. The evidence was there. It was the truth.

The Sang had crushed an oulma rebellion, and in turn, created an even greater enemy. Their Serrá, their wrath, had transformed the oulma into the first imuerte. The implications struck her harder than any lash. *Did Ebrahym know? Anayah?* Her heart sank. *All those Sanguinir secrets....*

"Where did you get this?"

Angorzhu traced the edges of the tome with care. **"From deep in the Luminean archives."** Sofia looked up into the eyes of the monster as he spoke. **"I, too, studied in the Fifth Tier. I, too, learned the ways of the Sang and their lies, their history of deceit."**

She felt the grasp of fire and flesh on her shoulders, like from her dream. **"Then I discovered what I could do with these hands."**

This was no dream. A nightmare, yes, but real. **"Think on your beliefs,"** Angorzhu whispered from the darkness as Sofia gazed at the writing. **"And on the ones whom you think you can trust."**

***

Sofia stirred in the dank black of her cell. Something pulled her up from the darkness of oblivion, where the nightmares were still imaginary, back to consciousness. Back to the real nightmare. A whisper called her name. Her thoughts played tricks on her again, feeding her lies.

The whisper again, louder, coming from behind the iron door. On bare, ragged feet Sofia crept to the door and put her ear to the warm metal. "Sofia?" she heard from the other side. "It is Anayah."

She reeled back against the wall. *Go away!* Not again. So many times she imagined hearing her friend's voice, a sweet melody to herald her rescue. So many times her hopes had turned to ash and pushed her toward a hopelessness there was no return from.

She cupped her hands on her ears to drown out the voice, hoping the delusion would disappear and torment her no longer.

"Sofia?" the whisper said again. "It is me. I am here, Sofia. We are going to get you out. Hold on."

"Go away!" Sofia screamed. "Leave me alone!"

The door groaned open. Two dark silhouettes standing in the doorway to the cell blocked the light from the corridor. Sofia cowered from the massive shapes as they lunged for her. Glowing eyes glared at her from the blackness. She clawed at the corner of her cage, digging against the iron and stone for an escape where there was none.

Anayah and Ebrahym knelt beside her, clutching her emaciated wrists and limbs with powerful hands. Sofia blinked to dispel the visions, but they remained.

The Sang released her. Sofia touched their faces with long, blackened fingers, the tingling sensation racing through her like a spark of life reanimating a corpse. They were real. *Real.*

The faces of the Sanguinir were as she remembered, like the memory of a sunrise long ago. It had been so long since she had seen beauty it was if seeing it for the first time. Tears escaped from Sofia's eyes as she looked upon Anayah and Ebrahym. Her friends, her saviors. She pawed at them, sobbing, making sure they wouldn't vanish again.

"I knew I would find you." Ebrahym said, cupping her head. "But we must move Sofia, we must hurry."

She nodded, wiping the tears and mucus from her face. The Sang helped her to her feet and, seeing her for what she was, could not hide the shock in their amber eyes.

Sofia took stock of herself. Her clothes were tattered, barely covering her intimate parts. Her scarred and ravaged skin was blackened by soot and grime and blood. She didn't want her friends to see her like this. Where there was once a proud, defiant warrior, a withered shadow now stood. *Would they ever forgive the things I've done to survive?* The shame was almost too much to bear as the heavenly eyes pierced through her.

"It is all right," Ebrahym said as he pulled her close. She flung herself at him, squeezing as tight as her muscles allowed. The tears came again, harder now. Zaniyoatli lied. Angorzhu lied. Irazi had not claimed another trophy after all. Ebrahym had escaped, somehow. She was ashamed to have ever doubted it.

"I knew it," Sofia whispered. "I knew you'd come." She could not remember the touch of love, only pain. The simple embrace was so foreign to her it made her weep all the harder. She wanted to stay in the Sang's arms, but after a moment Ebrahym pulled away.

She noticed for the first time Ebrahym's single wing tucked behind his shoulder. She knew where the other was. She'd sewed it into Irazi's foul cloak herself.

"Sofia," Ebrahym whispered. "I know you are tired and in pain. But we *must* move. Can you do that?" She nodded, not completely confident she could.

Anayah retrieved a set of armor from Ebrahym's pack. He forced a smile, and Sofia felt sunlight on her face for the first time in months. But she could see the sadness he hid underneath at the sight of her. Anayah unrolled the garments on the floor and helped Sofia's stiff limbs into them. The armor was black and minimal. Ebrahym kept watch at the door as she dressed. The armor felt good on her skin, loose as it was—a welcomed reminder of her former self.

"I'm sorry, Anayah," Sofia said as she fumbled with the buckles. "They took it from me. I—"

"Took what?" said Anayah, still buckling parts of Sofia's kit.

"My bracelet. They took it when I was…"

Anayah smiled with tenderness. "Here," she said. The Sang pulled a chain up from around her neck, revealing the golden knot encircling a lion's head, the necklace Sofia had given her before the tournament.

"This has kept me safe. Now you carry it." She draped the medallion over Sofia's, neck and it rested on her protruding collarbones. Sofia clutched it tight.

"Are you ready?" Ebrahym asked. Sofia nodded. Anayah retrieved a glowing vial from her belt and handed it to Sofia. "Drink." Sofia downed the liquid. It bled through her like warm honey, oozing from her core to her extremities.

"Anything?" Anayah asked.

"I don't know. It feels warm…"

Anayah shot Ebrahym a concerned look. "It is not working."

Ebrahym clenched his powerful hands around Sofia's arms. "You have to concentrate, Sofia. It will not work unless you will it to. Find your Serrá. It is still in you. Find it," he instructed. Anayah nodded, affirming.

"I can't," Sofia said, hanging her head. "There's nothing left. Nothing."

Anayah pushed Ebrahym aside. "Now it is I who am sorry."

"For what?"

"For this." The back of Anayah's armored hand crashed into Sofia's cheek. Blinding pain stung one side of her face. Anayah struck her again, this time a hard punch to the gut, and she gasped. "I know it is there, Sofia. Find it!" Anayah hissed again as her knee drove into Sofia's side. She slumped over, spitting blood onto the filthy floor.

"This is not the woman I knew. Sofia would never lie down."

The fire…

Another blow came, and another. *I…am the fire.*

Sofia clawed through the long dead embers of herself for the spark. Angorzhu had done his work well. There was little of herself left, piles of ash, dry and brittle, blowing in the wind. Dust and smoke swirled as she searched on hands and knees.

There! A tiny glowing speck, long dormant, lying in wait. It was the rage. The anger. The thing that separated her from everyone else. Her *power*.

Angorzhu, Zani, Irazi. The faces of her tormentors stoked the fire. She felt the whips against her flesh, the choking poisonous ash. The rage grew. She cupped the tiny ember clinging to life and nursed it back to health with her breath. And what she had done to survive. How she hated it. Hated herself. With each exhale the spark pulsated, flickering gently, gaining strength, then ignited like a newly birthed star exploding into life.

I am the fire.

Another fist careened toward Sofia's head. Her muscles remembered, shaking off their torpor and moved on their own, trapping Anayah's blow and countering fast with a strike of her own. Anayah's head snapped to the side as Sofia's fist connected, a trickle of blood streaming from her split lip. Sofia stood in disbelief, staring at her scarred fist. The scars of her crucifixion were still red and puffy.

"There you are," grinned Anayah.

The fire. Sofia felt it now. A lifetime of pain and suffering melted away, followed by a burst of energy that surged through her like lightning. Whatever she'd drunk multiplied the effect, focusing her Serrá into a concentrated beam.

She sucked rapid breaths to keep pace with her pounding heart. She felt...*alive*. The feeling pulled her in every direction at once. Her mind sharpened, vision focused. Her muscles shook with purpose, waiting to be unleashed. She flexed with anticipation.

"What the hell was that?" Sofia asked, panting.

"It is called wildfire," Anayah said. "We borrowed some from the Host's armory. All of it, in fact."

"They are coming," Ebrahym called out from the door. Anayah handed Sofia a sword. *Her* sword. The one that belonged to Nilayah, the one she thought she'd lost in the battle with Irazi. Ebrahym must have recovered it during his escape.

Her hand remembered the grip and the weight, like the handshake of an old friend.

"Are you ready?"

Sofia nodded, trembling.

The talons of the imuerte sentries sounded through corridor outside of the cell. They were coming to summon her once again to the torture pits and Zani's side. *Not this time.*

The Sanguinir pressed against the walls as the door swung inward. The impès skittered inside, confused by the empty interior.

Sofia was upon them before Anayah or Ebrahym could even react. She cleaved the head off one in a single strike with a desperate howl. Without pause, her sword found the gut of its companion and tore it open from side to side. It cowered and squealed on the ground as Sofia's boot heel found the creature's head, over and over, until it was a mass of brain and skull seeping into the stone.

Sofia took a deep breath and exhaled slowly, craning her neck toward the sky. Anayah and Ebrahym nodded as if they understood, though obviously surprised at the gruesome display of violence. *They don't understand. They could never understand.*

"Come on," Sofia said, leading the way. "I know the way out." Anayah and Ebrahym followed Sofia into the labyrinth of tunnels.

She knew them intimately. Early in her captivity, she had studied them, looking for an escape should the opportunity arise. She'd made mental maps and counted the steps. Now she sprinted through the tunnels, the wildfire pumping through her.

Through the dungeon, down the little-used corridors, out of the cellblock. They passed through the forge where smelting furnaces that never cooled belched hot ore into crude molds. The imuerte crafters there paid attention to little beyond their work, and the trio easily navigated around them, sticking to the shadows.

Sofia and the Sang emerged from inside the massive stalactite, the inverted mountain of Mictlani, to one of the many narrow paths carved onto its face. She whispered thanks that the bridge, hundreds of meters long and suspended with thick iron chains, was empty. If it hadn't been, there would have been nowhere for them to hide.

There was an ebb and flow of the inhabitants of Mictlani. Sofia had learned to read the patterns as the hordes came and went. Sometimes the city would swell like a bloated insect nest, bursting at the seams. Other times, it was an eerie ruin.

Thankfully, it was the latter. They raced across the bridge and scrambled through a large opening carved into the rock face.

Sofia knew the passage; it led to a large hall used for dark rituals and gatherings. The chamber would be empty now, for there was no gathering in celebration of a great victory on the field, nor preparations being made for one. *I hope.*

For a moment, the gamble seemed to have paid off, but a sweet smell in the air stopped her cold. The odor was all too familiar. Sofia gestured for caution as the warriors followed her lead through the shadows into the great hall. Her heart beat against the inside of her armor like a smith's hammer.

The gouged rock formed a kind of coliseum pit, with rows of seating rising up around them., Sofia saw her in the center of the diocese of sorts, lounging in the middle of the altar, brushing her hair.

"It's good to see you up and about, my sunshine," said Zaniyoatli, her sweet voice ringing out in the emptiness. "And you brought friends," the imuerte squeaked with delight. "How wonderful."

She stood from the throne, confidently striding naked toward them, unabashed. A cruel grin split across her face. Long talons pierced the ends of her fingers, extending like thin knives that flicked with excitement. Pale tentacles emerged from within her ghostly hair and reared up, showing their teeth.

The imuerte took her time. Her hips swayed provocatively as she shot a look toward Ebrahym. "This one, in particular, is quite handsome. Though he appears a little damaged."

"The things you did to me..." Sofia managed through her rage.

Zani giggled. "I remember the lash being in your hand more than mine, sunshine. Now, put your toys away and go back to your room. It is time for *me* to play."

"You...Oro," Ebrahym said as he recognizing her.

"And Zara," Sofia said through gritted teeth. "The one who betrayed Terafiq at Ilucenta."

Zani smiled wickedly, curtseying. "The most beautiful wolf among pathetic sheep."

Sofia charged forward, blinded by a thirst for vengeance. Anayah and Ebrahym moved to support, but the tendrils sprouted from Zaniyoatli's spine and struck like vipers in all directions. Zani screamed a banshee's call that echoed through the caverns.

Others will be here soon. Sofia could not outmaneuver the snapping tendrils. Even empowered by the wildfire, the eel-like monsters were too fast, so she stopped trying.

She pushed forward with brute strength, letting the teeth-lined mouths snap at her frail body. They bit. She bled. *It will take more than that to stop me now.* More jaws clamped on to her body, trying to hold her in place.

Ebrahym and Anayah swung wildly as more and more tendrils appeared to the sound of Zaniyoatli's cackling. Their halos activated, and the glow surrounding their heads brought the first true light to this place since time began.

Sofia pushed forward, unrelenting, her anger driving her forward like a plow. She howled with rage. The stone beneath her boots cracked from the force. The imuerte's porcelain face transformed from one of confidence to hesitation as Sofia inched toward her.

Anayah and Ebrahym sensed the plan. Rather than contend with their own mass of tentacles, they turned their blades on the ones holding Sofia in place, severing dozens with swords set aflame.

Ichor spewed from the severed limbs as Zaniyoatli screeched again. It was cut short. Sofia, freed from the tentacles' grasp, plunged her sword deep into the imuerte's gut. Sofia twisted the blade, enjoying Zani's face squirming at the pain.

"You taught me about compassion," Sofia whispered. "Now I have none."

Zaniyoatli's dead, black eyes flickered as she smiled defiantly. "Then my work is done, sunshine." She sputtered as the gore flowed from her mouth. "The end is already in motion."

"What do you mean?" Sofia demanded, grinding the blade again.

Zaniyoatli laughed. The sounds of approaching imuertes echoed in the tunnels. "Your precious Luminea. Our brethren, led by our Achontli, march upon it. All is in place. Very soon, Angorzhu will claim what is his and—"

Sofia roared and ripped the blade up and up, through the sternum, between Zaniyoatli's breasts, nearly to the base of her throat. Blood and entrails poured onto Sofia, as did a wash of relief. The tendrils wilted and fell to the ground. It felt as good as she'd imagined so many times.

"Sofia?" said Anayah with a hint of disbelief at the display of carnage.

"I'm fine," Sofia said, gore still dripping from her soaked hands. She looked around absently, coming down from the ecstasy of the release.

On the floor, near the body of Zaniyoatli, she saw caught sight of something: the book of Angorzhu. She could have sworn it was not there a moment before, but she hefted it into her arms, feeling its power.

"What is it Sofia?" Ebrahym asked, turning back as he and Anayah prepared to move.

She looked at the engraved leather cover, stained the color of blood. She thought of leaving it behind, letting the abyss claim the words of its master. But something prevented her. She wanted it.

"It's the truth, Ebrahym," Sofia said. *The truth you wouldn't tell me.*

PART VI

—

SALVATION

And Lo! She made the journey home.
Armed with truth and purpose,
To face whatever end.

Nephahi Epoye XXVI 9:6

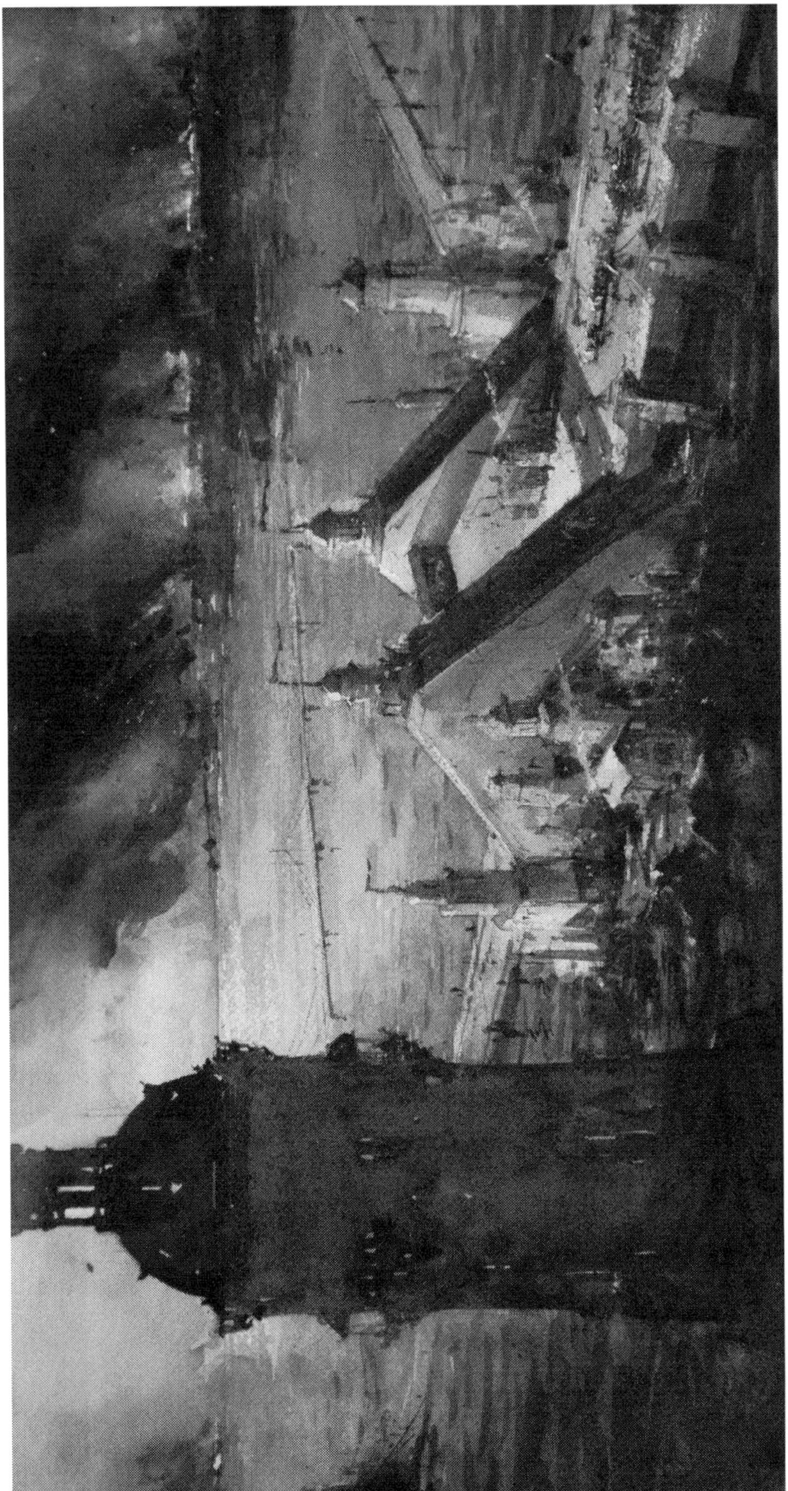

38

Sofia leaned on the bow of the skyship, basking in the glow of the rising sun. It was a small craft, much smaller than any of the floating galleons used by the Host in war. The cockpit was barely larger than the cell she'd left behind. But it was enough to ferry one broken oulma and two Sang back to Luminea.

A lifeboat.

The lines creaked as the morning thermals pushed against the hand-carved ailerons. From a few thousand meters up, Sofia gazed out at the desert coming to life. The dunes shed their evening coats of purple and warmed to the color of peaches.

Even in the weak light of the morning, the sun's ray were harsh and unfamiliar. She closed her eyes and savored the warmth on her skin and the smell of the breeze as if it were the first time. But the moment was too short. Mictlani stirred in the blackness of her mind. It was always there. Flashes of blood and fire and the sounds of screams boiling to the surface.

Sofia opened her eyes, heart racing, reminding herself it was over. Her hands clenched the railing of the skyship and whitened her knuckles. *But was it over, really? Would it ever be?*

Even if they made it back to Luminea, she wondered if she might never really return from the place underground. Part of her would never leave, and the void left inside of her would be ever filled with nightmares. The things she'd done to survive...how would she ever forget?

While some scars lay hidden from Ebrahym and Anayah, some evidence of her suffering was obvious. Although fresh clothes covered her ravaged body, it was no longer caramel and toned but pasty and thin. Once underway, Anayah spent hours applying Sanguinirian salves and ointments to Sofia's wounds help her body heal. Neither of them said a word as she did. Afterward, Anayah took to the sky to scout ahead.

Sofia's eyes traced the contours of the dunes as her thoughts rewound the events of their escape. The details were indistinct, perhaps a side effect of the wildfire. She remembered the bridge leading out of Mictlani and Zaniyoatli's blood on her hands. And the book she recovered, Angorzhu's book, that now rested at her side.

There had been winding tunnels and caves after that, more dark places that'd all run together. Eventually, she and the Sang had emerged from the Inferna. She remembered the evening chill, distinctly crisp. Cold, like when she'd first touched down on the tundra before Matías had died.

They'd run until Sofia could no longer keep up, and Ebrahym had carried her the rest of the way on foot. At some point, they'd reached the skyship Anayah and Ebrahym had used to travel west and had stashed in the sand. Sofia recalled vague images of the two Sang piecing the machine together as she'd lain nearby, watching their dark silhouettes work against a starry sky.

Ebrahym adjusted some of the craft's control lines from the stern. The propellers tilted slightly, whirring on their new course toward the west.

He was darker in complexion than Sofia remembered. Protruding from his robes was a single, feathered wing rustling in the breeze. She turned toward him, the span of the cockpit between them. Neither Anayah nor Ebrahym pressed her to recount her captivity—they saw the story written upon her body. But even in the presence of her friends, she felt the divide between them. Like the wedge she'd once felt between herself and Alana at the Conventa, only now, a chasm between her and the rest of the world.

"They made me think you were dead, Ebrahym," Sofia said after a few minutes passed in silence. There were so many things to say. She almost laughed, thinking of the hot-tempered, naive woman she'd been when they'd first met. She'd burned with questions then. Now, she was simply tired.

"After Irazi took you, the imuertes fled without a fight," Ebrahym explained. "I took up your sword and followed, but I lost them in the tunnels. I searched for days before making my way back to the lamasery."

"Your wing..." Sofia said, glancing at Ebrahym's one remaining feathered limb. Her fingers twitched at the memory of stitching its likeness into Irazi's cloak. It made her want to vomit.

Ebrahym didn't glance back. "Hmm. Poison on Irazi's blade infects me still. Despite my efforts, I cannot Will it to grow back or seal the wound." The memory of the dismemberment replayed in Sofia's mind in vivid detail. She shuddered.

His expression softened into a grin. "You would not believe what I found after returning to the lamasery."

"What?"

Ebrahym chuckled. "Messenger birds. The lamasery had a dovecote untouched by the attack, where a few hearty survivors roosted. Simple creatures that may prove to be the greatest heroes of us all. I fattened up the strongest one of them and sent him on his way to Luminea with a message for Anayah. She received it."

"And she came," Sofia said.

Ebrahym nodded. He held his breath. "I failed you," he finally said. "I was not strong enough. It was foolish to descend into the abyss. Prideful. I cannot imagine what you endured there. I am sorry, Sofia. With all that I am, I am sorry." She could see the pain burning behind his golden irises, a shame that cut deeper than any blade.

"It's not your fault. This is war," Sofia said. "You found me; that's all that matters." She turned her gaze back toward the horizon. "I don't know how, but you did."

"I cannot explain it either," Ebrahym said, "but an impulse drove me on. I could not leave, and while I waited for Anayah's reply, I searched the desert. I sensed your presence like the faintest hint of flowers on the breeze. It took many weeks, but the feeling guided me to you. Once she arrived, we continued to search for months to find you."

Sofia peered at the horizon, looking for familiarity. "Where are we?"

"Hundreds of kilometers south of the lamasery, east of the *Duna Intunis*."

"So, your halo led you to me?" asked Sofia. Ebrahym sounded his agreement. She sighed heavily. "Everything they did...*made* me do...I don't understand why they didn't just kill me. It doesn't make any sense."

Ebrahym pondered the thought. "I do not know."

"There were times when I wished they had," Sofia said. "Ended it, I mean." There was a long pause before she spoke again. The skyship creaked and gently moaned. "He stopped the imuertes in the north," Sofia said. "Before Matías...*changed*, remember? Angorzhu. He wanted to see what I would do."

"He...spoke to you? You saw him?" Ebrahym asked. Sofia nodded, and he held his chin in thought. "So, he is curious about you."

"He was toying with me. He still is." Her hand made its way to the red tome at her side. Ebrahym's eyes followed.

He spoke again. "Something stayed his hand. He could have killed you many times, but he did not. Perhaps you are more important to him than you think. Your dreams," he said, the idea coming to him. "Consider this: what if the vision you had of the attack on Espleña was not an *intentional* warning? Perhaps it was not a trap at all. Is it possible Angorzhu has no control over what he shares with you, or...you with him?"

Sofia's brow deepened. "I don't know. He kept me alone, the dark..."

"To conceal his true designs?" offered Ebrahym. "Luring you to the desert may have simply been the bait. Once he had you, the Hell Lord had the secrecy he needed to make his war. Otherwise, you may have divined his plan."

Sofia shook her head and shuddered, recalling the touch of Angorzhu's hand upon her face. "It's possible, but there's more to it than that. He *wanted* me there. Close to him." Something held her back from revealing everything.

Ebrahym sat next to her. He put his arm around her, and she recoiled at the touch, the reflex honed and automatic. The imuertes had done their work well. Ebrahym muttered an apology. Sofia did the same. Then they sat a while in silence before either spoke again.

"He showed me this," Sofia said, handing Angorzhu's book to him. She had been dreading this moment, this test of Ebrahym's character. "It describes something called the Unspoken War, among other things."

Ebrahym placed the book on his lap, scanning the pages. "*Grandir Infama*. The Great Shame..." Ebrahym whispered, visibly surprised. "Few know of this, even within the Host."

The sting of betrayal hit home. Not just the lie, but that the enemy of enemies had revealed the truth to her. "It's true, then. The Sang created the imuertes after the oulma rebelled, and the Divine Sphere to control everyone to keep it from happening again."

Ebrahym slowly paged through the book. "Yes, it is true. Long before my time or the time before my aurola's descension. All that I know of it comes from ancient writings. I recall one passage:

The shepherds did turn against their flock;
Against they who would rebel against rule
And lo! The mighty came to fear the weak.

And amongst holy places, fires burned,
Where the mantled sowed wrath upon the field.
And reaped evil harvest from the ash."

Ebrahym closed the book and eyed its menacing cover.

"It's all a lie, then," Sofia said. "The Host, honor, duty, the Way—all of it. A lie built by beings that cannot lie, only hide. That book belonged to Angorzhu before he was an imuerte, before he learned the truth. It's what drove him to become what he is."

The Sang hung his head. "I am sorry this is how you learned the truth of things. But it was not the Way to tell you."

"To hell with your Way!" Sofia yelled. "I believed in all of this, in *you*! I rotted down there for *months* believing it." Fresh tears came as the rage bubbled up. "And for what? So Terafiq can play queen of the court with all her little knights? I've seen the repercussions of pride first hand. I've watched oulma be transformed into monsters. I won't be part of this. Not anymore."

"This changes nothing, Sofia," Ebrahym shot back. "We are losing the war. The campaign has been a long and bloody one during your absence. Despite events in the past, there are oulma and Sanguinir alike fighting and dying for one another." His eyes bore down on her. "You of all people should understand one should not be judged merely by the sum of their past."

The point hit hard. After all, it was her past, her memory of the Afore, that made her an outsider.

Ebrahym paused before speaking again, his voice calm once more. "After my communion, I soon learned about the dark history of the Host. Yes, everything you say is true. But I wanted to believe I could make it better. I fought then for the oulma, and I still do. Why do you think I exiled myself with you, Sofia? I was looking for another Way.

"I cannot imagine what you went through in the Inferna. What you endured—it would have broken the bravest of the Host. But you still have a choice. If what Zaniyoatli said is true, then Luminea is in danger; we must act."

He was right. She had a choice now. As she met Ebrahym's hard stare, she remembered the words Matiás once said to her. *Would you sacrifice yourself to save them?* Not for the Host or glory, not for spite or pride. But because it was right, despite the injustice on all sides. Maybe there was still a chance to prove there was a better Way. Perhaps the umbra could be saved. Perhaps the Host could change. And in trying, perhaps she might find peace.

"What do you want me to do?" Sofia asked.

"Rest," Ebrahym said. "For you have earned it. And if you do have a link with the Fierno, we may yet divine the plan Zaniyoatli spoke of. So, sleep now, and let the dreams find you again."

"Please don't ask me to do that," Sofia said, rubbing her tired eyes.

"You must, Sofia. You know it."

***

The familiar scene materialized from the blackness of sleep: the cramped, run-down bedroom, the holy trinkets, the mattress that no doubt bore witness to the conception of the life growing inside of Sofia.

She sat on the bed, caressing the flesh separating her hands from the unborn child within. With effort, Sofia lurched from the mattress and righted herself. Her toes mingled with the cheap, worn rug. Nearby, the oval window cast a familiar reflection back at her. But it was not her own. There were parts there that were close approximates—hints at a likeness. But the emerald, smoky eyes were larger and sad. Sofia's strong jaw was replaced by a shallower one, and the face staring at her from the glass was slender, more gentle.

Sofia touched her cheek, as did the woman in the mirror. She reached out to touch the fingers coming toward her, but she blinked, and the reflection changed.

Zaniyoatli, thick blood pouring from her mouth, smiled back at her with hungry, black eyes. Darkness swirled behind the apparition. Sofia cowered, but slithering limbs tightened around hers and pulled tight. She wrestled with the tendrils, but they dragged her down into and through the floor as if it were sand, deep into the darkness waiting below.

She opened her eyes to fire and smoke. A creature with no lips whispered lies into her ears. She tried to break free, but iron held her arms and legs, spread away from her center, exposing the life in her belly to the pack of monsters that surrounded her.

Foreign fingers probed at her, their chattering, excited owners debating something Sofia could not understand. She screamed, or tried to, but no sound escaped her throat. She felt the sting of scalding metal on her flesh, violation more than pain. She mouthed the sound of terror once again as her eyes rolled back, slipping once more into the dark.

Then she fell. Not down, but inward. The horror of Mictlani and the imuerte torture pits dissipated into darkness. Her being condensed into its vital essence. But this was not the darkness of a pit. And it was hot, but not like the scalding sulfuric mats that bubbled in the imuerte capital. This was comforting. Life-giving.

Sofia felt energy pulse through her at a rhythmic beat. She was one with it, connected and entwined with it. And for a moment, Sofia hung there in the dark, perfectly at peace.

The blackness compressed around her. The pressure was enormous; the weight of the universe imploded around her. It forced her further down where a single point of light appeared. It was dim at first, no more than a flickering candle. Then it grew larger, white and blinding. She moved toward it by no will of her own.

On all fours, now, Sofia crawled up a rocky slope toward the light. The tunnel was long and dark, the way sharp and difficult. She was naked, and her hands and knees were soon scraped and bleeding as she climbed on, pushing onwards to the brilliance above like a thirsty beast toward water.

Sofia crested the surface, her vision momentarily overwhelmed by the daylight above. The sprawling vista of the Orvida came into view with rolling, green and gold fields and towering clouds. Luminea lay just below, brilliant and shining like shards of gold and glass protruding from the pristine waters of the Aecuna.

She scanned the shore and the farmlands beyond only to find great sinkholes opening up as the ground fell away, swallowed up by the void. Creatures of all manner of terror poured forth from the maws. Black filth oozed from the wounds and covered the land.

Drums from deep within the earth echoed across the hereafter.

Sofia sensed the ground trembling and looked behind her. A nightmare incarnate clad in black battle armor dripping with blood and gore charged up the tunnel. Angorzhu. His eyes burned like gems forged of pure fire. At his back, a horde of thousands at his call charged with him. Sofia stood paralyzed as the Hell Lord roared with a fury that cracked the world's crust like a meteor, shattering her mind to pieces.

Sofia snapped awake and slept no more.

Zani had spoken the truth. The imuertes were coming for Luminea, and they were coming soon.

39

The ruins of Ilucenta, towers and temples dark against the fog, emerged from the mist like gravestones. Ancient, lonely reminders of tragedies long past. They dotted the horizon; an endless sea of gray and more numerous than Sofia could count.

It was strange to see the place again. She remembered how she once was: a woman wandering the empty avenues of the desolate city, lost in a world she did not understand. Like her point of view, high above the city in the tiny skyship, she was different now.

Her perspective had changed, but the eerie tension of Ilucenta had lost none of its potency. A foreboding unease seeped into her bones.

Ebrahym steered the skyship into the wind. The craft banked into the breeze as patches of gray clouds passed by. Anayah was gone. She'd left to warn the Host soon after Sofia's vision of the battle to come. But Sofia's word carried little weight now. They would need hard proof to convince the Hierarch Terafiq, the remaining Eros and the High Council to abandon the front and defend the city.

Ebrahym, still one of the Host and incapable of speaking anything but the truth, needed to see it with his own eyes. And so, too, did she. Her dreams told her it would begin here, in Ilucenta, where it'd all started. Where the Fierno had once lived as a man; where he'd once brought war to the world.

It was also the one place Sofia would avoid at all cost if she could. Having only just escaped from the clutches of the Hell Lord, she had no desire to walk back into them. But this was the only way.

Sofia peered over the edge as Ebrahym piloted the vessel in silence, feeling his way through the minuscule updrafts and currents. For once, she wished she could see the ground clearly as she peered over the railing, searching for signs of movement in the mist below.

Slowly, the towers materialized as the massive structures they were. Ebrahym navigated them as if floating down a winding forest river, following the wind where it went, weaving through the great trees of stone.

"There!" Sofia exclaimed, breaking the silence. "Look." She pointed into the mist where blooms of warm light poked through the shroud. *Fires.*

Ebrahym pulled a handle, and the skyship lurched. "Hold on," he ordered. They descended through the mist, dropping altitude gently so as to not to reveal their position. The glowing lights beneath them grew and multiplied by the hundreds.

They were the same fires Sofia remembered from Mictlani. No longer contained by the dark. Now, they were free.

"Closer?" Sofia asked with some hesitation as Ebrahym banked around a tower. Her muscles ached at the ready. She could feel the presence of the enemy growing.

"We must. Terafiq will never be convinced by a few fires. I must see them myself."

Sofia reluctantly nodded her agreement.

She scanned the horizon, orienting herself by her recollection of the city layout, searching for a dome shape among the dark silhouettes—the one in which she'd first encountered the imuerte. She spied it lurking at the edge of her view, the great bulbous sphere rising from the mist. Sofia shot a glance back to the Sang, and he nodded knowingly, steering toward it.

A terrible screech echoed through the lonely ruins. Black shapes appeared in the distance. A massive swarm, like flies shaken from a carcass. Dozens, then hundreds. They formed a chaotic, angry mat against the gray sky. Sofia's stomach tightened at the sight.

"Hold on!" Ebrahym called. He jammed the tiller hard. Sofia clutched the railing and helplessly watched the swarm approach.

The black cloud howled as it undulated forward in a single, indistinguishable mass toward them. It was a ball of winged death that would shred them in seconds. Ebrahym steered toward the nearest tower, a pillar scattered with protruding, elaborate terraces and balconies. Wild calls sounded as the swarm began their hunt, searching for prey.

Ebrahym yanked back on the lever to control pitch, and the skyship craned upward. A long shadow covered the ship as they nestled under a massive terrace like a baby chick under its mother's wing. There, Ebrahym slipped into a deep meditation, Willing the craft to stay aloft.

The sound of the winged creatures was now a sustained, high-frequency screech. The cries slithered up her spine and into her brain. The first of the imuertes screamed past. The rest followed a heartbeat later; a mad gust of leathery wings, tails and talons. Sofia held her breath in silent prayer as the swarm thundered just above them like a black, raging torrent. The screeching grew to its zenith as the bulk of the horde passed by and then fell again as the imuertes moved on.

Sofia sighed in relief as silence returned to the ruin. Ebrahym took up the controls once more and headed toward the dome in the distance.

The bottom half of the temple was hidden in the mist, but the top was clear enough, and so was the oculus at its peak. The hole, ten meters wide, was the same one she'd once gazed at from below, from inside of the temple, before she'd found the body of Nilayah and fled through the cellar. The large plaza she remembered crossing so long ago teemed with burning fires obscured by the mist.

A war camp.

She retrieved a coil of rope from a nearby storage locker and cinched it to the railing. "Can you keep this aloft while we go down?"

Ebrahym glanced up at the rigging. "Yes, but I will be of little use otherwise. My Serrá must remain focused."

"In and out," she whispered. It was a gamble, but Sofia hoped the temple would be empty and they would have a safe vantage to observe the enemy from behind secure doors.

Below the skyship, the mouth of the dome looked like that of a giant serpent leaping from a gray sea to snap them up, suspended mid-bite. Sofia looked for movement inside before tossing the rope into the gaping mouth. The rope passed through the barrier between light and shadow and uncoiled with a whirring sound until it hit the ground below.

They waited for a moment. Silence.

Ebrahym was the first over the side. His wing stretched out by instinct to help him balance. It was a sad sight. She had seen him soar into battle like a hawk, fast and terrible as a storm. Now he appeared a maimed sparrow, awkwardly trying and failing to do the natural things that other birds do.

Sofia swung her leg over the side and inched her way down the line, willing strength into her hands until she slipped into the darkness. It wasn't until her feet touched the marble floor that she realized the fear of heights had left her completely. She chuckled grimly at the thought. If her captivity had taught her anything, it was that there were far greater things to fear.

Inside, the temple was cool and still. The sound of drums and clamoring hummed just outside of the heavy doors. The place was as she remembered. Nothing changes in the Orvida. The pews and furniture still lay strewn about, broken and splintered from the last days of the siege long ago.

"All right?" Ebrahym asked. Sofia nodded, dusting the rope fibers clinging to her hands and clothing. He moved toward the door, two massive slabs of wood standing between them and the army making ready just outside.

"Wait," she whispered. "Follow me."

The two slipped into the nearby alcove with Sofia leading the way. On the landing, just as before, she found the body of the dead Sanguinir. *Nilayah*.

She hadn't changed. The Sang's corpse was just as Sofia had left it, still and pale against the stone, adornments splattered with blood. Cuirass missing from her chest from where Sofia had taken it.

Looking upon her once more, Sofia was not frightened as she had been before. She knelt next to the body, drawing her sword, Nilayah's sword, from her belt. She rested it gently on the fallen warrior's lap with a kind reverence.

"Thank you," she whispered with her fingertips on the battered blade.

"I didn't know who or what she was when I was first here," Sofia said, turning to Ebrahym. "But she saved me. Gave me this," she said, patting the blade. "I wish I could have known her."

"You do," Ebrahym said, coming to his knees as well. He made a Sanguinir a gesture of respect. "Part of her lives on in Anayah now."

"Is this how we'll end?" she asked, eying the body. It was cold, the golden light long since faded from Nilayah's eyes. "Even if we succeed and Angorzhu is defeated, will another rise in his place? Are we doomed to fight the same war forever?"

"It is our duty to endure," Ebrahym reminded her, resting Nilayah's arms across her chest, "so that others may join in the light."

"I know. But when is enough enough?"

"Not until we are free from ourselves. Imuertes or not, the war inside of each of us is the one we must end. It is one that rages on in times of peace as well as war. In times of sorrow and happiness."

Ebrahym stood. "There are but two choices, Sofia. Two ways all stories in the Orvida end. We may walk into the Dawnlight, through the Great Seal to the beyond, or we may fall in pursuit of it. Nilayah knew this. As do I. As do you. With luck, we will find ourselves there one day. But we can only wage one war at a time. Come."

Ebrahym pulled her to her feet, and the pair of them ascended the steps toward the doors. Sofia found the slide covering the opening for them to see out. The Sang placed his hand on hers and nodded, and they pulled the slide. A rectangle of light appeared like a waning geometric eclipse.

And beyond the tiny window, madness.

Even through such a small opening, they could see the magnitude of terror that awaited Luminea. Fires. Plumes of green, sulfuric smoke. Stacks of iron-forged murder. Standards bearing the severed heads of oulma and beast alike. A sea of mangled forms clamoring in palpable excitement.

And in the center of the square, once a gathering place for peaceful oulma, was now a grisly source of amusement for the army. Crucified Sang and oulma scattered the plaza erected on metal frames.

Fires burned at their feet. Sofia recognized some of the Pax unit markings on the tortured oulma nearby. She kneaded the scars on her hands anxiously.

Lesser imuertes hurled spears at the captured Pax for sport. The Sang shouted defiantly at them, challenging the imuertes to turn their weapons upon them rather than the weaker oulma. Even in pain, their entwined voices were beautiful among all the ugliness.

Sofia lowered her head, shaking with rage, with fear. Her body remembered Mictlani, and the pain. Part of her wanted to burst through the door and take on the army herself. The other half wanted to hide in a hole. Ebrahym did not blink, as if committing every detail to memory was his responsibility. It was.

"Is the army here? The Pax?" Sofia asked, her gaze fixed on the prisoners.

Ebrahym shook his head. "I do not think so. These are captured tribute from other fronts. I feel no others here."

"What do they want with them?"

"They will try to extract the Sanguinir's aurola and use the halo to forge stronger, fouler kin." He said, watching the torture unfold. He placed his hand on Sofia's shoulder. "They are beyond our reach. No good will come from joining them."

She looked again, through tears. In the distance, half obscured by fog, the lumbering heralds, the ogorantè, paced patiently. A gong rang out, reverberating across the assembling horde. They shook with revelry, chanting and howling at the sound, a din that rattled Sofia's mind to the core. The urge to lose herself in the sound tore at her mind. The largest among them pounded the earth as they howled with such force dust from the temple walls shook loose and covered them.

"I have seen enough," Ebrahym said. "The Hierarch will hear my testimony."

As they turned to leave, something caught the attention of an imuerte on the fringe of the crowd. The creature craned its deformed head skyward, pointing with a gnarled, clawed hand. It hissed to its kin nearby who slithered up to gaze skyward.

They see the skyship. Sofia and Ebrahym exchanged glances and turned away from the door. She slid the viewport closed slowly to avoid detection. The wood inched closed until a pale, spindly hand burst through the opening.

Startled, Sofia let out a yelp and smashed the slide against the creature's hand. It screeched to its comrades nearby, who clamored at the door, scratching at the wood with talons of steel.

"I must not engage," said Ebrahym, eyeing the porthole in the dome, "lest the skyship fall."

"Go!" Sofia called as she hurled loose furniture and broken beams against the door. It began to shake as the imuertes on the other side put their weight into it.

"*You* have to make it back to warn everyone. I don't." She could feel the growing sensation of dread, the imuertes' dark whispers seeping through. Though hardened against it from months of torture, she was not immune. She felt despair taking hold. "Go!" she cried.

Ebrahym lingered for a moment longer than any other Sang would. Sofia nodded her permission, and he dashed toward the rope.

Sofia sprinted down the stairs to the corpse of Nilayah once more. "I need your help again," she said as she picked up the sword, just as she had a lifetime ago. Only this time, she would not run. She took one long look at the fallen Sang.

I won't fail you.

She climbed the steps two and three at a time back to the doors. Slashes of light appeared and splinters flew as the imuertes clawed through. Ebrahym was nearing the porthole as he ascended the rope, working his way upward, hand over hand.

The first imuerte, an oily creature freshly born from some corrupted womb, burst through the ancient wood. It slithered through the opening and tumbled wet inside the temple. It clamored to its feet and lurched toward her, howling.

Blood pumping, Sofia planted her feet and waited. That ember Anayah helped stoke back to life flickered. Sofia knew the imuertes' ways now, their secrets. There was nothing to fear. There was nothing more that could be done to her. Their worst had not broken her. She felt the grip of the imuerte's aura loosen.

The creature rushed forward predictably, all four limbs scraping against the polished stone. A pair of horns protruding from its head aimed at her. Gore and spittle flew from its mouth.

Sofia stood her ground in a high guard. Teeth and claws lunged the final few meters, but she stepped aside at the last moment, pivoting on her back foot as her blade came down in a high arc. The two halves of the imuerte continued a few more meters before skidding to the floor.

She spun on her heels. More imuertes wormed their way through the ever-widening opening. The door's iron hinges groaned, stressed near the point of breaking.

Terafiq had once said Sofia and she were alike, each of them willing to fight to their last.

But this would not be her last.

A lúpero's howl echoed through the temple. Its massive head gnawed at the opening in the wood so that its body might fit through. Filthy death children, pasty and disturbing in proportion, chittered about and beyond, the entire army seeming to have mobilized.

Anayah had always been the gifted one, Sofia thought as she closed her eyes. The Sang had the power to move water and make stone an ally, talents Anayah had learned in the Conventa long before she had wings. Sofia had never been exceptional at the art, but it was her only hope.

Her attention narrowed on the two stone columns flanking the door. Like heavy trees, they bore the weight of the elaborate arch suspended above. She imagined them as such, ancient elms towering above.

In a forbidden grove, the trees stood alone, covered in dew and surrounded by wildflowers. She walked toward them on bare feet. The grass was cool between her toes. When Ebrahym was a farmer, he had asked the earth to grow. She would not ask. She would not beg. She would command, and the earth would obey. That was her Way.

The ax was heavy in her hand. Sofia hefted it on to one shoulder, fired her hips forward and let the blade sing. The head dug into the bark with a thud. Again and again, she flung the blade into the tree, chipping meat from it until it cracked like thunder. Splinters flew as the tree splintered and fell, dragging branches and leaves to the ground with it.

She opened her eyes. Only the briefest of seconds had passed. The stone column beyond her extended hand crumbled, collapsed by her Will.

Surprised, she watched blocks of stone larger than a man move for the first time in millennia. The beautiful arch, with all its ornamentation, fell away as if eroded by a flood and came crashing down upon the imuertes below. The entire temple shook off a layer of dust as the hewn boulders slammed into the earth.

The wound cauterized, and the imuertes ceased to flow through the doorway. Sizzling gore and bone and meat pulverized by the boulders covered the stone tiles. Beyond, muffled roars bellowed.

Sofia took one last look at the carnage before heading toward the rope. She wrapped one hand around the line, tugged hard, and ascended into the light.

40

The skyship slowed to a crawl, pushed along by the light breeze, gently weaving through the sunbaked towers toward the center of Luminea. The view was as breathtaking as when Sofia had first laid eyes on it.

The familiar tiered districts rose up from the water of the great sea, eons of buildings built on top of one another with their red stone roofs and brightly painted facades. The elegant sprawl of Luminea passed under their hull as they listed along in the midday breeze.

Despite the beauty, Sofia nervously tapped her feet against the wood, anxious to be back on solid ground. There was no time to waste gawking at vistas. Soon, war would be here.

Sofia paced along the railing. The small vessel of wood and canvas and steel and rope had served them well. And they were lucky. The imuertes had not followed them out of Ilucenta. Ebrahym and Sofia had slipped into the mist and made their escape. It was the only time Sofia remembered feeling grateful for the haze.

But it had been worth the risk. Ebrahym's golden eyes had seen what was coming for them; the massive army staging at Ilucenta, preparing for the final assault. The High Council and the Hierarch still believed the demons were far off, scattered and weak. Ebrahym had seen the truth.

Now, they had to make the others believe it.

Sofia's neck craned as she fixated on the arcs of light dancing upward from the heart of the city. The Dawnlight was more beautiful than she remembered. It was, in some ways, both the cause and ultimate culmination of this war. The light from it wound its way up through the heavens with a radiance that burned brightly, even in the midday sun.

Although seeing the very symbol of Luminea brought a moment of comfort, her thoughts lingered on the army coming to take it. Soon, they would be here. Foul creatures would swarm the pristine avenues below. Screams would replace the sound of song, and towers would fall. Darkness would overtake the light.

Not if we can help it.

Thinking of Anayah, Sofia fiddled with the gold trinket around her neck and slipped it under her shirt. She wondered what she would say to the High Council if given the chance to speak.

Ebrahym pointed the craft to the west, over the last wall to the Fifth Tier, the Seat of the Host, where the Dawnlight burst forth from the temple at its center.

Like Ilucenta, it had become a staging ground for war. Skyships ten times the size of their own, and more larger still, hovered over the ground as neatly ordered *legios,* the Prime Auxilia legions, prepared to depart. Banners and lines of flags hung from skyships and shook in the breeze. Sanguinir messengers darted through the air like frantic sparrows, whizzing by them as Ebrahym steered the craft toward a nearby tower littered with jetties.

Even the famed *lioneers,* the heavy cavalry of the Choir of the Lion, assembled en masse. Sanguinir cavaliers corraled the great cats in the plazas, some of the noble beasts honey-colored, some white or striped, and all gilded to the teeth with adornment. Oulma warily approached to strap armor to their flanks.

Sofia flung a line to an oulma waiting at the dock as Ebrahym sidled up to it, the wood creaking as the hull made contact. The fleet prepared to disembark around them, and the port, such as it was, buzzed with activity.

The dockhands cinched the lines to their small craft and dropped a plank spanning the gap between the dock and the vessel. Sofia grabbed her gear, hopped over the plank, landed on the dock with a thud and righted herself to solid earth. It was good to be back.

"Welcome home," Anayah said as she appeared amidst the crowd. She wore a grim expression on her otherwise perfect face. She was in her full battle armor now, a further sign that all was not well.

Sofia's mind flooded with memory, to the time before her exodus. The Conventa, their training under Bethuel's keen eye, and her friendship with the woman she once knew as Alana. If it were possible for Sofia to feel a sense of home, this was the closest thing to it.

"Perfect timing," Sofia said. Ebrahym must have sent word once he'd felt Anayah's presence. Anayah pulled Sofia close. "How are things?" Sofia asked, pulling away from their embrace.

Anayah shook her head. "Not well." She glanced back to the guards standing at attention behind her. They saluted Ebrahym as he stepped off the deck toting bags of equipment. "I did not earn any favors by straying from my duties." Anayah hesitated. "Tell me it was worth it."

"It was," Ebrahym said, appearing alongside them. He still wore the dusty robes from their escape. It was a strange sight among the vibrant hues of Luminea. "I have seen it myself."

Sofia nodded. "Ten thousand at least," she whispered. "And those are only the ones we could see. They came from underground in my dream. I think they mean to burrow from Ilucenta to Luminea."

"Then we have little time," Anayah said, gesturing them forward. The Sanguinir warriors following Anayah filed in behind Sofia and Ebrahym. It was hard to tell if they were escorts or guards. "Sofia, it will be a public hearing of your claims."

Sofia let out a desperate laugh. "Terafiq always did know how to make the most of a situation."

"This is no time for games," said Anayah with all seriousness, her voice low. "From what I gather, the war goes ill in our absence. The oulma are scared. I feel the Divine Sphere weakening. But the Host is prideful, and the Hierarch insists on continuing the campaign on the frontier. I feel vengeance has blinded her. To retreat now and defend the city would be a show of weakness."

"How so? The strategy is sound."

"It does not matter, Sofia. *You* are an outsider. They have made you so," Ebrahym offered. "Trusting you would undermine everything they have built. That is why you were exiled in the first place. Add to that your captivity—"

Anayah nodded. "Even Ebrahym's testimony will not easily sway Terafiq's course, and she will use any opportunity to bolster moral. Even if that means making an example out of you."

Sofia held her chin in her hand. Once, the oulma rebelled against the Sang's control. The Great Shame. That's why the Sang forged the Divine Sphere and feared those outside of it. But even the Host would bend to the Will of the people lest there be bloodshed again. Sofia might be able to turn the public display against them.

"I guess we'll need to convince the people instead."

***

While the High Council prepared to assemble and hear Sofia's testimony, she was confined to quarters, a small apartment that overlooked the Market Strand. But there were no trades happening today. No musicians playing on every corner. No sounds of life.

She turned from her post at the window, breathing in the crisp, sulfur-free air, and wondered how long it had been since she'd slept in a bed. The simple comforts of a home were a distant memory. A pile of blankets, stripped from the bed, lay in the darkest corner of the room where she rested but did not sleep.

Not knowing what might happen next, and needing something to pass the time, she decided she might as well look presentable. She poured a bath, pumping the steaming water by hand using the brass pump.

After peeling off her dusty, greasy clothes, she stood for a moment in front of a mirror. A woman she did not recognize stared back at her. Scars and bruises were more prevalent than not. Ribs and joints pressed against her thin flesh, replacing the muscle that was once there. Her fingers wandered around her dry and flaking lips and sunken eyes, all framed by knotted mats of black hair. She was a shadow of herself.

Disheartened, she slipped into the warm water and sighed, closing her eyes.

After her escape with Ebrahym and Anayah, she learned that eight long months had passed since her capture. Everything was different. She thought of the soldiers heading to the various fronts as she lay soaking in the tub. Entire legions set out from Luminea to answer distant calls to glory, and for some of them, death.

Even after her ordeal, it was hard not to feel guilty that she was here and not fighting alongside them. She wondered how many more would fall before this was done.

There was a knock on the door that stirred her from her thoughts. "May I come in?" a sweet voice asked.

Sofia called out and was surprised to see Nesta standing in the doorway. She appeared as delicate as ever, almost hovering in pearlescent robes of silk laced with sparkling gems. Her face was hidden behind the veil she wore, but her dim, amber eyes were piercing, searching. "How are you feeling?"

"Better," Sofia lied. "It's good to see you."

Nesta bowed slightly. "I must admit, I am surprised to hear you survived," she said as she floated to the nearby stool, inspecting Sofia's exposed arms as she did. "And intact, so I see. Not many could have." Sofia said nothing, preferring not to think of the scars. She slid her arms under the suds.

"You told me once that no one would come for me," Sofia said. "I'm glad you were wrong."

"As am I."

"Then why all the guards?" Sofia asked, nodding to where the other armed Sanguinir waited just outside. She could hear their armor rustle and creak as they stood watch.

"Why do you think?" Nesta questioned gently. "No oulma or Sanguinir has ever come back from what you have endured...not even I. That kind of darkness does not wash away clean. You may have changed in ways you do not even realize," Nesta pressed. "The Hierarch is not taking any unnecessary risks. I am inclined to agree."

"I understand," Sofia said, unwilling to fight the point further. Always the suspicion, the mistrust. She longed for the simplicity of the desert.

"So, tell me," Nesta asked.

"About my vision? Didn't Anayah tell you?"

"No, not that," Nesta interrupted. "The rest of the story. How you survived." Sofia shifted uncomfortably in the tub, suddenly exposed. She instinctively hugged her knees to her chest and tried hard not to think about the horrible things she had done to stay alive, but they came in flashes she could not control.

"You were made to do evil," Nesta said, peering at her, seeing through. Sofia nodded. "I fear those scars are much deeper than the ones I can see. I would not wish to trade my wounds for yours, Sofia. I have not the strength to bear them. I can only imagine how you—"

"See this one?" Sofia asked, pointing to a knotted scar on her forearm. "They chained me to an umbra, some poor bastard long since mad. Drove a spike through my arm like a leash and chained us together. They threw us in a pit to see which one of us would kill the other first." She stared off, silently reliving the torture. "I used the chain to climb out a week later. I became like them. I obeyed. I endured." She trailed off and looked to see Nesta's gaze fall to the floor. "It was the only way."

Nesta hung her head with sadness. "I will not deceive you, Sofia. Many in the Host believe you to be—changed."

"I *am* changed." *Now I know the truth.*

Nesta nodded, her jewels twinkling as she did. "Many see these...*visions* of yours as a deception, a ploy to sow suspicion among us. After what happened at Espleña—"

"Believe me or don't. It makes no difference. They are coming for us all," Sofia said defiantly. After the pits of Mictlani, there was little Terafiq could threaten that would even come close to what she had endured. If the Host thought her a traitor, so be it. She would not have the truth weigh on her and go unspoken.

Then a thought came to her that hadn't before: she had never considered what would happen should the Council and the Hierarch actually *listen* to her.

The Sanguinir would rally their forces from the frontier to defend Luminea from the coming imuertes assault. In that one, final battle, Sofia would likely find herself among them. With the entire Inferna threatening to devour Luminea, the defenders would need every sword arm they could get.

And there, on the field, she would find him again, the Hell Lord. She imagined him from her vision, a being of fire, of metal and blood, a warlord titan coming up from the center of the earth to make ruin on the surface. Once again, they would meet face to face. She felt it as plainly as her own heartbeat.

There was no other way it could end. Not her story.

Sofia remained lost in her thoughts until the bath went cold, not even noticing when Nesta left.

***

"Free oulma of Luminea, hear me!" the Sanguinir boomed. Sofia didn't know him, but the caramel-skinned orator commanded the crowd of tens of thousands with his voice unaided. He was a stout member of their kind, with flowing chestnut hair knotted with braids woven with feathers. A helmet shaped like an eagle's beak covered his eyes. What part of him remained unarmored was decorated with paint and brightly colored bands of cloth. He was dressed for the occasion.

His audience of oulma had gathered for the spectacle in droves. The Sanguinir paced upon the amphitheater stage, ash-grey wings spread wide, working up the crowd. The theater's half-dome, opening to the crowd like a mouth waiting to close on the pageant unfolding within, was fashioned from polished marble and flanked by huge winged statues and columns. Thick plumes of incense-laden smoke billowed up from the gold braziers nearby

"Your honored Altuma Concilia," the orator continued, "and the Hestium have assembled you here, my good oulma, to hear the words of one who has returned from the East bearing a message." He pointed toward Sofia and Ebrahym seated on stage, awaiting their summons.

"In her wisdom," he continued, "the Hierarch Terafiq, eighth of her name, banished *this* one"—he motioned to Sofia—"from our city to protect all of you from her *strangeness* and her possible ties to the enemy. In these dire times, chances cannot be taken. Praise Terafiq, the wise."

The crowd echoed the phrase back. Terafiq and the Legatès, as well as the other Eros were seated in a long line on a raised platform suspended on stone columns like judges in a court. They listened, unmoving, playing along with the ceremony.

The orator spread his arms wide. "Now! This woman returns to us, she claims, from the very heart of the Inferna itself with a message, a prophecy." He let the words hang and the anticipation build. The crowd waited.

He pointed to the crowd. "The Hierarch wishes *you*, citizens of Luminea, brave and free oulma, to hear what she has to say firsthand, for it concerns the fate of us all."

An absolute silence descended on the scene. Sofia stood from her simple chair, the small sounds of her every movement echoing out toward the audience. She stood facing the High Council and the high-ranking Sanguinir, happy to have the crowd at her back. The feeling of thousands of eyes upon her was reminiscent of the torture pits.

But in that moment, she felt oddly at peace. She recalled the magical desert twilight and the calm that came with it. There was nothing more to be done to her. This was her reckoning and absolution.

"My name is Sofia," she began. The brass horn just in front of her mouth magnified her voice through a long cylinder. Her words carried into the distance. "It is not a name I chose. I remembered. It came with me from Afore." She let the confession flow, feeling weight shed moment by moment as she spoke.

"I know other things," she continued. "I know that I am different from you. Some say I have a bond with the enemy. I know now that this is also true." A ripple of whispers raced through the crowd, though Sofia barely noticed. The crowd and everything else began to melt away.

"But I also know that I am *not* one of them," she said. She pointed at the Sang, before gesturing to the crowd. "Nor am I like the Sanguinir, nor my fellow oulma.

There was a time when answers meant more to me than anything. But in my search, I found that all I need to know about myself is this: I will not run any longer. I have found my Iriva, my Way. That is what brought me back to you."

She took a breath. "The imuertes are coming. I have seen it in my dreams, and Catan Ebrahym has seen it, too, with his own eyes. His word is true, and he will testify in kind." Whispers raced through the crowd.

"Soon, the horde will be at our gates. Soon, the Fierno, Angorzhu, will be here to destroy the city of Luminea. Soon, whatever I say here will cease to matter, for there will be an army of thousands at those walls." Sofia scanned the faces of the High Council, statues carved from stone as she pointed toward land. Terafiq, in all her grand battle gear like a god of the sun, feathers and banners littering her frame, stared down at Sofia.

We are the same, you and I, the Hierarch had once told her. *We will do what is necessary.*

Sofia pulled her sword from her belt and held it out, hilt-first, as an offering. The same blade that had saved her more times than she could count she offered to her judges. "I have seen the Inferna. I have seen the fire that is coming for us. I've lived it. If that makes me a monster, so be it." She paused, waiting for the moment. "Hestium of the Orvida, protectors of the Dominion di Esanya...cut me down if you feel it right."

Terafiq's eyes narrowed. *She knows I know the Sang's secret; that they created the imuertes. Once slaughtered the oulma in a bloody war, the Unspoken War.* If the crowd knew, they'd turn against the Host in a heartbeat. But where would that leave them? The Sang would never call her bluff either. They wouldn't dare resort to desipar, lest they reveal its possibility.

Armed with the truth, Sofia could have exposed them right then, but she held back. That was not for pride or spite. What she did, she did for the people at her back. It would take everything they had to survive.

"Whether in battle against the imuertes or by your hands, I will accept my fate. As the Sanguinir say, I will endure. Take my life if you must, but listen to my warning."

The agitated crowd erupted in shouts of both judgment and adoration. The oulma voiced their own verdicts in a cacophony of sound amplified by the enclosed theater. But the din faded away as she closed her eyes, looking inward.

There was nothing left, nothing to fear. She had been stripped to her core by the imuertes and Sang alike to the point that there was nothing but Sofia left. Just Sofia.

Terafiq rose to her feet like a newly formed mountain emerging from the sea, face hard like granite. She raised a hand to silence the crowd, and tens of thousands of oulma obeyed. Looming from her stone perch, she gestured to Ebrahym to approach.

"Catan Ebrahym of the Corum di Leon, twelfth of your name," she thundered. "You are of the Hestium, and bound by your aurola, you cannot bear false witness."

"I cannot."

"And so, you vouch for this oulma and her claims?"

Ebrahym and Sofia exchanged glances. "What she says is true."

"And why did you take to the waste at her side? Why did you neglect your duty, and risk your aurola for the likes of her?"

Ebrahym bowed his head, considering the words. His gaze rose again before speaking, his voice strong and confident. "Because I believe in her." The crowd fell silent as the pair stood there, awaiting Terafiq's decision. Sofia's fingers reached out and found Ebrahym's hand. His eyes remained fixed ahead as he closed his hand around hers.

"Very well," the Hierarch called, her dual voices intertwining in commanding authority. She was outmaneuvered for the moment but would not waver in her authority. Her voice bellowed across the city as a god's would.

"Send word to the front! Rally all wings and legios. We will make our stand here."

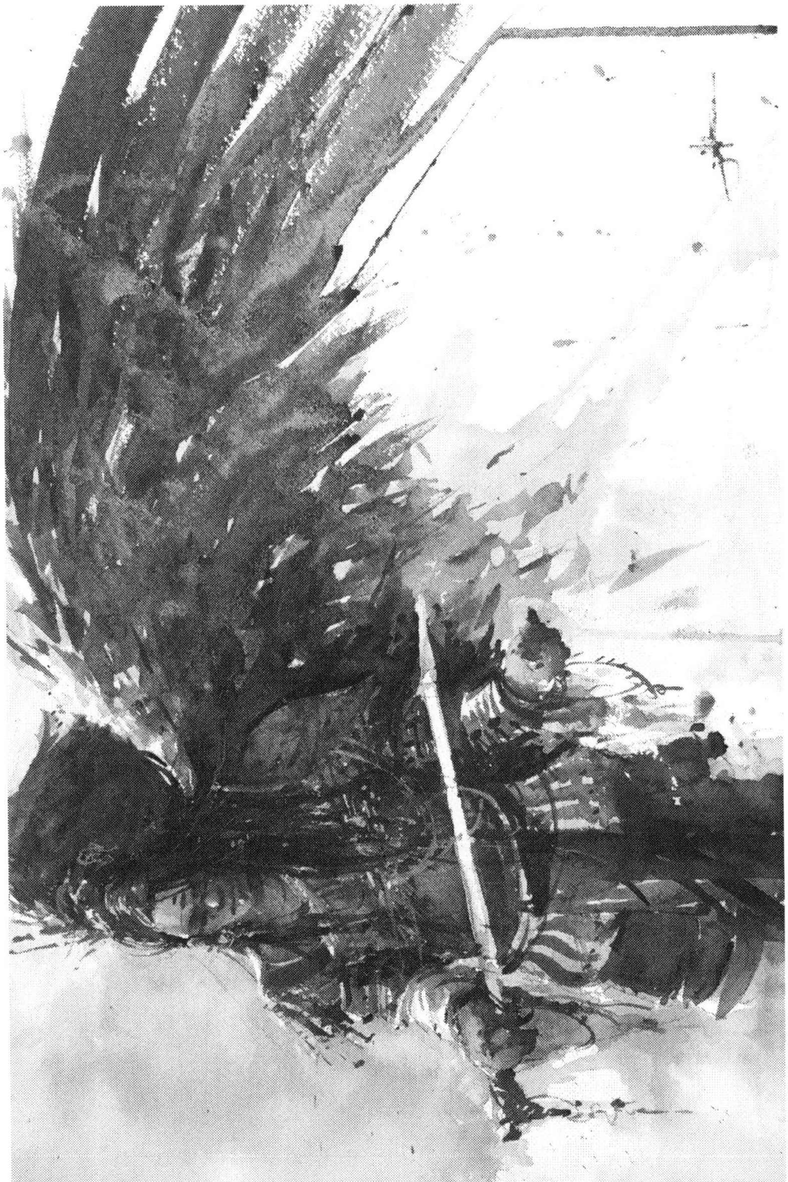

41

Dressed for combat without knowing why, Sofia walked across the dustfield where alumna practiced disarming techniques and hurled one another into the dirt. Her forearms ached just watching them.

The Conventa itself remained unchanged since her time, still foreboding and spartan. But there was a different energy surrounding the place now. A desperation in the air mixed with courage. There were so many alumna. The recruits filled the Conventa to the brim, and it swelled with anxious tension.

No longer did the school of war limit admission to once a century. That was not enough. The number of possible aurola remained fixed, of course. Even in the midst of war, no new halos had descended from the Santcu Arcam to aid their kin. These oulma were replacements. Honored few would carry on the mantles of the fallen Sanguinir. The rest would bolster the ranks of the Prime Auxilia.

And from what she had heard about the front, the Pax would need them. Doom approached, and yet, all they could do was wait. Imuerte burrows could erupt at any second, puncturing the countryside with black pits spilling darkness across the land.

Sofia desperately hoped she was wrong about the whole thing, that she was just mad. But in her heart, she knew it was the truth. They were coming.

She found Bethuel, the Raven, in his typical green and black armor, hands clasped behind, watching over his flock. His black wings fluttered in the wind, rustling softly like leaves in a tree.

Why had he summoned her? After Terafiq gave the order to withdraw the Host from the frontier, there had been a flurry of frantic activity. Not even Ebrahym or Anayah had been allowed a moment's pause. But a Sanguinir messenger and a suit of training armor had appeared early that morning, so here she was. At her hip, Nilayah's sword, polished and freshly honed, hung loyally in its scabbard.

Bethuel nodded to her as she approached. She signaled her respects instinctively, as if a recruit again. "So, you survived," Bethuel said. His eyes remained fixed on the sparring alumna.

"More or less," Sofia said, standing at attention. "I suppose I partially have you to thank for that."

"Indeed." The Raven did not show his usual flair. He was colder than she remembered, sobriety replacing his odd combination of flamboyant charm and cruel discipline. "Follow me."

Deep within the Conventa, Bethuel led Sofia through the winding stone halls to an underground gallery, someplace new. The place looked to be carved from the earth itself. Stone columns hewn into twisting designs. Murals depicting great battles covered the walls, and broken weapons hung on display with care, carefully preserved artifacts of war.

"My personal sparring court," Bethuel said, taking his cloak off, his wings ruffling. In the dim candlelight, jagged shadows cut across his face. A pair of golden embers burned from them. "Do you know why you are here?"

"No." *But it can't be good.*

"You played your hand well," Bethuel said as he unhinged the heavier pieces of his armor and placed them on a carved wooden form nearby. "I gather you know the truth of the Host's past and the nature of the Divine Sphere."

"I do. Control."

"In a manner of speaking," the Sang said. "Truth be told, I never agreed with the Hierarch's strategy. But it was not my duty to question it." He removed his chestplate to reveal a leather vest underneath and exposing the intricate tattoos that covered his arms. He drew his sword, feeling the edge with his fingers.

"What is your duty now, then? Do Terafiq's dirty work?" Sofia asked, hand on her own blade. She inched toward the center of the sparring area where there was more room to maneuver.

"To discover the truth."

"You heard what Ebrahym said. They are coming."

"I do not doubt your words," he said, glaring like a bird of prey. "Only your heart."

Bethuel pounced. He came at her in a flash, like a swarm of ravens pecking for her eyes.

Sofia struggled to keep up with him. Even at her best, keeping pace with the master swordsman would be a challenge. In her weakened state, it might be impossible.

A desperate, solid parry gave Sofia a moment of breathing room. The dance started to come back to her.

After months of atrophy, her muscles slowly began to remember their training, their hours of swordplay, their months of fatigue and conditioning. This was not the blunt work of slaying imuertes. This was a dance, and she struggled to remember the steps.

Bethuel pushed harder and pressed his advantage, hoping for her to break. Sofia matched his effort, her footwork clumsy at first, but the ballet began to emerge from the recesses of her muscle memory. He stepped; she pivoted, countered. She advanced. It was precision choreography, each warrior playing their part.

In the midst of the duel, her mind began to fall away and her concentration with it. Thoughts of her captivity flooded into her mind like a poison threatening to paralyze her. The raw anger came as intensely as ever. The sound of a hammer driving spikes through her flesh pounded in her brain, the siren sound threatening to pull her into the darkness.

Bethuel's steel came harder and faster. The blade bit at her defenses and worked its way toward her vital regions. An errant strike caught Sofia's forearm. The flesh opened up and left a streak of crimson upon the Raven's blade.

Sofia boiled with rage, the pain igniting that dormant, smoldering anger within her. It seemed more potent now as it surged through her veins, made stronger by the suffering she had endured.

The Raven beat her into a corner. She felt a prisoner in that dark cell again, helpless and angry. Everyone was to blame. Everyone was her enemy. The Raven no longer stood before her, instead replaced by the terrifying form of Angorzhu. Her torturer and her savior, the one who'd kept her alive and made her long for death. She hated the fact that she owed the imuerte her life, was forever indebted to the monster.

And so, she unleashed hate. Sofia exploded out like a desperate animal and came down with a blow from on high, a ruse that the surprised Bethuel fell for.

He raised his guard while she whirled around to his flank, driving her elbow into the Sang's exposed ribs. With the other hand, Sofia trapped his wrist and used the Sanguinir's weight against him, simultaneously disarming him and driving him to the ground. She did not yield but came down hard with the blade that drove into the stone floor as Bethuel rolled away and sprung to his feet.

Sofia couldn't see the shock on the Raven's face. All she saw before her was a monster.

I will destroy him. I WILL DESTROY HIM. She fought in the darkness, hacking her way toward the vision of Angorzhu standing before her.

Bethuel dodged her next attacks and maneuvered his way inside her guard. His legs entangled hers and toppled Sofia, and she landed hard on her back. She screamed with rage as he pinned her arm behind. Gasping between frustrated growls, Sofia flexed impotently against his grip, fighting her own joints until they throbbed with pain.

"I knew there was darkness in you," the Raven said as she struggled. "From the first moment, I could see it. And now, it has taken hold of you. The Hierarch wanted to know for sure. Yours are secrets only violence reveals."

Sofia thrashed again, her voice deep and primal. The rage spoke. "I—WILL—END *HIM*."

"You are too dangerous! Just as my beloved, Nesta, once was," Bethuel said with a sadness that reached her through the haze of fury she was lost in. Her muscles eased, the tide of anger pulled back toward the sea and the beach was calm again. The Raven released her, slumping to the ground.

"Just point me in the right direction," Sofia gasped as she came to her knees. "And let me finish this."

He eyed her cautiously. A bead of sweat trickled down the Sang's cheek. "There is only one end to that road." Never had she seen him so unguarded. "You can turn from it if you wish. Nesta can help you."

"Why do you care?"

The Raven rose to his feet and helped her to hers. He looked at her with pity. "No one deserves to endure what she has. What you both have. I convinced the Hierarch to allow you to take refuge in the Temple of the Dawnlight."

"No," Sofia said without hesitation. She would not run and hide underground. She would never find peace that way. "I—"

The entire chamber shook with such force it drove both warriors to the ground. The sound was monstrous, a low, grinding din of stone mountains colliding. It rumbled through the very bones of Luminea, to the core and the Dawnlight itself.

Dust shaken loose from the ceiling clouded the room and masked the torchlight, making the already dim room dark and eerie.

Sofia opened her eyes and remembered the impenetrable fog on the beach so long ago. Smaller, secondary quakes ripped underfoot as Sofia and Bethuel struggled to find their feet. They looked at one another, and a silent conversation unfolded in a heartbeat:

The imuertes are here!
Yes, they have come.
We can't defend the city with so few.
It does not matter. We will fight.
Yes. We will fight.

Without another word, the Raven and Sofia sprinted out of the sparring room toward the city above. Sofia could already hear screaming echoing through the streets. The dark plumes were already rising into the sky like forest fires when they reached the surface.

Bethuel did not wait for her, and took to the sky as soon as he had clear air above, leaving her behind. Politics were for peacetime. Now they needed every sword they could get, including hers.

The alumna scattered across the dustfield stared at one another, then at the sky, not knowing what to do.

"To arms!" yelled Sofia. The trainees hesitated. "The imuertes are here! Defend the city!" Sofia screamed with an authority she did not know she had.

The alumna filed out of the courtyard toward the armory. Sofia followed them as the novice warriors scrambled to don whatever weapons and armor they could find. Their hands shook with fear. Sofia pitied them; they had no idea what was coming.

She pushed her way through the crowd and headed for the Conventa gates. She passed through them and hurried toward the closest tower, one of the four flanking the pyramid Temple of the Dawnlight.

Across the square, frightened oulma ran in every direction, each thinking their way was safer than the others'. Sofia wove through them, burst through the doors at the base of a spire and sprinted up the winding stairs. Her lungs burned from flight after flight, but she needed to see. She needed to face the enemy.

And when she finally emerged from the stairway to the open terrace overlooking Luminea, the great sea of Aecuna and the country beyond, she did.

They had come.

***

"Quite the sight," Sofia said solemnly as Anayah gazed out past the island's walls to the shores of the Aecuna. The Sanguinir leaned on the ancient stone in full battle armor. Layers of gold and steel laced with crimson silk. Plumes of feathers and a battle standard bearing a lion protruded from her back. Wings painted with designs and dressed with ribbon. Glory incarnate.

Beyond the polished stone walls of Luminea, where once rolling farmlands and villages sprawled, there now was a single, continuous black scar across the land. It was as if an enormous blade had sliced the earth open and the wound had soured.

Thick plumes of black smoke raged as the landscape burned beneath scalding feet and hooves and claws.

"The bridge defenses hold, for now," Anayah said, eyeing the grim view.

"For now," agreed Sofia. She panned her spyglass to the fortified structures where the bridges from Luminea met the mainland. Makeshift ramparts and fortifications had gone up there quickly after the imuertes pits emerged in order to hold the monsters' ground access to the shore. Sofia could make out the squads of Prime Auxilia manning siege weapons under their Sanguinir commanders, master engineers with allegiance to the Choir of the Bull.

Beyond, she saw the giant, smoldering carcasses of the igdracio. The creatures, domesticated to bore through the deep earth to make tunnels for imuertes hordes, broke through the crust with such force the very earth shook and shattered with their coming. She and the Raven had felt them while underground. Now, their duties fulfilled, the carcasses of the beasts were slowly being devoured by the imuertes forces as they entrenched themselves along the line. Even from this distance, the stench was unbearable.

Their number was difficult to estimate. Sofia wondered if anyone really wanted to know for sure how many there were. Thousands upon thousands. Twisted umbra and monsters of all shapes and sizes risen from the darkness and assembled under the banner of Angorzhu.

Sofia could see his mark crudely displayed on filthy banners and burning effigies. The Orvida had turned inside out, and what was once contained in the

Inferna below now covered the surface. And somewhere out there, he was waiting. She could feel him.

"Any news on reinforcements?" asked Sofia.

"Scouts were dispatched the moment the Hierarch ordered the withdrawal," said Anayah. "But many were lost or forced to turn back when scores of those cursed winged nightmares appeared. We have received word that some of the legios are inbound. But for now, we are on our own."

Ebrahym appeared from a stone entryway leading down into the access corridors between the great walls. Even on the secluded island, the walls of Luminea were built to withstand a siege. Sofia hoped they wouldn't need to test them.

"Well?" Sofia asked.

"The order is to attack at dawn," said Ebrahym. He, too, was clad in gleaming battle armor, though he stood out from his Sanguinir brothers and sisters with his single, feathered wing. On the barren shoulder sat a gilded quiver filled with heavy javelins. "The Hierarch seeks to break the enemy before it can become established and organized." Sofia and Anayah looked at one another.

"Attack?" repeated Anayah in disbelief. "It is futile. There is little we can do against that," she said, gesturing to the nightmare waiting just beyond the shore.

"Ilucenta," whispered Sofia. The two Sanguinir looked at her. "This is how they took Ilucenta. This is how *he* took it. Angorzhu slowly strangled it..." Sofia thought of the dream and the feeling of life-giving air escaping her as the vision of Angorzhu crushed her through. At that moment, she understood the Hierarch's plan. Terafiq might be prideful, but she was no fool.

"Their numbers are too great," Sofia said, focusing once again on the situation at hand. "Even with all the defenses we can muster, eventually they will wear us down. Two months, two years, two centuries—it doesn't matter. They won't stop."

"Attack while our forces are their strongest," Ebrahym said, considering the point.

"Cut the head of the snake," she whispered, repeating the words they'd shared before descending into Irazi's lair.

She glanced where Ebrahym's missing wing had been and hoped that this time, things would be different.

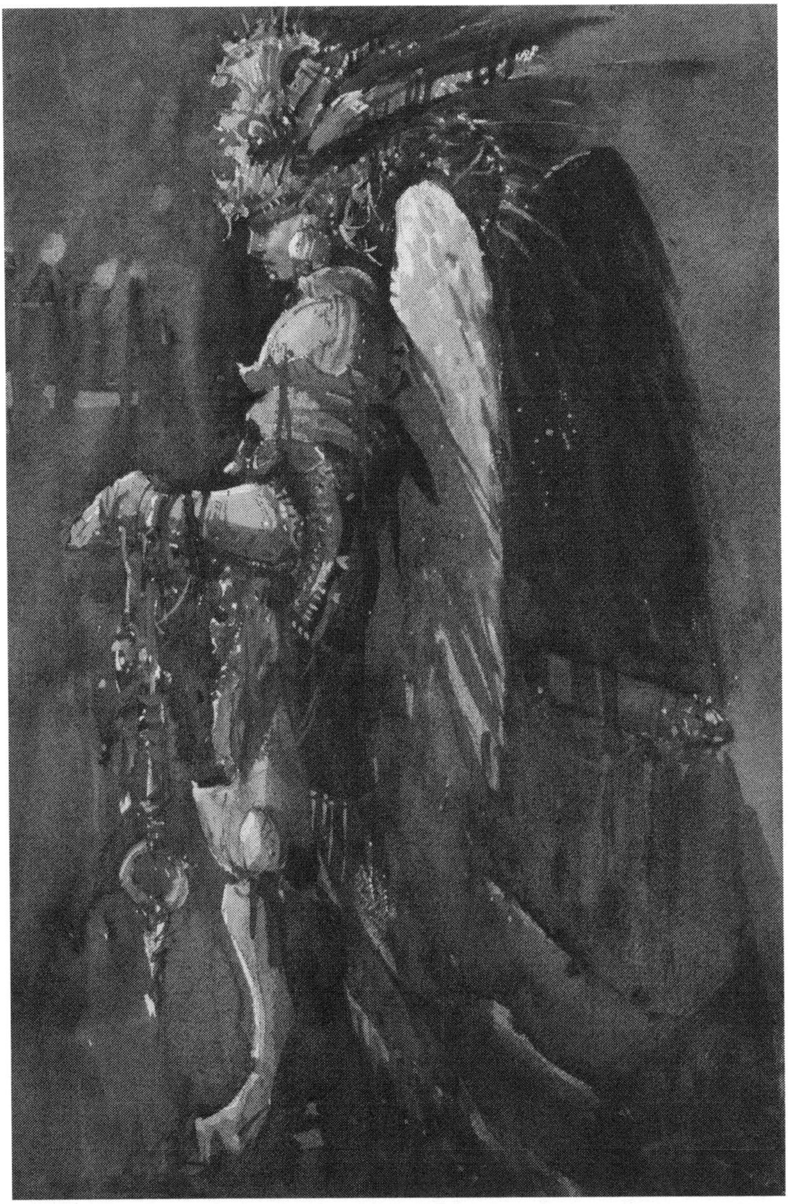

42

The morning damp lingered well after dawn. A weak breeze carried with it the pungent taint of sulfur. It intermingled with the incense and pyres that scattered the square.

The Host assembled for war in all its glory. It was a sight to inspire the most cowardly of men to arms.

Hundreds of Sanguinir stood in full battle regalia, absorbing the first hints of the sun as it rose in the east. Each warrior was unique in their battle gear. Each a symbol and summation of lineages thousands of years old. Decorated armor covered their powerful frames. Plumes of feathers fanned out to the side or ran along the spines of curved helmets, and banners of silk woven with sigils and stories of valor snapped in the breeze. The warriors stood at the ready like statues, their faces marked with symbols and lines across their flesh, and jewels pierced it wherever they could.

And as was done before all great battles, the wings of each Sang warrior had been blessed and decorated so as to appear defiant in the face of the darkness that lay ahead. A thousand fearless, golden eyes burned from beneath armored helms.

It was a fraction of the Host's total strength, however, despite the glorious sight. Sofia wondered if it would be enough.

She adjusted her own helmet to better see. Most of the Sang were still engaged in faraway fronts, some unaware that their home was under siege. But the few who remained did not stand alone. Grouped into tight battle formations, individual wings of Sanguinir warriors from all the Choirs formed compact phalanxes alongside Prime Auxilia foot soldiers. They were divided into neat units, and each of them was as colorful as the individual Sang who commanded them.

In total, the arrangement of squads and their support troops nearly filled the largest and most massive courtyard of the city, three thousand strong, all waiting in silence for the word to march upon the bridge and finally meet the enemy.

Even the Sanguinir cavalry that remained in the city had mustered. To protect the flanks were squads of lioneers. Sofia could only imagine the carnage they would inflict this day. The feline steeds snarled and growled in anticipation as their masters patted their massive heads.

Behind them, great stags, clad in blue, opalescent battle gear, stood at graceful attention as their swordsmen handlers comforted them from finely crafted leather saddles. Even the artists had mustered for war.

Above their ranks were the archers, the most talented in the air, hovering gracefully, silver bows at the ready. The Corum di Aquila, the Eagles, peaceful monks who were less keen on war than even their Stag brothers and sisters, were unmatched in the air. Their Way was to never touch the ground in battle, and they hovered now like a flock of white doves suspended above the rest of the army.

And positioned in the rear guard, hearty Bulls maneuvered the siege engines into place. Builders at heart, they were the masters of the weapons of war. Their dark green armor gave them the look of forest gods emerging from the earth to answer a call of war.

The golden-armored Sanguinir of the Corum di Leon, the Lion warriors, assembled on foot to form the central advance. As the tip of the spear, they would drive through the ranks and pierce the heart of the imuertes horde, Angorzhu himself.

Among them, the finest of the Prime Auxilia ranks millennia of war had to offer. Oulma generals, veterans of a thousand battles and adorned with the scars to prove it, were dressed in their finest battle attire. Heavy with medals and sigils of past victories, they stood proudly at the front of the battle column along with the other officers.

And at their head, a living goddess of war. The Hierarch wore exquisite gold plate. Her pauldrons curled skyward, each section honed to fit her powerful frame, accented by a cloak of crimson inlaid with gold weave. Its end burned with magical fire that would never cease, just as her commitment to her duty was eternal.

She walked slowly, like a statue coming to life. The sight of her caused a ripple through the entire army as thousands of winged and unmantled warriors alike knelt before her as she ascended to a stone pulpit designed for this one occasion.

Sofia stole a glance across the army as she knelt. Seeing the might and glory of the Host, defiant and proud, she better understood Terafiq's decision to meet the enemy head on.

It was prideful. Perhaps foolish. A leader might say they were better fit behind a wall, shouting with a voice drowned out by the din of combat. But Terafiq's place was in front of the charge. Sofia respected her for it.

No matter the strength of the Host's defenses, eventually, the imuertes' numbers would overcome Luminea's. But Sofia knew that if given the choice of a slow death on her knees or a quick one on her feet, Terafiq would choose the latter. And so would she.

The Hierarch climbed to her pulpit and pounded the hilt of her sword against the stone four times, once for each Choir at her command, for the four directions, the four elements. The holy quaternity of their beliefs resonating in a simple gesture.

"My brothers! My sisters!" Terafiq called out. Her voice roared across the open square, two fierce octaves intertwining as if lightning and thunder spoke as one. "I am Terafiq, eighth of my name, Hierarch of the Host, Spear of the Dominion and High Protector of the Light," Terafiq paused, letting the still reverence infect the crowd.

"But today, I stand before you as none of these things. Today, I am only Terafiq, and I look upon you as a proud mother. You are my family, my kin. This is my home. This is *your* home. And the great enemy is there now, at our door, ready to burn it to ash.

"Long ago, this horde claimed another city that once belonged to us. I was there, as were many of you. And like you, I wept for the city we lost and mourned the people in it. But this evil will not claim another!" A cheer erupted in agreement. "Ivá," they called.

"Look, there," the Hierarch continued, pointing to the black horizon. "Our enemy seeks to destroy everything we are sworn to protect, to infect the very light that guides us," She pounded her sword again against the stone. Three thousand echoed back at her.

"But know this! They will never foul the Dawnlight while I draw breath. Their kind will never set foot among the Tiers, never ascend to the beyond. That is a blasphemy that I cannot allow. One I *will* not allow! Will you?" A resounding salute and defiant calls echoed across the battlefield as the soldiers pounded their shields.

"Will you?!" Terafiq challenged again. Again, the crowd cheered back at her their resolve. Sofia's blood was up, her skin prickling at the words. It was not hard to understand how she'd ever thought the Sang divine.

"Do not fear the darkness, my brothers and sisters," Terafiq roared. "We will bring the light to it before this day is done. Trust in the Divine Sphere that protects us!" Then Terafiq drew her sword, and it sang from the sheath, glinting in the sun. It burst into white-hot flames like a geyser of fire.

"Per a Sphaera Divinia, per a Dominion di Esanya, per di Luminea!" The roar of the troops erupted like a rising storm. Sofia called out until her throat strained, as nearby warriors banged against their shields and stamped their feet.

"BY OUR WILL!" the army called out as one.

"The Way be done," Sofia whispered to herself, the sound lost among the roar.

Trumpets blared up and down the battle line, and a defiant hymn sung by hundreds of Sang warriors rippled through the army. Harmonies layered on top of one another like ancient strata.

Sofia recognized the melody hidden in the complex tapestry of song. It was the same one Ebrahym had sung when they'd first met, the one that had given her courage. The feeling of protection surrounded them like an invisible dome, an aegis not of metal or stone, but of Serrá, the collective Will of an army marching with singular purpose. Though she was outside of their Divine Sphere, the melody helped her remember her courage.

They descended the Tiers like a winding, carapaced insect, six thousand legs working in unison toward the great bridge that spanned the Aecuna and connected the island city to the shore.

One by one, the units left the golden towers of Luminea behind. They marched valiantly in columns across the bridge, uncontested, though Sofia watched the skies for winged ambushers. When none came, she wondered why the enemy would allow them to ready and position their forces. Angorzhu, in his pride and his arrogance, wanted them to come with all their might and fury.

He wants us to fight.

As the army assembled on the charred field, the broken shore of the inland sea, the horde entrenched in the countryside came into view like a thick mass of flies. As they, too, took up some semblance of formation, Sofia recognized some of their grotesque forms, large and small alike. She remembered them from the darkness of the Inferna, somehow all the stranger in the light of day.

Even at a distance, across the battlefield to come, she could see the same foul marriages of men and beasts, men and metal, men and the parts of other men, forming the other line. Rotten. Twisted. Representations of their own suffering and driven to war by whips.

The war bands congregated on distant hills, now ground down into mud and ash. Chained lúpero howled, waiting to be released. The blasphemous heraldry of the imuertes lieutenants rose from the mass. Their crude banners depicted cursed symbols, and the parts of dead things denoted their clans and their preference for cruelty.

Farther away still, the ogorantè sounded their gongs for war. The drums whipped the horde into a frenzy, held back by a dam about to give way.

The army of Luminea halted at the ready. The battle hymn mingled with the imuertes' war chants in an eerie din.

At the flanks, the cavalry units waited to dive at the imuertes' lines sideways. The Eagle archers floated overhead, awaiting the signal. Thick cords groaned as the siege engines wound tight, ready to unleash fury.

They waited.

Sofia's heart pounded under her plate. She stumbled a bit, grasping the shoulder of the oulma next to her. He clasped her gauntlet with his own and encouraged her with a nod. She looked to the warrior opposite her, and the lithe woman in gold did the same.

Staring out ahead, it was as she'd foreseen it, but she'd never imagined her place in it. The time of visions and dreams was over.

Terafiq took her position at the head of the army, pointing her sword high, singing louder than the rest. Every soldier followed suit, and then she began to move. The army of Sanguinir and oulma warriors moved with her, matching her pace as one.

Their advance quickened. The sound of thousands of heavy greaves thudding against the earth grew into a thunderous roar as the Sanguinir and oulma charged.

Sofia glanced above to see their winged allies loosing arrows into the enemy lines to slow the tide. Flaming meteors soared overhead and exploded into the enemy ranks. The imuertes, too, began their charge. The black meat grinder of iron and claws lumbered to battle.

Then she saw him. Angorzhu himself, riding to war.

The imuertes leader was atop a monstrous, six-legged creature with legs thick as the oldest trees. Smoke and fire surrounded his form, and he bellowed so fiercely it hit the charging defenders like a gale, momentarily slowing their push.

A hundred meters became ten in a matter of seconds. Time slowed enough for her to notice the silence just before the armies met. They hung there in space and time. Winged warriors encased in golden shells leaped forward. Bloated, distorted monsters swinging crude weapons roared. Arrows rushed overhead. Fire erupted from the enemy line.

Sofia heard the crunch and squish of a spear impaling the man next to her. It was only the beginning.

The Hierarch and the Sanguinir leading the charge disappeared into the enemy ranks like a comet impacting the earth, exploding into madness. The army lines merged, oil and water, the darkness plowing deep into the ranks of the light.

Utter chaos broke, as thousands of ravenous imuertes fell upon the defenders' swords and shields with a deafening clang. Sofia couldn't move, let alone fight, stuck between the stalled warriors in front and the anxious ones still pushing from the rear. The sound alone was enough to break a man.

A mob of imuertes pierced the main line and entangled Sofia's phalanx from the right. Unable to strike or even move, her only option was to hold her ground and support the warrior in front of her. The mass of men and metal began to crack as more imuertes burst through the line.

Ahead, the Sanguinir at the front of the column made headway toward a foul-looking battle standard that signaled an imuertes lieutenant. Blood-covered Sanguinir wings, steaming with gore, led the way.

Sofia followed their lead as the battlefield broke apart into a hundred smaller skirmishes. Up close. Brutal. Bloody. The imuertes lieutenant was a frightening creature with a bulbous frame, charred flesh and crazed eyes. It seemed its head was more mouth and jaw than not, and lined with fangs. His banner displayed a collection of bones from unlucky umbra long dead.

"To me!" Terafiq cried over the din as she led her unit toward the creature. She cut through ranks of imuertes like leaves, her followers trudging through the gore in her wake.

Sofia had never seen so many Sang activated by war at once. Hundreds of glowing discs masked their eyes in rings of light. Blades aflame, conjuring wind and lightning from the sky, it was as terrifying as it was beautiful.

Sofia struggled to keep from stumbling as she pressed on, transfixed, hoping to avoid being trampled by her fellow soldiers.

The bloated imuertes lieutenant, seeing a prize before him, seized his moment for glory and leaped at Terafiq, slashing wildly with a crude ax as he screeched. Terafiq parried the attack and landed a solid counter with her heavy, gauntleted fist. Stunned, the creature didn't even see the blow that separated its head from its obese, mutilated body. Sofia only caught a glance of the victory as she held off a pack of gangly imps biting at the army's flanks.

A victorious cry burst from the warriors around her, but it was short-lived.

She felt him coming.

Like a landslide after a flood, Angorzhu, on his mount, plowed through imuertes and oulma alike toward the Hierarch, crushing many of his own in his path to reach her.

Sofia tried to scream, but the din of combat made it nearly impossible. Terafiq turned to see the threat and raised her guard in time, her blades slicing the flank of Angorzhu's mount as he rode by. But the force of the impact as too great. She was put down as the creature thundered past.

"Protect the Hierarch!" Sofia heard Ebrahym shout somewhere nearby.

Sofia tried to disengage from the gnashing teeth and claws before her, but there were too many. By the time she disemboweled the pack of chattering foes, Angorzhu and Terafiq were locked in combat.

It was as if two primal, opposing forces were manifested. She could feel the energy emitting from each of them. She felt their power wax and wane as they exchanged titanic blows.

Angorzhu howled and laid into Terafiq's shield. The clash of the Hell Lord's hammer upon the Hierarch's blades rang out like thunderclaps across the field. Sofia's ears hummed.

Sanguinir fought to come to their leader's aid, but the mass of Angorzhu's minions bogged them down, their bodies a willing sacrifice to slow their foe.

Sofia worked her way to the perimeter that had opened up around the lords of war.

Terafiq parried a blow that sent her skidding on her heels. Shouting ancient words, she pounded her fist into the ground, splitting the earth open. The crack chased toward Angorzhu until he stomped his massive hoof, sending a shockwave and dust throughout both armies.

Then he charged. It happened so fast. One moment, Terafiq was there. Then, she was not.

The Hierarch fell.

Laid low by an impact that would have split a mountain in two, Terafiq lay sprawled on the gore- and blood-soaked ground, dazed.

Angorzhu pulled a spear from a skewered imuerte nearby, hefted it in one hand, and drove it through the Hierarch's chest with a sickening crunch. All who witnessed it cried out helplessly. The impaled Terafiq stiffened for a moment, then softened. Her song ended. The Sanguinir lay still. The crimson pooled beneath her, staining the feathers of her wings red. The Hierarch's gaze remained skyward, unblinking and unmoving.

Terafiq, eighth of her name, Hierarch of the Host, was gone.

Angorzhu roared triumphantly. Pure terror plowed through Sofia's defenses and demolished the courage she had left. Cold, overwhelming sadness drowned her. For a moment, a thousand smaller battles ceased. Imuertes and Sanguinir and oulma alike stopped to look.

In the distance, a horn signaling the forces of Luminea's retreat sounded.

"No," Sofia whispered. The sorrow choked her. All was lost. The city would fall, and like Ilucenta, it would become a tomb. *Is this how it ends?* She looked toward the beast who felled the Hierarch and felt the rage build. The sorrow evaporated as quickly as it came.

No.

There was only anger. There was only *him.*

Sofia dredged every ounce of fury from her being up from the darkness. In a fraction of a second, she summoned and relived a thousand painful memories. She was back in that dark place. But she was not helpless now. *I will show them terror.*

Sofia unleashed on the nearest pack of enemies as the oulma around hesitated. She hacked the limbs off some twisted brute and slashed through a thick, bony creature to reach the Hierarch.

She pressed, her sword finding flesh and bone and teeth alike until her arm burned. She drove toward the fallen Sang as the imuertes began to rally, urged on by Angorzhu's call. Amidst the chaos, Ebrahym and Anayah appeared at her side. Both nearly covered in black ichor from head to toe, their halos burning, they put down a pack of lúpero with blades aflame.

"Now is our only chance!" Sofia yelled through labored breaths, shaking with anger. "We can kill him!"

Ebrahym wiped steaming ichor from his face and spat. "No, Sofia! We must regroup, the battle is over!" he shouted.

"Ebrahym is right," called Anayah. "Our moment has passed! We risk more by lingering."

"No! I have to!" said Sofia, her eyes fixed on the corpse of the Host's leader.

Adrenaline and raw fury dumped into her veins. The sounds of battle faded away. Sofia's vision focused in on the Hell Lord and nothing else. There *was* nothing else.

As she wove through the charging imuertes, gutting the ones she could, she wrested control over her shaking limbs. A troll-like creature, a lumbering hulk twice her size, burst into her view, beating its scarred chest with rage.

I am the fire.

Sofia closed the distance, leaping off the creature's knee to put her sword to its throat, slashing it open. She never even stopped to see if the thing truly fell. She pushed on with a strength and speed she did not know she had. It was wild. She channeled some raw and ancient spirit of war itself. Then, she saw the Hell Lord, standing over his fallen foe.

Sofia was a few meters from him, closing fast from the side. She found her opening, limbs tensing in anticipation. Ebrahym called from behind.

Angorzhu caught sight of Sofia barreling for him. In a dark flash, he yanked the spear from Terafiq's chest and hurled it toward her with such speed she did not have a chance to react. But Ebrahym did.

The spear hit the one-winged warrior square in the chest as he dove in front of Sofia, shielding her from the lance. The force slammed Ebrahym into her, sending them both reeling into the dirt. *No, no, no!* Sofia scrambled to her feet, rolling her savior to his back.

The spear protruded from his shield, having pierced through it, his arm, and chest underneath. Blood emptied from his body. Sofia's rage went with it, leaving her hollow inside.

She cupped Ebrahym's face, oblivious to the battle raging around them. Anayah was screaming something nearby. The fallen warrior coughed, gasping for air. "Retreat," he repeated, over and over in a hoarse whisper. His halo faded so she could see his eyes. "My duty is done. Leave me."

"No!" Sofia hacked the shaft down with her sword and hefted the Sang onto her shoulder. His weight was enormous, and her legs seized, overwhelmed. *Endure.*

She called to Anayah. The Sanguinir nodded and summoned all her power to rip a bloody path through the imuertes' lines back to Luminea. Sofia followed Anayah. Scores of Prime Auxilia, exhausted but still on their feet, protected Sofia's flank as she trudged through the sulfuric mud mixed with blood.

Am I dead? Tell me. She'd asked Ebrahym the question long ago. He'd never answered her before she'd begun to climb that cliff face overlooking the oasis. The words lingered in her mind, willing her on. Each step felt like that climb now, up the sheer face with the imuertes close behind, hauling a heavy burden. It wasn't a message she carried now, but she would deliver it.

She would deliver it.

43

Ebrahym lay still and cold as the last light faded.

They moved him from the healing house to a courtyard. The other fallen warriors lay there: hundreds of oulma and the occasional Sanguinir, all mangled and filthy. All hastily relocated to make room for more wounded who might still have a chance.

Sofia sat next to him now, her eyes puffy and red. Pink streaks ran down her face where the tears had washed the grime of battle away. She held the Sang's hand, hoping that wherever he might be, he could feel it. There was no tingling sensation now, no crackling energy between them. Just a cold shell. Whatever had made him more than that was gone.

It was quiet in the courtyard, away from the wails of pain echoing through the hospital. Out near the walls of the city, the survivors rested and regrouped, wearily bolstering the defenses of the city proper after losing the bridges to the mainland. They were surrounded and leaderless. The three remaining Quato Eros did the best they could to maintain spirits. But with Terafiq gone, the Host and its army verged on collapse.

Sofia turned Ebrahym's hand in hers. She traced the lines of his palm with her nails. Among the rings that adorned his fingers and wrist, there was one she'd never noticed before. A small, silver ring on the third finger of his left hand. Its simplicity stood out against the other gold rings carved into the heads of tiny lions or winged figures notched with gems. This one meant something different.

As she worked it off his finger, she remembered the fang, the tooth she'd carved from the lúpero's corpse. She had carried it to remember the feeling of power. Now, she would carry Ebrahym's ring to remember the consequences of it.

She heard footsteps behind her, but she didn't turn to meet who made them. A warm hand rested on her shoulder with the same electrifying sensation she wished Ebrahym's had.

"It's my fault," Sofia murmured, clenching the ring. "I should have listened. He told me to retreat. And now he's gone." Her anger had caused this, her bloodlust. She had wanted Angorzhu's head; nothing else had mattered. And now the Sanguinir who'd protected her, who she'd followed to heaven and who'd followed her to hell and back, was gone.

Oulma in white robes appeared and hefted Ebrahym onto a stretcher. "What are you doing?" Sofia scolded. "Get away from him! Get *away*!" Sofia shoved the gentle aides in frustration. Anayah pulled her back, holding her as the healers did their duty. Sofia scrambled to her feet to follow Ebrahym's corpse, but Anayah pulled her in close, embracing her tightly. Sofia squeezed, harder and harder, trying to drive the pain down somewhere dark where it might never be found.

"This was not your doing," Anayah said, as a mother would soothe a child. "He believed in you."

"He shouldn't have."

"And is this how you would honor him?" Anayah asked with an unfamiliar sharpness to her tone. Sofia pushed the tears away, shaking her head. She inhaled sharply, regaining her breath.

"I can't, Anayah—"

"You would yield? Ebrahym lays down his life for yours, and that is how you repay him? The fight is not over. To be Sanguinir is to endure, Sofia. Remember that."

"I am no Sanguinir," Sofia said softly.

Anayah looked deep into Sofia's eyes with a gaze harder than steel. "Follow me."

***

Sofia walked down the aisle, Sheer linen robes of white skirted the stone tiles that were cold on her bare feet. Through a pungent cloud of incense, she passed by a few scattered Sanguinir warriors, still clad in their grungy battle gear. Even in times of war, some traditions are worth honoring. Sofia tried to read their perfect faces. Their divine veneers masked the sadness she knew was there.

One such witness was the Seer, the blind, ancient Sang Sofia had first met after arriving in Luminea. The Seer stood near the altar, the smooth skin where her eyes should be reflected the light from above.

In the Conventa, Sofia learned divination was not the Seers' only role. They were stewards of the aurolas and observed the extraction and transition from one host to another. It all felt so clinical. A fallen Sanguinir was treated as nothing more than an ineffective, spent shell to be replaced by another. Remembered only by a name carved into a stone wall.

The small gathering began to sing. It was the same hymn Sofia had heard at Anayah's haloing, but now they sang for her. The melody was thinner now. It was mournful. The sounds drifted up into the high rafters of the temple, echoing like shouts in a deep cave.

Once, Sofia would have given anything to experience this single moment—to be eternally bound to another being, a halo, and know the truth about her place in this world. She'd nearly cut down her friend in a fit of rage to have the honor.

Now, she couldn't have wanted it less.

She kept a steady pace toward the altar in the center of the huge and nearly empty chamber while her nerves threatened to shake her apart. The cathedral around her was dizzying. She steered her gaze away from the towering arches and frescoes and toward the intricately tiled floor ahead. She climbed the steps, taking note of the cool marble underfoot.

Upon the dais, the three surviving Eros stood, the absence of Terafiq noticed by all. Rahazad, the giant Eros and leader of the Choir of the Bull, stood at the center, encased in heavy bronze armor. The story of war covered it with gouges and punctures. His brown wings were still smeared with the ceremonial markings painted on before battle. Until the war was won, the feathers would not be washed clean. That was the Way. Rahazad was the strongest warrior of the three Eros and had assumed command upon Terafiq's death. By the grim expression on his dark face, he took no pleasure in that.

The two remaining Eros, Halphyus and Verivryn, flanked Rahazad, who stood nearly half a meter taller than either of them. Among them was Anayah, likewise still in armor from the battle. Blood and gore stained all of them.

Anayah passed Sofia the slightest of nods as Sofia found her place in the stone circle in the center of the platform. The chorus began to rise, and the hair on Sofia's arms pricked up. There was energy buzzing about, like charged lighting in a storm cloud, waiting to be released.

A hooded Sanguinir, a disciple of the Seer and shepherd of the aurola, placed the gilded chest at Sofia's feet and slunk from sight. It was the same chest Anayah had opened during her ceremony. But to Sofia, it was a funeral urn, a memorial. Her heart told her what lay inside: The aurola Ebrahym carried with him for hundreds of years. His halo. *Marahi*, Nesta had called it. The only part of him that remained. They were likely finished burning his body by now.

Sofia paused, taking in the moment. An upsurge of raw emotion welled inside of her, a potent concoction of sorrow, fear and reverence. She swallowed hard to push back the anxious tide. She took a breath.

The hymn built to its climax, and Sofia's skin rippled as her body struggled to process the sensations. She twisted the metal latch, lifted the lid of the chest and stared inside.

Silence enveloped her. Pure and absolute.

Blinded by light, she found herself enveloped in a stillness so complete it disturbed her senses. The cathedral vanished, along with the flock of Sanguinir it contained. Here, space was expansive and devoid of form or shape; there was only light.

She called out to the sterile, white void.

"We are one," the light answered in a sweet voice.

Sofia wheeled to find the source of the voice, only to discover it was within her. She felt the words appear inside of her mind, but they were not her own. The voice, such as it was, was ancient, with weight and authority to it. But it was not a man's essence. Sofia could feel it. It was a female power, fierce and alive.

"Hello?" Sofia said aloud to the thing inside. "Are you Marahi?"

"We are," the voice from within said.

Sofia shielded her eyes from a bombardment of images that flew at her. She moved from one place to another so fast her mind could barely register what she was seeing.

Some of the images were familiar. She recognized the spires of Luminea, but they were smaller, different. Snapshots of war placed her in the thick of battle as if she were seeing through the eyes of other Sanguinir warriors from different times.

Meditation and ceremony interrupted scenes of battle training and soaring high above green fields. *Flying!* Sofia was aloft, slicing through the air above the Orvida plains.

A second later, she was back in the same cathedral she was in a moment ago, repeating the same ritual. But it was not her kneeling upon the stone. She was a man now, lean and strong with pale, blue eyes. There was a boyishness to him, not the stony, noble visage of an Sanguinir warrior. He was just a man, wingless, with kindness to his gaze yet unclouded by amber fire. The man who would become Ebrahym opened the small chest and stared into the light. Sofia's heart wrenched and ached at the sight. She wished she could have known his name.

Espleña. She was in the city of Espleña now. Sofia had never been there, but she knew where she was.

It was as she'd imagined it in her dream, her vision before the imuertes attack. Her body, Ebrahym's body, moved independently, her mind simply a passenger. Around her, the layered buildings and narrow streets of Espleña burned, filled with ash and smoke and screams.

Sofia felt Ebrahym shout orders and rally his men as she called to them herself. She felt Ebrahym's fear for them. A moment later, the nearby barricade splintered, and a horde of nightmares spilled through.

She watched him fight valiantly through his own eyes, moving with grace and deadly speed from one foe to another. His blade opened imuerte flesh and cleaved bone. The memory seeped through time and space, and Sofia felt the rush of battle.

Then she was herself again, alone in the darkness.

The beast appeared in the shadows at first. The great, gnarled horns pierced through the smoke, the rest of the nightmarish form following soon after. The man-beast lumbered forward, its powerful form towering over her.

Pure, white-hot eyes burned from beneath a heavy brow upon which the fiery symbol burned. *Angorzhu.* He stood before her, a god of terror, of violence. Sofia willed her body to run, but it would not, paralyzed with fear. The beast roared. It hit Sofia with a gale force, and she heard the screams of ten thousand tortured oulma. Sofia shrieked as Angorzhu approached, a bloody hammer in one hand and a jagged sword in the other.

Sofia raised a defiant blade that appeared in her hand, but her foe pummeled her to the ground. At once, lesser imuertes were upon her, tearing at her flesh and burrowing into the weakest points of her armor. She thrashed desperately to defend against the swarm, but the claws and fangs of the creatures held her.

Darkness enveloped her. Suffocated her. Consumed her.

Sofia opened her eyes to meet the wide gaze of the Sanguinir lords and Anayah looming over her.

She was back in the cathedral, naked upon the dais, covered with a thick layer of inky soot. Around her, the floor had been burned black in every direction, the holy chest before her now a pile of ash.

Silence had replaced melody, and the cathedral was still. The Sanguinir glanced at one another, clearly not having expected to see what they'd witnessed.

Is this what Alana saw? Sofia supported her throbbing head with a hand. *No.* This was something altogether different. The barrage of sensations left her overwhelmed and weak.

She clutched her chest, recalling the words described in Angorzhu's book. The Unspoken War, the deeds of the Sanguinir, the truth. She *felt* all of it now, *knew* all of it. She felt the ache of regret the Host shared, the Great Shame. She felt the faith and power in the Divine Sphere and the threads of connection between her and the Sang around her.

Anayah helped her to her feet, wrapping her in a crimson cloak. She felt swallowed up by a landslide, weak and stiff all over. But there was something else. Not just the knowledge the communion with the aurola had unlocked. There was fear in Anayah's eyes. *Fear*. It was the look of one trying to hide when consoling another already too far gone to save.

"It is done," she whispered and held Sofia close. Sofia stared at the black soot covering her shaking hands.

44

Sofia touched the name *Ebrahym XII* etched into the stone.

The lettering was fresh and sharp and chiseled with perfection. The names of countless Sanguinir and oulma warriors lost in the centuries surrounded her, deep in the tombs below the Dawnlight. Ebrahym, Matías, Terafiq—oulma and Sanguinir alike. Hundreds more since the first days of the siege.

She sat cross-legged in front of the of the memorial wall, staring at the cold, silent marble. A pair of newly formed wings crossed awkwardly behind her, fresh feathers splayed on the stone tiles. In the reflection of the polished stone, two amber points of light stared back at her. Golden irises had replaced green. As she stared into her new reflection, a pale comparison of the Sanguinir that came before her, Ebrahym came to mind, and she wanted to weep. But the tears would not come.

In her lap lay Angorzhu's heavy tome. It described everything she now knew as a Sang herself. Despite his malice, his hate, the Fierno was as he was because of what he had learned. It had driven him to become the monster he was and, in no small way, helped set him on the path to war.

Sofia wondered if she would have done the same in his place.

She took a deep breath and shifted her wings, feeling the connection of new muscle. The aftereffects of the haloing were harsh but didn't linger. But other than her wings, Sofia felt largely unchanged. She couldn't hear the woman's voice that had spoken to her from the void, the voice of the halo.

Something was wrong; she could feel it.

Whereas Anayah's former self had been consumed in light when she'd looked into the chest, Sofia had experienced the opposite. Anayah described a pillar of darkness that had descended through the cathedral and enveloped Sofia as she and the halo entity had merged.

The inky cloud had smothered the light. Fire and ash had swirled in a volcanic cloud, and a chorus of screams had drowned out the Sanguinir song, defiling the place with foul presence. Anayah said the Sanguinir believed it was a bad omen. But Sofia was one of the Host now, and they needed all the help they could get.

Sofia came to her feet and walked along the lonely corridors of the tombs. As she passed by a burning brazier, she took one last look at the tome and tossed the book into it. The pages blackened and crumbled among the flames as she walked away.

She climbed the long stairs from underneath Luminea to the light above. In the worn faces of the oulma passing by her in the street, she saw a longing, a need for someone to tell them everything would be all right. That the Sanguinir would prevail. That Luminea would stand. That they would win.

But she had no answers for them. Bound by some property of the halo's device, she could only speak the truth. And the truth was, she did not know if any of them would survive.

After her patrol about the city, Sofia wound her way back to the Fifth Tier and the Temple of the Dawnlight. She descended deep into the earth once more, stair after stair to the giant cube of stone that held the Sanctu Arcam itself. The light beams emerging from the hardened gem at its peak ebbed and flowed peacefully, unaware of the doom that approached. There were no lively debates here now, no circles of curious oulma delving into ancient teachings. The hall was empty and still.

Sofia found Nesta, the sole caretaker, it seemed, deep in thought. The Sanguinir did not look up as she approached. Sofia envied her peacefulness.

"Welcome, Sebrahi," Nesta said, eyes still closed.

"My name is Sofia." There was something about losing her name and accepting the Sanguinir lineage title she could not accept. Nor did she wish to think of Ebrahym every time her name was called.

Nesta shook her head. "You dishonor the mantle. It is not a name, but a title of respect. You are the thirteenth in your line—"

"I need your help," Sofia said, sitting next to the wingless woman. "Tell me how to talk to it. The halo. During the ceremony…It spoke to me. Showed me things. It was trying to tell me something but…I can't quite describe it. Now I feel nothing."

"They are close now," Nesta said. Sofia could see dark, blotchy masses on her neck. Nesta's eyes were pale and milky. Her sickness was growing.

"We are fading," Nesta continued. "There is not much time. The Divine Sphere is weakening. There are too few Sanguinir with the Serrá to maintain it." Seeing Nesta's weakness and remembering her tale of captivity, Sofia felt a surge of inspiration. She would not give up or wither. Even if the end came, she would meet it on her feet, fighting.

"That's why I need your help. I'm of no use to anyone like this."

Nesta nodded. Sofia followed her lead and adjusted herself on the floor, wings crossed. She knew the basic principles of the communion, but the trancelike state eluded her. Nesta instructed her to relax and slip away from her body. She chanted the ancient words. Hours passed. Slowly, the layers of Sofia's mind peeled back. Sensation, memory, pain—all stripped one by one until there was nothing left. She drifted. Sometimes back to the torture pits of the Inferna, then to the lighthouse and the caravan. But Sofia followed Nesta's voice, and the thoughts fell away. In the center of herself, she found it.

There is a cave, Nesta described, *and in the cave there is a single candle.*

Sofia saw it. An endless void with one tiny flickering light struggling against so much oppressive blackness. Beyond it was total nothingness. Sofia knelt in front of the candle, staring at the tiny flame. Nesta's words drifted away like incense on the breeze. The candle flickered, and a figure moved in the shadows.

Sofia was not afraid; she felt its goodness. Ebrahym's form emerged from the darkness. He was whole again, a pair of delicate wings illuminated by the candlelight hovered behind him, and his eyes burned brightly.

"You're gone," whispered Sofia.

"Yes," Ebrahym said. "But part of me is still here. Like the others before me, back to the first."

"I have questions."

Ebrahym smiled. "You always do. Come, Sebrahi."

She appeared, suddenly, on a green hill, walking through the grass behind Ebrahym. He had both his wings again. Sofia flexed hers, opening them wide as effortlessly as she would her own arms. She could feel the tips of the feathers vibrating in the morning breeze, a sensation that was difficult to describe but entirely how she'd imagined it.

The sun was freshly risen, and the dew was nearly dried upon the tall grasses Ebrahym led her through, up the hill toward a craggy formation.

There was nothing extraordinary about the rise, though the view from the summit, once they reached it, was incredible. The cliff protruded from the earth, the only one of its kind for hundreds of kilometers in any direction, and a river flowed at the base of the slope that opened wide to yet more grasslands in the distance.

Sofia inched to the precipice slowly, eying the drop-off, swaying in the gusty winds that rolled over the peak.

"I know this place," she said.

Ebrahym nodded. "*Nidalda*, the Nest. Are you afraid?"

"Yes."

Ebrahym smiled again. "In the Afore, it is said the mother bird pushes the chick from the nest to awaken its instinct."

"But not here," Sofia challenged.

"No. Here, the Choir of the Bull works to keep the Orvida in natural motion. Either way, survival is a powerful motivator. You must have faith in the aurola, and it must believe in you."

"So, what's the trick?" Sofia asked.

"Simple. Let go."

Sofia's toes hung over the rock ledge as she closed her eyes, letting the wind spill over her. Anticipation churned in her stomach. The drop-off was absolute, a sheer plummet toward the river below.

For so long, she'd feared falling, of letting go. She feared trusting anything other than herself, including the being that now resided inside of her. It was only one small leap. Her body resisted the idea, as ancient programming for survival fought for dominance in her brain. Sofia opened her eyes and pressed her feathery wings outward as far as they would go, struggling to stay standing against the additional wind they gathered.

The thought of staring at the open road from the lighthouse passed through her mind for a moment, and she recalled the fear of the unknown she'd felt before walking into the desert a lifetime ago.

She breathed deep.

She opened her eyes.

She jumped.

For a moment, Sofia thought she was aloft, the next she was screaming toward the ground.

She thrashed and spiraled wildly, trying to right herself. Tucking her wings tight, she entered a dive that accelerated her pace yet allowed her to slow her rotation and eventually stabilize. The white rapids breaking on the rocks below were quickly becoming larger.

Sofia tried to feel the wind, but through the noise and force it was all a blur. Then, as she cut through one layer of air she felt it: a thin stream of warmth rising from the stone wall. Sofia knew it was now or never. She trusted the feeling and snapped her wings open, flexing the powerful knot of muscles protruding from her back. The initial force nearly tore the wings right off her.

Suddenly, all was silent. The only thing Sofia could hear was her own heavy breathing. She glided with the speed of the wind and felt its subtle variations. Slicing through the convection zones, finding the right currents, sliding into the grooves and maintaining altitude, she felt at home in the air.

She laughed aloud. *I am flying. Me!* It was incredible, a childish dream made real. Tears escaped her eyes as she hooted and hollered, her tiny shadow racing across the fields far below.

Ebrahym called out to her. He floated just to the side, his wing tips occasionally grazing her own. "Now, follow me!" He pumped his wings and rose, finding a stronger current. Sofia followed less gracefully but soon found herself in the clouds where the air was thin and cold.

The pair darted through the fluffy haze before diving deep, both Sanguinir howling with joy as they plummeted toward the ground before braking at the last moment. Ebrahym and Sofia screamed over the grasses so close that her toes dragged along their tips as they tore across the green and gold fields covering the Orvida.

They flew for hours it seemed, days. Together they soared over the fields and streams until the grass gave way to sand. Faster now, and the sand yielded to a forest of gnarled dead wood. From above, it appeared a tangled nest of thorns. Sofia recognized the terrain until the fog rolled in, obscuring the ground below.

ALL THAT WILL BURN

The heavy air was more difficult to navigate, and Sofia stuck close to Ebrahym as he cut through the mist.

Sofia saw him dive through the fog. She arched, tucked her wings together and hurtled toward the ground. The earth emerged a few moments later, and she spread her wings wide. Sofia glided over the sand and touched down in the soft surf.

She was back where she'd begun so long ago. The gray, desolate beach she'd emerged from as a newborn, naked and lost. Before her, a single path of footsteps, her own footsteps, trailed off into the mist.

"Follow them back," Ebrahym said, nodding.

"Where do they lead?"

The Sanguinir beside her said nothing. Ebrahym did not look like himself now. Sofia remembered the moments where she had seen Ebrahym differently, more feminine and gentle. The guise returned. His face softened. Then there were multiple faces, masks, as if transparent figures overlapped one another.

Amid the blur, the commonalities of the visages resolved to a singular form—distinct, but undeniably female. Dark hair surrounding a noble face, soft, loving eyes of green gazing deep into Sofia's being.

It was *Marahi,* the ancient, divine being from the realm of the Dawnlight. Sofia knew the aurola, felt its presence within her, even now as she stared at its avatar before her. The vision smiled reassuringly, knowingly, and pointed into the fog where the footsteps led.

Sofia began to walk.

45

The city street choked with all types of traffic. Old cars, buses, bikes and throngs of people fought to make headway through a sea of humanity baking under a blistering sun.

It was muggy. The glare was intense. Everything looked superheated, bleached of its color.

Sofia looked around, searching for a point of reference. A moment ago, she was in the fog, and now, here. But here was not the hereafter. Not the Orvida. This was the world of the past.

The Afore.

The sights and sounds of the crowded metropolis pulled at her. She felt this place. She *knew* it.

Old buildings sagged as they sat stacked on top of one another, deteriorating and crumbling. There were no grand towers among the Tiers here. No vast temples and sprawling plazas. Only cramped, crooked streets funneling humanity from here to there. This was a city shaped by modern, human hands and under siege by entropy and time.

Telltale signs surrounded her: worn electric lights and signs, some flickering weakly, tangles of power lines running shortsightedly overhead and pungent garbage scattered underfoot. A dog sniffed at the refuse and passed by Sofia's leg. Smoke from a nearby vendor filled the air with the smell of burning oil. The rawness of it was overwhelming.

Three children, with bronzed skin and large, dark eyes, precariously balanced on a single bicycle as they flew past her, laughing. She had never seen children in person before. They were so small.

A car horn screeched as a taxi flew past. Around her, people spoke in a language Sofia knew to be her own. The one she spoke before Anayah had taught her the common tongue of the Orvida. *I know these words.*

She tried to say hello to random passersby, but she was a ghost to them.

Then she saw the figure—the blurred form of dozens and dozens of Sanguinir stacked over one another in a fragmented, hazy figure of a woman. *Marahi.*

Sofia navigated the traffic to reach her. As she approached, a hundred smiles on a hundred melded, transparent faces welcomed her. Marahi nodded as she approached.

"¿Qué es este lugar?" Sofia asked. *Where am I?*

The aurola said nothing. It craned its multi-faceted head toward a narrow flight of stairs, then ascended them to toward a shabby structure that was worn by heat, moisture and neglect.

The sounds of trumpeting music and laughter, mixed with the cry of an infant, drifted nearby as Sofia and her guide made their way up a winding flight of stairs. Past a corridor of doors, they came to one marked fourteen. The four was the only number there, the stain in the shape of the number one standing watch next to it.

Marahi gestured for Sofia to open the green door. She hesitated for a moment, then pushed it inside.

It was dark inside the apartment. It was a shabby place. It was *the* place.

The paint was peeling, the floor stained, yet it was clear that some dedicated hand worked to keep the gloom at bay. Bright colors and cheerfulness forced itself upon the place. Candles depicting saints, paintings of tropical places, colored fabrics pinned to the walls—it was all too familiar.

Sofia drifted through the apartment until she reached the door to the bedroom. She could hear someone crying on the other side.

Sofia's heart began to race. *No, it can't be. Not the dream.* On the other side of the door the events she'd relived a hundred times were about to unfold; she could feel it. Only this was no dream. She knew she was not actually *here,* but at the same time, this was no manifestation of her mind. The hot moisture gathering under the thickness of her hair beaded down her back. This was *real.*

With a deep breath, she pushed her way inside and was in the bedroom. It was exactly as expected, though the small details were more distinct, sharper. Sofia could feel the carpet between her toes and smell the cheap incense lingering in the air.

On the bed was the woman—the woman Sofia had seen a hundred times before in her dreams. The same faded blue-green dress scattered with stars. The same golden cross dangling from her slender shoulders.

As always, she was heavy with child. Sofia went to her, kneeling low to see her face. It was beautiful, different than she had seen before. It was more *accurate,* and she understood why. Sofia stared at a face that was neither her own nor a stranger's, but right on both counts.

Mama.

She knew it. In every part of her, she knew it. The dark curls, the fierce green eyes and generous lips. Sofia saw herself in this woman. A part of her *was* this woman. Daughter placed her hand on her mother's belly, and Sofia felt the tiny essence kicking within. *Her* essence.

"We discussed this, Maria," said a deep voice from behind.

Sofia turned to see the massive man brooding in the corner—skin like leather, heavy brow and jaw and cunning eyes. The sinewy muscles of his tattooed forearms were tightly wound, containing some deep rage. Blocky and primal, symbols of jungle secrets long past marked his exposed shoulders and neck. There were feathered monsters and scenes of battle tattooed there. Scattered throughout the apocalyptic imagery were slogans and numbers.

Somehow, Sofia knew they signified allegiances. Criminal ones. A lifetime of knowledge came rushing back to her from the Afore. A world of pain and guns and murder, of bodies and money and blood. The details were dark and elusive. But she felt echoes of chronic loneliness, desperation, and the ache from an endless struggle against it. But there was something else. Something left undone...

The woman named Maria rose from the bed and went to the giant, her touch momentarily softening the golem. "Do you not love me, Luqa? Do you not want to start a family? God wants me to keep our baby. I must obey Him."

With surprising speed, Luqa hurled a nearby chair into the air. It smashed into the adjacent desk, splintering the flimsy particleboard. Cheap trinkets scattered. Maria screamed. She always screamed.

"You will obey *me*!" he roared. Sofia shoved at the giant and pounded his broad chest, but she was only a witness to the scene, a phantom.

Blood pulsed through thick veins on the side of Luqa's skull. His eyes were wide and darted about, seeking for a target to release his rage upon. As if possessed by some force and then exorcised a moment later, Luqa's face relaxed, his body sighing back to a state of calm.

"I am sorry, my love. I...you know how my temper can be," he shook his head and glanced at a pile of papers that had spilled from the gutted desk onto the floor.

His own face stared up at him from a photo, in portrait and profile, along with other photographs and police reports. Sofia knelt alongside him to read their detail. She recognized the format of the case file. *Assault. Trafficking. Murder. Extortion. Kidnapping.*

Luqa stooped over the evidence. "Y-You never speak about your work, your family," Maria said, trembling. She rubbed her belly anxiously. "I wanted to know what kind of man you are, what kind of father you would be." Luqa rose from his knees like a statue coming to life.

The final gear in a complex clockwork slid into place with a click. If this woman called Maria was her mother, then this man, the man named Luqa, was her father.

Father.

***

Snap. The world materialized from darkness. Pain. *Where am I?* The sting across her knuckles sunk into the bone. Her small hands lay flat on the stained table and swelled like tiny, dirty fruits. The room was old and musty. She always hated the smell of it. There was a cross with a man on it hanging on one wall. On another, a worn painting of a crow perched on a branch.

"I will ask you again, Sofia," the man in black said, holding the stick with gnarled hands. "Why did you leave the grounds? It is a sin to lie."

It was, so Sofia said nothing. She looked for Marahi, but there was only the man in black before her. She felt tiny in his presence, trapped in a smaller, weaker version of herself.

The man in black leered over her like a jagged shadow. His hair was black. His eyes were black. The only light about him was the white slash at his throat. When she didn't answer, he snapped the stick across her hands again, and she whimpered aloud.

"I asked you a question. Where do you go each night? What are you looking for? Everything you need is here, with us. With Him."

***

The fire burned into the night. The children watched from across the street as the women in white clutched them close, crossing themselves and whispering prayers. They sang hymns to calm the children and each other.

An errant candle had done the place in, or so they guessed. It was His will. The inferno consumed the building to its bones, until they turned black and crumbled.

Sofia watched the fire. She relived the guilt of a child who kills an animal for the first time just to see what happens. The sensation was just as potent as it had been then. Incomprehensible shame. The weight of the world resting upon a small pair of shoulders too weak to carry it.

Was this my fault? She hid the tears from the younger kids. She didn't want them to see. The soot wouldn't rub off her bare feet, so she licked her fingers and rubbed them again, not realizing how burned they were. The fire raged on.

***

The concrete cell was a cold, menacing box with a single light burning above. The woman across the metal table was a severe sort, hair pulled tight and restrained into a bun, her womanly figure masked by a dark blue uniform. The angles of her face cast deep shadows, hiding any emotion. She eyed an array of papers before her.

"What do you want?" the woman asked, eyeing the files. "To be a mule all your life? To get used up and tossed out like all the rest?"

Sofia snapped her gum and picked absently at a scab. Her new tattoo was still healing, but she was impatient to show it off. The heavily scripted *Mama* looked ok, but Carlos had messed up the wings flanking the word.

"Look," said the officer. She intertwined her fingers and rested them on the table. "I know you got a shit deal. But you're not the only one."

Sofia shot her the best apathetic stare a teenager could muster, complete with eye roll. *Who does this bitch think she is?* her younger self wondered.

"The cartels took my family, too," the woman said, watching Sofia closely. Sofia feigned disinterest, but the sting of ancient history still had bite. "They tell me you are looking for your father. Is that true?"

Sofia tried not to let her intentions show, but the woman saw through the mask. Sofia *was* looking for him, always had been. A notebook stuffed under that mattress of the wanna-be tough guy she was crashing with had the newspaper clippings, maps and old photos to prove it. Her father was out there, somewhere.

And when I find him, I'm going to kill him.

"I can see it in your eyes, kid." the officer grinned. "You're the type to not let things go. So, I'm giving you a choice. Go back to the street, to whatever hole you're living in..."

Or? Sofia raised her pierced eyebrow coolly.

"Or," the officer said, coming to her feet. "Come work for us, and I'll teach you how to fight people like that. You never know, maybe one day you'll find that son of a bitch."

* * *

Emptiness.

"Is she going to be ok?" a woman's voice asked in the black. Sofia's eyes wouldn't open, no matter how she strained. The voice was at her side, but it might as well have been a million kilometers away.

"The doctors don't know," a man answered. He sounded tired. "She took three in the chest. Lost a lot of blood."

Oh, God. Was I shot? Where am I? She struggled against unseen chains, a prisoner in her own body. *I'm here!* She screamed, but the void would not let her voice escape from the pit.

"Jesus," the woman whispered. A hand grabbed hers in the darkness. The sensation was acute and sharp, intense among all the nothingness. It squeezed tight. Sofia couldn't squeeze back. "It's hard to see her like this."

"Yeah."

"How are you holding up?"

The man sighed. "Four years we've been partners." Sofia felt his hand take hers. "Can you imagine it? Going through life knowing your only living family member is the monster who killed your mother? What she's been through to find him—"

GODDAMMIT LET ME OUT!

"How long was she undercover?" the woman asked. "She would never tell me."

Anayah?

"This last time? Six months. She was close on this one. *So* close to getting that son of a bitch. She always said something was leading her to him. In her mind, it was inevitable."

"It's not your fault this happened."

Ebrahym? Anyone?

The man's voice dropped to a whisper and came close. "Fia, I'm sorry. I let you down. But I swear I'll get him for you. I promise."

Something buzzed just outside consciousness, a loud, uninterrupted tone. It mingled with other sounds into a strange melody. *What is that?*

"Sofia? Sofia! What's happening?"

"Somebody! Help!"

"Don't give up!"

***

She was back in her parents' apartment.

Sofia's mind raced as she watched the scene unfold, powerless.

"You want to know what kind of man I am?" Luqa repeated. Her father stalked Maria like a jungle cat in the shadows of the canopy. Sofia could see that every muscle in his being begged to be released, restrained by a will that crumbled by the second. She knew the feeling well, and it sickened her to see its origin.

Her mother's back found the wall as she cowered from the volcano set to erupt. Luqa's face was inches from hers. Sofia tried to push her father away, fighting to get between them, but there was nothing she could do.

Luqa continued in a whisper, "I am the kind of man who has done terrible things, yes. I kept them from you because I love you. Parts of my life are not meant for you to see. I do what I must to survive. But *this*," he gestured to the evidence at his feet, "*this* is betrayal. Everything I have done was for you, and this how to you repay my love? My trust? By spying on me?"

Maria tried to respond, but Luqa's hands were already around her thin throat. He squeezed. She gasped.

Maria clawed desperately at the stone face looming over her. Sofia screamed and beat her father impotently with her fists until Maria stopped struggling and slumped against the wall. Luqa finally released his iron grip. His eyes burned with tears.

Sofia watched, transfixed by the bizarre nature of the scene, as the giant picked up the woman and laid her gently on the bed. His hands shook as he did.

On the bed, next to the body of her mother, she noticed something she hadn't before in all the times she'd watch this play out. In a half-finished cross-stitch, she could make out a single word surrounded by flowers. *Sofia.*

Sofia collapsed in terror, screaming as she held what was to be her first blanket close to her chest. The world caved in around her. She desperately tried to wake Maria, shaking her in frustration, but she was dead. The fire had left the green eyes.

Luqa stood silent witness, tears leaking from the golem of a man. He gently took Maria's hand in his and slipped the silver ring from Maria's left hand and squeezed it in his own.

The sound of the front door opening followed by another woman's voice calling out for Maria broke the silence. The voice was old and raspy and felt like home. Nana? Sofia watched Luqa hurry his way through the window and down the fire escape as the elderly woman entered the room. She called out Maria's name and screamed. She rushed to the phone, trying to get the words out. The phone receiver dangled by the cord as the woman rolled up the sleeves of her worn blouse, crossed herself with wrinkled hands and put an ear to Maria's belly. A tiny heartbeat fluttered.

"Hold on, child," she whispered.

***

Sofia opened her eyes. Nesta sat opposite her, as calm and reserved as ever. She was back in the sanctuary of stone, in the heart of Luminea. Back in the Orvida, the hereafter. It suddenly felt alien again. Too polished, too perfect to be believed.

"Did Marahi speak to you?" Nesta asked. "What did you see, Sebrahi?"

Her nightmares, Sofia realized, were not memories at all. Only dreams remembered. Even as a child, she had known the story of her mother. She had imagined it in every detail. She had lived the rage every day of her life, and held onto it so tightly she carried pieces of it with her after death.

"I saw my mother, and my father," Sofia said, testing the words. Her fists shook with rage. "Angorzhu."

I'm coming, Father.

I am coming.

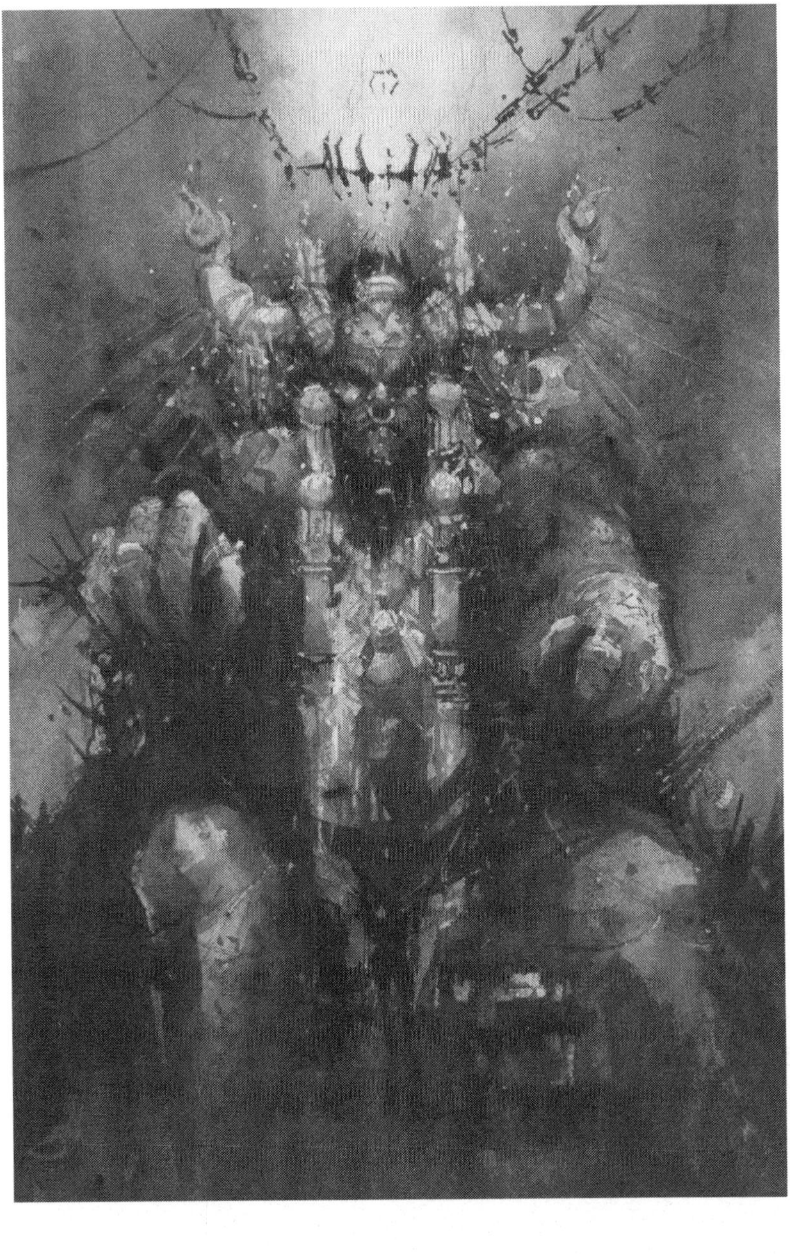

46

Anayah led Sofia, now Sebrahi, as she was called, along with the other newly mantled Sanguinir warriors, many of them replacements, to the foundries of Luminea, deep within the Choir of the Bull's home quarter of the Fifth Tier. The Anvil, some called it.

The delicate feathers attached to her back absorbed the sun's early light and energized her. In small groups of newly mantled Sang, they followed Anayah through the streets until Sofia tasted metal in the air.

Pinging hammers called to them as they approached. Enclosed within a walled plaza of stalls and workstations, a hive of metalworking churned. Inside, forges burned hot, sparks flew, and the singing of metal on metal rang out in time. The smiths worked nonstop, building new siege devices, ballista bolts, arrows—everything they would need for a long defense.

At first glance, the sight of molten metal and fire resurrected nightmares from Mictlani, but the thoughts quickly passed. The glistening men and women working the forges did so not out of fear or hate, but of hope. A few were Sanguinir, master builders, winged smiths bearing the telltale green of their Choir and metal jewelry wrapped around their limbs. Sweat poured from them. Not from the heat, but from the exertion of their Serrá to bend the metal.

Sofia tugged at the chain around her neck. On it hung Ebrahym's silver ring, and next to it, the lion pendant Anayah had given her.

They were met by a Sanguinir giant, the largest Sofia may have ever seen. A meter taller than her at least. Sweat gleamed off his bulging arms, honed over centuries by the hammer. The man's thick, black beard perfectly contrasted his oddly pristine, green apron. Embroidered on it were four bulls interlocking horns in a crossed symbol. Decorative metal studs covered his body as if he were metal underneath and it poked through the skin wrapping.

"Good to see you, Anayah," he roared over the sound of hammers and anvils. He nodded toward the flock that followed her. "And the baby birds, too. We will need them."

Anayah embraced him and pulled away. "It is good to see you, too, Micajah. Are we prepared?"

"Of course," the giant nodded toward Sofia, standing at Anayah's side. "This is the one?"

Anayah nodded toward Sofia. "This is the one."

Micajah saluted the new Sanguinir and personally welcomed each of them to the Host by ritual, reciting their name and gesturing his respect. Sofia did not get the sense he was a being of protocol and pleasantries even in the best of times.

But these new Sang were not honed by centuries of war. Fear was everywhere, and they needed courage. They needed to believe that now they were more than they were yesterday.

Through the maze of smelting furnaces, Micajah led Anayah, Sofia and the other Sanguinir into the armory. Finely crafted weapons hung on display around every corner, ready to taste imuerte blood.

The new Sanguinir dispersed to arm themselves. Meanwhile, Sofia and Anayah slipped away from their comrades and followed Micajah through a series of locked doors and private chambers.

The giant brought them to what looked like a trophy hall. Special war gear used by only the most venerated Sanguinir warriors gleamed in stasis. Each piece rested within a stone alcove lit by perfectly placed glass windows above. Light streamed down from overhead and glinted off the plate and blades as if the equipment were fresh from the forge, still hot from the fire.

Sofia followed Micajah toward the end of the hall where a specimen of gold and white plate hung motionless. The armor was beautiful. Shaped for a woman, reliefs of lions covered its surface between lines of scripture and names of warriors past. They flanked the image of a sun rising over a tiered temple relieved in white gold. A great plumed helmet hung above it, the headdress of red accented with metal spindles and delicate beads. Sofia reached out to touch it, pausing in reverence.

Micajah nodded his permission, and Sofia traced the inlays with her fingers. The metal hummed beneath her fingertips.

"Yasbrahi, the Mornshield, once wore this plate as she defended Ilucenta," Anayah said as she eyed the armor like a complex painting.

"Nesta..." Sofia said, still tracking the lines of the armor with her hands.

"Yes. She wanted you to wear it."

"Me?" Sofia shot a surprised look to Micajah. He bowed slightly, hands clasped behind his massive chest.

"Yes," Anayah said. "Twice now, Marahi, your aurola, has faced this evil. With Yasbrahi at Ilucenta and with Ebrahym. Twice now, the Fierno has taken our leader from us, taken our friends." She trailed off. The wound Ebrahym's death left behind was still fresh. "Tomorrow, when the siege resumes, we will meet him, Sebrahi. In all our glory, we will meet him. To whatever end, united."

"Ivá," Sebrahi said, nodding at the gravity of Anayah's words.

The armor fit perfectly, each joint snug but flexible. Sebrahi felt powerful enclosed in the armored plates. As Anayah helped secure the final pieces, tightening the segments with leather straps and buckles, Micajah emerged with a blade laid across his forearms. It gleamed near white, as if fashioned from pale silver or white gold instead of steel. He offered it to her with deep reverence.

Sebrahi took the blade with a nod, feeling its weight. She sliced the air and sensed the incredible balance of the weapon.

"Thank you," Sebrahi said gently. The giant smiled with pride.

"It suits you."

"It is time," Anayah said, cinching her own pair of short swords to her waist. One was the blade her aurola had once carried, the one Sofia had taken from Nilayah. It was better she have it. Sebrahi hoped it would serve her friend as well as it had served her.

Through the windows, Sebrahi could see the deep, scarlet sky darkening as the sun continued its journey beyond the horizon. Night would soon find them again, and with it, the imuertes would come.

Yes. It was time.

***

The defenders stood there, silent. In ranks ten deep, they ran along the wall in either direction as the sun slipped out of view to the west, opposite the imuertes' encampment. The coastline and beyond, once rolling green hills of life describable as heaven, was a ruin—trampled and burned by the hellish invaders.

Now, the falling sun bathed it in crimson light. The limbs of Luminea and the Sanguinir stronghold were destroyed, the body broken, the enemy positioned to strike at the heart.

After the fall of the Hierarch, on the heels of the retreating invaders, the enemy took the bridges and the ports, razed the markets and boroughs, and drove the defenders to the innermost stronghold. Two Tiers remained, with few defenders left to hold them. But hold them they would.

Hundreds of human eyes, burning amber and otherwise, gazed out at the ruins of the lower Tiers of Luminea. The Dawnlight at their backs cast an eerie, timeless glow onto the carnage below. Ethereal light mixed with a bloody sunset to illuminate a lifeless scene.

It reminded Sebrahi of Ilucenta; the ruins in the mist, devoid of color and life. She recalled the ancient remains of the Sanguinir warrior she'd found there, Nilayah. Sebrahi wondered if she had felt as Sebrahi did now, on the precipice of oblivion but determined to face it with eyes open.

The sun continued to sink, and the army held at attention. Sebrahi's mind drifted from the ruins of Ilucenta to the vision, the truth, Nesta had unlocked.

Marahi had shown her the true nature of her dreams. Angorzhu, the Hell Lord that marched against them now, was her own flesh and blood. The monster of the Afore had murdered her mother. The monster in the hereafter had killed thousands more. But something told her the revelation was still incomplete—something was missing.

Concentrating, Sebrahi reached out beyond herself to that other consciousness residing within hers. She asked Marahi to see far, and the being obliged.

Sofia perceived the entire Luminean army as one organism, one living thing. She felt other Sanguinir doing the same, picking up on her thoughts, separate nodes of light connecting across the battlefield. Sebrahi could hear Anayah's thoughts as they stood shoulder to shoulder. She was reciting chants and rituals of battles Sebrahi did not know. She could sense Bethuel down the line with the other Sanguinir lords, and even Nesta, deep beneath the Dawnlight, meditating. Heartbeats aligned and sounded in unison. Thoughts aligned and became a singular web of ideas. The warriors were one, the last defense of Luminea, the sword and the shield.

A song escaped Sebrahi's lips, low at first but it quickly gathered strength. She could sense the otherworldly voice singing with hers, that ancient, womanly voice of her halo. It followed her melody in multiple octaves and in perfect harmony. Anayah joined the chorus, as did the Prime Auxilia around them.

The anthem coursed through the ranks until every voice called out defiantly to the darkness. Hearts united, Sebrahi sensed them rising in pace and spirit, emboldened and prideful. The melody amplified over the wall, a resolute song of hope against the coming darkness.

Below, it began. Imuertes pooled against the defenses. Lesser lieutenants growled orders to underlings. Whips sang, and darts, arrows and flaming debris assailed the defenders.

Between volleys, Sebrahi saw specialized creatures with long, sharp talons leap onto the sheer face of the walls, driving their claws into the ancient stone. From their backs, molded into their flesh, jutted crude metal anchors and chain. The imuertes stacked on one another, digging in deep as smaller creatures clamored over them.

Sebrahi grimly acknowledged their cleverness as the webbed climbing nets began to creep up the wall like growing vines.

She sang louder as the army tensed at the ready. The melody reverberated through her being and those around her, encouraging all to stand their ground. She put everything she had into the chant, every hope and every promise. Every confession. Every loss.

She could see the dead, lifeless eyes of the imuertes climbing toward them and the hordes clamoring in the ranks behind. The hymn reached its peak as Sebrahi heard the resounding order to attack echo in her mind.

At once, arrows and spears sailed over the wall at the attackers below. Purified water, stored in giant cisterns, was set free, spraying from orifices in the structure. The creatures slowed but were not deterred, for the whips of fire drove them onward.

The first of their ilk summited the wall under a volley of flaming projectiles. With her sword, Sebrahi met one besieger, a wretched creature with a distended jaw and bleeding, empty eye sockets. The head and body of the thing toppled to the ground below in separate pieces.

More creatures followed. Many more.

The thunderous din of war eclipsed the hymn as chaos broke out all along the wall. Hundreds of small skirmishes erupted, each one a desperate battle for survival.

Sebrahi unleashed on the attackers. The disk of light emanating from her helm blinded her for a brief moment, then resolved to let her see far. She was a tempest now, powerful like an untamable river. The halo whispered to her, moment to moment, perceiving things before they happened.

What training had given her, the mantle multiplied tenfold. Sebrahi struggled to keep up with the flurry of information—a wild swing from charging attacker, an off-balanced foot, an unpredicted collision. She could see them all unfolding at once, outside of time.

A grotesque imuerte slashed with a jagged piece of iron, but Sebrahi opened its gullet and moved on without missing a beat. As she spun to her rear foot, a fiery dart sailed over the wall and struck the spot where she'd stood a moment before.

She flowed through the cascading events as they unfolded, leaving in her wake a mound of unidentifiable imuerte flesh. The aurola opened her mind to the entire battle, and for now, the defense was holding.

We are winning.

She sensed Anayah below and looked. The gate leading to the next Tier creaked and strained under the impact of the attackers. It was dozens of meters wide and groaned like some great beast held captive in the earth.

Sebrahi glanced over the wall to see the hulking forms of domesticated monsters, dozens of meters high, rampage through the ranks. They crashed into the ancient doors, trampling many of their own kin. The wall shook as ancient stones stirred from eons of slumber. Anayah coordinated the reinforcement of the gate, but Sebrahi knew it was only a matter of time. *I know*, said Anayah, using her thoughts to communicate over the din.

The black tide would not stop, not while their leader still lived. Sebrahi called out with her thoughts to the other Sanguinir on the wall as the chaos of battle continued around her. *Brothers and sisters, we must find Angorzhu! We must break this army, now!*

"Here," said a voice from the ether.

Sebrahi recognized the voice. She sensed Bethuel as a spark of cold light in the haze of the battlefield in her mind, the Raven's unmistakable icy and sharp demeanor as apparent as if he were standing right in front of her. Bethuel's presence was moving fast. Her former tutor and two other Sanguinir were already in flight, beyond the wall, screaming toward the Hell Lord's war camp.

A pack of lúpero scrambled over the wall near Sebrahi, surprising the Pax soldiers holding there. One of the hounds mauled the nearest warrior, instantly slashing his chest to ribbons in a spray of crimson.

Sebrahi grabbed a lance from a nearby rack and hurled it clean through the hound. It drove into the stone behind with a thud. As the other Prime Auxilia tried to pull their comrade to safety, Sebrahi hacked through the hounds as they snapped and bit. She mistimed one blow, and one of the lúpero locked her forearm in its maw. The teeth punctured through the plate and the bone and flesh beneath. The creature's jaw foamed with putrid toxins. Before she could bring her sword to bear, something else leaped onto Sebrahi's back followed by another. Pain shot through her sides as she felt claws and teeth burrowing through her armor.

Sebrahi turned inward, summoning the fire. She drifted back to the lighthouse so long ago, the place where she'd realized that fire could not burn her. But she could not escape it, either. *I am the fire.* She imagined herself ablaze, setting her Will to it. *I am the inferno. I am the star. I am the cleansing fire.*

And a second later, she was.

Beams of light erupted from her body as she burst into white-hot flames. Sebrahi's very skin illuminated, blinding the surrounding imuertes long enough for her to free her sword arm. Her blade emerged at the top of the lúpero's skull, driven up through the jaw. She whirled, shaking the clinging creatures to the ground. She slashed at their eyes with her hardened wings of razors.

She recognized the mark upon their twisted, gore-covered corpses. *A feather.* They were the same chittering creatures that followed the imuerte lieutenant...

Irazi.

Sebrahi heard Anayah call out the imuerte's name a moment before the gate gave way. Sofia dispatched the gangly imps ahead of her with a few deft strikes and looked over the edge. Below, a stream of nightmares poured into the higher Tier, led by the Wingtaker himself. His cloak of dismembered Sanguinir wings dragged behind as minions followed, hoping to present their master with new trophies.

One of those once belonged to Ebrahym.

The thought burned hot in her mind, and Sebrahi dove toward the ground on the friendly side of the gate to join the defenders there. She pulled her wings tight, accelerating toward the earth like a falling star. The chilling screech of the imuertes echoed across the field.

Sebrahi touched down, cracking the stone beneath her as she fell to earth, the flames around her dissipating. A phalanx of Prime Auxilia formed up to meet the clamoring horde waiting on the other side of the weakening gates. The ancient barriers hadn't failed completely. Not yet.

Through massive splinters big enough for streams of imuertes to begin flooding through, she could see the giant monsters pounding on the barrier with armored skulls. The Pax engaged with the first of the horde as it seeped through. It was only a matter of time before the trickle of creatures became a torrent.

The tall, spindly nightmare reared up from the stream of imuertes pouring through the gate. "You!" screeched Irazi with glee, pointing toward her. "I know you. And look! You've brought me new trophies of your own."

Brave defenders rushed the imuertes lieutenant. Irazi's wicked blade lashed out. Half a dozen Pax in the rank and file lost a limb or worse. Flesh hit stone with wet thuds. Men screamed. Irazi screeched in ecstasy, awash in the chaos.

Anayah was close. Sebrahi felt her presence drawing near as the imuertes thickened. More of them streamed through the weakening defenses.

Sebrahi heard Anayah's voice in her head: *all at once, take that monster down!* Sebrahi signaled her understanding and bolted toward Irazi, her wings splayed wide. Bait. The target was too tempting for the creature to pass up, and his rotten skull laughed with glee.

He bobbed to meet Sebrahi, scythe at the ready. Anayah cut left, barreling toward the Irazi's flank, staying low in the fight.

Irazi saw her coming at the last moment and wheeled, swinging his blade wildly. The edge tore through Anayah's thigh, and she fell to the ground, her armor scraping against the stone as she skidded.

Sebrahi came up on Irazi from behind, hacking through his neck at the collarbone. She wrenched the blade free as the creature howled, and she cut again, deeper this time, crunching down through the chest and through the cloak of trophies, nearly to the opposite hip.

The creature let loose howling death throes as the foul, life-giving substances flooded out of him. Sebrahi beat her wings to avoid his last desperate attempt to rend her and watched from above as Irazi toppled to the ground in a slick, steaming mess. The nearby imuertes scattered, lost without their leader.

The Wingtaker is dead.

Sebrahi rushed to Anayah and touched down as a few Prime Auxilia, still standing, covered in gore, encircled them.

"I am all right," Anayah said, struggling to her feet. "But soon, we will not be." She nodded toward the buckling gate.

The living battering rams were more visible than not, pounding through the last metal reinforcements. Beneath, what remained of the lioneer cavalry bravely plowed through the ranks, claws, spears and teeth mauling the enemy. But they would not be enough to turn the tide.

"None of this matters if Angorzhu lives," Sebrahi said, catching her breath. "He is close. I can feel it, Anayah. I can feel him."

Anayah nodded. "Go. I will lead the stand here." Anayah tore her cloak into strips and cinched them tight around her leg, and Sofia helped her to her feet.

The two warriors looked at one another as they once had long ago, knowing what it meant. At that moment, they were without amber eyes and wings at their backs, without armor or the steaming gore that covered them, without the hidden scars. Simply two friends again. But Sebrahi knew where her path must end, and it was not here.

"Goodbye, Alana," Sebrahi said, pulling her friend in close. She tried to memorize the feel and the smell of the moment, knowing it might be the last time she would see her friend.

"Goodbye, Sofia."

Sebrahi smiled reassuringly. Anayah grinned and donned her helmet, nodding proudly, once again a being of war. She turned and raced toward the crumbling gates and likely her doom, shouting orders and rallying the Pax.

Sebrahi lingered for a moment, beaming with pride. She leaped into the air, flying toward Bethuel and the others heading for the front. As she soared across the field, she glanced back and wondered if she'd ever see her friend again.

47

I'm too late.

Sebrahi beat her four-meter wings with all the strength she had. The muscles from her jaw to her hips ached with exertion. She screamed toward Bethuel's essence through the swarm of chaos, as flaming arrows and demons buzzed past her. In every direction, Sanguinir tangled with winged foes as if painted in a fresco, frozen in time.

She concentrated on Bethuel's aura. It appeared to her a fading light in the ether's fog, a distant, twinkling star. She could not detect the two other Sanguinir with him, and she imagined the worst had befallen them.

She caught sight of the Raven across the darkened, bloodstained field, at the heart of the horde itself. Torches and fires illuminated Angorzhu's war camp. At the foot of a makeshift throne were heaps of tattered Pax banners, discarded helmets and bloody weapons, dismembered bodies of fallen friends on display. Angorzhu's minions streamed like ants toward it, carrying trophies from the front line to lay at their master's feet. But the throne itself was empty.

As she slipped though through the acrid haze of war, only a few hundred meters up, the obscenity grew.

One of the tributes to the Fierno was the Hierarch's violated corpse. Terafiq's body hung near the crude throne, crucified upside down, stripped of her armor and of her wings.

Steady, Marahi said to her through vague impressions and sensations. *Do not fear.*

There, in the middle of Angorzhu's camp, she saw them: The Hell Lord and Bethuel. They clashed arms amid the imuerte horde; the eye of the storm.

As she spiraled down, dodging projectiles, Sebrahi wondered where the rest of the Host was. Had the Raven challenged the Fierno alone? *Pride.*

She called out to that strange ether once more and realized it was not ego that drove the Raven to face the Fierno alone, but desperation. There were so few lights now, so few of the Sanguinir still fighting in the darkness. They flickered and dimmed.

Soon the battle would be lost, and with it, the war and everything else.

Bethuel deflected a flurry of blows from Angorzhu's mighty blade, his own singing with each parry. Even at a distance, Sebrahi could see that the hulking Hell Lord was toying with him, holding his minions at bay, enjoying the sport of it. Her heart sank.

Nearby, the blood-covered bodies of the other two Sanguinir who followed the Raven lay in the mud, filthy and still. Even more scattered the field beyond. A tangled trail of grisly death.

Sebrahi touched down just as Bethuel let loose a counterize, a series of deft swings that forced Angorzhu onto the backfoot. Cinders cracked and popped across the Fierno's flesh. Flames erupted from his horns. Blood wept from his banner. Angorzhu stumbled for a moment, slipping to one knee.

But it was a ruse. Bethuel went in for the killing blow—the beast's feint had fooled the Sanguinir.

The Raven lunged desperately. Angorzhu pivoted and exploded with fury and surprising grace. And with a single, powerful blow, he split Bethuel's flank apart and sent him careening toward the ground. The Sang cried out in pain and frustration.

"No!" Sebrahi called out.

She cut through a score of lesser imuertes to reach a bloody circle that had opened around the Hell Lord and the downed Raven.

Angorzhu snorted hot steam and roared, pacing back and forth, savoring the kill, lost in the bloodlust. Fires raged around them. Bethuel pulled himself along on his elbows toward his blade just out of reach, refusing to give in. The imuertes chief loomed over him, the red light emanating from him casting a bloody glow onto the wounded Sang.

Watching the beast, Sebrahi realized no essence of the man that was her father, how little good there might once have been, remained. He'd strangled her mother to death with a baby Sofia inside of her. He'd killed countless more as the beast Angorzhu. Even so, Sebrahi resisted giving into the rage. For all her hate, for all her desire to avenge Ebrahym, the Hierarch and the countless scores of others, she would not succumb to it.

Knowing now where it came from, she would have no part of it. She had spent her whole life in the Afore and the hereafter consumed by helpless anger, hunting and hating the man she'd never known. And people had died for it.

No more.

The creature before her was a monster, yes. Completely consumed by a lifetime of pain and terror unleashed on the world. And despite the truth of his crimes, despite everything, Sofia pitied him.

The Fierno plowed through the mud and moved in for the kill. The Raven closed his eyes and raised his chin in defiance. Hefting his blade above his head, Angorzhu bellowed a call for blood. His steel came down toward the Sang like a meteor.

A sharp clang rang out across the battlefield like a cathedral bell, deep and pure. Sofia's blade held firm against the Fierno's. The force of the blow nearly drove her into the dirt like a spike, but she found the strength to hold firm.

He snorted sulfuric air into her face. Again, he struck with a roar, driving her shin-deep into the mud. Splinters of steel where the swords met sparked and disappeared. But she would not yield.

The beast's eyes, *her* eyes seared at her from black pits of rage. He slashed wildly, trying to put Sofia off-balance, but she anticipated the move and parried the weight of the blow to the side and countered, slicing a deep gash across Angorzhu's chest. The imuerte glanced down and touched the molten fire pouring from him. He cocked his head at her. He sniffed the air.

"You are changed."

"Yes," Sofia said. Two voices spoke as one.

"You know the truth," Angorzhu snorted. **"I can smell it."**

She nodded, her golden eyes ablaze. "I have seen the Afore. I am your blood."

"Then embrace me. And with it, victory," Angorzhu roared, gesturing to the carnage of the battlefield. He pounded his chest. **"This is your birthright."**

"I will not."

"That creature in your mind preaches illusions! Lies! We are what we are. This campaign is just a glimpse of what is to come, of what we can accomplish together. I am primal chaos incarnate. I am the cleansing fire. And so, too, my seed, are you. Beautiful and terrible like the storm."

"Yes, part of me came from you," Sebrahi gritted out. "But the other part, from *her*."

Angorzhu's eyes narrowed, knowingly. **"*She* betrayed me. And she was weak."**

"She stood up to a monster," Sebrahi said, gazing up at him. She tossed her plumed helmet aside and held her sword in a high guard. "As will I."

Angorzhu kicked Bethuel away, no doubt crushing bones as he did. The Raven crumpled into a pile of bodies nearby.

Angorzhu hefted the gore-stained, serrated shard of metal that was his sword and threatened it her direction. **"Very well. You shall die then, like your mother."**

Angorzhu came at her, again and again, his strength a limitless font of vengeance. Even her aurola struggled to anticipate his movements. He drifted in and out of the shadows like a ghost, his massive form shifting from one place to the next. Sofia swung wildly in the darkness and flames. Panic began to creep in with each desperate parry. Each time, the Fierno drew more blood. An errant strike caught her behind the thigh.

Sebrahi stumbled.

The shadow came.

A blade materialized from the darkness and plunged into Sebrahi's gut with a wet crunch of buckling armor and ripping of flesh.

The feeling of metal inside her body was a strange one. There was no pain at first, only surprise and a slight sensation of pressure. Then, cold.

Sebrahi gasped and blinked. Angorzhu drove the blade deeper until his face was inches from hers. His hot breath poured over her. She felt her body drifting away with the blood pooling at her feet. She looked down at her crimson-stained gauntlets. There was so much of it.

Oh, God, I've failed again.

I've failed you all.

"Disappointing," the Fierno growled. He twisted the blade. She heard it grind organs and bone but felt no pain.

"How could you do that to me?" Sebrahi said. She spoke the words, but they were not her own. She felt the presence of Marahi inside of her taking form, and from the haze of time and distant memory, it began to sharpen. As Sebrahi spoke, Marahi's voice became her own. Angorzhu hesitated.

"How could you do that to *me*, Luqa?" Sebrahi said. "To our baby?" Angorzhu recoiled like an animal from fire.

"What game is this?" the imuerte growled.

"It is no game, my love, and no deception. Do you remember this?" Sebrahi held up the silver ring hanging on the chain around her neck, the one Ebrahym had worn to honor his aurola. She continued, "The ring you gave me wasn't even real silver. You told me that in another life, you would have bought me a diamond. But I didn't care. I only ever wanted you. And *her*."

Angorzhu cowered, the beast shrinking, transfixed by the sound of the voice. **"M-Maria? My...Maria?"** the imuerte stammered. Angorzhu dropped his blade into the mud, stunned in a daze. He staggered toward Sebrahi, reaching for her from another time.

"I am here," said the voice of Maria. Her voice was ancient and commanding now, as if the very stars themselves were speaking. Sebrahi realized the last and final truth of things. *Marahi*. The aurola once joined with Ebrahym and all the eleven before him, was her mother. *Maria*.

She had been here the whole time. She was what had driven Ebrahym to protect her, to defy the Way, to love her. It was a mother's love she'd felt radiating through him in all those soft moments. It was the love she'd never known, reaching out over time and space to find her, to watch over her.

The sound of Maria's voice withered Angorzhu's presence. His ferocity waned by the second. Once so mighty, the Fierno dropped to his knees, groveling toward her.

"You were here, my love?" Angorzhu pleaded. **"I searched for so long. I waited...to beg your forgiveness. I was so...alone."** Angorzhu groveled at her feet, clawing at her boots. He looked through Sebrahi's eyes to the being within her. The pain from the wound began to shine through the shock. Sebrahi dropped to her knees and held the monster close. The battlefield faded from consciousness as time slowed.

"Yes, my love. I came here, long ago," Maria said through spurts of blood-filled coughs. Sebrahi's body was giving out. There was barely human quality to her voice. "For a thousand years, I worked to free myself of you, to forgive you for what you had done. And I did, Luqa. I found my peace and passed on, through the Dawnlight and...beyond." Sofia's arm gestured toward the Dawnlight still visible through the haze of war.

"You've seen it? The beyond?" Angorzhu asked. **"Tell me, Maria, please. Tell me what lies there."**

"Through the Dawnlight is a universe you cannot begin to imagine. Humanity lives among the stars, outside of time, outside of form, united. But ours is one realm of many. We explore the furthest reaches of them all, searching."

"Seeking what?"

Sebrahi smiled. "Truth, and those worthy of it. There is still work to be done among the heavens. Few of us choose to make the difficult journey back here to act as guides. Aurola, they call us. Halo. But I came back for a different reason, for I knew one day *she* would come. Our daughter, Luqa. I knew one day Sofia's life in the Afore would end and she would find herself here." Tears streamed and evaporated off Angorzhu's skin as he shook his head violently, wishing to not hear the words.

Sebrahi placed her hand on the top of the Hell Lord's head. "I came back to protect her and this world, my love, from you."

"Forgive me," Angorzhu whispered. **"Forgive me."**

"We do," said the voices of Sofia and Maria, in ethereal unison. With the last strength in her body, Sebrahi came to her feet. She helped the cowering Fierno to his. But Sebrahi no longer saw the beast. Before her was a being of pure radiance in the shape of a woman. In its light she felt in the womb again, warm and content, ready to stay there forever. This was the being known as Marahi. It was Ebrahym. It was her mother. It was herself.

"Mama?" Sofia said.

"Yes, baby," Maria said. She smiled and extended her hand. "It is time."

"Where are we going?"

"You'll see. But you're not finished yet."

She was back on the battlefield. Pain. Blood. Around, the imuertes crept toward her, unsure what they were seeing. Bethuel, too, clutched his wounds and stared in disbelief.

She turned inward. Once more she was in the cave Nesta described. There was the single candle inside the abyss. Sebrahi reached for it, willing it to grow.

Everything dredged up from the blackness, manifested. Her fear. Her pride. Her selfishness. Matías appeared from the shadows, candlelight flickering off his face. Behind him, scores of Pax and oulma Sebrahi had left in her wake.

Casualties. Victims of the caravan attack, fallen soldiers from the Espleña massacre, the siege of Luminea. All were tied to one another, links in a chain leading back to her.

They stared at her without judgment, waiting. She did not turn from their gaze.

Then, Ebrahym appeared from the crowd, his eyes afire once more. A gentle smile crept across his face, and he gave her a nod and gestured toward the candle.

Sebrahi looked at faces of the lost and understood. *Sacrifice*. It was not enough to slay the beast. This would not do. This would not honor these fallen. Her thoughts drifted back to that night when Matías had asked her if she would sacrifice for something greater than herself.

As she stared into the candle, Sebrahi whispered to them. "I will."

The candle before her suddenly became two, then four, and then multiplied until the entire cavern was filled with the glowing sticks of wax. The space had no end, continuing forever in all directions. Sebrahi found herself there, in the middle of the sea of candles, the eyes of all those who were gone upon her. Then, the cave's darkness gave way to blinding light.

Sebrahi ignited like a star being born in the cold darkness of space. Cleansing light bathed the battlefield, casting it in strange, artificial daylight.

The imuerte Angorzhu basked in the light with closed eyes. A sword found its way into her hand. She caressed Angorzhu's scarred face and slipped the blade into his chest, gently. He did not resist. Angorzhu gasped as the brilliant rays stripped the foul flesh from his bones.

Piece by piece, Angorzhu disintegrated like kindling in a fire.

A face of a handsome man remained in his place. His eyes opened, slowly, reverently, to meet hers. There was a kindness there she'd never seen beyond the monster. "Beautiful," Luquitas whispered as he touched her face. "Just as she was."

Sebrahi kissed his forehead as her father disappeared, absorbed completely into the light.

Beyond her body, she felt the light growing in dimension. It raced out in all directions, expanding at speed. The glowing sphere enveloped Luminea, then beyond to the Plains of Lumbra and Caldea, deserts of the Tierroa, and the Basuio, the ice fields to the north, and farther still. All of the Orvida bathed in her light. In the heart of Luminea, the Dawnlight pulsated with her in harmony, for she and it were one. Deep in the Sanctu Arcam, she could feel Nesta smiling. Elsewhere, Anayah belted a hymn of glory, tears forming in her golden eyes.

And as the sphere of light surrounded and engulfed the imuertes across the Orvida, it freed them from their twisted forms. Their foul visages burned away like thin, paper shells. Underneath, what remained burned bright and found peace.

Then they came to her. Rushing across the surface of the hereafter, the essence of every freed oulma drew to her by some unseen force. Beads of light pooling toward the sacred center. She felt their beings join hers, preparing for the next journey.

She took a breath and looked down at her physical body. The blood slowed. There was little left of it.

Then, the Sanguinir known as Sebrahi, thirteenth of her name, collapsed.

Somewhere far off in the dark, Bethuel pleaded to her to fight on. But her fight was done. She let go from the world and slipped away into the waiting arms of her mother. Into the Dawnlight, into the beyond. She could see her mother now, arms held wide, welcoming her home. Like falling into a dream, all physical sensations melted away.

Memories flashed before her, but she did not linger on them. Pain, war, fear—these came to her as she passed into the light. But they soon faded. Then came love, and it overwhelmed her.

She felt the goodness of every being in the hereafter, and they intertwined, becoming inseparable. Blissful, comforting warmth enveloped her, and she gave herself to it, collapsing into a single point. But this, too, passed.

Parts of her mind, her very self, burned away. Layer by layer, they disappeared until all that was left was the primal, eternal force that drove her onward. In the distance, an infinity of brilliance unfolded in all directions, formless and complete.

And at the brink, an unfamiliar road extended ahead of her. She cast off the last part of herself, all that remained of the woman called *Sofia*, and took her first step into the unknown.

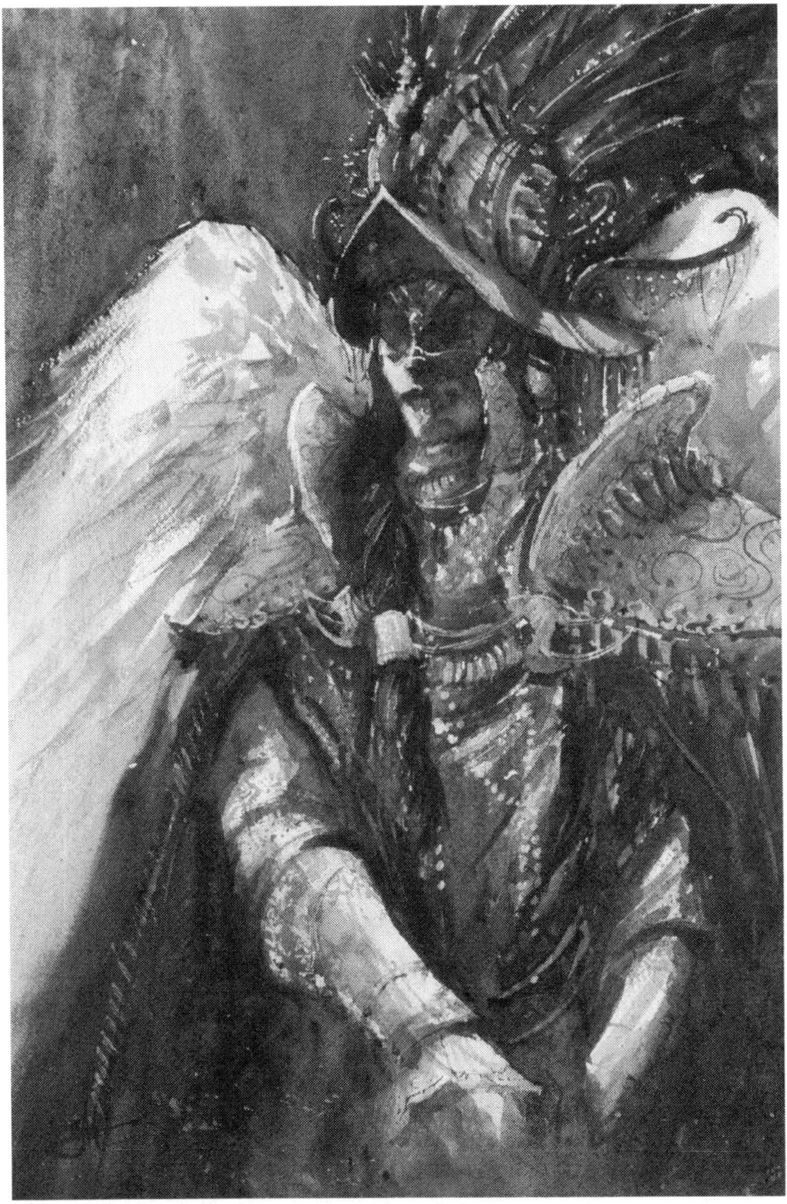

The story doesn't end here.

Visit AllThatWillBurn.com to explore a growing collection of artwork and writings from the Orvida and beyond.

About the Author

Judd Mercer is a painter, writer, designer and all-around creative who doesn't know the meaning of the word "bored." Afflicted early-on with a severe case of hero worship, Judd spent his suburban childhood as most nerdy kids do: pretending he was Batman, watching 80s movies on repeat, playing games and reading. Some things never change.

Today, as a co-owner and Creative Director at a digital advertising agency, Elevated Third, Judd spends his days in the real world tackling tough business problems. But on nights and weekends, he still escapes to an imaginary one, spending time in the studio making up entirely new problems (like how to write a novel) and slowly, painfully learning how to solve them. Judd lives in Denver, Colorado, with his wife, Katie.

Made in the USA
Lexington, KY
24 November 2018